CONFESSIONS OF A CASANOVA

Books by Chris Kenry

CAN'T BUY ME LOVE

UNCLE MAX

CONFESSIONS OF A CASANOVA

SUMMER SHARE
(with William J. Mann, Andy Schell, and Ben Tyler)

ALL I WANT FOR CHRISTMAS
(with Jon Jeffrey, William J. Mann, and Ben Tyler)

Published by Kensington Publishing Corporation

CONFESSIONS OF A CASANOVA

CHRIS KENRY

KENSINGTON BOOKS
http://www.kensingtonbooks.com

KENSINGTON BOOKS are published by

Kensington Publishing Corp.
850 Third Avenue
New York, NY 10022

All Kensington titles, imprints and distributed lines are available at special quantity discounts for bulk purchases for sales promotion, premiums, fund-raising, educational or institutional use.

Special book excerpts or customized printings can also be created to fit specific needs. For details, write or phone the office of the Kensington Special Sales Manager: Kensington Publishing Corp., 850 Third Avenue, New York, NY 10022. Attn. Special Sales Department. Phone: 1-800-221-2647.

Kensington and the K logo Reg. U.S. Pat. & TM Off.

Library of Congress Card Catalogue Number: 2004105212
ISBN 0-7582-0435-3

First Printing: October 2004
10 9 8 7 6 5 4 3 2 1

Printed in the United States of America

For my ever-elusive father

Acknowledgments

Thanks to John Scognamiglio, who never lost it with me, although he certainly had a right to. I owe you a case of Angel Foam.

What do you do when it quits being new?
—Lyle Lovett

Chapter One

Death is very anticlimactic. That's about the best I can say about it. You always hear about the white light, or about your life passing before your eyes, but that's not really how it was at all. Oh, there was drama, all right—people hovering around my body on the street, panicked yelling, the sound of sirens in the distance—but then everything just started folding in on itself, reducing the light with each fold. I remember staring up at the streetlight overhead and watching it grow smaller and dimmer until it looked just like that last little lingering star in the center of the television screen after you shut it off.

Probably it's jumping the gun, so to speak, for me to tell you what death is like because, that evening on the sidewalk when my spinning, spinning, spinning world came to a stop I didn't really die. No, the bullets, intended for the tiny target that is my heart, missed their mark entirely and lodged themselves instead in my right elbow and left thigh. I've since been reassured by my doctor and by a detective assigned to the case that the bullets probably were not fired with an intent to kill, which is supposed to be comforting. Someone just wanted to severely wound me, not actually kill me, so I guess I should feel happy, maybe even grateful, and I do, although I'd feel even better if I knew the shooter wasn't still out there, waiting for just the right time to jump out of the shadows and finish the job. If that is the case, then there's no time like the present to launch the attack since I'm now what's called an easy target, a sitting duck, a fish in a barrel. The first bullet hit my femur and pretty much blasted it apart. The bone has since been pinned and fused together and the whole leg, from hip to ankle, encased in a creamy, plaster cast. When they first put it on, I remember looking at it and thinking what a nice canvas it would make. And to be honest, I would enjoy whiling away my idle, infirm hours sketching on it, but that's not going to happen because the second bullet—the one that hit my elbow—severed some tendony thing that operates my fingers. It, too, has been pinned, and fused, and repaired, but will require lots of physical therapy to get it working again. Until then, I pretty much can't do anything with my right hand; can't wave, can't make a fist, can't beat off or pull a trigger, and I most certainly cannot sketch, which is sure to make more than a few people very happy.

The detective, a shy, geeky man with a schoolboy crush on my mother, comes by a few times a week, always with the hope that I'll remember more details, or provide him some clue as to who might be responsible, but I never tell him very much. What I remember from that night is this: It was raining. I went to a café but left because it was crowded and I couldn't find a seat. I went to the bar next door. It was also crowded so I gave up and decided to go somewhere else. While I was walking back to my truck, taking a shortcut through the alley to get to my secret parking space, which evidently wasn't such a secret, I heard a voice (male probably, possibly female) say my name. I turned but I never saw who it was. I saw the flash of the gun, heard the shots, felt the bullets, saw the blood and felt the pain, in that order. Then I panicked. I stumbled out of the alley onto the sidewalk of Seventeenth Street. I fell down with a splash. Then there was the crowd, and the sirens, and the light folding in.

We go through the same scenario, the detective and I, almost every day, but there's never anything new, never any face that I can attach to the voice, but that's not to say there's a shortage of suspects. On the contrary. Roy, Gabriel, Arabella, Tom, James, Cleve, Reid, Peter, Louisa . . . the list could go on and on. Day after day they parade in and out of my hospital room, survey the damage with a smug satisfaction, and then write some colorful, dorky quip on my cast with the Magic Markers left behind for that purpose by the art therapist. I run my fingers over their rainbow-colored names and wonder which one of them had the supreme pleasure of autographing his or her work. I wonder, but I'll probably never know for sure since it could easily be any one of them—all suspects, each with an individual motive.

Motivation. It's something you think about when the list of possible suspects in your case extends to two pages. It's something you think about when you realize that most of the people you love, and who have loved you, are included on that list. It's something you think about when you're confined to a single unguarded room of a hospital with an immobilizing cast on your leg.

Although, instead of motivation, probably I should take a step back (figuratively, of course) and think about provocation, since the one thing I'm sure of is that my shooting was not a random act of violence. No, I provoked it and, some would say, I got just what I deserved. Some would say I got off easy, and I can't really argue with that. My actions were pretty despicable. So, before you figure it out for yourself, if you haven't already, now might be a good time for me to tell you that I probably won't be a guy you're going to like all that much. At least not in the beginning, maybe not in the end, either, and certainly not in the middle.

In polite society, I am what's known as a Casanova. In the lower ranks they'd probably just call me a slut. Specifically, I'm the kind of guy who'll make a great show of sweeping you off your feet only to drop you on your ass all too soon thereafter; the kind of guy who'll hold you in his arms and whisper sweet nothings in your ear while at the same time winking over your shoulder at someone new; the kind of guy that your mother (and certainly my mother) would have warned you about. In short, I am just the kind of guy you'd expect someone to shoot.

The funny thing about my getting shot (and I mean both funny ironic and funny ha ha) is that, when assessing my case, the Department of Social Services did not take motivation or provocation into consideration. In their eyes I am nothing more than the victim of a heinous crime and as such they assigned me a social worker who, after a phone interview and an assessment of my file, assigned a victim's advocate who, after a phone interview and an assessment of my file, assigned an art therapist who, after a phone interview and assessment of my file, actually showed up in person, and continued to show up in person three times a week, although always with one eye on the clock so that she wouldn't stay longer than the billable fifty minutes. The job of the Art Therapist is, as she put it, to help me "work through the feelings of victimization and find a way to express and process outrage and pain."

Uh, right.

Mostly she just irritates the crap out of me for 150 minutes each week with her pseudospiritual elementary school art projects. And yet, even though I can't stand her, I'll admit I admire the fact that she's managed to parlay the "skills" acquired in her dead-end job at a New Age retail store into a career that is covered by most major medical policies.

When Serena—that, of course, being the art therapist's name—found out that I was an artist (a label I would hesitate to paste on myself), she brought me a Big Chief tablet and box of waxy, colored pencils and tried to convince me to do a series of drawings about my shooting and the events leading up to it. That way, as she put it, "you can do physical therapy on your elbow while at the same time expressing your feelings of outrage on the theme of violation."

When I heard that one I turned and gave a weary look to the detective, who was lingering around the hospital that day, as he did on so many days, hoping that my Nordic Beauty mother might make an appearance. I looked down at the tablet, then back up at Serena and said, "I don't think this is such a good idea."

She cocked her head, and gave me a patient, empathetic look. The kind of look you give someone when you completely understand and pity their reluctance to relive what was surely a horrendous and potentially scarring trauma.

"No, really," I said. "This isn't right. If anything, I should probably try to express my feelings on the theme of being an asshole and learn how to process my guilty conscience. And I really don't think I should use a sketchpad to do it since that's what got me into this mess in the first place."

She looked confused so I explained, as concisely as I could, how in the months (okay, years) leading up to my shooting I had used pencil, paper, and my artistic ability to, well, flatter and entice men out of their clothes and into my bed. Or, as they'd say in the lower ranks, how I'd used pencil and paper to pimp for me. I told her all that and as I spoke (using up most, but not all, of the fifty minutes), I watched her expression as it changed from confusion, to disbelief, to outrage, to disgust, and by the time I finished my tale, it was clear to me that both she and the detective knew there were many, many adjectives that could be used to describe me, but that "victim" certainly wasn't one of them. What was even worse (and, I suspect, what bothered Serena more), was that I'd ruined the sketching exercise she'd planned for me that day and she would, therefore, need to come up with something else on the fly. She scowled. Then, feigning nonchalance, she pretended to stretch and consulted her watch. Seeing that we still had ten minutes to occupy, and clearly wondering how she was going to occupy them, she closed her eyes and settled into the lotus position, legs curled beneath her, her eyes closed. I glanced over at the detective. He shrugged. A minute later, having evidently reached a resolution, or received some sort of divine message, Serena jumped up and snatched back the Big Chief and the colored pencils.

"The Goddess has given you a gift," she proclaimed, wide-eyed, "and you have soiled it. You've used your talents for a bad end. And now," she said, waving a finger toward the heavens, "the Universe is punishing you."

Great, I thought to myself, so the Goddess pulled the trigger and the Universe drove the getaway car. Hard to believe that Kaiser Permanente was actually paying someone to tell me that.

"So here's what we'll do," she said, taking a plain spiral notebook and a mechanical pencil from her bag and setting them on my tray table. "We'll use a different medium and consult a different muse. I still want you to use pencil and paper, but for a different end. This time I want you to try and figure out your problems not by drawing, but by writing them down."

She then launched into a four minute and eighteen second explanation on how to write haikus and gave me guidelines for starting a journal. She was about to offer suggestions on short story formats that I might like to try when the alarm on her watch went off and she stopped.

"I'm afraid that's all the time we have for today," she said, hauling her macramé purse onto her shoulder and fixing me with a smug, plastic smile, "but I think I've given you more than enough to work on until our next meeting."

After she'd gone, the detective and I sat in bewildered silence. I stared down at the tablet. The pencil rolled off the tray table and onto the floor. The detective retrieved it, and as he handed it to me, asked, "What exactly did you mean?"

I waited for him to elaborate. When he didn't, I said, "What do you mean what did I mean?"

"I mean, what did you mean about using your sketchpad to, um, you know, *get laid*?"

Even though we were alone in the room, the last two words of his question came out in a shy whisper.

"I meant just what I said. I drew pictures of guys and then used the pictures to appeal to their vanity and, well . . ."

He waved a hand to show that he understood that part. "But that's all it took?" he asked. "Just drawing some pictures?"

"No, that's not all. That was just the start, really. The way to get past the doorman and behind the velvet rope."

"And after that?"

His inquiries seemed to have little, if anything, to do with my case, so I decided there wasn't any harm in answering them. Nevertheless, I studied him for a minute and asked, "Why, exactly, do you want to know?"

Like a startled turtle, he pulled back. His face reddened.

"I just, well, I," he stuttered, unsure of what he wanted to say. His eyes, behind the greasy lenses of his glasses darted from side to side like two minnows in a bowl, and he rubbed a finger back and forth on his lips. He took a deep breath, started to speak but then stalled. I knew where he was going, but decided to let him get there on his own. Eventually he said:

"Um, it's like, well . . . I'm not a guy who has . . . what you might call success with the ladies."

I looked him over: He was wearing a short-sleeved button-down shirt, with a collar that was frayed and pilled from scraping against the stubble on his chin. He wore a tie, too, but it was clear that it had been selected on price alone. And then there was the hair! Not much of it, granted, but what was left on the sides had been grown out and pulled back into a wispy ponytail.

"Okay," I said, "I see your point, but why would you want to know what I do to win over guys? Even if it could translate into winning over women, why would you want to know when you can see," I said, drumming my fingers on the cast, "what it got me?"

He nodded, but I could tell he wasn't dissuaded.

"Look," he said, moving closer but still whispering, "I'm almost forty and I've never been married. What's worse is I can count the dates I've had since college on one hand. I know I'm not much to look at but—and pardon me for saying so—neither are you."

I was offended and he must have realized it because he back-pedaled.

"Er, that's not what I meant. You're handsome enough. For a guy, I mean, but there's, well, nothing out of the ordinary, you know what I mean? Even so, you've got an army of guys coming through here each day and all of them, even that crazy blond woman, are still kind of in love with you. I can tell. They're angry all right, but they wouldn't even bother being angry if they didn't still feel something. What I wonder, is how you did it, and, well, if maybe you could give me a few pointers?"

I don't know why but I laughed at that. When I stopped, I told him I'd certainly think about it, and then changed the subject to my mother, who was due to arrive at any moment. What I hoped was that he'd just forget about it. I fully intended to do so, but later that night, after he and my mother were gone and I was alone again, my eyes kept drifting back to the mechanical pencil and the spiral notebook.

Maybe it was boredom with all the evening television programs, or maybe it was curiosity, or a desire to understand all that had happened, probably it was just vanity, but whatever the reason, I picked up the pencil and began to write. At first, I followed Serena's advice and attempted some haikus and prose poems, but after an hour of that I gave up and started journaling; just writing down what went on from day to day. That went on for a few days but I found that chronicling my hospital stay—who came and went, what disgusting food I had for lunch, how the machine next to my bed was clearly not dispensing enough morphine—was not very interesting, even to me and I concluded that writing about my present situation was stupid. Stupid because it seemed to willfully ignore the past and all the things I'd done to deserve being put in the hospital in the first place. Things that, believe it or not, I had thought a lot about. So, with those thoughts in mind I flipped the page and looked back into my past to try and figure out why I am the way I am, and did the things I did.

Psychiatrists, self-help books, and any of my angry ex-lovers could, I've no doubt, supply numerous labels for my behavior: Megalomania, Fear of Intimacy, Peter Pan Syndrome, Advanced Egotism, Malignant Narcissism, Love Addiction, etc., and in all of those bitter diagnoses there is undoubtedly some truth, but if I'm really honest (another label I would hesitate to paste on myself), I have to admit that the last one on that list probably comes closest to summing it all up: For me, love is an addiction. For me, there is no better, or longer-lasting, high. Other drugs give similar feelings of euphoria, but they are comparatively short-lived, and with them, if you want the feeling to last, you have to keep doing another hit, or bump, or line, or whatever. Love has a longer half-life. One dose can last for months, even up to a year and seven months, and sometimes even longer if there are great distances between you or adverse circumstances conspiring against it. But like all drugs, love eventually evaporates from your system. Some people can live on the fumes, the memory of that bursting bud, that poppy rush, but I am not such a person. And neither, I'm afraid, is my father.

My father. Inevitably, I turn to him as the real source of the trouble. I know that sounds like a cop-out, a throwback to the 1980s blame-your-parents-for-absolutely-everything era of self-help books, but sit tight and I bet I can convince you that my father is hugely responsible for my current fate. After all, what is Fate but Father with a few letters missing? Take aim and fire at the h and the r and there you have it: Fat e .

My particular fate was to have a conniving little charmer for a father. A dad with a proclivity for promiscuity. A dad hugely endowed with charisma, which he used to mesmerize any blond-haired, blue-eyed woman who had the misfortune to get caught in his cyclonic storm of seduction. A dad who skipped out on my blond-haired, blue-eyed mother when I was ten years old and who, despite his subsequent absence from my life, somehow managed to infuse me with a wisdom I probably would have been wise to forget. A wisdom that, I reflected, my little detective friend, the shy, sloppy sap, was now beseeching me to pass on to him.

I closed my eyes and thought about some of the things a father passes on to his son. On the nature side there is genetic material, for which I am, by and large, grateful, although I'd like to add about five inches. To my height. On the nurture side there is a long list of learned behaviors, and it is for those things I am less grateful.

Most fathers, at least most of the idealized ones on TV and in the movies, teach their sons useful things, like how to run the family business, or how to fly-fish or fix cars or wire lamps. Some teach their sons how to barbecue, or play baseball, or about their religion, and culture, and morals. But not my dad. No, my father taught me two things, and only two things: how to read a betting form, and how to make someone fall in love with me. With the betting, I have probably broken even. The wooing has nearly bankrupted me, both morally and financially, and is, I'm certain, responsible for my perforated leg and elbow.

I thought again about the detective and how he seemed more interested in the methods I used to seduce the suspects than in gathering any evidence that might convict the one who pulled the trigger. Then I picked up the pencil and tapped it on the paper, feeling a slight pain in my elbow. If I were to write down my strategies, codify them, so to speak, and offer them to the detective (along with some much-needed grooming and fashion tips), would I, I wondered, really be doing him a favor? Probably it would be the moral equivalent of teaching a child to smoke. And besides, he was already easily distracted. Wouldn't this make him all the more so, and even less inclined than he already was to find the real culprit in my shooting? Without hesitation, I started writing.

The Beginning

In the beginning, there is the Object of Desire (referred to hereafter as O.O.D.): the person you've scoped out and decided you want to pursue. Once you have that, you're ready to start.

Okay, let's set the mood. Background music is important. Cue up that Carly Simon song in your head. You know, the one from *The Spy Who Loved Me*. Got it? Good. Now remember, in the beginning, confidence, or at least the appearance thereof, is key.

Step 1. The Eye Game

In the beginning, before the actual wooing, there must be flirtation. This usually starts with eye contact and a slight smile. I learned from my dad that it is better to make several quick, furtive glances rather than one prolonged stare since the latter often has the undesired effect of frightening away the O.O.D. The smile should occur right after your eye contact has been detected, and is actually more of a shy, dopey grin. Since I can draw, this first step is almost too easy for me. I just take out my sketchbook and execute a quick portrait of the O.O.D. This gives me a reason to glance at him while at the same time making him curious to find out what I'm doing. Most men, at least most of the men I've known, are vain creatures. For that reason they are usually flattered when they realize they are being drawn. A few of them will get self-conscious and uncomfortable, some will even get up and leave, but most will stay put, and many will actually attempt to fix their hair or try to favorably manipulate the expression on their face. They needn't bother. I can usually tell which feature (high cheekbones, a square jaw, full lips, rounded triceps, washboard abs) they are most proud of and I make sure to accentuate that in my drawing. Realism plays a very small part in my work.

Step 2. The Approach

Once the O.O.D.'s curiosity has been aroused, the next step is to get up and walk over to him. Speaking to the O.O.D. for the first time can make or break anything that will happen in the future and so requires great caution. A good opening is vital to success. My father used to start with the line, *"Excuse me but aren't you _____*[insert name of beautiful model or actress here]*? No? Well, you certainly have her_____*[insert physical attribute here]. *Really, the resemblance is quite strong."* All conveyed in the faux Italian accent he was always trying to perfect to hide the fact that he's Mexican. He'd comment on the beauty of her teeth while staring lustily at her mouth, as if he could hardly hold himself back from kissing her right then and there.

Personally, I find that strategy a bit dated, more suitable to the empty-headed Barbies my dad likes to pursue, so I tone it down and use my sketch as an introduction. When I've finished, I get up and approach, as if I'm studying him in comparison to my drawing. Then, with an almost guilty tone in my voice, I'll say, *"I hope you don't mind, but I've been drawing you. You have great* _____ [insert physical attribute here]. *They're so* _____[insert appropriate adjective here]." Then I'll straddle a chair, flip open my sketchbook, and show him the drawing, pretending all the while that what I'm really excited about is having found such an ideal example of _____[insert physical attribute here] to draw. *"No, really,"* I say, when he blushes or protests. *"They're beautiful. I'd love to draw you again sometime. Could I? I mean if your girlfriend or wife wouldn't mind. No? You don't have one? I find that hard to believe!"*

I always make sure to say girlfriend or wife since there are few things more flattering to a gay man than to be told he resembles a straight one. It also makes him laugh and allows me to determine if there is, indeed, a rival at home, although that usually doesn't make much difference since those who have been dining on the dry toast of monogamy are usually the most eager to pull up a chair to an illicit feast. Oh, and the accent is important, too. Instead of faux Italian, I go for something vaguely, untraceably foreign; a subtle upward lilt on the last word in interrogative sentences, with a few odd inflections tossed in. Madonna has tried and failed to do this. Grace Kelly succeeded. So did Cary Grant. In fact, imagine yourself as Cary Grant (speech, looks, manners, dress, grooming, subtle humor, etc.) throughout this whole process and you really can't go wrong.

Step 3. The Ruse

Once you've broken through the introduction barrier and have maintained a conversation for at least, say, fifteen to twenty minutes, glance down at your watch and realize that you are late for an appointment. It is important to have a look of profound disappointment on your face. A look that says, *"I am torn between remaining in this halcyon nest with you and, uh, my commitment to teach a drawing class to underprivileged children in the projects."* The goal here is to make him see your angst and have him hastily scribble down his phone number. If he is not so bright, and let's face it, not all of them—and especially not all of the really pretty ones—are, you will have to relent and scribble down your number, which is not, as you'll see, such a bad thing.

The Middle

Once a phone number has been obtained, it is essential that you don't call right away. This is to ensure that the O.O.D. will think about you, if for no other reason than to wonder why you haven't called. If he should happen to call you first (which will obviously be the case if he has your number and you don't have his), listen to his message and then wait at least twenty-four hours before returning the call. As my father said, this waiting "gives time for the little seed you planted to germinate. And seeds always germinate better in the dark." Only once you are sure his curiosity has sprouted is it okay to call and set a date.

If, for some reason, the O.O.D. is reluctant to make a date, so much the better, for then you have what you, as a wooer, are really after anyway: the challenge. Like most everything in life, anticipation is much better than acquisition, and wooing is no exception. The pleasure comes from the chase, not from the capture. When the O.O.D. is reluctant to see you, the real lobbying can begin and you can get creative. I usually start with some sort of gift. The gift can be anything, really. Flowers and heart-shaped boxes of chocolates with sappy little notes attached might come to mind, and they were my father's gifts of choice, but I try to go for something more original. An example: One time, years ago, I wrote a request for a date on a piece of paper, stuffed the paper in an empty wine bottle, corked it, and then set it afloat in a five-gallon bucket of water, which I stealthily placed on the O.O.D.'s doorstep sometime during the night. Or another time, I remember I sent an engagement ring—the kind with a big plastic stone found in supermarket gum ball machines—along with a postcard of Siegfried and Roy on which I'd written a request that the O.O.D. go to Las Vegas with me and get married. Absurd, yes, but different from anything the O.O.D. has experienced before, and memorable.

Only after the lobbying has been successful and a date has been set do I decide where to go and what to do. I try to avoid dinner and a movie, since that scenario has been played out to its boring end, time and time again. I suspect that Adam took Eve to dinner and a movie and I've no doubt two thousand years in the future people will be doing the same, unimaginative thing. For me, evening picnics are much better. They take more preparation but are always memorable and are as close to a "sure thing" as you can get in the sex department. There is something wonderful about having a guy think you're taking him on a ho-hum date to a restaurant, and then confusing him as you veer off the road, stop the car in the middle of nowhere, and shut off the engine. There is an element of surprise, maybe even a tinge of fear, as you get out of the car and open the trunk. Fear that will melt into relief and joy when he sees you returning with a basket and a bottle of wine. By the time you've spread out the blanket, handed him a wilted daisy and lit a small candle; before you've even opened the basket or the wine, it's safe to assume that he'll be out of his clothes and in your arms before you get to dessert.

Miniature golf is also good as a first date since no one is very good at it and most O.O.D.s find it rather quaint. The same goes for bowling and skating (roller or ice), kite flying, concerts in the park, whatever. The important thing is to use your imagination and make an event out of it. Bring a bottle of wine, take pictures, make it out of the ordinary, something he'll look back on and remember fondly, even as he curses you under his breath and slanders you to his friends for all the things you did to him later. But I'm getting ahead of myself.

Making dinner for an O.O.D. is also excellent. If you can cook, great, dazzle him with your culinary prowess. If not, that's even better, for then the O.O.D. will see that you are really making an effort to impress him and will, more often than not, be thrilled with the result, however dismal it may be. In fact, in my own experience I've found it really is best, when entertaining someone who is gifted in the kitchen, to pretend that I don't know the difference between boiling and baking since then it gives him the opportunity to help and to show off his own expertise.

Like I said, first dates are usually great. The first six months to a year with a guy are usually great. It's what comes after that's difficult. It is difficult to keep things new and imaginative and exciting. At least it's difficult to do so with the same person, and for that reason, more than any other, you'll probably find it necessary to move on. You'll look at him one evening and think only about how you want to get back the shirts he's borrowed, and which of his CDs you want to copy. It is then that you'll know you're passing from the Middle to the End.

The End

At this point, I'm sure you're thinking of that other Carly Simon song. You know, the one about clouds in the coffee, the one that may or may not be about Warren Beatty. And you'd probably be right to do so, but it would be much more useful to choose the song by Simon, Paul—the one in which he tells you all about the fifty ways.

If you're like me, once the robin of infatuation has flown south, the first thing you'll want to do is take wing and follow it. When your stomach no longer does flip-flops at the sight of his number on the caller ID, when your gift giving starts feeling more like an onerous chore instead of a pleasure, it is time to move on. And the best way to do that is to stop calling and stop taking his calls. It's as simple as that. Simple, unless you've made things really sticky by moving in together (in which case you'll need to consult the following chapters).

Breaking up may be hard to do, but what is even harder is to come up with an original way to do it. The reason for this, again, is one of inspiration, or the lack thereof. That said, you have two options to consider when you decide to leave him:

1. Be the good guy, or

2. Be the bad guy

With either option, it is important to remember that nearly all breakups are trite. There is no new and improved, innovative way to do it so don't waste your time trying to find one. Just reach blindly into the magician's bag of platitudes and pull one out.

Lines to use for Option One:

It's not you it's me.

You're too good for me.

I'm at a crucial period in my career/art and I can't afford a relationship now.

I can't give you the love you deserve.

Lines to use for Option Two:

This isn't working for me.

We're incompatible.

I don't love you.

There's someone else.

Goodbye.

Things to keep in mind:

Choosing Option One will probably make *you* feel better, like you're a martyr sacrificing your own potential happiness for a higher principle. It probably will not make *him* feel better because he won't believe a word of it.

Choosing Option Two will probably make *him* feel better because he'll have the smug complacency that you were a rat and that it is better to be rid of you, although a few days, weeks, months, or in some cases even years down the road, he will probably rue the fact that he is, on some level, still in love with that rat.

While what you say is not really important, finding the right place to say it is, and for me, that place is a restaurant called The Hornet. For three reasons, The Hornet is an ideal place to deliver the sting: First, it is usually crowded so the O.O.D. will be less likely to make a scene, and it is noisy enough that if he does make a scene, it will probably go unnoticed. Second, The Hornet is relatively inexpensive, so if I get stuck with the bill when he leaves, I will not be out all that much. Third, The Hornet is centrally located so that if he storms out and leaves me stranded, I can easily walk, or catch a bus back home.

I realize this last section may sound brutal, or at least incredibly callous, but in the end there's no use pretending. We're talking about romantic love here, and as wonderful as it is, it does (like all things wonderful) have a most definite end. Wooing is all about the joy of the hunt. The capture and kill are tasks completed, and as soon as they're done, you just lift your head and start scanning the horizon for bigger game. That's how it works. Or at least that's how it used to work. It worked that way until one evening last summer when it all stopped working.

Chapter Two

First, I saw Meth, tied to the cherry tree in the front yard, tail between her legs. Then, rounding the curve, the house came into view. The three upstairs windows were open and the lawn below was littered with my belongings—clothes, books, easel, paints, laptop computer, the few pieces of furniture and kitchen items I could claim as my own—all heaped on the smashed remains of the Fiestaware I'd bought Roy for his last birthday. It looked like a closet had exploded, or like a giant piñata had been cracked open overhead. Or it looked like an eviction, which, unfortunately, is just what it was.

Closest to me, having been Frisbeed from the porch with the hope that it would land in the street, lay the obvious source of all the trouble: my sketchbook. Or at least what remained of it, since most of the pages had been clawed into tiny pieces and were blowing across the lawn like handfuls of tossed confetti.

In the nine volcanic months we'd been together, I'd grown used to Roy's eruptions of temper. He was always slamming doors and dramatically smashing things on the floor to make a point, usually about something important like how I'd left my dirty dishes in the sink or had forgotten to hang up a wet towel. Indeed, that magmatic personality was what I'd initially found so attractive about him. That, and his broad, tattooed shoulders, and the fact that he could cut my hair more perfectly than anyone before or since. But alas, in the end I was no Samson, and Roy had none of Delilah's magic.

In the weeks preceding my eviction, the romance between us had begun to cool, as it so often does with me, and Roy had grown justifiably suspicious. It was those suspicions, I realized, that had led him to invade the private world of my sketchbook. An invasion that had been all too successful since he'd found the sketches, and the names, and the phone numbers that I'd written down and been too careless to conceal, and he knew exactly what they were and what they meant since his own had once been among them.

But I'm afraid that's not the whole story. You see, a few days before our final fight, I had been involved, I'll admit it, in an afternoon of innocuous, insignificant, and in my view, really harmless heavy petting with someone who was not Roy. And that would have been fine (at least as far as I was concerned), except that after the encounter, when I returned to my van and pulled down the visor to look in the mirror, I noticed that I'd been scarred. There, on the left side of my neck, between chin and collarbone, was a large, oval, purple-speckled spot. A strawberry, a love bite, a territorial marker, the visible proof of passion's violent nature, a hickey.

I was angry, yes, but what made it worse was that I knew it had been given to me deliberately. I'd "played" with this particular guy before, many, many times, and was perfectly content to maintain our trysts as a sidebar to my committed relationship, but he, for some selfish reason, wanted more, and had indicated as much that very afternoon as we lay twisted in the sunny sheets. I remember he sat up suddenly, lit a cigarette, and said (prophetically, so it turned out) that this particular encounter would be "the last like this." *Like this* meaning on the sly in a motel room in the middle of the day.

I can't really blame him. He wanted what every gay man wants at some point or another—a boyfriend, a significant other, something more than a trick, something more than a one-night stand, something more than I was, at that point, willing to give, and as I gazed in the mirror at the welt on my neck, I knew that his giving it to me had been a final attempt to force my hand; an effort to expose me to my boyfriend as the cheating cad that I am, after which I would presumably be tossed out on my ear and go running back to him.

His plan was only partly successful.

There are many methods to conceal hickeys, a turtleneck sweater being the most obvious, but since this particular hickey was given to me in the summer, that really wasn't an option. Other techniques that can be feverishly culled from the Internet include pressing a frozen spoon on the wound (which doesn't work), running the teeth of a comb gently back and forth over the affected area while simultaneously blowing it with a hair dryer (doesn't work either), applying a poultice of baking soda and mustard (really doesn't work and is a stinky mess), or rubbing it with ice cubes, toothpaste, or crushed garlic (ibid).

Or after all those things have failed and you have less than thirty minutes before your boyfriend returns home from work, you can do the extreme thing that I did, and that is to make it worse. Most girls would do this with a curling iron, but since I am not (in the strictest sense of the word) a girl, and do not have access to such an appliance, I hastily devised the following procedure:

First, go to the place in the house where you keep liquor and pour yourself a shot of vodka. Make it a double if you've got a weak stomach. Then go out to the garage or down in the basement and get a sheet of 60 grit sandpaper. Once you have that, return to the bathroom and strip down to your underwear. Carefully fold the sandpaper in fourths and rub it repeatedly over the hickey, applying more and more pressure until you don't think you can possibly stand it—and then do it some more. Once the affected area looks more like a scrape than what it is, stop, and repeat the process on your forehead, chin, shoulder, and the side of your knee. If you haven't guessed, these other areas are done for appearance's sake. Scrapes on the neck are rare, so these others are to make it seem like you had a catastrophic fall on gravel, or asphalt or concrete. A fall in which you hit one of those convex concrete stops in a parking lot maybe, or some other raised object that could fit nicely in the recessed niche between your shoulder and head.

Once you are satisfied with the appearance of your wounds, dress yourself in some running clothes and go out into the backyard (if you don't have a backyard, a potted plant will work) and smear your cheek and wounds with dirt (don't worry, someone will lovingly clean them with disinfectant in a few minutes), then return inside, get a wad of wet paper towels, and pour yourself another drink. Make it a vodka tonic this time, with ice, maybe even a twist if there's time. Then take a sip, sit back at the kitchen table, and wait. When the dogs start barking their heads off indicating the imminent arrival of your spouse, remain seated, a dejected look on your face, and gently dab at the wound on your knee with the wet paper towel. Then, when he enters, sees you, and cries, *Oh my God, you poor thing, what happened!?* be ready with one heck of an explanation. It will probably hold for a day or two, maybe even a week, but then the suspicions will begin to surface. Like I said before, scrapes on the neck are rare, so no matter how good your sanding technique, it will probably still look like you were trying to hide a hickey. And he'll probably consider calling you on it. But here's the beauty of it: *Who in their right mind*, he'll think to himself, *would go to such an extreme to hide a hickey?*

Who, indeed?

In retrospect, the hickey suspicion was probably what spurred Roy on to the rape and pillage of my sketchbook. And I really should have known there was trouble that very morning when he violently shook me awake and gazed down at me through narrowed eyes. Should have known by his surly demeanor over breakfast, by the way he spanked my dog for begging and put her outside but then proceeded to feed his own yapping Jack Russels from the table. Should have known that he'd thumbed through the damning pages sometime during the night and was already plotting his revenge. Of course, I *should* have known, but I didn't. Roy was often moody and I was often running late, as I was that morning, so I didn't have the time or, frankly, the inclination to contemplate the source of his moodiness. It was when I couldn't *find* my sketchbook that I should have worried, but like I said, I was late, so I made a quick and fruitless search of the house and convinced myself I'd probably just left it in the van or at the coffee shop; convinced myself that there was no reason to bring it up and risk unnecessary incrimination so I just shrugged it off. I kissed Roy's inflamed cheek and headed out the door, figuring we'd hash it out, whatever "it" was, later that evening. Which brings us back around to where we came in . . .

The sun had almost set. I stared out at the littered lawn, unsure what to do next. I turned to the west and looked up at the darkening sky, streaked with angry wisps of pink and orange. Then I turned back to the east and looked up at the house. It seemed like every light was burning inside. I couldn't see Roy but I knew he was there: doors were slamming, Jack Russels were barking, curses were flying, and from the stereo speakers the voice of some self-righteous diva was pealing on and on about being wronged and throwing the bum out.

I grumbled, rubbed my temples, and started slowly up the steps, thinking I'd better go in and try to calm him down, try to make up some excuse and appease him as I'd done so many times before. Either that or confess all, grovel, and beg for forgiveness, which I'd also done so many times before, although not with this particular boyfriend. Weighing the two options, I stepped up onto the porch and reached for the door handle. I was about to grasp it but then hesitated, as if afraid it might be hot or give me an electric shock. I knew that I could, and probably should, go in; knew that was what he wanted, in spite of the overwhelming evidence to the contrary on the lawn, but I just couldn't do it. Mental pictures of what awaited me on the other side of the door scrolled through my mind: there would be rage and indignant tears from Roy, protestations of innocence, or depending on the signals I received, a confession and promises to change from me. And then, of course, there would be sex. There would most definitely be sex. Some of the best sex ever occurs in the aftermath of fights; that much I knew, and probably, on some level, Roy did, too, but that knowledge didn't excite me just then. It always had in the past, but not this time. The thought of all I would have to do and say to get from Point A to Point B E D seemed like more trouble than it was worth. I'd worked hard that day and more than anything else I wanted a shower, something to eat, and a soft place to sit down.

I lifted my glasses and rubbed my eyes. I looked back at the lawn and at Meth, whining and prancing expectantly, ears back and tail wagging. I looked at the neighbors across the street standing in their large picture window, evening cocktails in hand, looking at me and all my stuff. For a moment, I rocked back and forth on the balls of my feet wondering what to do.

Could I?

Should I?

Would I?

It turned out I would. I did a *demi*-pirouette, tiptoed back down the steps, and began collecting the pulverized vestiges of my life and hauling them down to my van.

In spite of my stealth, Roy must have seen or heard me because on my second trip down the meandering, Malibu lamp–lighted walkway the sprinklers came on, much to the amusement of my soon-to-be-former neighbors. I paused, grumbled, clenched the muscles in my neck and glared up at the empty, glowing windows. For a moment, I considered throwing something or shouting some obscenity, but instead I just gritted my teeth and got back to work, making three more soggy trips before returning to release Meth. As soon as I untied her from the tree, she ran, leaping through the shooting jets of water, to the van and jumped in the open door, wriggling like a seal, up and over the piles of my stuff to take her customary place in the passenger seat. She knew the routine. There had been six such moves in as many years and she had been around for three of them. She knew what the shouting and the slamming doors and the piles of clothes meant. She knew that this particular show was over and it was time to move on. Of course, she didn't know why—didn't know that it was because her owner had been exposed, yet again, as a charlatan, a seller of amorous snake oil, a thief of hearts. No, all Meth knew was that things had gotten bad and we'd better move on before they got worse. The moving didn't seem to faze her anymore. As long as she was not left behind, as long as she had her place in the van, as long as she was with me, all was right in her world. A dog's loyalty is something I should have studied.

I got in next to her and looked at her regal profile: the long nose pointing into the future, albeit with as much choice in the direction she was headed as a weather vane. She seemed eager to go, almost happy that we were leaving, but, then, that was probably because she had some inkling of where we were going. Somewhere in that walnut-sized brain, she must have suspected that we were returning once again to the soft, happy, treaty place. The place where there were no psychotic Jack Russels to compete with, the place where she would be allowed, even invited, to lie on the furniture. Yes, in Meth's mind, our prospects were definitely on the rise, but

I'm afraid I couldn't share her enthusiasm. Oh, I was certainly looking forward to the wonderful meals my stepfather would make, to my old bed, and to the comfortable furniture in the house I was familiar with, but what I was not looking forward to was the chilly reception I would receive; the minefield of quiet disappointment I'd have to walk through before I could relax; my mother's weary sigh when she opened the door and saw me on the doorstep, the click of her tongue implying that she hoped my stay would be short. I'd smile and nod my head, indicating that *Yes, she'd told me so.* Then, as quickly as I could, I'd sneak past her and go up to my room. It was not an inviting prospect. But as I looked in the rearview mirror at the messy trouble I was leaving behind, the place I was headed seemed not quite so bad.

Chapter Three

In my experience, one can go home again, numerous times, but it will never be even remotely the same as the last time you were there. A fact that is especially true if you have a mother and stepfather like mine, who are unnaturally obsessed with home renovation. If even less than a month had passed between my "visits", there would always be something radically different when I returned: Some new wall that had been torn down or erected, or a different sink and tub in one of the bathrooms. Paint colors changed with kaleidoscopic speed and the hardware to every door was slowly being upgraded with original brass pieces that they'd unearthed on one of their archeological outings. Their fever for home improvement had, in recent years, spread throughout the neighborhood and soon, in the front window of just about every house, the green and white permit signs began appearing, which was good, I suppose, since few places in Denver were more in need of renovation than the neighborhood where I grew up.

For decades, Curtis Park had languished; its name synonymous with violent crime and urban blight, which was too bad because as one of the city's earliest, and still largely intact, neighborhoods, it has wide streets bordered by mature, stately trees, and more examples of Victorian architecture than all of Denver's other neighborhoods combined. Fortunately, those charms were rediscovered by a new generation and Curtis Park has since then experienced a small renaissance. The charge toward gentrification, led by young, mostly white couples, both gay and straight, began in earnest about seven years ago, and hasn't shown any sign of stopping. Almost overnight, property values shot up and it soon became impossible to buy even the burned-out shell of a house for less than $300,000.

The house I drove to on the evening Roy threw me out was, from a renovator's point of view, spectacular: A three-story, patterned-brick Victorian with elaborate and elaborately painted trim. On the front lawn stood a gazebo, as elaborate and elaborately painted as the house, and next to that, a circular, multitiered fountain. Surrounding it all was an eight-foot iron fence, which had once surrounded an equally grand house in Denmark, and which my stepfather, Peter, had imported at considerable expense. It was a great fence—I had helped erect it one summer a few years before—and yet, whenever I entered the yard and heard it latch behind me, I invariably thought of prison.

The house had sheltered my family since the 1940s when my grandfather, according to legend, won it in a cock fight. Or at least that's how the story goes. My grandfather died before I could hear it from him, and my father, the principal raconteur of the family history, is, to say the least, an exaggerator. I suppose I could have asked my grandmother, Lola, about it, but that would not really have done much good since trying to pry facts about the house, or anything else, from her—a Spanish-speaking lunatic—was like, well, trying to pry facts from a Spanish-speaking lunatic. She lived in her own world of Mexican soap operas, and bingo, and church, talking more to her dashboard statues of the Catholic saints and her pet squirrels than to any of us, so whenever I asked her questions about the past, she just looked at me with her coy, bovine eyes and giggled like a schoolgirl. What I do know is that my father was probably born and raised in the house and that when he married my mother (because she was pregnant with me), he brought her to live there, too. The marriage lasted only about two years and from its dissolution came their unorthodox divorce settlement: My father moved out of the house (which he had always hated anyway), but we three—my mother, grandmother, and I—stayed on, and my father signed over the deed in lieu of alimony.

On the surface this might seem like it was a very good deal for my mother, especially when you consider that my father had always been lax about paying bills of any sort so it would have been safe to assume that alimony and child support would probably not be high on his list of priorities. But a good deal it most certainly was not. The neighborhood was rough, and the house rapidly decaying, which made the possibility of resale impossible. Add to that the stipulation my father tacked on to the transaction and it became even more so.

"I'll give you the house," he told my mother, "no strings attached. All free and clear, as long as Lola can stay until she dies."

Which might have been fine if my grandmother had been near death, which she was not, or been sane, which she was not, and if she did not despise my mother with all the feverish, Latin passion in her heart, which she most certainly did. My mother must have known she was getting a rotten bag of fruit, but she signed the agreement anyway and thus took over all of my father's biggest liabilities. It would be easy, I suppose, to think her stupid for accepting the deal but when you consider her situation, what choice did she have? She'd been a nineteen year-old au pair when my father, the gardener, planted his seed in her, and in the time they'd been together she had acquired no real money or skills. She was alone in a foreign country, and suddenly the single parent of a less than angelic child. Of course once my dad left, she could have just packed the two of us up and taken the first flight back to her family in Copenhagen, but she was proud and didn't want them to know her marriage had failed, just as they'd predicted. I hate to say it but she was also somewhat masochistic and for years sustained the hope that one day, my father would settle down and come back to her, so with few reservations she accepted his offer, batty ex-mother-in-law and all. She went on welfare, worked part-time during the day, studied accounting at night, and for the next eighteen years, the three of us lived together in the house.

The house!

The White Elephant.

The Booby Prize.

Casa Turquesa.

It's funny to look at it now, in its pristine state of perfection, and try to remember what a landmark of ugliness it used to be. Back then, it was just one eyesore on a block of similarly run-down and neglected eyesores, but what made it distinctly hideous was its paint color: a gaudy turquoise that had certainly been intended only for the bottom of a swimming pool, and which covered every conceivable exterior surface except the windowpanes. My father had always hated the color because it looked too Mexican and my mother had always loved it for the very same reason, which was good for her, because after he left, it was years before she could afford to change it.

But the paint was only the most obvious problem. On closer inspection there were rotting soffits and shutters, gutters so full of holes you could see the sky through them, and a herd of giddy squirrels coming and going through the gaps in the vinyl siding. The roof, with its seven layers of asbestos shingles, looked like an unevenly frosted cake, and the concrete walkway (also painted turquoise), leading from the sidewalk to the front door, had buckled and cracked from the roots of all the smelly ailanthus trees ("ghetto palms") that had taken over the yard. A yard that was itself nothing more than a weedy patch of hard clay surrounded by a stretched and sagging chain-link fence. For years the three of us lived under its leaky roof, endlessly complaining about the place but never quite sure how to go about making it better. Until Peter, that is.

Peter, who eventually became my mother's second husband, arrived late one autumn afternoon, won her heart, and almost overnight began to change the place for the better. The first time he saw the house, he was impressed, which surprised us both. It was as if he had x-ray vision and could see, beneath the siding and the turquoise paint, the bird within the egg. He walked around it that first afternoon and explained to us all the things that could "and really ought to be done" to renovate it, and of course, in time, my mother consented to do whatever Peter thought best. Very few people can refuse, or even argue with, Peter. There is something about him—his childlike excitement maybe, or the aura of masculine capability he exudes—that makes you want to do whatever he suggests. But probably, it is his eyes. Eyes that are a deep lapis blue, set off by hair and skin so fair they would make any Nazi proud. To say that Peter is beautiful is an understatement. He has a distracting, unreal beauty—the kind that makes you forget what you had intended to say and leaves you mumbling fragments. He seems immune to flattery so his personality hasn't been spoiled by vanity, which, of course, makes him even more beautiful, but again, it is probably his eyes. Eyes that focus on you whenever you speak because he is always paying attention, always engaged in what you have to say.

So, Peter moved in and soon thereafter began the process of removing the house from its cocoon. He stripped, cleaned, and polished everything that was worth saving, threw out everything that wasn't, and together he and my mother renovated the place from top to bottom, transforming it from neighborhood eyesore to jewel in the neighborhood crown. The siding was removed and the exterior paint sandblasted away, revealing an intricately patterned brick. The trim, gutters and windows were replaced and the sagging porch rebuilt. The ailanthus were cut down, wrapped in the chain-link fence and hauled away to the dump, their stumps and roots then rototilled into mulch. The gazebo was built, the fountain erected and plumbed, and the yard landscaped around them. Best of all, Peter built a series of hutches on the back deck outside of Lola's room, so that her squirrels (evicted from their attic home) could come and go in peace.

And a peaceful house it eventually became. Too peaceful. So, like the excellent and restless renovators they had become, my mother and Peter bought another decrepit mess of a house and began the whole process over again. They made so much money from the sale of that second house that they decided to quit their day jobs and start renovating for a living. That was seven years ago. In that time, they've renovated and sold twelve houses in Curtis Park. Of course, they didn't do it alone. They now have several employees and a cadre of subcontractors, who have helped make them the darlings of the Mayor's Commission on Urban Renewal.

For mostly sentimental reasons, they kept and continued to live in the original house, which, I reflected as I sped along in the soggy, doggy-smelling van, was lucky for me.

Meth began whimpering and wagging her tail blocks before we arrived, and by the time I pulled up alongside the curb in front of the house, she was shaking from excitement. I opened the driver's side door and she bolted over my lap, sprinting with cartoonish speed, up to the fence and squeezing her narrow body between the bars. I followed, in equally cartoonish slow motion, dreading the meeting with my mother and stepfather as much as Meth was looking forward to it.

When I reached the porch, I sat down to sort through the keys on my ring, trying to find the one, among all the useless souvenirs, that would open this particular door, but before I could find it someone unlocked and opened the door from the inside. I looked up. My mother was standing above me. I tried to smile but probably succeeded only in looking sick, which was how I was beginning to feel in my clammy clothes. She was dressed all in black, evidently ready to go out for the evening, and had her graying blond hair pulled back and twisted in the new style Peter had devised for her. Behind her, descending the stairs, was Peter, partially dressed in a tuxedo, an untied bow tie hanging around his neck. Meth pushed past my mother, jumped up on him, and licked his face, her muddy paws on his chest.

My mother smiled at the spectacle and then turned and looked back at me with an expression that surprised me. Instead of looking annoyed by my arrival, as she usually did, this time she seemed relieved, almost happy.

"Tony!" she cried, and then quickly turned to Peter. "Look, Peter, it's Tony! Come in, come in," she said, grabbing my arm and pulling me up and into the foyer.

This was odd. Certainly not the reception I'd expected. My guard went up. She eyed the soggy pile of clothes I'd brought with me to the porch and asked, "So, you're here for a while?"

In her voice, usually so calm and remote, I heard a high, hopeful note. She sat down on the step next to Meth and Peter, and all three of them looked up at me expectantly.

"Uh, yes," I said. "If it's okay, I mean. I was hoping to stay. For a little while, anyway. Things aren't, um, going well. With Roy."

"Have you eaten?"

Had I *eaten*? That was all she had to say? No reproach? No click of the tongue? No *I told you so*? I shook my head.

"No? Then of course you must come with us. Hurry and change.

You're soaking wet. And what happened to your face? Did you fall?"

"Uh, yeah," I said, fingering the scabs on my forehead and neck.

The clock at the top of the stairs began chiming. My mother gasped, looked at her watch and then at Peter.

"Could you just clip this, Peter?" she pleaded, giving him her arm and a pearl bracelet she'd been struggling with. "I've been trying for five minutes and I just can't get it."

Peter reached over the dog and took her slender wrist in his large, calloused hands, effortlessly fastening the tiny clasp and never removing his gaze, or his smile, from me.

"Yes, Tony," he said. "Why don't you come with us."

"Mmmm, maybe I better not," I said, thinking again of all my wet belongings stuffed in the van. "I don't think my clothes are . . . accessible."

"What's happened?" my mother asked.

I wasn't sure if she meant what happened with Roy or what happened to my face. Hoping it was the former, I said,

"Oh, you know. The same again." Then I leaned over, gave Meth a conspiratorial pat on the head, and speaking to her in order to avoid looking at my mother and Peter, I said, "We've been given the heave-ho, haven't we, girl? Yeeesssss. It was all your fault, wasn't it? Yeeesss. Just couldn't play nicely with the two Jacks."

My mother raised an eyebrow and shook her head. Peter chuckled.

"Okay, maybe it wasn't her fault, but we can talk about it later. You two better get going."

Peter rose, and began tying his tie, standing in front of the huge Moroccan mirror, but again his eyes were on me instead of the task he was executing.

"If you won't come with us," he said, "you should at least eat something here. There's plenty of food in the refrigerator, and half a bottle of wine on the counter. The sheets on your bed are clean."

"And what about her?" my mother asked, bending down again and stroking Meth's head. "She looks so hungry. So skinny. Do you never feed her, Tony? Peter, is there any of that ham left? Maybe you could give her some of that."

Before I could protest, Peter turned, put his nose next to the dog's, and spoke to her in Danish, the way he always did when he was about to give her a treat. She responded with a fit of Pavlovian hysterics and went tearing off down the hallway toward the kitchen, nails scuttling on the polished wood floor. Peter rose, and followed her, brushing the mud off his lapels as he went.

As soon as he had turned the corner and was out of sight, my mother grabbed me by the arm and pulled me into the living room. She closed the pocket doors behind us, and when she turned around, I saw that she was starting to cry. This startled me. Initially, I'd expected annoyance and had gotten a weird glee. Now there were tears, and I was suddenly afraid she'd moved beyond her usual irritation with my return, to feeling real sadness or despair.

"Mom, don't cry. I'm sorry. I'll only stay a couple days. Don't cry."

She shook her head and smiled, even laughed a little. "It's not you," she sighed, brushing my wet hair away from my forehead. "I would have been more surprised if you hadn't come back. No, I'm glad to see you. Really. It will make Peter happy. Lola, too."

Again, I was skeptical. And worried. The way she was behaving was the way I imagined people would behave when they were about to tell you they'd found a lump in their breast, or that they'd accidentally backed over Fluffy in the driveway.

She turned around again and peered through the small crack between the pocket doors. Seeing no one, she came back to the sofa, sat down, and patted the cushion next to her. I sat.

"It's Peter," she sighed, and her shoulders fell. My mother was not a sigher, or a crier, for that matter, so the two occurring together was a bad omen. My own shoulders rose up in anticipation of the worst.

"Peter? What? Is he sick?"

Peter was never sick, so that was a stupid question, but neither had Peter ever done anything (unlike me) to make my mother sigh and cry.

"Oh, no, no," she said. "Nothing like that. No. But he's leaving, Tony. Going back to Denmark."

My shoulders dropped. I gave her an impatient look and rolled my eyes.

"Is that all?" I said, and got up from the sofa. *That* was nothing, and I was a little annoyed that her tears had made me think otherwise. Peter threatened to go back to Denmark on a monthly basis but it was always more musing than threatening, and we both knew it.

"When your father left," she went on, ignoring my impatience, "that was bad enough. But to lose Peter . . ." she cried, waving a hand in front of her face, as if by doing so she could shoo the possibility away. "What will I do? I can't handle the business, and Lola, and this house all by myself. No, no, I just don't even want to think about it."

"Mom," I said, returning to the couch. "Relax. This is stupid. You know how he is. He won't go. This is his home now. He loves this house. He loves you. He loves me. He won't go."

"I hope you're right," she whispered, and then looked over her shoulder to see that Peter wasn't listening at the door. Satisfied, she turned back to me. "But I think he really means it this time. His mind seems more . . . sure. Do you know what I mean? He's not the same Peter. He's changed. Even with the houses, he hardly seems interested. He still works hard, as hard as ever, but with no heart, no enthusiasm. Can't you be nice to him?" she pleaded. "Please be nice. He loves you so. If anyone can change his mind, Tony, it's you."

She was right about that. My powers of persuasion were strong when it came to my stepfather but I was surprised that she, who'd scolded me whenever I'd used them on him in the past, was now actually suggesting I do so.

Peter had been good for my mother, but despite her belief to the contrary, he wasn't Jesus. I wanted to remind her that she had managed to live without him for years, and that she could certainly do so again if need be, but I didn't bother. I knew he wouldn't leave. He'd been dropping little bomblets like that for years and thus far—nine years after his arrival—they'd all been duds. In my mind, it wasn't even worth discussing so I changed the subject.

"Why so dressed up?" I asked. It was the wrong question. She glared at me.

"The dinner's tonight," she said, her voice ringing with the familiar maternal annoyance I'd expected to hear earlier. "I told you about it last week, don't you remember?"

I did not.

"The Sons of Denmark dinner. We're getting an award . . ."

"Oh, yes, yes," I said, faking it. "Is that tonight? I've been a day behind all week. Really. I'm sorry. I thought today was Tuesday, but of course it's Thursday. Of course. The Thursday night award dinner."

Her lips tightened and the crease between her eyebrows deepened into a trench, much like the one I was digging myself into. Lying to a mother is never easy, but mine was especially attuned to my brand of prevarication, probably because it was so similar to that of my father. In the silence that followed, I struggled to remember the details of the phone conversation we'd had the week before.

My mother and Peter, both Danish expatriates, were being honored by the Sons of Denmark fraternal order for the positive example they set as two successful Danish-American businesspeople who had bettered themselves and their adopted community. And I, her half-breed spawn, had forgotten all about it.

There was a knock at the pocket door. Peter leaned in and smiled at us, tapping his watch.

"It's after six, Louisa, we'd really better go."

"Yes, yes," she said, standing and smoothing the front of her dress. "Just let me get my purse."

She exited the living room and headed toward the stairs, pausing briefly at the mirror in the foyer to admire and recompose her unfamiliar hairdo. When she'd gone, Peter stepped into the room, took my hands, and pulled me up from the sofa. He put one arm around my back, and with the other held my hand and led me in a dance around the coffee table and back out into the foyer.

"Are you sure you won't come with us?" he asked, pulling me close and swaying from side to side. "I've got a suit you could wear."

I shook my head.

"No?"

Again, I shook my head and he responded by dipping me backward and holding me there, his face very close to mine.

"You ought to go," he said. "It would make your mother happy. We could all eat Danish food and get drunk on Carlsberg."

"I hate Danish food," I said, and that was not a lie. I was half Danish, but the other half was Mexican and I leaned toward my Latin roots when it came to cuisine.

"Yes, I know that," Peter said, still holding me arched back in a dip. "You always remind me if I forget." Then he kissed me. I didn't resist. When we came up for air, he straightened his tie and said, "Yes, our Tony hates Danish food." Then he kissed me again and said, "That much I know. But I also know he has a weakness for Carlsberg."

And Peter had a weakness for me. That much everyone knew.

My mother returned and stood once again in front of the Moroccan mirror, reapplying her lipstick and smiling at the two of us. I caught her eye and she gave me a conspiratorial wink.

"I'm ready," she said, dropping the lipstick into her purse and snapping it shut. Peter spun me around, gave me one last kiss and then went and stood behind my mother, his hands on her shoulders, admiring her in the mirror.

"Louisa," he said, addressing her in their native tongue, "you look fantastic tonight."

She blushed, gave a girlish, self-conscious shrug, and then linked arms with Peter.

"You sure you won't come?" she asked as they went down the walk toward the car.

"Yes, I'm sorry. It's been a long day. Have fun. I'll get some dinner and sit with Lola."

"Yes, do. I just told her you were here, but, well, you know. It's Simplemente Maria time and she doesn't hear anything when that's on. Mrs. Garcia is supposed to come by at 7:30 to check on her."

I nodded.

"She has had her dinner so she should be okay for the night but maybe you could go up and talk to her before she goes to bed."

"Sure."

I stood in the doorway and watched as they went down the sandstone walk to the car. Ever solicitous, Peter opened the car door for her and held her hand as she stepped in.

It was then, watching them, that I understood why even the remote possibility of his leaving distressed her: In so many ways, all but one, actually, Peter really was the ideal husband.

Chapter Four

I first met Peter on a boat almost ten years ago and our relationship has remained wavy and unstable ever since. It was the summer after I graduated from college and from a relationship with Boyfriend #2 (one of my art professors). A summer when I was, like so many other recent grads, traveling across Europe on a Eurail Pass to have one final bohemian jaunt before settling into the quotidian life of work, "marriage," and mortgages. At least that was how I thought it would be.

My journey began in Sicily—my father's fictional birthplace—and from there I slowly worked my way up the map, stopping in France, Czechoslovakia, Belgium, and Germany, before ending my trip in Denmark—my mother's nonfictional birthplace—where I was to stay with some elderly relatives in a small town outside of Aarhus. It was an eventful trip for me, although not in the way you might think.

When I left Boyfriend #2, (who assumed I would be coming back to him at the end of the summer, a more sophisticated and rounded individual), I was given, as a parting gift, a large sketchbook encased in brushed titanium, along with some expensive pens and pencils, and the advice that I "draw my way up the continent." Up until then, I had been drawing lots of dogs and flowers and pieces of fruit (I was smoking a lot of pot) and the time had come, as #2 put it, "to move away from juvenilia" and elevate the subject matter of my work.

And for a while at the beginning of my trip, that's just what I did, high-mindedly sketching every monument, church, and historic building that I could find, making serious drawings of the ruins in Sicily, and sitting for hours sketching different angles of architecturally complex buildings in Rome and Florence. By the time I got to Milan and stood before that daunting, depressing cathedral, the thought of drawing another organized pile of stones made me want to cry, and I came very close to chucking the brushed titanium sketchbook, the expensive pencils, and all of my artistic aspirations into the river.

Instead, I decided to have a drink. I went to one of the street cafes on the plaza and took the only open seat at a table in back—a table that had no view of the cathedral—and there I sat, sipping my beer, idly watching the people around me. To my left, there were two, old whining English cows, who wanted to be "as far away from the filthy street as possible." To my right was an adulterous Italian couple, who wanted to be just as far away from the street, but for a much different reason. The English women were tired and fussy and complaining about prices and the heat (but, nevertheless, drinking hot tea), and they kept applying and reapplying powder to their faces from small compacts. Thinking they might be a nice change from my architectural pursuits, I pulled out my sketchbook and began drawing them, trying to capture their expressions and moods and even their voices. The result was good, but not great, so I tried the adulterous couple. They grew conscious of my staring and the man shot me an angry look. He summoned the waiter for their check, and it was then that my eyes alighted on a more tantalizing subject.

If there is one thing that can be said about Italy, it is that the men are more beautiful than any scenery, painting, statue, or building you'll ever find. All that sleek, black hair and clear, olive skin; those lean, firm bodies squeezed into tight, fashionable packages. Why it took me two weeks to recognize them as suitable material for sketching, I'll never know.

The one who sauntered into my field of view that afternoon—

the waiter—had dark, heavy-lidded eyes, a huge nose, and an impassive, sexy expression. I sharpened my pencil and got to work.

Most people are curious when they realize someone is sketching them, but this one was different. The first time he caught me looking, he scowled and turned away. Remembering the angry look from the adulterer, I quickly turned my attention elsewhere and pretended I hadn't been staring, but he knew, and the next time I glanced up, his scowling expression had been replaced by a faint, almost devious smile. I took this as encouragement (although it was just as likely a signal that he would later bash my head in and steal my wallet), gave him a shy smile back, and then returned to the drawing. A few moments later, I got the peculiar feeling of someone looking over my shoulder. I turned and there he was, about five feet behind me, a little to the left, absently drying glasses with the crisp, white towel attached to his apron, his eyes on my sketchbook. Our eyes met briefly, for what seemed like less time than it would take electricity to travel down a kite string, and he gave a nod to the bathroom door. I looked at the door, then back at him, and then got up and walked to the bathroom.

The thing I remember most about the encounter was that when it was over (it really was quick, he had to get back to work and we were both excited), after I'd returned to my seat and he'd seen to the other customers, he returned to where I was sitting and was adamant about wanting something more.

"Paper," he insisted, in schoolboy English. "Give me paper."

Naively thinking he wanted me to pay the bill, or even to pay for his "services" I reached for my wallet. He laughed, put a hand on my shoulder, and waved a finger at me.

"No, no, no," he said. "Paper. *Paper!*" Finally, after much gesturing and mumbling from each of us, I realized what he wanted and opened my sketchbook. He nodded eagerly at the drawing I'd done of him, so I gently tore out the page and handed it to him. He smiled, took it, gave me a discreet pat on the head, and walked away, as happy as Narcissus.

Though I didn't know it then, I had reached an artistic turning point. After that bathroom encounter in Milan, I gave up on monuments, and statues, and buildings, and devoted all of my artistic attention to the study of men. Each morning I'd find a different café and sit down with my coffee, pencil and paper to watch and capture the endless display of male models in all shapes and sizes just waiting for me to immortalize them in a portrait.

With a good portrait, even more than a good photograph, you understand why some African tribes think a picture can steal your soul. A camera is stupid. It opens its eye and records an instant of time. A portrait is more intimate, albeit a calculated, one-sided, voyeuristic intimacy. Photography is like snatching a purse and running away. It leaves the victim stunned and helpless. Portraiture is less violent but more disturbing. It is the criminal stalking his victim before the strike. The victim may know he's being stalked but can never be sure if it is so, or if he is just being paranoid.

The first time I saw Peter, it was as a drawing subject. I'd spent a bleary two nights on trains trying to reach Denmark and arrived just in time to board an early-morning ferry; one of those massive, slow-moving boats crammed with carloads of summer tourists. I was tired and wanted only to find a place to curl up and rest when, suddenly, there appeared before my weary eyes a vision of such blond, blue-eyed, muscular masculinity that I forgot all about sleep. Almost without thinking, I abandoned my seat, picked up my belongings and followed him out on deck. After some meandering, he found a seat in the sun, removed his shirt, revealing a smooth, tanned chest, and sat with his head back and his eyes closed. I took a seat a discreet distance away although still well within his line of sight so that when he did open his eyes, he would inevitably see me working on my sketch.

Of course, as my subject matter, I chose his chest: the large pectorals, elevated and flat, like two mesas rising above the rippled terrain of his abdominals, and the whole expanse of it expanding and contracting as he breathed.

To my annoyance, he did not even once open his eyes. Or at least not when I was looking up. He just sat there, contentedly baking in the sun, oblivious to everything around him. Only after the boat had docked and most of the other passengers had disembarked did he open his too-blue-to-be-believed-and-yet-not-contacts eyes. He got up, stretched, yawned, put his shirt back on, and walked right past me without so much as a glance at me or my sketchbook, which I had, of course, left wide open to the page with his portrait.

As I watched him stride obliviously down the gangway, with all of his chilly Scandinavian beauty, I wondered if maybe it hadn't been a mistake leaving Italy.

Later that evening, dozing in the compartment of a small, glacially slow train headed north I was surprised (and yes, annoyed) to awaken from my drooling nap only to discover someone sitting across from me drawing *my* portrait. And not just someone, but the oblivious chesty sunbather from the ferry. I sat up quickly, as if in response to some loud noise, but the only sound was the slow, rhythmic click and clack of the train wheels. I looked around. We were alone. I tried to remember the simple Danish phrase for "What the hell are you doing?" but like any really important foreign phrase, it wasn't there when I needed it and would not come until after the moment had passed, so there I sat, mouth mutely open. Nor did he speak. He just glanced up at me, and then back down at the notebook in which he was sketching. Finally, the words came to me.

He smiled but didn't look up. Then, in low, languid, beautifully accented English, he stated the obvious.

"I'm drawing you."

"So I see," I snipped, also in English. "Please don't."

He closed the notebook and gazed at me with his azure eyes.

"That's hypocrisy," he said, mispronouncing it slightly. "You drew me without asking. Shouldn't I be able to do the same?"

I raised an eyebrow. So he *had* seen me. Nevertheless, I gave a deep (and deeply phony) laugh and said, "I wasn't drawing *you.*"

The intent, of course, was to make him feel vain and mistaken. It didn't work. He held my gaze for several seconds and said, "Now you are not only a hypocrite, but a liar, too."

In spite of his words, he wasn't angry. On the contrary, the corners of his mouth were turned up in a subtle grin.

"Yes, you did draw me. I saw you out of the corner of my vision on the ferry. You were waiting for me to notice."

I struggled to find something to say, some way to protest, but nothing came to mind.

"Let me see it," he said.

I could not help smiling, but made no move.

"I'll show you mine," he offered, again holding me in that steady blue gaze, "if you show me yours."

I grinned, my heartbeat quickening, endorphins rushing into

my bloodstream, but still I hesitated. I had no qualms about show-ing my work to him (few artists are really coy when it comes to that); I just wasn't sure I wanted to see the portrait he'd drawn of me. And the reason for that was simple: it was the fear we all have of suddenly hearing a recording of our own voice, or of seeing a photograph snapped before we were ready; a fear that we'll be pre-sented with a representation of ourselves that is radically different from what we imagine, and which is, nine times out of ten, not for the better.

In the end, vanity and the desire to actually touch the chest I'd so recently sketched overpowered my fear. I pulled out my sketch-book and patted the seat next to me. Like a spaniel, he came over and sat. I opened to the page with the drawing of his torso and handed it to him. He then handed his notebook to me, our hands brushing against each other during the transaction.

He looked at the page I gave him, a confused expression on his face, and I looked, just as confusedly, at the page he'd given me, which was blank. I flipped through the rest of the pages, all equally blank, and looked at him, about to protest. Without looking up from my sketchbook, he put a finger to his lips and emitted a "ssh-hhh," which I, for some reason, obeyed, and we sat, silently rock-ing, as he examined the rest of my drawings. He lingered over a few of the portraits but kept returning to one page—a trio of heads that I'd drawn, not in Italy, but in Marseille. I remembered that I'd missed my train that evening and had taken a seat at one of those seedy bars that cluster around train stations. The kind of bar that is packed with people all day long but is almost empty at night. The heads had belonged to three handsome Algerian men who'd been having a beer and telling stories after work. Their faces were weathered and expressive, and I had drawn them slowly, one after the other. The first one was laughing, the second, mute and serious, and by the time I got round to drawing the third, he was drunk. I'd arranged them all on the same page so that they appeared to be floating there, almost coming out of a mist. Like most of the por-traits still in my sketchbook, that particular one was of men I hadn't slept with, since when I did, I usually gave them the portrait as a souvenir.

"This is the best of them all," Peter said, pointing to the trio. I nodded my agreement and was glad he'd selected that one out of all of the others since it was the one I was most proud of. On impulse, I tore it out of the book and handed it to him.

"Then you should have it," I said. He was surprised, as I'd hoped he would be, and was about to protest, but I held my finger to my lips just as he had done and shook my head. I could tell he thought he should refuse, that it was something too valuable to accept, but in the end, he smiled and took it.

"But you haven't signed it," he said, looking at both the front and the back of the page.

"You won't get any money for it," I laughed. "I'm not famous."

"Not yet," he replied, "but maybe someday you will be and then I can tell everyone that I had a lover who was a famous artist."

For a moment, I did not know what to say. I chuckled nervously, signed the paper with a shaking hand, and gave the portrait back to him. He took it, placed it carefully in the compartment above his seat, and returned and sat next to me. Slowly, and with a confidence and assurance that I found very exciting, he took my chin in his hand and turned my face toward his, hesitating just for a moment before kissing me. Then he got up, locked the compartment door, lowered the shade on the small window looking into the corridor, and removed his shirt.

Chapter Five

That was the beginning of June, the beginning of Relationship #3, the beginning of Peter and Tony. I abandoned my plan to stay with the Aarhus relatives and stayed instead with Peter, who was house-sitting for his uncle. The uncle, Peter told me, was visiting his girlfriend in Brussels. What he neglected to add was that he hadn't yet left on the journey, so when I followed Peter into a hedge-surrounded yard I was surprised to find a nude, middle-aged man sitting in a chair under a shedding linden tree, reading a newspaper and puffing on a pipe.

"*Far*," Peter said, putting his arm around me as we approached. "I'm home."

The nude man looked up and squinted. Then he stood up, folded the newspaper, and strode toward us wearing nothing but his glasses.

"And you've brought a friend," he said, taking one of my hands in both of his and shaking it. I tried not to look down.

"I'm usually dressed," he said, sensing my surprise, "but I'm leaving tomorrow and needed to wash the clothes I was wearing and, well, it's a nice sunny day."

"Tony is an artist," Peter said. "He is probably used to nudity."

"An artist!" the uncle exclaimed, and then inhaled sharply.

"Yes," Peter said, "he's from Colorado. He draws portraits."

"Colorado!" he exclaimed. "Portraits!"

From the skewed expression on his mouth and the high magnification of his glasses, I could not tell if his exclamations were of pleasure or disapproval.

"The last portrait painter we had here was Peter's cousin, Pernilla," he said, with a sour look. "But she does mostly children and small pets, or Pierrots and ballet dancers, that sort of thing, all with giant heads and big watery eyes. You don't do children, do you?"

"No," I said. "No children. No Pierrots."

"Good. Then you must show me your work. If Peter likes it, I'm sure I will like it. You do like it, don't you, Peter? Yes? Then I'm sure I will like it. He knows something good when he sees it. Peter is an artist, too, as you must know."

I did not. I had known Peter for just about twelve hours at that point, at least six of which we had spent having sex in the train.

The uncle went on, "He carves such beautiful things. Steady hands and a good eye, just like his father. Come," he said, taking my bag and heading into the house, "I'll take you to your room."

Enveloped in a cloud of fragrant pipe smoke, I followed the tanned ass, crisscrossed like a waffle from the chair in which he'd been sitting, into the house. At the landing, I turned and glanced nervously back at Peter. He gave me a reassuring smile and a wink so I turned and went the rest of the way up the stairs. The uncle led me to a room on the second floor with two small windows looking out onto a thatched roof.

"You two should be comfortable here," he said, setting my bag on the bed and retrieving some clean towels from one of the closets. "Nice and quiet, this room. And the nice afternoon sun."

I heard Peter coming up the stairs. When he arrived at the top, he stepped past his uncle, came into the room and stood behind me, his hands on my shoulders.

"I didn't make any dinner yet," the uncle said, turning and descending the stairs. "And since I'm going away tomorrow, there's not much food, but don't worry, I'll come up with something."

"Let's hope," Peter groaned, "he can come up with some pants." Then he turned me around and began unbuttoning mine.

"Shouldn't we close the door?" I whispered. Peter shook his head.

"It would get too warm. And I can feel," he said, reaching a hand down the back of my pants, "that you are already quite warm." With his free hand, he pulled my shirt over my head and began kissing my neck and chest.

"But what about your uncle?"

"What about him? He has his girl in Brussels. You are all mine." I laughed.

"But what if he hears us?" I whispered.

"Are you going to be noisy?" Peter asked, excited by the prospect. Again I laughed.

"It is okay," he said, his face close to mine. "You don't have to be uncomfortable. When I am happy, he is happy. And you," he said, pushing me back on the bed and unbuttoning his own pants, "make me very happy."

Twenty minutes later, we returned downstairs to join the still smoking, still nude uncle, who was sitting in the same chair under the tree drinking a beer and thumbing through my sketchbook. He looked up at us, a guilty, amused expression on his face.

"You're very nosy," Peter scolded. "And you haven't done anything about dinner."

"No," he said, taking a swig of his beer and looking at his watch. "I didn't think you would be done so soon. And then I got distracted by the sketchbook. These really are very good, er, what is your name again?"

"Tony."

"Yes, Tony, really very good. You have a gift. I especially like the one of my nephew. It is Peter, isn't it? I thought so. But it's not really a portrait. It's more of a, oh, I don't know what you would call it, a chestlet, maybe."

Peter disappeared into the house and returned a moment later with two bottles of beer. He handed me one and I took a long drink. It was very cold and I felt it go all the way down into my empty stomach.

"Shall I see what I can make us to eat?" Peter asked.

"We really may have to go out," the uncle replied. "There isn't much of anything, Peter. You're so picky about food so I didn't want to buy anything before you arrived."

Peter clicked his tongue and turned toward the house.

As soon as he was out of earshot, the uncle looked up and winked at me again. "There really is food," he confided. "I was just hoping he would offer to cook it. I am only an adequate cook, but Peter! Tonight we'll really have something to eat."

The conversation then returned to my sketches, and more embarrassed by the attention than flattered, I sought to change the subject. Earlier, on my way up the stairs, I had noticed several pieces of taxidermy mounted to the wall: two exotic gazelles and the head of an enormous water buffalo. Underneath them, mounted in descending rows according to size, were three guns. When I asked where they came from, he closed the sketchbook and looked up at the sky over the hedge, as if considering how to respond.

"They are souvenirs from my former life," he said.

"Did you live in Africa?" I asked, leaning forward in my chair.

"No," he said. "Texas."

I was confused.

"For many years," he explained, "I owned part of a big game ranch. A place where oil men could go for a weekend of African hunting. An amusement park for the rich. The heads and the guns are the only things I brought home with me when I returned to Denmark."

I nodded, and took another sip of my beer.

"How did you get into that?" I asked. "And in Texas, of all places?"

He laughed. "It was a woman, of course. She was from Texas so I moved there to be with her. Her brother was my partner. It was a silly profession," he said, "but I have to say that what I do now is even sillier."

"And what's that?" I asked.

"I own a different sort of game park," he said. "A shooting gallery."

He ran inside and returned a moment later with a pistol. A long, silver-barreled six-shooter with an ivory handle, which he loaded and handed to me. It was comically large, but very heavy. He went and stood in front of the linden tree, his back to me, and carefully placed his empty beer bottle on his head.

"I want you to try and shoot the bottle," he said.

I thought surely I'd misunderstood his Danish so I responded in English.

"You want me to what?"

Without turning around he said, "Shoot the bottle. Go ahead. Even if you miss, you can't hurt me."

"I'm not going to shoot you," I said, again in English and then repeated it in Danish.

"Right," he said, still keeping his back to me, "you're going to shoot the bottle."

Just then, Peter appeared in the doorway, two new bottles of beer in his hands. He rolled his eyes, strode across the lawn, and took the gun from my hand, replacing it with one of the beers. He took a drink of his own beer, set it down, and then, without a moment's hesitation, aimed the gun and fired straight at the uncle. The gun made a popping sound and a large blue splat appeared on the back of the uncle's head. Peter fired again, hitting him in the back this time, causing a purple splat to appear, and then one more time hitting him with green on his left ass cheek. The uncle was giggling so hard that the bottle toppled off his head. He turned around and was disappointed to see that Peter had done the firing.

"Oh, now you've ruined it," he said.

Peter shook his head, made a scolding sound with his tongue, and returned to the kitchen, taking the pistol with him. The uncle, his backside now covered in paint, ran to the spigot on the side of the house and began hosing himself off, still laughing like a madman. Then, shivering from the cold water, he ran inside to dry off and, I hoped, get dressed.

Alone in the yard, still bleary-eyed from travel, exhausted from sex, and buzzed from the beer, I wondered if my own Danish relatives would be as eccentric as this one of Peter's seemed to be.

A few minutes later, the uncle returned, dressed in khaki shorts and a Hawaiian shirt. He sat once again in the chair opposite me.

"Your Danish is quite good," he said, almost with a note of suspicion. "But you don't look Danish. Were you adopted?"

"No," I said. "My mother's Danish, but my father is from Mexico."

"Mexico!" he exclaimed. "I've always loved it there. Where is he from?"

I shrugged.

"He's never told you? You've never been?" he asked, not concealing his surprise.

"No, never."

"But why not?"

I sighed, took a big drink of my beer and then an equally big breath, and tried to explain, as concisely as I could, the story about my charming, philandering, rarely seen in captivity, faux-Italian father, who had always wanted to erase his Mexican background. Then I took another breath and told him about my lunatic grandmother, who for all I knew probably thought she was still in Mexico, and about my poor, hardworking, romantic mother, who had always dreamed about a trip south of the border but had never been able to afford it. The story quickly became too convoluted for my limited Danish, despite the added fluency from the beer, so I gave it up. I also began to realize that the uncle knew more about me and my life than Peter did, which made me feel strange, so I turned the conversational telescope around and asked him about Peter's parents.

"Peter's parents," he replied, "died when he was quite young," and he offered nothing more. I kept waiting but nothing came. Curious, but not wanting to seem morbid, I asked, "So, who were his parents?"

He looked at me steadily and sucked on the pipe. It had gone out.

"His mother," he said, tapping the ashes out onto the lawn, "was my youngest sister."

"And his father?"

"His father . . . was a mess. Maybe a bit like your father. I mean no offense to you, but I was very fond of my sister and not so fond of my brother-in-law. But maybe it is more for Peter to tell you than me."

We talked about distant, harmless subjects after that—about Texas, and paintball, and the differences between American and

Danish beer—until, just as the uncle had predicted, Peter appeared, having succeeded in making a highly edible masterpiece from seemingly empty cupboards. We ate at a table in the hedged-in yard, the evening light lasting until almost eleven. Then we sat in the twilight, passing around a bottle of fruit wine that the uncle had made himself, and gazing up at the stars, Peter's hand in mine.

Later that night, when we were alone in bed together, I asked Peter about what had happened to his parents.

"They overdosed," he said matter-of-factly. "First, my father, then six months later, my mother. Hers was probably a suicide."

"I'm so sorry," I said. "I shouldn't have asked."

"Don't be silly. It's all right. It was a very long time ago."

"How old were you then?" I asked.

"When my mother died? Five."

"That must have been hard."

"It was much harder on my uncle, really. He was close to my mother and had introduced her to my father. He still feels guilty for how it all ended."

"Do you miss them?" I asked, and then felt stupid for asking something so obvious.

"Sometimes. To tell you the truth, I don't really remember them all that well. I've been with my uncle for so long."

The next morning all that remained of the uncle was the lingering smell of pipe smoke and a note telling us to enjoy the house.

I stayed with Peter the entire month of June, making short trips every now and then to visit my elderly relatives, who had fretted about what to do with me during my visit and seemed relieved that I had found a friend to keep me entertained. It was an idyllic month, to say the least. We were young, we were virile, we were smitten with each other, and although we didn't have any money, neither did we have any rent to pay or any real obligations to the outside world. It was one of the few times in my life when I have felt truly free. A time when the happiness just seemed to pile up, day after day.

When I remember that month, somehow the sky was always blue, the leaves on the trees lush and green, there were always ripe strawberries in the field behind the house, and the sex was great.

Most mornings, we would ride bicycles to the beach and lounge in the sun, Peter carving pieces of wood and smoking, while I sketched the suitless Danes as they played paddleball or badminton, their liberated breasts and genitalia bouncing to and fro. If we needed money, we would sometimes set up a little booth at the beach where I'd draw portraits and Peter would sell some of the small wooden figurines he had carved of the characters in Andersen's fairy tales. Then, in the evening, we'd lazily walk our bicycles back to the house, talking all the way.

Some days Peter would go out in the morning and buy delicatessen food and a fresh loaf of bread and we'd pack them in shoulder bags and set off riding though the forest, or along the coast until we found an isolated place to have our feast. There, wherever "there" happened to be, we ate and drank and Peter (who was wild about country music and Western movies), played old cowboy songs on a harmonica while I sang along, improvising the words.

In the evenings, we made experimental cocktails using the contents of the uncle's bar and Peter cooked experimental dinners using the contents of the cupboards, which the uncle had, in fact, stocked before he left. After dinner, we'd play backgammon or watch movies, or I would sketch him while he read to me.

Since the uncle was an avid pipe smoker, each room on the lower level of the house had at least one pedestal ashtray, suspended from which were three or four carved pipes and the accessories needed to clean them, and the kitchen cabinets, although stocked with food, contained at least as much tobacco.

Pipes, like fedoras, elbow-length gloves, and hip flasks, have been essentially abandoned in our healthy, utilitarian age. There are still some older people who smoke them, but when you're young ("young," in this case, being under the age of forty), it is difficult to smoke a pipe without exuding an air of theatrical affectation. Peter was familiar with the practice but I was not and decided that I wanted to learn. So after dinner one night, we sat down and he tried to teach me.

"It is like starting a campfire," he said, packing the tobacco tightly in the bowl and lighting it with a thick, wooden match. "Weren't you ever a Boy Scout?"

I shook my head.

"The idea is to keep inhaling, keep supplying oxygen to the fire until it has the energy to burn on its own. Even then you have to keep puffing or it will go out."

I tried, coughed, tried again, it went out. I tried a third time and, by puffing like a fiend, managed to get it going. Then I threw up.

I gave up pipe smoking after that, but Peter stuck with it and soon it, and an evening walk, became a part of our routine. We walked along the quiet streets, sometimes all the way down to the beach, and talked and talked and talked until the light faded.

Talk.

Let me take another break here and add some more advice for my friend the detective. Talk is, arguably, the most important part of the wooing process, and the part where most guys make the biggest mistakes. Ideally, the conversation that takes place between two new lovers will lay the foundation on which to build the rest of your relationship. It's like learning another language: You teach him yours and he teaches you his, and if you're smart and you love him and want to make him happy, you remember what he's told you. You remember what's important to him and why, and if he loves you, he does the same. If you are serious about becoming a World Class Wooer, then there are a few things you should know about conversation.

1. It's not all about you.

That sounds simple and obvious but many people just don't get it. When they first meet someone, they'll talk on and on and on about themselves and relate everything the other person says back to their own experience. In short, their "I"s are too close together. Don't be that way. It's like playing a board game and never letting the other person have a turn.

2. Ask a lot of questions.

At the risk of offending with yet another generalizing sweep, I'll say that most people, gay or otherwise, love to talk about themselves—what they know and what they do—and the only thing they love more is when someone feeds them a string of leading, open-ended questions to enable them to do that. Therefore, if you want to succeed, the poser of interesting, open-ended questions should be you.

3. Remember what they've told you.

For me, this part is easy. When I first fall in love with someone, as I did that June with Peter, and have done with someone, to various degrees, roughly every eight to ten months since puberty, every ordinary thing they say becomes extraordinary in my mind. In every little story they tell about family vacations, or birthday parties, or when they played the part of a tree in the elementary school play, I see poetry. Tales of their parents' divorce or the death of a beloved family pet are to me, epic dramas, so remembering them is easy.

That said; let's look at two not infrequent scenarios:

Scenario 1: Long Term Relationship (LTR)

Suppose you've set your sights on some square-jawed, blond crew-cutted, big-bicepped specimen of male beauty sitting alone at a bar or a coffee shop, and after approaching and talking to him for, say, forty-five minutes, in which time he's told you all about his motorcycle trip across Australia, or his job restoring antiques, you decide that he is someone you might be interested in seeing for more than one night. The strategy to get him is, believe it or not, relatively simple: Just listen and ask a lot of questions. I know, I know, you know nothing about motorcycles or Australia, and don't really care about antiques, restored or otherwise, but that really doesn't matter. Just listen, ask questions about what you don't know, and then let him have the joy of explaining it to you. I guarantee it will work. Modern-day members of royal families have to engage in this sort of diplomacy every day. Princes and princesses rarely know much about any one thing; instead, they're trained to talk somewhat intelligently about any subject that arises, and when they can't do that, they've been trained to cultivate a look of intense fascination.

And that is what you need to be able to do, too. Intelligence on your part is not necessary but curiosity (or at least the illusion of it) is essential.

Example:

I once carried on an hour-long conversation with a broad-shouldered, narrow-hipped beauty about the electromagnetic forces in silt-sized feldspar granules—and that was the beginning of a six-month relationship.

Scenario 2: Short Term Relationship (STR)

Suppose you've set your sights on a tall, black-haired, thick-lipped, soulful, blue-eyed drink of water with an enticing bulge in his crotch sitting at a bar or a coffee shop, and after approaching and talking to him for, say, forty-five minutes, in which time he's told you all about the exciting world of system administration, or given you a detailed description of the drive-train mechanism on a Ford Taurus, you decide that you don't want (nor could you bear) anything more than a one-night stand or some afternoon delight. At that point, you can do one of two things:

1. Leave and try your luck elsewhere, reassuring yourself that soulful blue eyes and a potentially big dick are not all that hard to find, or
2. Grit your teeth, feign interest a little longer, and try to hurry things along, knowing all the while that once you get him into bed, you probably won't have to listen to him talk for at least fifteen to twenty blissful minutes.

If you choose Option 2, there are several things you can do to expedite the conversation but one of the best is, believe it or not, to use my dad's strategy and stare at his mouth. Not like you're staring at a bit of food stuck in his teeth, or at that white stuff that sometimes collects at the corners of the lips of big talkers, but like you are so attracted to him you can hardly keep yourself from kissing him right then and there. If the conditions are right (i.e., you are in a "safe," nonhomophobic environment), then do kiss him. He probably won't resist and once you've done it, once you've crossed that line, it is easier to say something like, "I really love talking to you but maybe we could go someplace a little more private." Then, of course, once you get him to that private place, you make sure his mouth is otherwise occupied.

Troubleshooting

Sometimes, I have to admit, the topics of conversation an O.O.D. can come up with, especially those that are work related, can be just too boring and tedious. I'll put up with a lot if I think a guy has potential to be something more than a trick, but when I see that it's not going to be anything more than sex, I am usually less patient. And let's face it, the possibility of sex, even the possibility of great sex with a spectacular guy, is often not worth the inane, vapid palaver you have to endure to get it. In those tiresome situations, you'll try hard to listen and ask pertinent questions, but more often than not, your own body will betray your mental boredom: your eyes will glaze over and cross; you'll stifle yawns and begin to fidget. Then, if the O.O.D. does, by some fluke of personality, stop yammering long enough to catch a whiff of your boredom, all the progress you've made over the course of the evening can be instantly lost and you'll end up going home alone.

There is, however, a solution, a simple way to alleviate your ennui and avoid trouble: just change the subject. I know, I know, you're thinking that if you change the subject, it will become even more obvious that you're bored and that will offend him as much as the glazed eyes, yawning, and fidgeting; and yes, that is a risk. Subtlety is important. Diplomacy is important, but change the subject you must! If he's going on and on about the chemical composition of envelope glue, or the highlights of his 401K plan, or even about some dumb sitcom you're not at all interested in, why should you suffer through it? Martyrdom, no matter how beautiful he may be, is overrated, so just look at your surroundings and try to find an adequate and subtle transition. Maybe point at a passing car and ask what kind it is, and then ask him what kind he has and what kind he's always wanted. Or even better, derail the conversation with a compliment: look at his shirt, maybe and comment on how well the color goes with his eyes or how nicely the cut of his jacket accentuates his broad shoulders. The point is, steer him toward something else. Granted, this isn't always easy to do, and for that reason I have taken time out of my oh-so-busy convalescent schedule to assemble a helpful list of potential topics about which most O.O.Ds will probably have something to say:

- **Music**
  This can be a good segue, especially when you are in a bar or in a car. Cock your ear sideways and listen, as if you've just noticed the song that's playing and are trying to identify it. From there, ask him what kind of music he likes. Most guys have strong opinions about this and usually like to share them. Make mental notes of his preferences for use in future romantic evenings.

- **Goals for the future**
  His, not yours. Your goal, after all, is to get his clothes off and get him in bed. I suppose you could, with the right penetrating gaze, risk confessing that fact (i.e., "my goal is to make love to someone as beautiful as you"), but I wouldn't recommend it. It will either work like a charm, or absolutely fail. The odds are about fifty-fifty.

- **Coming out**
  This is a sure thing since all gay men have experienced it, at least to a certain extent. Most will have a lot to say about it, good or bad, and their stories are usually so interesting that you won't even need to pretend that you're paying attention.

- **Parents and siblings**
  He'll either like 'em, and have a lot to say, or he'll hate 'em, and have a lot to say. Be wary of those who give an indifferent shrug when this topic is brought up. You've reached a dead end.

- **Places he's lived/traveled**
  Again, this is where that intensely interested look you've been practicing gets used, even if he's talking about Boise or Fort Wayne.

- **Ex-lover(s)**
  Again, his not yours. This sounds like stepping into a mine-field but don't worry, it's perfectly safe. He'll want your out-rage, shock, and sympathy, not necessarily in that order, so be ready with the appropriate reaction. Again, I warn you, do not mention any ex-lovers of your own. It sounds stupid, but in my experience (and there's a lot of it), I've found that in the back of his mind, in the deepest recesses of his subcon-scious, he wants to believe that you haven't had any other lovers.

- **Places he's always fantasized about having sex**
  Don't you answer until you've heard what he says. If he persists and insists that you go first, smile and say, "In your bed."

- **Injuries**
  This is something to try when the rest is not working. Broken limbs and trips to the hospital are stories most people love to relate. Again, practice your shock, sympathy, and sometimes humor.

Since there are two sides to every coin, here then is a short list of topics to avoid:

- Social diseases you've had

- Old boyfriends (yours, not his)

- Any money troubles you may be having

Definitely stay away from those topics, but there is one thing that's even more important to be careful about and that is The Wandering Eye: that magnet lodged somewhere behind your cornea that gravitates likes a compass needle toward beautiful specimens of the male sex. All gay men suffer from it at one point or another. It may seem to be like an involuntary response, like breathing or your heart beating, but it's not, and if you want to make a successful conquest, you must learn to control it, especially in the beginning. You must make your O.O.D. believe that you only have eyes for him, and again, the more you show you are interested in a man, and by "interested" I mean curious, intrigued, enchanted, and fascinated, the more success you'll have.

One final thing to remember: Although it is important to talk, to ask questions about the O.O.D., and to remember what he's said, it is much more important to avoid talking about yourself. I realize that sounds self-effacing and timid, but it's really quite the opposite. It's a subtle method of engineering his curiosity so that it will eventually boomerang back on you. To put it another way, not talking about yourself on the first few dates is a lot like investing money: It's not much fun in the beginning and it can take a while to get a tangible return but eventually you'll probably be glad you did it.

The strategy, as plainly as I can put it, is this: By not revealing too much about yourself, you will, eventually, make the O.O.D. wonder about you. That is precisely what you want: to become an enigma, a man of mystery, someone he'll become curious about. Think of all of the intensely private celebrities—the Greta Garbos, Jackie Kennedys, and J. D. Salingers. They are proof of the theory that if you want to enflame curiosity, it's important to maintain a theatrical silence about yourself. Make it seem like you've got something worth knowing and then don't tell it. That is what I did that first June with Peter, and as you'll see, it worked.

Oh, and one more thing before we return to the story. When the boomerang comes back and it is time for you to talk, make sure you portray yourself favorably. Some people call this putting your best foot forward or making a good first impression, others will say it is polishing the apple or pulling the wool over their eyes, but I prefer to think of it as nothing more than self-portraiture. Let's face it; no one is ever completely truthful about themselves in the beginning of a relationship. You try to present your good parts first, use them to sell yourself, make the O.O.D. fall for you. Then, once he has, you can relax and let some of your less attractive traits float to the surface. He might not be thrilled with what he discovers but at that point he's already in love with what he see as "the real you," so the warts won't matter so much. Or to put it in terms that just about everyone can understand, it's like fibbing on your résumé: you say whatever it takes to get the job. Once you've got it and have been working for a while, your boss is probably not going to fire you just because you're not quite as fluent in French as you said, or because you've "forgotten" how to set up Excel spreadsheets.

So, when I met Peter that first June, I did what I thought was necessary to get him: I asked a lot of questions and did not tell him much about me. I was deliberately vague, almost evasive about my life, and the self-portrait I painted was in hazy hues with no definite outline. I certainly didn't mention that I'd screwed my way up the European continent; did not tell him that each missing page of my sketchbook represented a man I had slept with; did not tell him that the sketchbook itself had been a gift from my last boyfriend—the one who was then anxiously awaiting my return. No, I did not really tell Peter much about myself at all. And that, my friends, was by design, not mistake. I knew he was worth having, knew after that first encounter on the train that he was more than another "sketch model." Almost from the very beginning, I knew that he was someone I could love, so I played the game necessary to get him and soon, just as I'd planned, just as I've outlined above, he was in love with me.

Even though we were both in love almost from the start, we were both very careful never to actually use the *L* word. Careful, because it was tacitly understood that at the end of June the romance would have to end. When June ended, "we" would end. No illusions, no delusions, no confusion. We were different people from different countries with different lives. I would go back to the States and try to decide on a career, Peter would go back to the career he was on his way to establishing in Copenhagen, and we'd both have a wonderful memory to keep us warm through the long winter.

Yeah, right.

Oh, I left all right, on the first day of July, just as planned, and Peter went back to Copenhagen, but I knew he wouldn't forget about me. I knew the boomerang would come back around, and when it did, I knew we'd be together again, so my departure did not cause me all that much grief.

When I returned home, #2 was at the airport to meet me. I greeted him coolly and on the drive home told him I'd had a change of heart over the summer and didn't really want a boyfriend at the moment. It was a transparent lie and as such, he saw right through it.

"There's someone else," he said, his voice low and flat.

"Don't be silly. I just think it would be good for me to be on my own for a while. Good for my art."

"Who is it?" he demanded. "Where did you meet him?"

I sighed, said there wasn't any "him," and it just got worse from there. More accusations, more lies, and then the groveling and bargaining began: the offer of an apartment together in town, a joint checking account, an open relationship, anything, if only I would reconsider. I tried to let him down as gently as I could, but didn't succeed. When one person is determined to hang on and the other is determined to pry their fingers off, an ugly struggle is bound to ensue, and for a month after I got home that is precisely what happened. He called and wrote letters, he slept in his car out in front of the house, he bought presents and flowers and tried everything he could to get me to change my mind, but it didn't work. It rarely, if ever, works. As soon as one party in an affair finds someone else and transfers his affections, there is no way short of a lobotomy to sway them back, and the only thing for the one left behind to do is drop it and move on.

Not surprisingly, the two weeks after I got home were agony, but only partly because of the difficulty I was having dispensing with #2. The other difficulty was trying to play it cool with Peter, and I spent most of my time waiting for him to call and restraining myself from calling him. There'd been no commitment, no promise to call from either of us, but my ego wouldn't let me believe that he wouldn't do it. Finally, eleven days after I got home, when I was just about to give up and had almost lost faith in my strategy, a letter arrived. A letter Peter had written and mailed the very day of my departure. In it, he said everything that I hoped he'd say: that he missed me, that he couldn't stop thinking of me and hoped it wasn't just a summer fling. He said he'd known after the first week, almost after the first day in the train, that he was in love with me but had said nothing out of fear of scaring me away. He'd tried to shrug off his feelings for me early on, to dismiss them as nothing more than infatuation, but it was no use. He was miserable and wanted to hear that maybe I was just a little bit miserable, too. He said, and I quote, "It seems I did most of the talking when you were here and now that you're gone I feel like I never got the chance to ask you so many things, Tony. Please, tell me that I'll get another chance again very soon."

After that letter, once I knew I had him hooked, the romance really began. There were long and shockingly expensive phone calls, in which we giggled and murmured and said nothing, really. Letters (novellas might be a better word) saying how much I missed him and loved him traveled across the Atlantic along with sketches I'd done of him, and of me, and of us. I sent sappy cards and mix tapes, books I wanted to share with him, and lots and lots of embarrassingly bad poetry.

From Peter I received wooden boxes he'd carved, filled with sand and a tiny vial of water from our favorite beach. There were his own mix tapes with cleverly decorated cases, books by Danish authors he wanted me to read, and of course, his own embarrassingly bad poetry.

Finally, after almost two months of mutual pining, there was my offer. No, maybe that's not the right word. There was my statement, my suggestion, my request. Oh all right, I'll admit it, my plea, my begging, groveling plea that since he was, by his own admission, so miserable without me, maybe he ought to consider bridging the gap between us. And why not come to Denver? It was as good as anyplace else. We could always leave if he hated it. But he wouldn't hate it. I was sure of that. How could he? I'd be there, we'd be together and together we'd have months and months and months like June. We'd make our life together one long endless June!

I didn't exactly word it like that, but you get the idea. I wanted him and he wanted me and I was sure, I was absolutely certain (as I usually am in the beginning of affairs), that he was The One. He was not "Mr. Right Now"; he was "Mr. Right on the Mark!" I was sure of that. I just knew it.

What I know now is a little different. What I know now is that the person I should trust least in matters of the heart is the one I see looking back at me in the mirror. It's not so much that I lie to myself, because I don't, really (or at least not all that often), but that I want to believe. I want to believe so badly that I don't see the possibility that I may be wrong, won't even allow that possibility any air to breathe, and so I mount campaigns. Campaigns that involve subtle manipulation, charm, gifts, flattery, etc., to win his heart and mind, only to be surprised, usually disillusioned, and yes, frightened, once I've succeeded.

When the gods really want to punish you, they give you exactly what you think you want.

Chapter Six

After discussing it on the phone with me for about eight minutes, Peter agreed to come to Denver. He moved into the house with my mother and grandmother and me, and together we laughed and loved and were happy, all under one roof.

For the first two months, Peter and I didn't spend much time at home. I had an old, beat-up Nissan back then, and soon after his arrival we loaded it up and traveled all over the state, indulging Peter's Western fantasy. We climbed peaks and camped in the mountains, went rafting and kayaking and horseback riding, picked peaches on the Western Slope, fished in mountain streams, and saw all the sights we could possibly see in two months. It was great fun while the money lasted, but soon our wallets were empty again and the autumn was half over so we returned to Denver.

Denver in November. There are few places on earth more brown, dead, and ugly than Denver in November. Nevertheless, we returned, energized and in love, determined to make a life together. Of course, it wasn't as easy as we'd hoped. Money was a problem and it soon became apparent that we could no longer just saunter along, carefree, living off my mother's largesse. We needed our own place to live. We needed jobs. It wasn't pretty.

Since we both have art degrees, finding a job was not easy for either of us. I had just graduated, and had no work experience whatsoever. Peter had a little, but that consisted mostly of selling the wooden puppets he carved to tourists on the street in Copenhagen. Not that his lack of work experience mattered all that much since he was on a travel visa and couldn't work legally anyway.

In our free time (which was pretty much all the time), we decided to collaborate on some artistic projects, designing our ideal house and an ideal line of furniture to go in it. I did the sketches of our preliminary ideas, while Peter determined what would be technically feasible, and then working together we honed a common aesthetic vision. A vision that seemed doomed to be forever trapped on paper since we had no money to buy materials or tools to realize it.

Yes, the lack of work and money were problems, no denying that, but eventually we did come up with some solutions. There were ways to overcome our difficulties, and together we brainstormed and tried to think of something that we could do.

"What if we go back to selling sketches and carvings on the street?" Peter suggested one evening, as we sat in front of the fireplace roasting marshmallows on coat hangers. "Just until we make enough money to get a studio and start working on the furniture."

"I don't think that would work," I said. "It's not as easy to sell things on the street here. You need permits and licenses, and with your immigration status, that might not be such a good idea."

"Well, what about day labor?" Peter asked, stuffing a marshmallow in my mouth. "I'm a good carpenter. I see all those men waiting down the street for the construction companies to pick them up. Maybe we could do that."

"Maybe," I mumbled, "but I think they might get suspicious about a 6-foot 2-inch blond man standing on the corner with a group of Mexicans waiting to be picked up for low-paid illegal work. We'll just have to think up something else," I said, and put my arm around his shoulder.

"Yes," he agreed, "we'll have to think of something else."

And, in time, we did think of something else. Unfortunately, the something else we thought of was something that made both of us miserable (but is, nevertheless, what I continued to do, although in a refined form, up until the day I was shot). The something else that we thought of was a job that would, in theory at least, enable us to make money under the table, had a minimal start-up cost, and was, in a way, artistic. We would have paint, we would have canvases (albeit very large canvases), and in the summer we would be able to work *en plein air*. We became (drum roll, please) house painters.

House painting can be described in many ways, but the adjectives "glamorous," "exciting," and "wildly profitable" will probably never be used. It was vaguely interesting sometimes, if we were doing a mural or using some bizarre color scheme, but mostly it was just backbreaking, mind-numbing, four-letter-word work, and I hated it. Neither of us knew a thing about it so, predictably, for the first six months we made a ridiculous amount of mistakes, usually of the costly variety: a gallon of red paint would accidentally tip onto new, white carpeting, or an unsecured ladder would blow sideways off a roof and land with a crash on the hood of a car. Once, we even spent an entire day painting some exterior shutters only to discover when the homeowner returned in the evening that we'd been working at the wrong address and that the shutters we were supposed to be painting were on the house across the street. And then there was always the problem of our bidding, which was either so high that we wouldn't get the job or so ridiculously low (more often the case) that the client would jump to sign us up before we realized our mistake.

It was terrible, and I was miserable, and probably so was Peter, but you never would have known it from the way he behaved. Peter was, and still is, about as far from a brooding Dane as you can get. He's like one of those people that Paxil ads promise you will become after popping their pills: indefatigably cheerful, smiling, and humming his way through any and every adversity. That is Peter. You could ship him off to Stalin's Siberian gulag and he'd see it as an opportunity to make snow angels.

Day after monotonous day Peter would paint and chatter on and on to Sally Homeowner as if they were the best of friends, totally oblivious to the fact that just five minutes earlier she'd been shrieking at us for dripping paint on her petunias. He'd smile and sing, even as he knelt in some spider-infested window well or scrubbed inch-thick grease off the wall behind a kitchen stove, and at first, I'll admit, I found his optimism comforting, encouraging even. He seemed always able to find the daisies sprouting in a pile of shit, but as time went by and the work and our lives became more tedious and difficult, I began to wonder if maybe he wasn't crazy or even a little retarded. I just didn't get it. I mean, what kind of rose-colored glasses was he wearing? Certainly not the same prescription I had. No, in my gray view we were living with my mother and my crazy grandmother in their run-down house in the ghetto; we were broke, not making enough money, and yet working harder than either of us had ever worked before; we were driving a car held together with duct tape and prayers, and if it failed us, we would be screwed. For lack of a better term, life sucked, but Peter seemed oblivious to the misery of it. No, worse than oblivious, he seemed to be actively enjoying it. I just didn't get it.

But then, I've forgotten to mention that in addition to being perpetually happy, Peter was also clairvoyant. He could see into the future, and what he saw was a time when we would not be so miserable. He knew that we would not always be house painters; we would not always be poor; life would not always be so bleak. The sky would clear and the weather would get warm again. There would be money in the bank and we'd have a place of our own. Maybe we wouldn't have that Danish June, or at least not all of the time, but there would be new experiences together and we would be happy again. Together. That much he knew.

But then, I don't think I need to mention that I was not clairvoyant; I had no sixth sense, no faith. I could not see down the road. Oh, I thought I could, but all I saw was more of the miserable same. His glass was half full and mine, well . . . I felt like a big snake had coiled itself around my neck and was slowly squeezing the life out of me.

It's funny, but what I remember most about that awful time was that we used to check out a lot of Westerns from the library. Thank God for the movie section of the library because we were so poor then that even renting a movie was totally out of the question. I'm not really into Westerns but Peter, who had the foreigner's romantic notions of the Old West further fueled by his uncle's tales of Texas and our summer travels in Colorado, couldn't get enough of them. We would lie in bed at night watching all the Technicolor films (in which the women always seemed to have bouffant hairstyles and Sophia Loren eye makeup), and when they ended—after the gun-slinging cowboy and the prim schoolmarm had ridden off into the sunset together, after the credits rolled and the story was over—I remember wishing that someone, anyone, would tell me what exactly happened next. What happened after the hero and heroine rode off into the sunset? What happened when night fell, or even worse, what happened the next morning when they woke up in their log cabin or teepee, when all the excitement of the story was over and they went back to the drudgery of everyday life?

Our painting career continued, and as each day passed, I became more and more surly and impatient. So surly that sometimes I would not talk to Peter all day, or if I did, it was only to grunt responses to his questions or to tell him where to paint, all the while trying (and failing) to maintain my paper-thin veneer of civility. Finally, one night, as soon as the evening's Western was over, Peter turned off the TV and said, "I think maybe I should not paint with you anymore."

I rolled over and looked at him.

"Really," he said. "I'm not any good at it and maybe it's not good for us to be together night and day all the time like this."

"Just great," I snapped, although secretly relieved. "You do that. Do what you want. But how am I supposed to do all the work by myself?"

"You can do it," he said. "There hasn't really been enough work for two."

"Yeah, but what will you do? We don't have any money, remember? And it's not like you can just go out without a green card and get a job."

"Well . . ."

"Well what?"

"I've already found one!" He squirmed out from under the covers and sat Indian style on the bed, taking both my hands in his. "Sort of a job. You know those girls from down the street, Stephanie and Judy, the ones who bought that Italianate on the corner."

"The lesbians?"

"Yes, the ones I helped with the drywall last weekend. They called again yesterday evening—you were out somewhere—and they want to hire me to do some carpentry work! They also gave my name to James and Thomas, the neighbors next door to them, and they also have work I can do. Doesn't that sound fantastic?"

"I guess," I shrugged, and then turned away to face the wall. "But I don't know what you'll do when that's done."

"Oh, I think more work will come. People are starting to see how nice the buildings are around here and they're spending money. You should give out some of your cards."

I groaned. Peter lay back down beside me. He kissed the back of my head and stroked my hair.

"It will be good," he said. "You'll see."

So, Peter gave up painting and moved on to carpentry and renovation. We saw each other only in the mornings and evenings after that and my days were, once again, my own. My work, minus the cheery chatterbox, went more smoothly, and with the change from spring to summer I began getting more work and making some money. Or at least not losing so much.

Peter, on the other hand, began making a lot of money, and seemingly with little effort. He had done such a beautiful and meticulous job skim coating the lesbians' walls and salvaging their oak trim that word of his "Old World" carpentry skill spread fast through Curtis Park. But it wasn't just his skills that made him popular. It was, to quote the rhapsodic neighbors, "his charming little accent," "and those beautiful blue eyes, and that hair!" (he was wearing it long then), "and so friendly! You just won't meet a nicer, kinder person!"

In my observation of the canine species, I've noticed that dogs share many emotions with humans. Unfortunately for the dogs, jealousy is one of those emotions. They do seem immune to resentment, however, which is more than I can say about myself. Over time, I began to resent Peter with a passion. I resented that he was more skillful and talented than I (or at least that was how I saw it), and that he was making more money. I resented that he was tall, and blond, and that his shoulders were broader than my own. I resented that he had come into the neighborhood—my neighborhood (albeit by my invitation)—and charmed the pants off everyone. I began to feel more Mexican than ever, and by that I mean more like a second-class citizen, more like the kind of trashy wetback all these new, renovating yuppies were trying to push out so that they could restore the neighborhood to its *fin de siècle* grandeur. Ironically enough, it was me, the envious little Mexican, who secretly entertained fantasies of turning Peter in to the INS and having him deported.

Still, through my thick veil of rancor even I could see that the neighbors were right: Peter was wonderful. And that only made me feel worse. If he was so great, then what the hell was he doing with me?

Me: Mr. Inadequate, Mr. I-Have-No-Skills-or-Money, Mr. Moody, Mr. I. M. Whiney, Mr. Surly.

And surly I surely was. With every one of Peter's triumphs, my resentment increased. Every time he took me out to dinner and picked up the check, or paid one of my bills without telling me about it, I openly seethed. In spite of my spite, Peter never stopped encouraging me (which I, of course, found condescending). When he began making money with his carpentry, the first thing he purchased, even before he bought much-needed tools for himself, were art supplies for me (which made me mad). He praised my work to everyone that he worked for and carried a big stack of my business cards in his wallet to distribute (read: Poor Tony needs help). He praised me to the skies as a wonderful boyfriend (a lie), and brushed aside all of his many suitors by telling them how happy we were together (ditto).

In retrospect, I see how kind it was. I see how much he loved me, but all I saw then was my failure in comparison to him, and worse, my failure to give him a life even remotely resembling the one I'd promised him. Then things got even worse.

Ever since he'd arrived, Peter had returned again and again to the topic of *Casa Turquesa* and all that my mother could do to improve it. He had already done some improvements himself: converted the garage to his carpentry shop, fixed the stairs leading to the cellar, cleaned up the yard and planted a garden, but there was so much more potential hidden in that pile of bricks and he never stopped trying to convince us of that. At first my mother just smiled, thinking it nothing more than the silly exuberance of an artistic boy, but after hearing his praises trumpeted throughout the neighborhood and seeing some of the work he had done, she started to think that maybe he might be right. She began asking small, shy questions about how to strip the paint-globbed door hinges, and what could be done about the leaky toilet. Soon, she was openly wondering about the possibility of installing skylights, and if our old floors would sand out as beautifully as the lesbians' had?

"Do you think it would be possible . . . ?" she asked again and again. And again and again Peter answered in the affirmative. He could change things, he could turn them around, he could make them better, and so the two of them began huddling together in the evenings making plans.

Initially, I was a part of the plans, too, and for a while, the renovation did bring the two of us closer together, but in time, I'm afraid I made it into just another wedge. I had my own work to do during the week but Peter made the house his job, my mother his employer, and together, all day, every day, the two of them worked, side by side, harmoniously plotting and deciding without bothering to ask my opinion. Of course, I didn't need to be asked—it wasn't my house after all, it was my mother's—but I couldn't help feeling left out. A feeling that wasn't helped by the fact that often, when my mother and Peter were together, they'd revert to speaking rapid-fire Danish. I cannot tell you how many evenings, over cocktails or dinner, one of them would suddenly mutter something to the other in their native tongue and then put me off when I inquired about a word I didn't understand, saying "Oh, it was nothing," or "It was just something about the house."

And probably it was nothing, probably it was some trivial talk about cabinets or knobs, but it made me insanely jealous and angry every time they did it. And they did it often. More and more as time went by, until soon we could almost make it through an entire meal without a word of English being spoken. Oh, I wasn't completely shut out. I knew Danish. I'd grown up hearing it spoken, and my mother had taught me enough to carry on a conversation, but I'd never really had much of an opportunity to use it, and I certainly wasn't about to start opening myself up to verbal ridicule with either of them. They'd giggle at my pronunciation mishaps, or correct my grammar and vocabulary, and that was more than my poor, wounded ego could then take.

I don't like to make excuses for my behavior (shaky, elaborate rationalizations, yes; excuses, no), but I do think my feelings of exclusion from the renovation of *Casa Turquesa*, even though I'm sure it wasn't intentional on either of their parts, were valid, and that those feelings were partly responsible for some of the terrible things I subsequently did.

Like murder, there are degrees to infidelity. It can be a chance occurrence, or one of cold-blooded premeditation. For me, in this instance, I have to admit it was probably the latter. In the midst of my ego crisis, I remembered the Milanese waiter and how enchanted he'd been with my sketch. Then I remembered the many other "café men" that I'd picked up, like so many checkers on a board, on my way north. I remembered those men and that summer and was nearly overwhelmed by a nostalgia that suffused my whole body with warmth and excitement. Soon, of course, the nostalgia wasn't enough so I decided to go after the real thing.

One day I was driving home from a painting job and, almost without thinking, turned a different direction. I parked my truck and walked to a sidewalk café in Larimer Square, wondering if the wooing system I'd developed would work as easily in America as it had in Europe. It did, and soon I began leaving work early, sometimes as early as noon, and going back to that café, or to one of the many others that were then springing up in the city. The speckled painting whites I wore made me look even more artistic and became, together with my sketchbook and box of pencils, my peacock feathers; the glittering lure I used to troll the waters. Fifteen minutes of sketching and twenty to thirty minutes of witty banter usually got me forty-five minutes to an hour of sex, after which I would hop back in my van and head home, feeling smugly fortified against the Danes of Curtis Park.

With my little afternoon dalliances, I began to feel like I had something to call my own, some little acre I could claim that Peter and my mother could not have any part of. Of course it was stupid, and worse than that, deceptive and mean, but for a while it was the only thing that made life with them bearable. Soon, the short-term seduction just wasn't enough. It was like tossing paper airplanes when you really wanted to be a jet pilot. I wanted something more, something stronger, and that something, I concluded, was a new relationship.

Life with Peter, I convinced myself, had grown stale. He was the x for which I'd found the solution in my life's algebra, the completed jigsaw puzzle, the discovered *Titanic*. What I needed was a new script to follow from the very beginning, another exciting story-line to jump into. What I needed was someone new who could challenge me; make me feel like the good, smart, capable, and hand-some person I'd been the summer before. It wasn't hard to find him.

Jason was just twenty-two years old. He was young, beautiful, smart, and kept. He had a wealthy lover in his fifties who paid all of his bills and gave him pretty much anything he wanted. An as-piring, but lazy, novelist, Jason was happy with his arrangement as it gave him the leisure to pursue his craft. Although fond of his lover, he, too, was bored. Which was why he remained behind at the coffee shop one day after his friends had left.

I remember exactly how and where he was sitting that first day: slouched in a chair by the street, left leg crossed over right, deftly twiddling a pen between his fingers. I took out my sketchbook and began drawing. Nicely shaped head, thick black hair and eye-brows, a mouth I could see had the potential to do oh, so many things. I let him catch me studying him and the dance began. He raised an eyebrow and then turned away, pretending to be uninter-ested. He finished his coffee, set down the cup, and turned back and looked at me, this time lowering his sunglasses. I smiled. He returned the smile. I waited another moment, finished the sketch, and then got up and approached.

"Hello," I said, standing in front of him but looking down at my sketchbook. He gazed up at me, wondering if he should be an-noyed or not.

"It's rude, I know, but I've been drawing you," I said, tapping the sketchbook, still not looking at him. He sat up straight.

"Now I can't say for sure," I said, pulling up a chair and sitting down, "but something about your face makes me think you might actually be able to smile."

The smile appeared. I boldly took his chin in my hand and turned it to the side, as if studying his jawline. (It's horrible to say but I remembered how much I had liked it when Peter did that to me, so I "borrowed" the tactic.)

"You see," I said, pointing at the sketch, "I was right. I tried to imagine it here but I didn't quite capture it."

He raised his glasses to get a better look.

"It's beautiful," he said, eyeing the portrait critically, "but it's not me."

"It's not anybody else," I protested. "Don't be silly. Art imitates life. It's almost a mirror image. Here," I said, tearing the sheet from my sketchbook. "Will you sign it for me?"

He looked at me, confused.

"Sign it? Aren't you supposed to do that?" he asked.

I smiled and held out the pencil. "It will be much more valuable if you sign it."

He grinned and rolled his eyes, but accepted the pencil and printed his name in block capitals.

"So tell me, Jason . . ." I said, and then left him dangling a moment. "Will I get the chance to draw you again?"

He gave me a look of pretend shock and then laughed.

"Oh, you're slick," he said. "Very slick."

I smiled, locked my eyes on his, and stared.

"I've got a boyfriend," he said. "You should probably know that."

I pretended not to hear.

"A very jealous and possessive boyfriend," he added.

"Who's out of town on business, perhaps?"

He shook his head.

"Then that makes two of us."

"So, you've got a boyfriend," he said flatly.

"Uh, yes. But not one with a smile like yours."

He rolled his eyes again.

The conversation went on easily from there. He told me all about his boyfriend and his life, I told him next to nothing about mine, and we began our affair. An affair that was even more heated because it was illicit, of course, but also because it took so frickin' long to actually consummate since neither one of us had a place of his own or any money. There was a lot of making out in cars, afternoon rendezvous in the park, sometimes a dinner on the sly, but actually finding the time and the place to have sex proved difficult. Finally, a friend of his came to the rescue and allowed us to use her apartment while she was at work as long as we promised to wash the sheets and walk her dog when we were done. We agreed, and so it was there, on her pink canopy bed, surrounded by teddy bears and dolls, and under the curious eyes of her basset hound, that we made love several times a week.

In Jason, I found the challenge and adoration I had been looking for. Also, our situations were similar: He felt obligated to his lover, I felt obligated to mine, but together, for a few hours a week, we both felt sweetly free from obligation, which probably would have been fine if I'd left it at that. Well, not fine, really. We were both being unfaithful no matter how I might try and paint it, but no real harm would have been done to the outside parties if we, no, if *I* had been content to keep it just an affair. But I wasn't. I couldn't be happy until I'd convinced him to leave his lover and come away with me.

Good wooers are always somewhat emotionally detached from their situation. It's not love we want but success: To be wanted more than to want. To win the game, yes, but to win against seemingly outrageous odds. And that, I'm afraid, was my goal with Jason. In a perverse way, it can all be explained, as things often are, by Scripture—The Garden of Eden. We Adams always think the forbidden fruit is the sweetest; the apple high up on the tree has to be better than the one hanging right in front of our faces. It's the old Protestant work ethic: If it doesn't take effort to get it, then it probably isn't worth having.

So, I worked and I wooed Jason away from his lover, I left my lover, and together we set up house together in a spacious LoDo loft neither one of us could afford. Which brings us to Edmund.

Believe it or not, the night I was shot was not the first time someone pulled a gun on me. No, the first time was years before when Edmund, Jason's lover, confronted me about stealing his boyfriend.

Edmund was (and still is) a doctor. A surgeon. Ironically enough, the very surgeon who removed the bullet and bone fragments from my elbow and is solely responsible for the reconstruction of my leg. In the weeks following my surgery, he took a certain amount of glee in limiting my pain medication, which he was certainly entitled to do. I wouldn't be at all surprised, a few months down the line, to find that he'd intentionally left the scalpel inside me.

The first time I met Edmund was the day after Jason told him he would be leaving and moving in with me. Understandably vexed, Edmund got the address of the house I was working on and drove over to confront me. I was high up on the third level of a house, painting exterior dormers and saw his big, black Audi pull up next to the curb. He got out, still dressed in green hospital scrubs, and approached. When he saw where I was, he called up and asked if I was Tony. When I said yes, he climbed to the top of the ladder, called me some rather unflattering names, and then climbed back down. When he reached the bottom, he lowered the ladder, effectively stranding me on the roof. Then, still cursing, he got back in his car and drove away.

The next day at about the same time he arrived again, this time to apologize for his actions the day before, and to ask if I would mind coming to his house when I'd finished work that afternoon. I agreed, wrote down the address (even though I already knew it since Jason and I had sometimes used the house for surreptitious lovemaking when Edmund had been out of town), and arrived on the doorstep that evening at around five-thirty.

The house was a large, pink, Art Deco box in the Belcaro neighborhood. It seemed out of place in Colorado, and Edmund, who answered the door wearing a brown sweater and tweed slacks, seemed out of place in the house. He invited me in, offered me a drink, which I declined, led me to a living room toward the back of the house (a room I'd never seen on my previous visits), and then went off to the kitchen to fix a drink for himself.

While I waited, I examined the surroundings. The furniture, keeping with the style of the house, was sleek and modern. There were two opposing sofas with a long coffee table in between and in the corner a piano covered with picture frames.

Edmund was still a handsome man, but it was clear from some of the earlier photographs that he had once been extremely handsome. Time had, as time is wont to do, taken its toll on his face and body. His waist was no longer as thin; his hair was gray and thinning, and the skin around his eyes and mouth was etched with lines. None of it was unattractive—it just made him different, but yes, less attractive than he had once been.

When Edmund returned, he took a sip of his drink, sat on one of the sofas, and indicated that I should sit opposite. I sat and I waited. He stared at me for several seconds, as if sizing me up, a demonic grin on his face.

"So," he said, slapping his palms down on his thighs and lean-ing to the edge of the sofa. "You two are going to move in together."

I nodded.

He nodded back. I watched his jawbone clenching and imag-ined the sound of his teeth grinding.

"You know he's lazy," he said.

I smiled.

"He spends most of the day reading women's fashion maga-zines and he'll probably forget your birthday. He'll expect you to pay for everything and he snores."

The slander didn't surprise me. It's the fourth reaction to being dumped. The first, second, and third, in no particular order, are shock, sadness, and anger.

"I know all that," I said. "And you know it, too, but if you can put up with it, why do you think I wouldn't?"

He leaned back in the sofa and narrowed his eyes.

"I'm just saying," he said, "he's high maintenance."

I nodded.

"So," he said, taking another sip of his drink. "Where will you two be setting up house?"

I almost told him about the LoDo loft we'd just rented but then thought it might not be such a good idea.

"I think maybe you better ask Jason about that," I said, and then added, "but really, you don't want to know."

"Yes," he said, "I do."

I knew that was true for two reasons. First, he wanted to know because he wanted to hear that it was a filthy hovel of which his pampered boyfriend would soon grow tired. Second, he wanted to know because he wanted to have someplace to drive by late at night and stare up at the window and torture himself with the knowledge that we were inside making youthful love. I considered both of those things and said again, "You don't really want to know where it is."

He looked up at me from under hooded lids and clenched his jaw. Then he reached into his back pocket and retrieved his wallet. He removed five one-hundred-dollar bills and set them on the table. I looked up at him and shook my head, sadly.

This was the fifth reaction to being dumped: deal making.

The money was enticing, but not nearly as enticing as the high-principled feeling I got from refusing it. He took out another five hundred.

"Look," I said, pushing the money back toward him. "I love Jason. I don't want your money."

He laughed.

I shook my head and got up to leave. It was then that he moved from the fifth to the sixth reaction and I heard the gun cock behind me. I turned around and saw the pistol trembling in his steady surgeon's hands. Perhaps it was all the Westerns I'd been subjected to with Peter but I instinctively put my own hands up.

"What are you doing?" I said, trying to sound more bothered than frightened, and not really succeeding. "Put that away."

He was starting to cry.

"Why do you have to do it?" he said. "Why? You can find someone else. You know I can't compete."

Suddenly I was more afraid he would use the gun on himself.

"I know he's just staying with me for the money," he said. "For what I can give him, and that's fine. I don't care about any of that. In love you pay one way or the other, and believe me, my young friend, money is the least of it."

I kept my eyes on the gun.

"I quit smoking for him," he said. I lowered my hands.

"I smoked for thirty-one years, and I quit for him. Now I work out with a sadistic bitch of a trainer four days a week. She puts me through the motions on those stairs and bicycles that don't go anywhere and all those Spanish Inquisition weight machines! And I actually tip her when we're done, can you beat that! And then there are all those little blue pills. Thank God for the little blue pills! But you wouldn't know about that, would you. You can't imagine what it's like to need them. Can't imagine what a fucking godsend they've been. Oh, and how could I forget the music. All that hip hop, trip hop, trance and dance, or whatever the fuck it is, always blaring from the speakers. Let's hope you like music and magazines and muscles because that's pretty much gonna be what your life consists of from now on!" he said, tossing off a bitter laugh. "I know it sounds like I'm complaining, but I'm really not. I never complained to him. I put up with all of it. I even put up with you when I found out. Oh yes, I knew, almost from the beginning. Of course, I wasn't thrilled. I was mad as hell, but I put up with it. I figured you were just a little side dish to keep him occupied while I was at work. And why couldn't you have just left it that way?" he demanded, waving the gun at me like a scolding finger. "Why couldn't you just stay on the side? Why do you have to take him away?"

He was crying, the silent, convulsing, agonizing-to-watch type of crying, and I could think of only one thing to remedy it, so without really thinking too much about it, I did it. I approached, took the gun from his hand, tossed it over to the sofa he'd been sitting on, and then started kissing him. And not gently, either, but holding the back of his head with one of my hands so that he couldn't pull away. With my other hand, I untucked his shirt and fumbled with his belt. He resisted at first but was too exhausted and confused to really protest. I pushed him back on the sofa, pulled his pants down around his ankles, and then took off my own clothes and jumped on. I know it was a largely symbolic, largely hollow gesture but I let him fuck me, without lube, or anything, and, well, what can I say, other than that he didn't seem to need Viagra and it hurt like hell. When it was over, I got up, got dressed, and took the gun, which was the real reason I'd done something so distracting, and again went toward the door. When I reached it, I turned and looked back. He was propped up on both elbows, his hair disheveled, looking bewildered.

"I'm sorry," I said, and then went back out to my car. A week later Jason moved out of Edmund's pink house and into the loft with me.

Of course, our relationship didn't last, and of course, it was my fault that it didn't last. I could present and dissect the reasons it ended but I think a story Peter read to me on the beach that magical June illustrates it best.

Danes are fiercely proud of their little country and Peter is no exception. He was always giving me books and offering to read to me from the works of Danish authors so that I could learn more about our shared heritage. I loved it when Peter would read to me and, above all else, I loved it when he read the stories of Isak Dinesen. Although she was Danish, most of her work was written in English, and there is, to my mind, nothing better than hearing her elegant prose read to you in Danish-accented English, with all of its oddly elongated vowels and subtle swells of inflection. The Danish accent on English is as rich and soft as velvet or fur, and can be just as seductive.

The story I'm thinking of was, if I remember rightly, from a book of Dinesen's essays on life in Africa, and in it she gives an account of hunting a large, iridescent lizard; the skin of which she thought might make a nice pair of shoes or a handbag. The story goes like this: One morning she awoke, looked out her window, and saw one of the lizards sunning itself in the yard. She immediately sent a servant to fetch her rifle and when he returned she took aim, being careful not to hit the best part of the hide, and fired. As soon as she did, and as soon as the life oozed out of the thing, so, too, to her dismay, did all of the color and iridescence.

Men are my iridescent lizards. Wooing men is the way I hunt them. Whenever I catch one, all of the color inevitably goes out of the romance, and that is what happened with Jason, and with Peter, and with all the others before and since.

When I left Peter that first time, he reacted with a cool grace. He was angry, yes, but thought it was just a phase. I was young; it would pass. Surely, one day, once I'd explored what I needed to explore, slept with whom I needed to sleep with, had the odyssey I needed to have, I'd come back. And for that he was willing to wait.

Although Peter reacted with cool grace to my departure, my mother did not, and for months after I left, she refused to speak to me. Her silence, however, came only after she treated me to a rather sizable piece of her mind as we both stood on the front lawn. Her last words were, I remember, sharp and succinct, although still spoken in her low, modulated tone:

"I don't understand you, Tony. This is crazy. As crazy as the craziest things your father and grandmother have done. As crazy as the squirrels in the attic. And until you stop doing crazy things, I want you away from the house."

Then she turned and went back inside, closing the door on me.

It was during my absence that my mother married Peter in a lavish ceremony under the newly constructed gazebo. I was not invited. It might seem strange that my mother would marry my gay lover but she certainly had her reasons, three of them, to be exact.

First, she was ashamed of what I, her son, had done and wanted to fix it. By marrying Peter, she could get him dual citizenship and enable him to live and work legally in Denver, which, because he was patient and somewhat masochistic, he wanted to do.

Second, she married him because the renovation on the house was only half done and she needed his help to finish it.

Third, and perhaps most important, she married him because she really did love him. I did, too, although I know at this point in the story that's not so easy to believe.

Chapter Seven

After putting my grandmother to bed and digging some of my soggy belongings out of the van, I got into bed and sat up reading until I heard the sound of the car in the driveway. Actually, Meth heard it first. She raised her head, vaulted off the bed, and ran down the stairs. A few seconds later I heard car doors closing and steps coming up the walkway. I looked at the clock: Ten-thirty. I set down my book, turned out the light and lay there in the dark waiting for Peter. He would come, I was sure, but ever the player, I thought it important to look like I hadn't been waiting, so I arranged myself in the bed to make it appear I'd been asleep for hours. It was a silly little game, and one that was hardly necessary to play with Peter, but at that point, I'd been playing it so long, I really knew nothing else.

I heard the key in the door, heard them come in, heard their voices as they talked and laughed and greeted Meth. They went through the house turning off lights and locking doors, Meth's nails clicking on the wood and tile floors as she followed them. I heard their footsteps as they padded up the carpeted stairs, heard them say good night and head to their respective bedrooms. Then I listened to the water in the pipes as they brushed their teeth and flushed the toilets, and then . . . silence. I knew the next sound I heard would be Peter's soft knock on my door. I looked at the clock again: Ten forty-seven. He would arrive in less than a minute. I was looking forward to it, enjoying the sweet, tense anticipation. I'd always enjoyed sleeping with Peter, even after we broke up. It was like ordering a cocktail I liked but hadn't had in a while, or like putting on a favorite shirt that has been packed away all summer: familiar, comfortable, comforting. Just what I wanted after the evening of drama I'd endured.

I looked at the clock again: Ten-fifty. Maybe he was shaving. I'd hear the knock before ten fifty-five, no doubt. I waited. Ten fifty-five came and went but no knock. I waited. Eleven o'clock, eleven-oh-five, eleven-ten. Not only did Peter not come but Meth didn't either, and that really bothered me. I got up, turned on the light, and got my sketchbook. I quickly drew a crude map of the second floor of the house with my room and Peter's room clearly labeled. I drew an ornate X in my room, like the X that you'd see on a pirate's treasure map, and then took a red pencil and drew a thick line from Peter's room to the X. When I'd finished, I stood up and looked at my reflection in the mirror on the back of the door. I glanced back at the clock, then back again at the mirror, adjusted my pajama bottoms and my hair, and then opened the door and tiptoed down the steps to the living room, where I plucked a bright pink zinnia from the vase on the mantel. Then I crept back up the stairs and down the hall to Peter's room. The door wasn't closed so I didn't knock but just went in, closed the door behind me, and flipped on the light.

There they were, the two of them, in the same bed! Peter sat up, blinking and squinting. Meth buried her nose in the covers like the traitor she knew she was.

"Tony?"

"I woke up and didn't see the dog," I said, a banal tone in my voice, "but here she is."

I went over next to the bed and gave her a pat on the head, although I'd rather have given her a good pinch.

"She just followed me in here," Peter said, sitting up and leaning forward to pet her. We sat for a few moments stroking the dog in silence, each waiting for the other to speak. I took the initiative.

"I have three things for you," I said, scooting over next to him and gently booting Meth onto the floor. "The first is this." I handed him the flower. He rolled his eyes. Then I leaned over and kissed him.

"That was the second."

He was smiling.

"The third," I said, pulling the folded paper from the waistband of my pajama bottoms "is this map, since I can only conclude that you tried to find me earlier but must have lost your way."

I unfolded the map and leaned in close to show it to him.

"See here, this green square represents your room. The red line is how you get from your room to my room, represented here by the blue square."

He leaned over, kissed me, and pulled me down onto the bed. Without another word, we did what we'd done so many times before, and just as I expected, just like so many times before, it was good.

"So tell me," I said, when it was over and we were lying together in the dark. "Were you going to keep me waiting as some sort of punishment for not going to the dinner?"

I couldn't see him in the dark but I knew he was smiling.

"Well, okay," I said, "if that's the case, you won. You got me."

"Ahhhhh," he sighed. "I don't think so."

"Yeeeeesss, I think so. I'm here, aren't I?"

"You are and you aren't."

"Oh, I'm here," I said, and placed his hand down the front of my pajamas.

"You may be here now," he said, taking back his hand, "but you probably won't be tomorrow. And soon I'll be gone, too."

The departure threat. I made a dismissive clicking sound.

"You've really upset her with that," I scolded. "Did you know that?"

"Yes," he sighed. "I know, but there's not much I can do. I don't mean to upset her. I'll miss her, too, very much, but it was always temporary. She needs to find someone of her own," he said, and then added after a pause, "and I do, too."

I said nothing. I had heard it all before. It was Peter crying wolf again. I put my arm around him, pulled his head down so it was resting on my shoulder, and gave it a few little pats, not unlike those I habitually gave to the dog. It was a condescending thing to do, a way to diminish the gravity of what he was saying, but at least I didn't pull his head under the covers and fart, which was another charming little game I resorted to whenever a postcoital conversation threatened to get too serious.

"Now why would you leave?" I asked, although it was more statement than question. "You have everything here. You've got the house, lots of friends, the business is going well—why would you just walk away from all that?"

It was Peter's turn to make the dismissive clicking sound.

"Yes," he said. "Why? I have many things, many things that make me happy, but I don't have you."

I had heard that before, too. Many times. Too many times to take it seriously. Next would come the comparison, the conceit, the poetic image. He did not disappoint.

"I feel like a diver," he said, "looking for a ring lost at the bottom of a lake. I'm almost at the point where I'm going to give up and return to the boat."

All I heard in that sentence was the "almost." He went on speaking but he might as well have been speaking Swahili since I was drifting (to continue the watery metaphor) in and out of sleep, rocked into unconsciousness by the gentle pitch and roll of his voice.

When I woke up, the sun was streaming in around the edges of the window shade. Peter was still in bed beside me, our legs intertwined, his arm around my waist. Somehow, I got up without waking him and went into the hallway. I yawned, stretched my arms above my head, and looked out the window. It was a beautiful morning, all green and blue, so I decided to go for a run. I whispered to Meth,

"C'mon girl, let's go outside."

But she pretended not to hear me again, didn't even lift her head, so I left her and went on my own.

When I returned to the house an hour later, my mother was up and busy arguing on the phone with one of her subcontractors. She smiled, gave me a little wave, and then returned her attention to the conversation. I went upstairs, showered, dressed, and went to fetch Meth. She was still curled up with Peter, and again, when I called her, she refused to come.

"Meth, come on, girl, come on," I whispered, but she continued to ignore me and buried her nose in the comforter. Peter half opened his eyes and smiled.

"You must have told her what a good lover I am," he said with a yawn, throwing an arm around the dog and scratching her stomach.

I rolled my eyes. "You're not helping. I'm late already and I have to drop her at the track before I pick up Gabriel."

Meth was a racing dog and trained with my partner, Cleve, several days a week. Lately, we'd been grooming her for higher classes of races and she showed great physical promise, but as you can see, she had a stubborn streak.

Peter smiled, sighed, and pulled Meth into a spoon position. "Can't Cleve take her to the track when he goes?" he asked.

"He's already gone," I said. "And he probably doesn't even know that I got here last night."

Peter nodded but continued stroking the dog's ribby torso.

"I can take her," he said. "I've got to go out that way anyway. What time does she need to be there?"

"Cleve's got track time starting at one o'clock, so that means she's got to be there no later than noon."

Peter raised his head and looked at the clock on the bedside table. "Not a problem."

"You sure you don't mind?"

"I don't mind," he said.

I approached the bed and gave them both pats on the head. Peter grabbed my arm and pulled me down on top of him.

"You can say goodbye to the dog like that," he said, kissing my neck, "but as a human, and a sometimes revisited ex-lover, I think I deserve a bit more."

Relieved of my dog delivery responsibility, I was no longer pressed for time so I didn't resist. Thirty minutes later, I was dressed again and heading down the walkway to the van.

Curtis Park is much safer than it was when I was growing up, but it is still not safe enough to go to bed and leave the car windows cracked open, which was too bad because when I got in the van, it was like entering a terrarium. I briefly considered taking my things inside and hanging them up to dry, but then I looked at my watch and realized that in less than half an hour's time I had gone from being late, to having lots of extra time, to being late again, and

I could easily picture my helper, Gabriel, pacing the sidewalk in front of his building, nervously looking up and down the street wondering if something had happened to me. I got in the van, rolled down the windows, opened the vents, and headed up to Capitol Hill.

Although Peter had moved on to another, more dignified and profitable profession, I was still a house painter, although a considerably more refined one than when I'd started out. I no longer did exteriors and rarely, if ever, did any standard painting indoors. Instead I had become a faux painter, which, when you took away the French name, meant that I was very good at making things look like what they were not. I could, for instance, make plain old drywall look like marble, or wood, or granite; I could mimic the wallpaper from the Versailles bedroom of Marie Antoinette; I could stencil the perimeter of any room with cherub-laden vines or *fleur-de-lis*, or a parade of pink and blue geese wearing boots and carrying umbrellas. But, my real specialty was murals, Impressionist knockoffs, to be specific: Monet's water lilies, Renoir's feathery nudes, Pissarro's landscapes, all remarkably easy to execute on the cheap, textured walls so prevalent in the boudoirs and bathrooms of today's bourgeois mansions.

About four years ago, word of my talent began spreading through the suburbs, and I was suddenly in demand. For the first time in my painting career, I had more business than I could do by myself, and for the first time since my disastrous partnership with Peter, I decided to try to find an assistant. To that end, I posted a help-wanted sign in my local paint store and soon thereafter hired a string of unbelievably annoying and useless helpers.

House painters are not, generally, the stablest members of society (a generalization I am, of course, aware that I epitomize). The work is uninteresting and tedious, and does not require all that much skill or training. For those reasons, it is a profession that appeals to some of the lower elements of society.

My first employee was a paunchy man in his thirties. He didn't drive so I had to pick him up each morning, which would have been fine if he'd even just once been ready when I arrived. Usually he was not even awake and I would have to park the van and go bang on the door of his apartment. Several minutes later he'd come stumbling out, reeking of booze and cigarettes, his Walkman blaring Led Zeppelin. Only later did I learn that his "lunchbox" was filled with nothing but little airline-sized bottles of liquor, from which he would sip every fifteen minutes. He lasted two days.

The second was punctual, sober, and quiet but a horrible painter. The kind who thought you could roll every surface and who considered the use of drop cloths a foolhardy waste of time and money. I spent most of his first and only day fixing his mistakes and cleaning up after him.

The third was punctual, sober, quiet, a decent painter, *and* a kleptomaniac, who would remove things from shelves we were supposed to paint with no intention of ever putting them back.

The fourth, thank God, was Gabriel, and yet, when I first met him, his appearance made me think he'd probably be worse than all the others combined. He is my height (i.e., short), somewhere between the age of forty and fifty, and has a face and body like a bulldog: big head, no neck, and arms that hang at his sides like muscled parentheses. He is nearly bald but keeps the little hair he has buzzed so short that his balding is not noticeable. And then there are the eyebrows, although I hesitate to use the plural when describing them. I suppose there were two of them once, but they have long since grown into a single black hedge that shadows his deep-set eyes and perpetual frown. The overall visual effect is of a tough thug: the kind of person you could imagine felling you with one angry punch, which is ironic because in the entire city of Denver there is probably not a gentler, more soft-spoken person. He is the kind of guy who will take the time to carefully envelop a spider in a tissue and release it outside rather than squash it underfoot.

Gabriel was one of the last children to be raised in an orphanage before such places were abandoned in favor of foster care. His orphanage was run by Jesuits and consequently he is fiercely Catholic, although his faith was a thing about which he never pontificated. In addition to being gentle and devout, Gabriel was also, thank God, an excellent painter—methodical, careful, and meticulous almost to a fault.

I remember being exasperated by his professional integrity the first day we worked together. Because of my three previous helpers, I was behind schedule and rushing to finish. Gabriel was moving slowly, taking time to paint under the windowsills, and above the door frames—places we could easily have passed over since, unless someone was lying on the floor or standing on a ladder, they would never be seen.

"Don't worry about that," I whispered. "Skip it. No one will know."

Gabriel hesitated a moment, his brush suspended midstroke. Then he replied with absolute seriousness, "I will know," and without looking back at me, he continued painting. His response annoyed me at the time, but later, after we'd finished and I saw how pleased the client was with all the detailing, I decided to hire him full time. We worked together for three years and in that time he never did anything to make me regret my decision. His job was to go ahead of me on each project and prepare "the canvas" for my artistry, which meant that he did all the grunt work I found distasteful: he moved the furniture away, erected scaffolding, if necessary, removed pictures from the walls, and patched any holes or damage. Then he caulked along the baseboards and around the door frames, carefully masked everything off, and applied two even coats of the base color—the background color of the mural.

The only downside to Gabriel was that he didn't have a car. Because of that, I had to pick him up each morning and drop him off in the evening, which was not all that difficult since he lived in a residence hotel just east of the capitol building. The hotel was also less than a block away from the Cathedral, which enabled him to walk to Mass in the morning and evening.

His building had once, I'm sure, been quite fancy, but over the years, it had followed the entropic lead of the neighborhood and become a place for aging, solitary men with few possessions. Meals were provided in the mornings and the evenings in the dining room, and there was a communal TV and telephone in the lobby. It was a run-down, dreary place but there was an easy camaraderie among the men and I suspected that to orphan Gabriel the simple group setting seemed completely natural.

I remember one of the few times I saw his room, a small studio with an attached bathroom. It contained a bed and a nightstand, a small round table and two hard-backed chairs, and neatly arranged in one corner, his painting tools. No plants, no pictures, nothing but a Bible and some back issues of *Reader's Digest*. Nothing, it would seem, to indicate that the occupant was anything more than a temporary guest. And yet, had he been given money and space to decorate as he chose, I doubt that he would have changed anything.

I turned onto Colfax, made my way up Capitol Hill, and there, as I'd feared, was Gabriel, pacing beneath the sagging awning, tool bucket in one hand, black metal lunch box in the other. His expression relaxed when he saw the van and he almost smiled. I pulled up next to the curb, and before I could stop him, he opened the sliding door and a pile of my soggy clothes tumbled out. He stood staring at them, a confused look on his face. I got out, went round to his side and began picking up my clothes off the sidewalk.

"Sorry about that," I said, hoping he wouldn't ask for an explanation. "And I'm sorry about being so late. I, uh, had to take the dog down to the track."

He nodded and stood awkwardly on the sidewalk, wondering where he should put his tool bucket.

"Here," I said, taking the bucket and pushing it into the mass of clothes. "I'll hold it and you push the door closed."

He did so and we got in the van and drove away. It was only after we'd been driving for a few minutes that he asked, "Are you moving again?"

The "again" in that sentence bothered me.

"Yes," I replied, and left it at that. More silence followed, which I soon felt the need to fill up with explanations.

"I'm not sure where, but yes, I'm moving. I've broken up with Roy. He threw me out, actually. That's why all the stuff is in the back. You know what a temper he's got."

"Do you need any help?" he asked, a look of genuine concern on his mug.

"No," I said. "Thanks, though."

"You're not sleeping in the van again?" he asked.

I shook my head, again bothered by his "again." "I'm staying with my mom and Peter. Just until I can find a place of my own."

"Good, then I'll see you on Sunday."

"Sunday?"

"Yes, when I take Lola to church. Peter usually makes us waffles afterwards."

"Oh, yeah," I chuckled. "I forgot about that."

The year before, when my grandmother's gradual slip into delusion began to accelerate, she started getting lost whenever she went out by herself in the rapidly changing neighborhood. Gabriel, who goes to the same church as my grandmother, heard of her troubles, and had generously offered to escort her. I'd seen so little of my family in the past six months that I'd forgotten he was still doing it. Since I feared that the next thing out of his mouth would be a request that I join them, I quickly changed the subject.

"So, about today," I said. "I know you're not wild about being at Arabella's again—"

Gabriel gave a small grunt.

"—but she does pay well."

"Some things," he said, folding his arms across his chest, "are not worth the money."

"Now, come on. It's not that bad."

"You don't know," he said, shaking his head. "You leave in the afternoon, before things get messy."

It was true. Several days a week I left early to go to the coffee shop, giving Gabriel cab fare to get home.

"Do you want to know what happened yesterday?" he demanded.

"Probably not," I mumbled, dreading what he was going to say. "But tell me anyway."

Our client, Arabella, loved to tease Gabriel, and never more so than when I wasn't there to deflect it.

"She was smoking her marijuana."

I nodded. That was nothing new. Arabella smoked joints like cigarettes.

"She's troubled," he said, "I know, but what made yesterday different from all the other days is that afterwards she insisted on helping me."

"Helping you?" I said. "Helping you do what?"

"Paint!"

"Oh, no."

"Yes! She insisted. And you know you can't argue with her when she's like that."

I nodded.

"She kept lifting up her blouse, as much of it as there was, and threatening to take it off if I didn't give her a brush and some paint."

"So how much damage did she do?" I asked, lifting my glasses and rubbing my eyes, trying to keep myself from smiling.

"Oh, not all that much," he said, "at least not to the walls. I gave her a brush, and some paint, and tried to show her what to do and how to do it, but you know how she is; she ignored me and dunked the brush in the bucket, just like a donut. Paint went halfway up the handle. It was a drippy mess and she was wagging it all over the place. Then the phone rang (one of her beaus, most likely), and she marched off to the kitchen and gabbed for almost an hour."

"So . . ." I ventured, "then it wasn't *that* bad."

He held up a hand. "I'm not finished," he said. "While she was on the phone, she kept tossing the dripping brush in the air like some majorette's baton, trying to catch it as it came down."

"No!"

"Yes. The brush is ruined."

"I'll buy you another one," I said, knowing how careful Gabriel was to keep his equipment clean. "I'm sor—"

He held up a hand again.

"Then," he continued, "after her phone call, she went and passed out on the living room floor. I heard the thud, I hear it almost every afternoon about that time and I went to see that she was all right. She was, and I was able to get the brush away from her and clean her up a little. I moved her up onto the sofa, and went back to work. Then, later, after she woke up and went to the kitchen to get some water, she noticed that there was paint all over the floor and forgot that she's the one who put it there. Well, she came charging at me, all headachy and angry, and actually scolded *me* for being careless and sloppy!"

"I'll talk to her," I said.

"There's no point. She won't remember any of it."

"Then don't worry about it," I offered.

"Look, Tony, I just want to do my work. I don't ask much else. I'm quiet. I work hard. Don't take any more jobs from her. It's too much. Let's just get out of there."

"I'll talk to her," I said. "Maybe I can get her out of the house more often."

Gabriel just sighed. He shook his head, and gazed out the side window.

Arabella was difficult, no question about that, but she was also my best customer, and unlike some of the others, she accepted any bid I gave her and was liberal with advances. A former stripper who had married well—and often—she had too much money and not enough ways to spend it. For various reasons that will soon become apparent, Gabriel and I were the ones on whom she had lately chosen to squander it.

When we arrived at Arabella's house, it was almost ten o'clock. She was, as usual, not awake yet, so again I twirled through the keys on my ring until I found the one for her front door. I'd been to the house several times a week for the past ten months, but I was still never quite prepared for the shock of color that greeted me whenever I stepped into the foyer, an unearthly shade of peach, which Arabella had selected from the color deck more because she liked the macabre name—*Isadora's Scarf*—than because she liked the color. It blazed from the walls and ceiling, and was made even more hideous and unbearable by the high-gloss white that we had used to paint the trim. We entered as quietly as we could, and set down our tools. A moment later, we were startled by a noise, much like the amplified mewing of a large kitten. We stopped, looked up and saw Arabella at the top of the stairs, arms stretched out in a yawn. She was dressed, as usual, in some frilly, filmy teddy thing, her hair loosely piled on top of her head.

"Tony!" she exclaimed, her voice a studied facsimile of Ann-Margret's. "And my sexy Mr. Gabriel."

She then sailed down the stairs, ran across the foyer, and leapt on Gabriel's back, her mane shaking free and cascading over his shoulder. Gabriel stood rigid, unable to do anything because his hands were full. He blew the hair away from his face and shot me an impatient look. Arabella stuck her tongue in his ear and Gabriel shook her off, dropping the bucket of tools and the stepladder in the process. She landed with a thud, the brushes, rollers, and screwdrivers all scattered around her. Gabriel bent down to pick them up and a laughing Arabella rolled over onto her hands and knees to help him.

"No. Please," he said, averting his eyes from her breasts swinging pendulously before him, barely contained in their lacy hammock. "I've got it."

"Let me help you," she giggled.

"I've got it. Really!"

"No, I'm the one that made you drop them," she laughed, "Don't worry about it. Really. Why don't you go show Tony the work we did yesterday."

"Oh, all right," she said, bouncing up and snatching his hat from his bald head. "I need some coffee first, though. I'll make some for all of us."

Then she flitted off through the dining room toward the kitchen and I helped Gabriel pick up the tools.

"I'll talk to her," I said. Gabriel just grumbled.

To get to the kitchen, I had to walk through the dining room, where I paused for a moment to admire the first mural I'd done at Arabella's: a wall-sized version of Manet's "Le Déjeuner sur l'Herbe," with Arabella's face and hair imposed on the naked woman's body. The mural had taken nearly two months to complete, partly because Manet's style, unlike the other Impressionists, was more precise and finished, and partly (okay, mostly), because I had gotten behind schedule, taking afternoons off to, uh, practice my sketching. In spite of the slow progress, or perhaps because of it, Arabella was thrilled. So thrilled, in fact, that she immediately commissioned another mural—a towering version of Boticelli's "Birth of Venus"—looming over the enormous sunken tub in her bathroom. During the painting of it, I made the mistake of telling her that Venus was emerging from the surf where Zeus had spilled his seed. I say it was a mistake, because that bawdy aspect of the subject matter appealed to her and spurred her on to become an amateur student of Greek mythology. Armed with a junior high textbook, she read other stories, got new ideas, and commanded me to paint other murals in other rooms, all on the same Greek theme. We made it through two rooms, drew up sketches for four others, and could potentially have painted a mural on every wall in the house, keeping me busy on into the next decade, when I had a fit of conscience and decided I'd better rein her in. I suggested that rather than murals in every room maybe she ought to consider just repainting the rooms plain, straight colors (a plan that would provide work for Gabriel) and have me paint a gallery of faux niches in her circular foyer, each occupied by a different bawdy god or goddess. She thought that was a brilliant idea, so that was what we were doing. Gabriel had painted the walls and ceiling the shocking Isadora's Scarf, and once he'd finished, I set to work on the niches—hideous pink and orange and light blue faux marble with clamshell scallops—to be occupied by whichever character she saw fit. The whole room looked something like a giant feminine douche box.

Arabella handed me a cup of coffee as soon as I entered the kitchen and then immediately flitted out to take one to Gabriel. When she returned, I was about to ask her to please ease up on the teasing, but before I could get a sentence out of my mouth, she cried, "I can't believe you did it again!"

I was confused.

"Uh, what?" I asked, suddenly nervous. "Did what again?"

"Now, don't be coy with me," she scolded.

I was still confused.

"I thought *I* was bad," she said, "but this is the second one since you've been working here, and that's, what, less than a year?"

Then it hit me. She knew about Roy.

"News travels fast," I sighed.

"I'll say. My phone rang at eight o'clock this morning!"

"Roy?"

"None other. He wondered if you were here yet, and asked to have you call him as soon as you got in."

I nodded, took a sip of my coffee, and examined the rim of my cup.

"The poor thing," Arabella continued. "I've heard that same anguished tone from enough of my own jilted men to know just what happened. What was it this time, Tony? Cold feet?"

"Not that it's any of your business," I said, "but since I know you won't let up until you've got the whole gristly story to chew on, I'll tell you. I didn't leave Roy, Roy threw me out."

"Well, he certainly wants you back this morning."

"Hmmm, I doubt it."

"Oh, please!" she cried. "You know he'd take you back in a second. So what's the plan, wait awhile and make him grovel?"

"No," I said. "That's not the plan at all. The plan is to get on with my life and let him do the same."

"So you've already got another fish on the line! What word do you gay men use for 'mistress'? Is it 'mister'? No, that doesn't sound right. I know it can't be lover, because Roy was your lover. What could it be?" she puzzled.

"Listen, I don't know," I said. "I'm sure you'll come up with something, but there's not a mistress, or a mister, or whatever, on the line, or waiting in the wings, or anywhere."

"Ahhh," she said, raising a finger, "maybe not a serious one, but you got caught doing something with someone, didn't you."

"Huh?"

"Don't 'huh' me. Remember who you're talking to. We're a lot alike, you and me. I've been caught letting strangers drink from the private reserve a time or two myself."

"All right," I said. "Yes, I sort of got caught."

"The sketchbook?"

"I think so."

"Ha!" she cried, slapping her thigh. "I love it!"

I groaned.

"Odd," she said, cocking her head to one side and looking off into space, "but I don't think I've ever been caught like that. No, I'm pretty sure I haven't. I've always been careful. Never kept a diary or a secret phone book, or anything messy like that. I usually have to confess everything and even then, I have to chase them away. I know how not to get caught and you do, too, which is why this surprises me a little. I can't imagine you being so careless and sloppy." She paused to consider the problem, taking a big sip of her coffee.

"You know what I think?" she continued.

"I wasn't aware that you did that much at all," I grumbled.

"I think you must have left the sketchbook lying around on purpose," she mused, more to herself than to me. "Yes, of course you did. You wanted to get caught. You wanted him to throw you out. That way you could avoid having to sit down like an adult and say, *'You know, Roy, you're just not as great as I thought you were.'* Yes, of course, that's it."

"Miss Marple, have you got anything to eat?" I asked, looking around the kitchen. "I didn't have time to grab breakfast."

She reached in a tin on the counter and pulled out a bag of biscotti, handing it to me absently.

"Not that there's anything wrong with your method," she went on, walking over to the refrigerator. "In fact, it's probably a little more humane than my brute honesty. At least you let them be the martyr, give them some righteous anger to feed on. My being honest just makes them feel, well, inadequate."

She handed me a bottle of milk and a container of yogurt but no glass and no spoon.

"Who's to say which method is better? Either way you end up walking away trying to shake the sticky mess off your hands."

She paused, lit a joint, and inhaled.

"No, my friend," she stuttered, "neither way is fun." Then she exhaled a plume of smoke and added, "But don't worry, it gets easier the more you do it.

"Do you need me to model today?" she asked, a hopeful lilt in her voice.

In her leisure time—whenever she didn't have lunch plans or a Botox appointment—Arabella liked to play the part of "The Artist's Model." A whim I was usually happy to indulge since she was essentially paying for my company more than anything else.

That particular day, we were working on the Helen of Troy niche, so while I laid out the drop cloth and set up my paints and brushes, she ran upstairs to retrieve the bed sheet she'd fashioned into Greek drapery. Gabriel passed through on the way to the bathroom.

"Did you talk to her?" he whispered.

I shook my head. "No, but I definitely will."

He shook his head, grumbled something incomprehensible and went down the hall.

Although Arabella loved the idea of being an artist's model, her posing would last only about ten minutes, usually more like five, and sometimes as little as three, before she'd slump down into a chair or run to get a drink or a cigarette or go to the bathroom. I had told her that all I really needed was a photograph of her (she'd given me several) in the pose she wanted, but since she seemed to need an excuse to idle the day away talking to me, and since, again, she was the one paying the bills, I never argued.

We broke for lunch at noon. Arabella had disappeared to answer the phone an hour before and had not returned. Since I had no lunch, Gabriel offered to share his with me. I thanked him and together we sat in the sun by the pool and ate bologna and cheese sandwiches prepared for him by one of the men in his building. I had thought about leaving at lunchtime and going to the coffee shop, as I'd done so many times that week, but after the scolding from Gabriel about my absences, I was feeling remorseful. Not to mention afraid of running into Roy, who would not be above tracking me down for a confrontation.

Arabella appeared again just as we were finishing up lunch, still dressed in the Greek costume but with hair that was a different color than it had been that morning and freshly painted nails that she was fanning.

"You're quite the do-it-yourselfer today," I commented.

"Huh? Oh, this," she said, pointing to her hair. "Yes, I can be when I need to. But it's your fault that I had to be."

"My fault?"

"Yes."

"How so?"

"Well, I have a date tonight that I kind of forgot about until late yesterday afternoon so when I remembered I called Rolf's right away to make a hair and nail appointment. That was yesterday afternoon! A whole day in advance. Of course I got that bitch receptionist, you know, the one with the Transylvania accent. '*Zer ees no vay vee kun vit you in on such tiny notice.*' Such snobs. Anyway, it didn't really bug me that much because I figured you could pull some strings with Roy and get him to squeeze me in, but since I don't really want my hair washed with someone else's bitter tears, I thought I'd try and do it myself. So you see, it's your fault. What do you think?"

"Very nice."

"And . . . ?"

"And I'm sorry."

Gabriel packed up his lunch box and returned to the room he was working on upstairs. I got up and returned to the foyer,

Arabella skipping along ahead of me, ready to resume her role as the face that launched a thousand ships. We all took our proper positions and did what we were supposed to do, without pause or distraction for a good ten minutes, mostly because Arabella was still philosophizing on men.

"Of course my beauty has made men want to pursue me . . ."

I was not sure if she was speaking as Helen or herself.

"Ever since I was a little girl. I'm sure it will change when my looks fade (that's why it's good that I've got money), but maybe it won't change. I mean Mae West never had a problem getting men. Marlene Dietrich had young lovers. Older women can teach a young man a lot. Look at Cher, look at Madonna. Look at Demi. You should think about it, Tony."

I tried hard to ignore that last part.

Maybe it was the mention of singers that did it, maybe it was the angle of the sun streaming down on her as she posed, or maybe it was just that Arabella had been conditioned over the last ten months to know when it was time. Whatever the reason, she looked at her watch, dropped her props, jumped off the pedestal, and made a dash for the Media Room (not to be confused with the Medea Room, which was upstairs), stopping along the way to pluck my car keys from the hall table where I had left them right next to my turned-off cell phone.

It was, after all, ten minutes past one o'clock. The news at the top of the hour was over, the superfluous midday traffic had been reported, the round of annoying and fast-talking commercials had been played and that brought us back once again to "our program." Or maybe I should say *my* program. I had nothing to do with its daily presentation but it was undeniably pointed, like a well-aimed gun, directly at me. A bit of vengeful spite dispensed every day by an ex-boyfriend and perversely administered by Arabella.

There were speakers wired throughout the house, even on the front and back patios, so there was no getting away. I heard Arabella turn on the receiver and switch over to AM. There was a loud buzz followed by a series of squelching noises as she adjusted the tuning. A commercial for an assisted-living complex was just finishing up. That was followed by an impossibly harmonious chorus of voices singing out the station's call letters and jingle, and then the all-too-familiar voice of James.

"Welcome back, ladies and gentlemen, to hour number two of 'Afternoon Delight,' right here on KLZY, your home for the best of the past on the AM dial. It's good to have you along with us on this beautiful Tuesday afternoon. We've got some excellent music on deck so stick around. Let's see, Doris Day, Nat King Cole, Bing Crosby, Johnny Mercer, Petula Clarke, and Eartha Kitt. Yes, it's a veritable cavalcade of singing greats for your listening pleasure, so sit right back, relax, and enjoy.

"But first, it's time once again for the most popular part of our program. The time we allot every day for all you jilted lovers out there. The ones who've been cast along the side of the road like some old apple core. It's a sad time, it's a depressing time, oh heck, it's time for a little harmless revenge, and from the stack of requests I have before me, I can see that there are more than a few of you out there with someone you'd like to dedicate a song to. Yes, it's the time in our program that we devote to the scamps, the Don Juans, the Slick Sams and Casanovas that so many of us have had in our lives at one time or another. It's time once again for Radio Romeo."

(Here the voice dropped an octave and became more modulated and intimate, as if he were whispering into the microphone.)

"Today, ladies and gentlemen, I'd like to direct our program once again to a very special listener. Yes, you know who you are. Now, like I said, we have a lot of requests but I'm afraid I'm going to have to push them aside for just one day more. Yes, it's dealer's choice today, and let me tell you why. It's because, my friends, the one for whom this program was developed, the one who so notoriously abused the once fragile heart of yours truly has, so my reliable sources tell me, done it yet again to yet another poor guy. Can you believe it? Broken another heart. So, yes, today's installment of Radio Romeo is devoted to you, my feet-of-clay-darling. Without further ado, here's Miss Marilyn Monroe with her version of 'After You Get What You Want You Don't Want It.' "

I marched toward the Media Room with the intention of turning the song off, but before I could, Arabella emerged and locked the door behind her. The key, along with my car keys, was clenched in her fist. I walked slowly toward her.

"Give them to me," I said sternly, trying not to smile. "Enough is enough."

Gabriel, his book on tape interrupted by the earsplitting broadcast, appeared at the top of the stairs, a pronounced frown on his face.

I made a lunge for Arabella, who was, despite her age and addictions, remarkably agile. She made several evasive moves and then did a fake to the right. I fell for it and dove to the floor. She squirmed past me on the left, her squeals now adding chorus to the song, and began a feline climb up the outside of the banister. I got up, ran after her, and tried to grab her leg, but I succeeded only in grabbing one ankle and the hem of her stupid toga. She kicked with her free leg so that I couldn't grab it, but somehow, in the blur of painted toenails, I managed to grab more fabric and began pulling downward. The fabric stretched and then ripped. Arabella shrieked and giggled but kept up the violent kicking. More ripping, more screaming, then, finally, her sweaty hand began losing its grip on the high-gloss banister and she was forced to drop the keys. As soon as I heard them hit the tile floor at my feet, I let go of the sheet. I bent down, scooped up the keys, and made a break for the front door, grabbing my cell phone from the hall table as I went. As I closed the door behind me, I turned and saw Arabella, both breasts exposed, clinging to the banister and laughing hysterically while a horrified Gabriel looked on from the top of the stairs.

"I'll be back!" I called to Gabriel, and then closed the door on the both of them.

Even outside I could still hear the song blaring from some hidden speakers. It wasn't until I was back in the musty van with the door shut that it stopped. I turned on the ignition, backed out of the driveway, and drove. I'd go back in a few minutes, but just then, I needed a break. Gabriel was right; we did need to move on.

I drove to one of those twiggy suburban parks, the kind they build in drainage ditches and call "Open Space," and I sat for a while watching a group of bikinied little girls make water balloons at the drinking fountain. Despite my previous attempts to avoid listening, I couldn't resist the temptation to turn on the radio then and hear what new slander James might have to sling at me but there wasn't any more. Just a series of commercials and then a simple introduction to the promised Doris Day song.

* * *

I met James, The DJ, #6, in an unusual way. Or rather, an unusual twist on the usual way. There was the same sketching and eye contact, the same delivery of the drawing, and the same deluge of compliments, but the difference was that I met him not in a café, but at a smoky bingo parlor, where I had escorted my grandmother one Friday evening. James was doing some promotional work for the radio station and was the "celebrity number caller" that particular evening. With his young, clean-cut, gentlemanly looks and his deep, radio announcer's voice, he had the audience of mostly blue-haired old ladies in a swoon. My grandmother tugged at my sleeve and whispered to me, "*Ai, hijo, es muy guapo!*" and I remember thinking to myself, "This guy has got them all duped." Of course, Rock Hudson and Liberace had fooled these old ladies, too, but I wasn't fooled. For me, it was the shoes (highly polished box toes, as flat and thin as the bill of a duck) that gave him away. It's not that straight men wouldn't wear them, because I'm sure some of them would, but it is highly unlikely that such men would also pepper their bingo host banter with quotes from Peggy Lee songs and references to *All About Eve*.

I played a few games with my grandmother, studying him while I did so, but then I gave control of my bingo cards and marker over to her and took my sketchbook out of my bag.

Since it was his face and his voice everyone seemed so enchanted with, I decided to focus on his feet. After all, that is what I'd first noticed about him. I drew his right foot, expensively shod in Kenneth Cole, then drew the other unshod, and unsheathed from its thin, patterned sock. I had no idea what his foot actually looked like so I drew the foot of Michelangelo's "David" instead, figuring that a foot didn't get much better, or more flattering, than that.

Although I was drawing his feet, I kept glancing up at his face from time to time, to ensure that I had captured his attention. As one of only three males in the audience, and the only one of the three with hair that was not white, it would have been hard for him to miss me.

At the end of the evening, I let my grandmother do the rest of the work. While she stood with the other fawning old ladies in a semicircle around their matinee idol, I calmly put the finishing touches on my drawing. Soon the ladies dispersed, gathering their handbags and cigarette cases and heading to the bus in the parking lot, and my grandmother was the only one left. I continued to sit at an empty table in the center of the room and pretended to be focused on my drawing. Then, just as I'd calculated, starstruck, demented Lola was led back to me on the arm of none other than the star of the evening.

"I noticed your shoes," I said, seemingly apropos of nothing.

He looked down at his feet and then back at me, confused. I picked up my sketchbook and handed him the drawing. He looked at it in silence.

"It must seem strange," I said, doing my best Cary Grant, "I know it must, but it's a little game I play sometimes, trying to imagine what's inside. I mean, sometimes I'll draw a house or a building, and then try to draw the people I imagine living there. Or maybe a woman's handbag and the imagined contents. I've done essentially the same here with your shoe," I said, tearing the heavy sheet from my sketchbook and handing it to him. "Please," I said. "I'd like you to have it."

He accepted the picture and continued to stare at me, his confusion and doubt dissolving into a smile. I glanced at my grandmother and saw that she was staring at James the same goofy way that he was staring at me and I knew then that the portrait had been enough. The seed had been planted, was already beginning to sprout. Anything else I said to him would be too much, would spoil the moment, so I picked up Lola's sweater from the back of the chair, put it over her shoulders, and told her we'd better go.

"Uh, thank you," he called out as I walked Lola toward the exit. I turned, smiled, winked, and then continued on my way.

The next day I made sure to bring a radio with me to the job site. Usually I listened to books on tape with Gabriel but that day I made him listen to the radio, tuned, of course, to AM1430. We listened from the time his program began, a little after noon, until he went off the air at four o'clock, and it wasn't until three fifty-five that I heard what I was waiting for.

"I'd like to give a big thank-you to all you folks who came out to Swingo Bingo last night. We had a great time listening to some of our favorite big band and swing songs before we got the bingo pot turning. Of course, in my eyes, all of you ladies out there are winners, but I'd like to extend special congratulations to Betty-Madge Rosenhart. Betty-Madge was our big winner, taking home a pot worth two hundred and seven dollars. You can bet there was some wild partying afterwards at Francis Heights when they wheeled her back in. I heard they had a keg of Ensure to celebrate. Oh, I'm just kidding, of course. I'm sure Betty-Madge is dividing her winnings evenly between the church and the IRS. Then, if there's any left over, maybe she can even get some of her prescriptions filled. Again, I'm kidding, just kidding, so don't call me. Oh, too late. I see the switchboard lighting up already.

"Before I sign off and let Morton take over for the evening drive, let me say thanks again to all of our listeners for coming out last night. And thanks especially to a woman and her grandson, whose name I didn't catch. I'd like to send this song out especially to you. Here's George Gershwin's *Rhapsody in Shoe*, er, I mean *Blue*. *Rhapsody in Blue*."

It was a nice start to a nice affair. And indeed, our eight months together were rhapsodic, a mix of disconnected but nonetheless harmonious parts. James was the only man since Peter who could hit the wooing ball back across the net. He was always giving me little gifts and planning outings and dates and dedicating songs to me, and perhaps that's one of the reasons it didn't work between us. I was good at doing those things for others but was, frankly, a bit embarrassed when someone did them for me. I should probably admit, too, that I went a little overboard in the gift giving department with James. People who love retro kitsch are always easy to buy for and I loved finding things to give him probably as much, if not more, than he enjoyed receiving them. A monogrammed smoking jacket, a cocktail shaker in the shape of a rocket, bowling shirts, back issues of *True Romance* magazine, a set of Bongo drums, boomerang-patterned bolts of cloth, I LIKE IKE bumper stickers, a stuffed Marlin, clusters of colored resin grapes, and countless vinyl records.

If buying gifts for James was easy, then planning dates was even easier. Take him to any black-and-white movie, to any nightclub with a faded diva doing her act, any thrift store, any boxing match where he could sit close and smoke cigars, any seedy bowling alley, or diner, or soda shop. And we were always taking weekend road trips: to Vegas, to Carhenge, to Cadillac Ranch; to Kansas to see the largest ball of twine, to New Mexico to see a two-headed cow, or to Branson to see the Osmonds. Wherever. And when I look back, it seems our time together those first few months was like one of those fast-talking, fast-paced romantic comedies from the 1940s: always on the go, always fun and funny.

As time went by, he began suggesting that I move in with him, kept telling me how much nicer it would be to wake up together and not have to drive across town every morning. And to that end, he began wooing me with music on his radio show (although always careful to keep it gender neutral to avoid alienating his aged fans).

"I'd like to send this one out to that very special someone of mine. Here's Nancy Wilson singing 'You'd Be So Nice to Come Home to,' " or "I'd like to send this one out to a very busy painter out there. Here's Glen Campbell with 'Gentle on My Mind' " or, "Here's 'Won't Last a Day Without You' by Karen and Richard Carpenter."

Eventually I gave in. I just shrugged my shoulders and moved in. And that was a mistake, because as soon as I did, things changed. I know, I know, change is inevitable, so everyone keeps telling me, but there must be some way to keep that early magic alive, some way to keep the lizard iridescent, or at least so I hoped. Up until I moved in, our time together had been like the party scene in *Breakfast at Tiffany's*: loud and colorful and intoxicating, like a carnival, or a street parade, or our own music video, always fun and interesting, never dull, but as soon as I moved in, that all seemed to change. James seemed to lose his spark, his fire, his verve, and became the most retro of all retro things—a fifties housewife—and developed a daily routine from which he did not want to veer. I'd try to rally him, try to get him to pick up and go out to some drive-in on the Eastern Plains, or suggest we get drunk on sidecars at some fancy hotel bar after work and then go bowling or invite lots of people over for a croquet party, but more often than not, he declined, saying, "Mmm, I don't really feel like it tonight. Why don't we just stay in for a change?"

He was content to spend his evenings at home with the feet I'd so lovingly portrayed, propped up on the couch while he sat in the blue television glow, watching AMC or Nick at Nite. And that might have been okay, except that then he started scheduling time in the evenings for us to do fun things like balance our checkbooks or dust the knickknack shelves, and would devote our precious free time on the weekends to something fun like weather stripping the windows, which also might have been okay if the onerous tasks had been tempered with some fun, but the former seemed to increase and the fun became almost nonexistent.

I wanted more. I wanted the flush and blush of the new, the excitement, the spontaneity; the slightly nervous feeling that makes you want to put your best foot forward. I wanted the first days of love, when people are kind and friendly, more carefree and less concerned with the mundanities of life. I wanted something heavenly, and the life James was offering was all too terrestrial. I'd fallen in love with his free and wild style, but once I moved in, that all seemed to evaporate.

I'm sure you can guess what happened, even this early on in my little narrative. With sketchpad under my arm, I returned to the coffee shop and moved up from feet to a pair of the most amazing, most perfectly muscled legs I have ever seen, but I'm getting ahead of myself . . .

I strayed, and I got caught. To use the foot metaphor again, I acted like a heel, and appropriately enough, the very next day James opened his radio program with another shoe song. A song by Sinatra. Not the dead Sinatra, mind you, but the Sinatra with the dead career: Sinatra, Nancy. Even now, I can still hear the echo of those ominous descending bass chords at the beginning, meant, I suppose, to represent the infamous walking boots, or maybe a scolding finger moving back and forth like a metronome. Whichever, the song was a clever choice and in that instant reminded me how much I loved James (or at least the ideal I had of him), and would continue to love James, even as I wished that he would move on and stop tormenting me.

The thing is, James did move on. He was angry with me, and hurt, as they all have been, but he grew strong, he knew how to get along, and the thing that made him forget about me was, as it is with so many broken hearts, a new love. A love he found, believe it or not, in the exact same way, at the exact same place that he had found me—at Bingo, with Lola. It was, of course, Peter, who was escorting Lola, just as I had previously escorted Lola, to another evening of Swingo Bingo. James and Peter quickly realized the connection but were, nevertheless, smitten with each other. In fact, once they realized the connection, I think they both got a perverse thrill out of it all, although the perversion was somewhat different for each one. James, I'm sure, loved the idea of getting back at me by dating Peter, my ex-boyfriend who is much handsomer than I. Peter, on the other hand, went out with James in order to get closer to me—to find out what James had that he, Peter, didn't have. To find out what had made James so attractive to me in the first place. Predictably, it got messy.

Although my breakup with James was rough, Peter's, I'm afraid, was even worse, because in the few months they were together James had fallen in love, but Peter, still in love with me, was unable or unwilling to reciprocate. And that little bit of circular misery, while bad for James's heart, had done wonders for his radio career.

"Pervert!" a voice cried, and a second later a water balloon smacked into the driver's side window. I looked over and saw the three girls, not one of them over the age of ten, standing with their hands on their prepubescent hips, staring at me.

"Whaddya lookin' at, Mr. Pervy?" one of them cried, and then all three ran squealing across the lawn.

It was so ridiculous I couldn't help smiling, but figured I'd better get away before they made more ammunition or ran to find Mommy.

Driving back to Arabella's, I turned on my cell phone to check my voice mail. There were two messages, both from Roy.

Message 1: Hey. It's me. We need to talk. Call me when you get this.

Message 2 (sound of techno music and hair dryers in the background): Hey, it's me again. We really need to talk (long pause). About yesterday, last night. You really pissed me off, okay. I guess I overreacted but, Dude, that seriously pissed me

*off (another long pause). Look, I need to talk to you. I've tried
everyone but no one knows where you are. Or they're not
telling. At least they're not telling me. I'm sorry, Tony, okay?
But let's talk. Please call me.*

I erased the first message and listened to the second again. Why,
I wondered, was it giving me a hard-on? Was I so whacked that
someone else's mental distress could turn me on? Or was it just
that I imagined again the great "makeup sex" we could potentially
have? Whichever it was, I couldn't help thinking that the little
water balloon Lolitas had not been too far off the mark in their assessment.

The rest of the afternoon, thank God, passed quietly. I had a serious discussion with Arabella about teasing Gabriel and she
promised to be good in the future. Feeling remorseful, she quietly
smoked half a joint and resumed posing for fifteen whole minutes
without saying a word. I was still annoyed and didn't really want
her there but figured that if she stayed with me at least I could be
sure she wouldn't be bothering Gabriel. At the end of the fifteen
minutes she took a break to smoke the other half of the joint, found
a spot in the sun, and sat flipping through various paint decks.
Soon, we were inevitably playing her favorite game: the one in
which she would read a series of paint color names (almost always
a noun or an adjective) and I would supply the necessary verbs to
make them into a sentence. She wrote down the sentences as we
went along, and after about half an hour, she would read back the
result. Her hope was that one day she'd have enough to make a
novel, or at least a collection of short stories. I'm sure there have
been worse things published.

"Okay," she said, flipping through some paint chips, "here are
today's principal players. We've got Dorian Gray and Savanna
Grass. Are you ready?"

"Yes," I sighed.

"Okay, go!"

"All right then," I said, pretending to really think about what we
were doing, "the first verb for our young couple will be 'meet.' "

Arabella, pencil and pad in hand, color chips spread out on the
floor, tapped the pencil against her siliconed lips and concentrated.

"Hmmm, let's see," she said, and began writing, " 'Dorian Gray met Savanna Grass at the Ye Olde Curio Shoppe on Baker Street.' Okay, next," she said, hastily penciling in the notebook.

"How about 'fly.' "

"Fly? As in fly a plane?"

"Yes."

"Okay, this will be easy. 'Dorian Gray's Sensual Heart flew into the Stratosphere when the Pale Silhouette of Savanna Grass . . .'"

She paused, waiting for another verb.

"Appeared."

" '. . . appeared in the Firefly Glow!' "

"Very nice!" I said, in my best kindergarten teacher voice. "Is that really a name, that 'Firefly Glow'?"

"Yes, see, right here," she said, proudly showing me the third color down on a strip of yellows. "Pretty, huh? Okay, give me another."

"Hmmm," I said, tapping the end of the brush on my own lips and staring up at the ceiling. "How about 'ascend.' "

She scrunched up her forehead for a moment but then grinned and began writing. A minute later she read,

" 'Dorian Gray's Corinthian Column ascended in response to Savanna Grass's Mauvelous Taffy Pull, and before long he . . .' "

"Cough."

"No, really?"

I nodded.

"Oh, all right then. 'Before long he *coughed* at the Storm's Approach. Tickled Pink, he . . .' "

"Blush."

" '. . . Tickled Pink, he blushed a deep Philosophical Grey, and his Corinthian Column . . .' "

"Ejaculate."

"Oh goody! '. . . his Corinthian Column ejaculated Dutch Cream all over her . . . Swiss Boudoir.' "

As strange as Arabella's chemical-induced and perverse interest in the color deck may seem it is by no means unusual. You'd be surprised at the number of people who choose a paint color by rolling a joint or dropping a Valium or having a few cocktails and then sitting back and getting stupid with the stupid colors and the incredibly stupid names.

I remember one client, suitably named Dottie, who sat out on the front lawn of her house, stoned to the gills, trying to choose a shade for some exterior window frames. She had the deck open to shades of purple and just kept repeating over and over, "I'm really getting lost in these plums."

Or the persnickety gay couple, who spent hours sitting on their calfskin sofa one Sunday morning with a pitcher of Bloody Marys and virtually thousands of color chips spread out on the coffee table, trying to decide "what color the Great Room wants to be." If only the Great Room had wanted to be mosaic, that would have solved everything. Then they could have just pasted all the color chips on all four walls and been done with it.

Ironically enough, paint manufacturers have started selling small samples of all their colors in pill bottles so that you can actually paint small sections of the colors you are considering and see how they will look on your walls. It sounds like a good idea but most people go way overboard with this, and by the time they're through, there are so many colorful empty pill bottles rolling around it looks like a forgotten scene from the *Valley of the Dolls*. Not to mention that their walls now resemble the side view of some psychedelic giraffe.

One of the worst things, however, is when the homeowner turns to me and asks, "What do you think?"

There are several No-Win Situations in life and that is definitely one of them. First, they don't really care what I think, and are only asking to take some of the burden of deciding off themselves. Second, if it turns out badly, I will be blamed. Oh, not literally. They are, after all, the ones who made the ultimate decision. But if I've been careless and said something offhand like, "Yes, that yellow seems nice," and then once it's on the walls, they decide that they hate it, they will inevitably turn to me and say, "But you *said* it would be nice." Or on the flip side, if I have cautioned them against the color and they went ahead and used it anyway, they will say that I didn't warn them loudly enough. But worst of all, if I have remained silent and left the decision entirely up to them, they will turn to me once it's done and shriek, "*Why didn't you say something?*"

This is not entirely the homeowner's fault. No, the real fault lies with all the magazines and home-decorating shows that have made paint seem more powerful than it is; have given the idea that the color of a wall can project an image of who and how fabulous you are. Their hope is that you'll see their color and the name associated with it and think "I am Dusky Rose" (or Whipped Cranberry, or Doric White) but really, you are still just a person who chose this color. Probably you did it on impulse. Probably you regretted it. Which brings up the really beautiful thing about paint: it can always be fixed. No matter how awful and hideous, it can, usually within a few hours or days, be redone. Your mistake can be completely eradicated. Granted, it will cost you, but in the realm of costly mistakes, its price tag is still a bargain.

But the most important thing to remember about paint color is that no matter what "energy" or "feeling" you hope to get from the color you've chosen, no matter what you hope it will say about you, the fact is that once the furniture has been put back in place, once the pictures go back up and life resumes, for all intents and purposes, the walls may as well be white. You probably won't even notice them.

At exactly 5:01, Gabriel silently descended the stairs with his bucket of tools. I smiled at him and motioned that I had just a few more things to finish up. He sat down on one of the paint cans and waited, looking down at the passed-out form of Arabella. I finished the section I had been working on and then got up and went into the laundry room to clean my brushes. When I returned, Arabella had been covered with a blanket, the scattered pages of the color novel had been recollected in their folder, and Gabriel was walking toward the bathroom, ashtray in hand. When he returned, having flushed the contents, he looked down at her and shook his head.

"She's really just lonely, isn't she," he said.

I thought about that for a moment and then nodded.

When we got in the van and drove home, I was, thankfully, spared another discussion of how we should not take any more work from her. Instead, we just listened to NPR and were quiet until we got back to his hotel.

"Same time tomorrow?" Gabriel asked.

"Yes, I promise to be on time."

He nodded and gave me that bulldog smile. He was about to

close the door but then hesitated. "You're not going to sleep in the van, are you?"

I shook my head.

"If there's anything I could do to help you out, you'd ask me, right?"

I nodded. "Hey, I'm all right," I said. "Really."

"Okay, then," he said. "Tomorrow morning."

As I got back into traffic and headed across town, I couldn't help wondering why he seemed so worried about me.

Chapter Eight

The aptly named Commerce City is not a pretty place. That the dog track is its most attractive feature says a lot. I started going to the track with my dad back when I was a kid and have harbored a nostalgia for the place ever since. In retrospect, I see that my father gambled not for the fun of it, but with the very pointed goal of supplying himself with a secondary source of income (a secondary source undetectable to my money-managing mother) to support his wooing habit. It gave him money he needed for the flowers and the cocktails, the silk scarves and dinners out. For me, the track was the one, really the only, place I ever went with my dad where he wasn't flirting with women. Mostly that was because the ones who frequented it were of the chain-smoking, trailer-dwelling, big-assed variety that didn't appeal to him. Minus the female distraction, his attention turned to the betting form, to the dogs, and to me, in that order. I remember him holding me up on the fence so that I could watch while he told me what was good or bad about a particular dog and explained, with mathematical precision, the odds for each race and what each bet was likely to pay.

When I first returned to the track in my early twenties it was, like I said, for mostly nostalgic reasons, with memories of a colorful place full of fast-talking men and big payoffs. The reality was, as reality often is, less shimmering than the memory, and when I returned as an adult, I saw that more often than not it was desperation that fueled their fast talk, and that most of the cheerfulness was alcoholically induced. Nevertheless, I kept going back because, like my father, I had a wooing habit to support and, like my father, found that gambling was as good a way as any to do it. Unfortunately, I didn't have my father's luck or "system" and would, more often than not, leave the track no richer than when I'd arrived. Until I met Cleveland.

Cleve was, to put it bluntly, a hustler in just about every way that word can be applied. Although just fourteen, he had the street smarts one acquires from, well, a life on the streets. When I met him, he had just run away from yet another foster home and spent his days and evenings at the track, working the stands hustling men to make bets for him, and then hustling them for a place to stay in the evening. Since I was not then, and still am not, interested in the sexual favors of a child, he was content to act as my bookie and to give me (for a small fee, of course) tips on which dog was likely to win. Tips I came to value since they were rarely wrong.

In recent years our friendship had taken a bizarre turn, making us co-owners of three dogs, and through an even more bizarre set of circumstances, Cleve had been taken in by my mother and Peter and was (in the same unorthodox way that Peter was my father) my brother.

When I got to the track that evening after dropping off Gabriel, the first race was just about to run. Meth was in the second, so thinking I might have a chance to see her before the race I walked over to the building on the west side of the stands where the dogs were taken to be weighed and examined. Just as I expected I saw Meth and Cleve standing with the rest of the dogs and their trainers, waiting to be admitted. After the dogs were approved by the vet, they were given over to the attendants (usually pimply high school students working for the summer) who would slowly parade them, one by one, down the straightaway to the starting line so that the people in the stands could get a look at them, and so that the announcer could introduce them by name and number.

Cleve's baggy pants were halfway down his ass, the excess fabric bunched around his ankles. He held Meth's leash in one hand and a cigarette in the other. Meth, anxious as always before a race, began hopping up and down like a coiled spring, trying to jump over the other dogs like they were hurdles. Cleve was trying to control her by ignoring the behavior, while at the same time keeping a tight rein on the leash but Meth, not wanting to be ignored, tried another tactic: She backed up as far as she could and then butted her head at not one, but two, of the other dogs. The first victim jumped away, pulling his handler with him, and while Cleve was apologizing to him, Meth turned and butted the dog behind her. But, instead of jumping away, the second dog turned and lunged. Given that all the dogs were muzzled, it was a useless gesture, but still, the other dog's handler was angered by it, and although I couldn't hear him, I could tell from his gestures that he was yelling at Cleve. Apologizing, Cleve led Meth to a spot away from the other dogs and knelt down in front of her. He hooked his hair behind his ears, clenched his cigarette between his teeth, and gave her that stare of his—a stare that indicated disappointment of the one she wanted above all else to please and perhaps other, unknown consequences if the behavior didn't stop. Surprisingly (to me, at least), it worked. Almost immediately, she calmed down and lowered her head in a gesture of submission. Cleve stood up again, and slowly led her back to their place in line.

Satisfied that the situation was under control, I left and went to the window to place some bets. Then I wedged in near the finish line and waited for the race to begin. The mechanical rabbit began its rickety journey around the rail surrounding the inside of the track and when it got to the starting line, the gates went up and the dogs shot out. Meth was in the middle of the pack and got boxed in early, which was not good because instead of trying to pass the other dogs, she made a game of keeping up with them only so she could, as she'd done while waiting in line, butt them in the rear. It was as if she enjoyed teasing more than the racing. The most annoying thing about it was that although she was almost always fast enough to win the race, it just wasn't a priority to her, and this particular race was no exception to that. She'd run fast and had energy at the end, but had been so busy butting the ass of the frontrunner that she came in second. Wisely, I had not bet on her to win, which was a little like betting on your child to lose in a track meet, but which gave me the money that I needed. I went back to the window to collect my winnings, then took the back stairs down to the kennels and was waiting there when the two of them arrived. Meth wagged her tail and jumped when she saw me. Cleve just rolled his eyes and shook his head.

"I know," I said. "I was watching in the stands. She's a little wound up. It's from living with those two Jacks."

I undid the clasp on the muzzle and Meth shook it from her head. She nibbled an itch on her leg, sniffed her butt, jumped up and tried to lick my face, and then went over to the water trough and began lapping away.

Cleve removed her jersey and hung it up in her locker. I noticed that he seemed to be gaining some weight and commented on it.

"Yeah, your mom and Peter feed me well. Did you remember to put twenty down for me?"

I nodded, took his winnings from my pocket, and handed them to him. Cleve had also, wisely, bet on Meth to place, not to win.

"Thanks, man," he said, and then stuffed the money in his pocket.

"What do you think about Peter leaving?" he asked, bending down to brush the dog. I wrinkled my forehead.

"It won't happen," I said. "No chance."

"You think? Seems like he's made up his mind to go, said he'd be gone at the end of summer."

"Look," I said with a sigh, "don't bet on it."

"Well, I guess you'd know," he said snidely, "since you're back with him again."

"What do you mean by that?"

"Dude, I saw your van out in front of the house last night when I got home and then saw you weren't in your bedroom when I went upstairs. It's pretty obvious."

"No," I said. "It isn't."

"Well, Roy's sure upset about something. He's called here about fifty times today asking if I know where you are. Guess you've got your little phone shut off."

I shifted the conversation back to the dog.

"It's probably best that she's not living with the Jacks anymore," I said. "Don't you think?"

"Yeah, but, well, never mind."

"What?"

"Now don't take this the wrong way, okay, I don't mean anything bad by it—and I am glad you're out of there—but maybe it would be better if she had some more, like, stability, you know, so she could focus on her training?"

"She's a dog," I snapped, as if that somehow explained everything.

"Hey, man, don't get offended. I just mean that, like, she's got some big races coming up. She's in great shape, she just needs, well, not so many changes."

"She'll be away from the Jacks," I yelled. "She'll be fine!"

He was undeterred.

"Yeah, but it would be better if you kept her at the house for a while. Just until you get back on your feet. Until your life's more, like, settled."

The irony of that stung like a slap.

Like I said, when I first met Cleve, he'd been a fourteen-year-old waif working the stands: befriending men so they'd place bets for him and purchase his advice or, as the evening came to an end and he sought a place to shelter himself for the night, befriending men so that they would purchase him. Later, once he'd attracted a somewhat loyal following, he decided to make some money on his recommendations and started running his own book. Since it was widely known that he attended almost every race and knew many of the owners, he was seen as more knowledgeable than most, and guys were willing to pay for his advice and trusted him with their money.

For a while, I trusted him, too, and he made good money for me. Over time, we became friends, sharing a compulsive love of dogs and gambling, but there our compulsive personalities split; mine branched out into love and sex, while his went to methamphetamines.

Like I said, whenever I was short of money, which was often, I'd try to increase the little I had by betting on what Cleve assured me was a "sure thing." Unfortunately, as his drug use increased, so, too, did his exuberant predictions of this or that dog's imminent success. Predictions that were right only some of the time, less and less often as time went by.

One particularly bad day, I came to the track to confront him about some money he owed me, and to find out why he'd stopped taking my calls. He wasn't there, so I drove over to the motel where he stayed sometimes. The office was empty, so I asked one of the men working on a truck in the courtyard if he'd seen him and was directed to the last Komfy Kabin on the right. I approached and knocked but there was no answer. Conveniently enough, the door had already been ripped off its hinges so all I had to do was move it to the side and step in. The room was dark, except for the TV. Cleve was sitting in front of it in a rocking chair. I knocked again but he didn't turn around.

"It's me," I said. "Tony."

"Yes," he said, a lispy slur in his voice. "You're here about the quinella payoff."

"Yes."

"It was a good pick, eh? I was right on the mark with that one."

"Yes, you were," I said, "but hey, that race was a week ago and, uh, I'd kind of like the money."

The speed of his rocking increased.

"That might be a problem," he said.

I waited.

"You see, it's like this: I kind of spent all of it on drugs."

His frankness surprised me, but still I kept waiting for the next part of the sentence. The part where he'd say, *"But don't worry, I'll have it for you next week."* When that didn't come, I said, "Well, since I'm guessing you didn't buy the drugs for me, what are we going to do about it?"

He got up and switched on the light. His face was bruised and he held one arm close to his chest, unable to bend it. Evidently, I was not the first disgruntled client to visit that week.

In addition to taking bets on dogs, Cleve often talked about wanting to breed and train them. I had always assumed it was just talk so I was surprised when he pulled a puppy out from under his shirt and handed it to me.

"Now take a look at this one," he said, smiling and revealing the gap that had until that morning housed one of his front teeth. "He's got the makings of a real champ."

I looked at the puppy: a still-blind thing wriggling in his palm. It looked more like a giant pupa than a dog.

"Her dad rocked!" Cleve said, and then gave his name as one of the top five greyhounds of the previous year, which I knew was a lie since that dog had never set paw let alone penis in Colorado.

"You won a lot of money betting on this little guy's dad, remember?"

"Yes," I said, "but I won a lot of money on that quinella, too."

"So you did. So you did," he said, nodding his head and looking at the floor. "And I'll tell you what I'm going to do." He handed me the puppy and, using his good hand to brush the hair away from his face, looked at me and said, "I'm gonna make you an offer."

Great. A nineteen-year-old hustler was going to make me an offer. I scanned the room. All the IV drug paraphernalia—the spoon, the lighter, the blackened foil, and the rubber strap—was in plain sight on the table next to the bed.

"You can either wait on the money. I'll probably have it next month, definitely the month after that," he chuckled grimly, as if he didn't believe it himself. "Or you can take this little champ here, the best of the litter!"

We were silent. He waited for me to make my decision. Bells and whistles and flashing lights on the TV indicated that someone had won a prize, or advanced to the final round. The puppy lolled in my hand making little mewing sounds.

"Cleve, this dog can't be more than a few days old. Where's the mother?"

He looked down and kicked at the carpet with one of his feet. Then he led me to the back of the room, where there were two empty dog carriers. He reached in one of them and brought out a small plastic laundry basket stuffed with a pink electric blanket. He unwrapped the blanket and I saw that it contained three more of the tiny pupas, all making the same little mewing sounds.

"Okay, so, like, the mother's gone," he said, and looked down so I wouldn't see him crying. "She wasn't a champion, okay, and neither was the dad, but they were worth something, and that's why they took them. I hid the puppies and I've been trying to feed them myself, but I can't hold my hands still," he said, struggling to keep his voice steady.

"Take the dog, take all the fucking dogs if you want, they'll probably die if they stay here anyway. It doesn't matter. I'm getting kicked out of this shit hole tonight so I don't know what the hell I'd do with them anyway."

He sat down again and stared at the TV. I stood, stupidly holding the tiny dog and staring down at the others, wondering what I should do or say.

"Look," he said. "Take the dog or don't but you better go. Some more pissed-off people will probably come soon, and trust me, dude, you do not want to be here then."

I didn't move. I stood in the grim room, the cheerful din of the TV in the background.

"Do you want to be here?" I asked. "I mean, why just wait around?"

"Yeah," he snorted. "Why. Where the fuck else would I go?"

I was silent and again wondered what to do, although there really was no question in my mind, no alternate possibility. Oh, I could have just gone, written off my loss and left him and the basket of puppies to fend for themselves, but I never really considered that. Instead, I took the dog and christened her Meth, since that is what Cleve had purchased with my quinella payoff. I also took the other three dogs and Cleve himself, loaded them into my van, and drove to the storage unit on South Broadway, where I kept all of my paint and supplies, and where, conveniently enough, I'd been keeping myself since the breakup with Jason and the subsequent loss of the loft. It was a windowless room with a toilet, a small sink, and a CD player, but that was about all. I'd been showering at the gym down the street, eating all my meals out, and sleeping on a cot that I'd purchased from the army surplus, so all I really had to do to make room for Cleve was shell out twenty bucks for another cot.

That first night together was strange. I had just finished brushing my teeth and was about to get into my cot when Cleve, sitting on his cot, asked, "So?"

"So . . . What?" I asked.

"So, you want to suck my dick?" he asked.

I wrinkled my brow, wondering where that question had come from.

"Okay, okay," he said, as if he hadn't got it at first, but now understood. He stood up, came over to where I was standing, and started undoing my belt. I grabbed his hands and pushed them away.

"What are you doing?"

"Look, I'll do anal if you really want, but there might be, like, a train in the tunnel."

"What? Gross!" I cried. "I don't want that. I don't want anything but for you to shut up and go to sleep."

He looked at me skeptically, but went back to his own cot and lay down, although neither one of us got much sleep. We took shifts caring for the dogs, feeding them cans of Ensure and pureed soup from a bottle when they got vocal, which was about every three hours, and tried hard to keep them warm. Despite all that effort, one of them died that first night.

I went to work the next day and Cleve stayed "home" to care for the pups. It would be nice to say that we fell into a steady routine but that didn't happen. An addict alone with time on his hands and no money is not a good thing. I came home on the fourth day to find my CD player, most of my painting equipment, and Cleve gone. Not a very nice thank-you for my efforts on his behalf but at least he had been considerate enough to make his bed before he left, and to time his departure so that the dogs didn't miss a feeding, details of which he explained in the shaky, misspelled apology note he left for me on my cot.

For three days after he left, I stayed "home" from work and cared for the pups, whose eyes had finally opened and who were now actually taking some steps. I went out only to get food, or to shower, and spent most of my time bottle-feeding, or hauling the filthy electric blanket across the street to the laundromat, taking the puppies with me in a backpack so they wouldn't get cold.

On the third morning, I was sitting and listening to the radio, trying to drink coffee and feed one of the squirming brats at the same time, when I heard a knock on the door. Hoping it might be

Cleve, and praying that it wasn't the owner of the building since I hadn't paid the rent and was probably not supposed to be living there, I walked over to the door, clenched the nipple of the baby bottle in between my teeth in order to free up a hand, and bent down to pull up the metal slider. I had it up about a foot and a half when I saw the well-toned calves of the new Mrs. Peter Carlsson. One foot supported her weight while the other rotated from side to side on the short, spiky heel of her shoe.

I froze.

"Tony? It's Mom. I have some mail for you. I don't know where you're living these days so I can't forward it. I was just going to push it under the door here . . . but I saw your van, so I . . . Can I come in?"

I couldn't very well push the slider down again and pretend I wasn't there so I pulled it up, squinting at the midmorning sun.

I must have been quite a sight—unshaven for three days, hair standing on end like a fright wig, a baby bottle in my mouth and a blanketed bundle cradled in one arm, but my mother's face showed no surprise. I took the bottle out of my mouth, said hello, then turned and retreated to the cot. My mother followed, her heels clicking on the concrete. She looked for a place to set down the mail and, in the process, assessed the surroundings, realizing no doubt that she had, inadvertently, found the place I was living.

"How long have you been here?" she asked, sitting on Cleve's cot and holding the mail in her lap.

"About a month."

"And Jason's here, too?"

"No, that's all over."

She nodded.

"That can't be a baby," she said, leaning forward to see what I was cradling, a look of dread on her face. "Please, tell me that's not a baby."

"No," I said. "At least not a human baby. It's a puppy. And it's a long story."

Her face relaxed when she heard that and she settled back down on the cot.

"Listen," I said, "I know I'm not in a position to ask you to do anything for me, but there are two more in that basket over there that need feeding. Would you mind helping out?"

She didn't mind, and over the course of the morning we sat across from each other on the cots, fed the puppies and told all that had happened in our lives over the past eleven months. Of course, most of what I told her were lies—that Jason had dumped me to return to his lover; that I'd found the dogs outside the Laundromat in a basket; that I was just living in the storage unit until the floors were refinished in the fabulous new apartment I was going to rent; that yes, I had plenty of work, and no, I didn't need any money.

She didn't believe much of it, I could tell, but she didn't argue and seemed genuinely happy to see me, and to see that, despite my dismal surroundings and unhygienic appearance, I was all right.

Later that evening, she returned with Peter and said I could move back home for a while if I wanted. I knew it would be awkward with Peter so I declined. Also, for some stupid reason, I was worried about Cleve and didn't want him to come back and find the place all locked up. However, I did need money, and that meant I needed to get out and work. I had one, and only one, crotchety client who was just about fed up with my frequent absences and slow progress (progress that was bound to be even slower now that most of my equipment had been stolen). I had a good two days' work left on the job and desperately needed to collect the final invoice in order to pay the back rent on my "home." So, with all that in my mind, I explained the situation as best I could to my mother and Peter, leaving out the parts about Cleve, and the drugs, and him stealing my stuff, and asked if they could help me.

"If you, or somebody," I said, "could just come by twice a day, just until the weekend, and help out with the feedings, it would really be great. According to this book I got at the library," I explained, pulling out the appropriately dog-eared copy of *Domesticated Orphan Babies*, "they still need to be fed about four times a day. That should go down to three times in a week or so. Right now I can handle the morning and the evening, it's just the two feedings during the day that I can't really do, and I can't take them with me because I'm doing an interior and the client is a real bitc—"

"We can help," Peter said.

"Yes," my mother agreed. "Peter is out most of the day, but I'm working from home. I can come by. Just give me a key and show me what to do."

Two days later, when Cleve returned, jittery and strung out and full of remorse, it was not me he found in the storage unit bottle-feeding the puppies but my mother, sitting on his cot, her long, blond hair pulled over onto one shoulder, her elegant legs slanted to one side. He was so mesmerized, and she, of course, was so kind and motherly and understanding, that he told her the truth about everything. When I returned that evening, she and Peter were packing up my few paltry things, and moving the two of us into *Casa Turquesa*.

"Don't argue," Peter said.

"Yes, don't," my mother agreed. "If you won't let us help you, at least let us help him."

Seeing the logic in that, I did what they suggested, and shortly thereafter, at my mother's behest, and with my promise to care for the dogs until he returned, Cleve entered a two-month residential treatment program. While he was gone, Peter built two doghouses ("villas" might be a better word) in the backyard, although that really wasn't necessary since, with the exception of Lola's deck, which was reserved for the squirrels, they pretty much had the run of the whole house. He built only two doghouses because after about a month I took the third dog, Meth, with me and moved out again. The capable Danes had everything completely under control and I really wasn't needed. I got an advance on one big job and put it all into getting a place of my own: a garage in an alley off of Fifth and Acoma Streets, that had been half-ass converted into an apartment. It had windows and heat and a shower, so for me, it was a step up.

When Cleve emerged from treatment, Peter gave him work as a carpenter's helper during the day, and at night, he would meet me at the running track at East High School and we'd exercise the dogs. Cleve, eager to get back to the greyhound track, began asking me, just like in the old days, to place bets for him.

"Listen," he'd say, while we watched our dogs tear around the infield, "I've been looking over the form for tonight's races, and if you want to make some money, I'd go with Shorty Sandra to win in the fourth. You might try a box with her, Cajun Igloo, and Sam I

Am. You got that? You think you could drop a fifty on it for me? If you're headed out that way, I mean."

"Sure," I said. "But why don't you just come with me?"

"Na," he'd say. "I don't think your mom and dad would like that so much."

Soon, with Peter's help, Cleve got a legitimate job at the track, driving the grooming tractor and cleaning up where the dogs left off, most of which he did in exchange for track time for our own three dogs. A week after that, he was back selling advice and running a book and was doing quite well.

Surprising to everyone, Meth, the dog with the least amount of training, showed the most promise of the three so we focused our attention on training her, devising a "sure thing" plan for winning dog races: a system of long-distance endurance training combined with sprint work. It was a system that had worked for me when I was on my college cross-country team and was proving to be fairly effective for dogs.

"Just think about it," Cleve said. "It might make sense for her to stay at your mom and Peter's for a while. At least until she's back to winning again. You wouldn't have to commute so much and you could come see her whenever it's convenient."

I was offended and didn't try to hide it.

"Hey, she'll always be your dog," he said. "You know that, but we've put a lot of work into making her great. It would suck if it got messed up when we're so close to making her really shine."

"You've got a lot of money on her for these next few races, don't you?"

"Yeah, I do, but that's not the point. At least not all of it. Call me superstitious but these three dogs mean a lot to me. I know you probably don't get it, but as long as they're okay, I feel like I'll be okay."

I didn't say anything. What could I have said? We both stood there staring stupidly down at Meth, who stared stupidly back at us.

"Just try and be good to her," Cleve said, clipping the leash onto her collar and handing the leash to me. "At least let her stay at your mom and Peter's place and don't take her tricking around town with you."

"I don't trick around," I protested.

"Well, whatever you call it. Just be careful—with her and with you."

He handed me the leash, and Meth started pulling me out toward the parking lot. Cleve followed.

"What did you mean by that?" I asked. "That part about being careful with myself?"

He put a hand on my shoulder.

"I meant you seem to be moving around a lot and not really getting anywhere. Can't say I'm sorry that Roy's out of the picture. He is, right? Out of the picture, I mean. Yeah? Okay. Look, I just want you to be happy, man, but none of these guys seem to be doing that for you."

"Well, I haven't really found the right one, have I."

"Yeah, whatever."

"No, I'm serious."

"I don't think you're ever serious when it comes to guys. You've had the right one about ten times over."

"You mean Peter."

"I didn't say that, but yeah. What's wrong with the guy? If he wasn't, like, my dad, I'd want him. But it's not just him, the others, too. I mean it didn't seem to me that there was anything wrong with a lot of those guys."

I was silent.

"Look, not to preach, or anything," he said, giving me a very fatherly pat on the back. "All I'm saying is I'm worried about you." Then he leaned down and rubbed Meth's ears. "And about her, too." She gave his face a lick. I opened the van door and Meth hopped in, curling herself up in the passenger seat. I got in and rolled down the window.

"The last race probably won't finish up here until about eleven o'clock," Cleve said, "so I won't be home till after midnight. If you wanna just leave her at the house tomorrow morning, I can bring her with me."

"Sure," I said. "Thanks."

I put the van in gear and drove away. In the rearview mirror I watched Cleve as he walked back to the track, and I saw his nineteen-year-old head give that disappointed shake. The same disappointed shake he'd given earlier that evening to my stubborn, head-butting dog.

Chapter Nine

Chastened by Cleve and resolved to be good, I drove straight from the dog track to Curtis Park without any sketching diversions. I took Meth inside, fed her and set up her bed at the top of the stairs by Peter's room, right where she liked it. Then I unpacked the mess of clothes from my van, hauled them downstairs to the washing machine and started a load. I went back upstairs to see if I could find my mother and Peter but found instead a note on the kitchen table. It was in Peter's handwriting and said that they had gone to dinner and then to a play and would not be home until late. I was directed to food in the refrigerator, and asked to please telephone Roy, who had called several times. I crumpled up the note and went upstairs to see my grandmother.

The stairway leading up to the third level of the house had always been dark and narrow, but when they'd replaced the roof, Peter had installed skylights, making it much less grim than it had been when I was growing up. He had also enlarged an ancient dumb waiter and made it into an elevator, which went from the kitchen up to the mother-in-law apartment he had fashioned for Lola in the attic. The attic was now one large room, painted pink, with four large dormer windows and a sliding glass door leading out onto a spacious redwood deck, which was where I found Lola, sitting and working on her needlepoint, squirrels scampering around her feet.

The deck, more of a tree house really, its support divided between the house and the massive trunk of a black walnut tree, was a testament to Peter's carpentry, engineering, and aesthetic skills. It was like a bridge between the developed and the natural world. A cool, leafy, surreal place, high up and away from earthly reality.

What made my visit to my grandmother's porch even more surreal that evening was the fact that in recent months, since her Alzheimer's had grown worse, she'd begun confusing me with my long-absent father. At first, the mistakes were subtle; she would call me by his name then quickly correct herself. But as time went on, the frequency of her error increased and her correction of it decreased until soon I ceased to exist as myself in her mind at all.

And then, of course, there were her squirrels.

Squirrels have always been a problem in Curtis Park. The majority of people regard them as a nuisance: nothing more than bushy-tailed rats that eat out of the Dumpster. But when the neighborhood "turned over" and citizens with more money began taking over, the squirrels went from being a nuisance to being a dangerous and destructive adversary that needed to be destroyed. They were accused of devouring gardens, of killing young trees by stripping the bark, and worst (and least truthful) of all, of carrying disease. Campaigns were organized to cut back their numbers or, better yet, get rid of them altogether but, luckily for the squirrels, there were people like Lola. People who regarded them as pets and fed them as such.

For the sake of illustrating the problem, I've taken the liberty of naming the two opposing groups—The Trappists and The Franciscans—according to their philosophy:

The Trappists, as their name implies, catch the squirrels in traps and relocate them to other, less desirable parts of town (Commerce City being a favored dumping ground). Some, however, are less charitable and will actually shoot the poor things out of the trees with pellet guns. Others will drown them by submerging the traps in a trash barrel full of water, and one woman (surely more deranged than even my grandmother would ever be), even went so far as to seal a trapped squirrel in a Hefty bag, connect the bag with duct tape to the tailpipe of her car, and start it up.

The Franciscans, on the other hand, are elderly people or PETA members, who loved any type of cute, furry little animals, and speak to them in high pitched voices and give them individual names. The Franciscans feel there is nothing wrong with putting out a bit of food for them each day, in fact, they feel almost a moral obligation to do so, which, of course, just encourages them to breed more and more, making more work for The Trappists.

Squirrels were first attracted to our yard because of the productive, and hugely messy, black walnut tree. Later, more of them came because of Lola's largesse. During one especially harsh winter, she started putting out seed for the wild birds. When they were bullied away by the squirrels, she just transferred her affections. Soon she was buying fifty-pound bags of peanuts and sunflower seeds from the Seed and Feed on Fifteenth Street, and supplementing them with any fruit or sweets she could pilfer from the kitchen. She and my mother used to have verbal brawls about it almost daily; my mother trying to explain how feeding them just perpetuated the pest problem we already had in the attic and Lola calling her cruel and hateful, and pelting her with made-up quotes from Saint Francis. No matter how the arguments started, they always ended in a firefight of Spanish and Danish obscenities, neither one of them understanding what exactly the other was saying but each saying it very loudly.

The battles escalated and soon my mother, who had control of Lola's money and her means of transportation, refused to buy her any more peanuts and sunflower seeds. Lola responded by stealing money from the collection plate at church and walking the ten blocks from Curtis Park to the Seed and Feed, buying the bags herself and then hauling them home in a wheelbarrow, right through the middle of downtown.

After that, my mother became one of the first Trappists, although the group as such wasn't really organized back then. She drove down to the Feed and Seed herself (which was, ironically enough, the only other building in the whole city painted the same hideous turquoise as our house), and bought three squirrel traps. With Lola at home all day, she couldn't really put them in our yard, so she conspired with the next-door neighbors, who were also sick of the squirrels, to place the traps in their yard. Then, when they were full, the neighbors would discreetly telephone and my mother would go pick them up and take them out to Riverside Cemetery, which was almost always deserted, so there was no risk that anyone (anyone living, at least) would witness her deed.

For a while, my mother's plan seemed to work. The squirrel population, while not actually declining, did seem to have leveled off, and it was only a matter of time, she figured, before the scales would tip in her favor. But, then, that was before Scarface.

One day, maybe she had to take me to the dentist or to soccer practice, or maybe the neighbors forgot to call, but for some reason, my mother forgot to check the traps. When she finally did so the next morning, all three were occupied and one trap, strangely enough, had two squirrels in it. Together we snuck them into the back of the station wagon, careful that Lola didn't see us, and headed out to the cemetery. The squirrels tended to freak out in the car, rattling around and making little chittery squirrel noises, but this time it was worse than usual and there seemed to be high-pitched squeals coming from one of the cages.

"Mom," I said, my voice shaky, "I think they're fighting."

She drove faster, and when we got to the cemetery, she got out, lifted the hatch of the station wagon, and we saw that the two squirrels in the one cage had indeed been fighting and were covered in blood. They both seemed to be alive so we quickly took the cages out, carried them down the hill away from the car and stood, as we always did when releasing them, on top of headstones. My mother poked at the traps with a broom handle until she hit the release buttons and the doors opened. The two single squirrels bolted as soon as the doors opened, but the two bloody brawlers were dazed and injured and didn't move. My mother poked again and again at the cage and finally one of the two—the dead one—fell out. The other would not emerge. Finally, after about two minutes, he came crawling out, but did not run away. He just sat there on the grass, staring at us with his one remaining eye, and making low, threatening noises. My mother kept trying to shoo him away with the broom handle but he wouldn't go. Then, angered by all the poking, he grabbed on to the handle with his little paws and began climbing, with alarming rapidity, toward her. She screamed, javelined the broom handle as far as she could, grabbed my arm, and leapt from the headstone, sprinting back to the car. She pushed me in, got in herself, and sped away with the hatch still open.

Weeks later, maybe even a month, she was at the kitchen sink washing dishes when a squirrel suddenly appeared on top of the fence and began chattering at her. This was nothing new, since there were probably close to ten squirrels in the yard at any given time. But as she looked closer, she saw that this was not just any squirrel. This squirrel had a torn ear and a crooked front paw, and he wasn't eating, or playing, or anything, just sitting and staring malevolently at her with his one eye.

After that, she bought a gun and began shooting the squirrels out of the trees on Sunday mornings while Lola was at church. But even that didn't completely solve the problem.

When Peter arrived, he, too, tried and failed, to get the squirrel situation under control. He allowed Lola to keep feeding them but persuaded her to feed them a new food. A food that would make our yard look less like a barroom floor and had "an extra special ingredient" that he had obtained from a veterinarian friend. This ingredient essentially sterilized the squirrels and did, at least for a while, slow down the population explosion, but not enough to really satisfy anyone. The squirrels still decimated treasured fruit trees, feasted on the vegetable garden and were generally little scolding, tail-flapping menaces that my mother continued to slaughter on Sunday mornings.

What finally solved the problem once and for all was the arrival of Cleve and the three greyhounds. As soon as their size eclipsed that of the squirrels, there were no more squirrels in the yard at all and fewer and fewer in the trees. Those that remained were the brave few, Scarface included, that Lola fed from her hand, and which were at that point nearly domesticated. These five or six sterile, graying, rotund beasts were fed so much and so regularly that they almost never wandered from the tree and spent most of their days napping in the dollhouse hutches Peter had built on the deck.

"Hello, Lola," I said, approaching and gently touching my grandmother's shoulder. Calling her "Grandma" only confused her, but calling her "Mama" troubled me, so Lola was the compromise.

"*Fernando!*" she cried, greeting me with my father's name. She set aside her knitting and stood up to give me a hug.

"Sit, sit," she said, shooing one of the squirrels from the chair next to her. "Tell me about Juana and the children."

"Uh, yes, Juana and the children . . ." I said, although that was the first I'd heard of them in my life. "Oh, you know, they're okay."

"Good, good. And the tennis?"

"Uh, okay."

"And you made peepee in the truck," she said, laughing. "You remember?"

I nodded. A good twenty minutes of such insane banter followed. Banter that was so insane it left me scratching my head and wondering who I was and if I'd forgotten all of my Spanish. Soon, thank God, Mrs. Garcia arrived, and I was able to sneak away, being careful to latch the gate at the bottom of the attic stairs so that the dogs wouldn't go up. I went back down to the kitchen feeling depressed, and wondering what to do with myself. I thought of showering, getting something to eat, and making it an early night, maybe watching some TV or reading a book and then going to bed, but that seemed such a waste of a beautiful summer evening, so before I knew it I was out the door, back in the van, sketchbook and pencils in hand.

From a wooing standpoint, St. Mark's coffeehouse is ideal: it is located on a wide, busy sidewalk where there are, at any time of the day or night, attractive men coming and going. But the best part is that right next door there is an artsy, black turtleneck bar called The Thin Man, so if the post-sketching coffee shop conversation with my new Mr. Tonight goes well, I can carry it on next door with a cocktail. Conversely, if it's not going so well (i.e., if the O.O.D. is playing hard to get), there is nothing like a little alcoholic inducement to soften the stone.

I found a parking place on the street, fed the meter, and then walked with my sketchbook and pencils, toward St. Mark's. It was mobbed; every table and chair was occupied. I stopped and assessed the situation for a minute. The patio for the bar next door was also crowded, but when I peeked inside, I saw that there were vacant seats so I walked in and took a spot at the end of the bar. From that position, I had an elevated vantage point from which I could look through the large, glass sliding door that led to the out-side, and I could both see and be seen from most of the seats on the patio.

I ordered a drink and quickly gulped down half of it. Then I calmly swiveled the stool around so that I could observe the patio. I crossed one leg over the other as an easel for my sketchbook, and began assessing the crowd: mostly groups of students, couples on dates having a cocktail before heading to dinner, or groups of friends meeting for a drink after work. I weeded through those people and picked out the few solitary souls, who, like me, were looking for something else.

I locked on to one of the attractive students. He was young for my taste but had cute ears that stood out from the sides of his head like a monkey's, and I was intrigued by the challenge of making them look attractive. I started drawing, got the subtle eye contact established, and had about a third of the drawing finished when a plump girl wearing unflattering hip huggers and a Hello Kitty backpack passed me on her way back from the bathroom. She crept up behind him and enveloped the big-eared head I had been so ar-dently sketching between her two ample breasts. She giggled, leaned forward, and gave him a kiss. I flipped the page and looked around again.

Two women and a man; probably a platonic thing. The women rose and said goodbye, leaving the man alone. He was attractive, mid-twenties, and very well groomed, his thick black hair nicely in sync with his black linen shirt and black boots. I focused on the hair. It was one of those studied messes—meticulously pomaded and fingered to look like he'd just gotten out of bed. Some people find that style pretentious, and probably it is, but as one who was always seeking to project a studied image of myself, I admired those who put such obvious effort into their appearance. Alas, this one was not to be immortalized or pursued, at least not by me. Five minutes after the girls left, a similarly disheveled boy arrived and sat down. Their subsequent body language made it obvious to me, and everyone else within spitting distance, that they were not brothers. I flipped the page.

He was sitting at the table right in front of me, a little to my right, so close that I hadn't noticed. His chair was facing the patio but he was looking up at me. I turned away, flustered. I turned back toward the bar, took a casual sip of my drink, composed myself, and turned around for another look. This time he turned away. I studied his profile: handsome, probably thirty, with a dimpled and stubbly chin. He had that gilded hair that, I theorized, came from spending a lot of time in swimming pools, a theory that was supported by the width of his shoulders and his muscular arms. The gilded hair was on his forearms, too, and it was one of those forearms that I decided, without a second's hesitation, to draw. I focused on the left one (he was a southpaw), resting on the table not ten feet away from me, flexing as he clutched the glass in his hand, casually rolling its base in a circle on the table top. A perfect pose interrupted, as so many things in life are these days, by the ringing of his cell phone. He set down the glass, retrieved the phone from his pants pocket, and flipped it open. In his "hello" I detected a Southern accent.

"No. I can't talk. I'm in some café, or bar, or something. No, we went over that . . . I said not now . . . I said you could have the china, not the china cabinet . . . No, it's a family piece . . . No, my family. Yes, but that's not really a reason I should give it to you. No . . . No . . . I'm through talking to you now. No. I'm hanging up."

He snapped the phone shut, but only for an instant before popping it back open and scrolling through the address book. When he found the number he was looking for, he pressed the call button and held the phone to his ear.

"Hello, this is Reid Alland, I've left you several messages this week and I was hoping for a response. I've been without water in the bathroom for three days now. I know you're waiting for a part but I'm wondering if you can let me know how long you think it will be . . ."

I listened and continued to sketch. There was an aluminum suitcase on the ground next to him, the kind that held some piece of technical equipment.

"I realize I'm not your biggest project," he went on, "but I was hoping we could wrap the job up soon. Please give me a call at your earliest convenience."

In spite of his politeness, I knew he was angry and for a moment I thought that maybe I'd better shake this one off the line and go after another, but I'd completed the drawing and had already wasted two sheets of expensive paper. It would have been a shame to waste a third so I got up and approached, sketchpad in hand, and stood before him, assessing him in comparison to the drawing. He had been about to take a drink but paused midway and gazed up at me over the rim of his glass, a questioning look in his eyes.

"I'm sorry," I said, continuing to gaze at his arm and make a few adjustments to the sketch. "I don't mean to stare but I've been drawing your arm."

I paused again to make a few more touch-ups with the pencil. Then I stopped, studied the drawing a moment, and dragged a chair over next to his.

"See here," I said, leaning in close. "You've got great definition, really nice, and you were flexing in just such a way to give me multiple views of the muscle, but then your phone rang and you moved so I had to do the rest from memory."

He blushed but accepted the drawing and studied it silently. When he handed it back, I gazed at it, as if reflecting on ways to make it better.

"I, uh, couldn't help overhearing," I said, still looking at the drawing.

"I wasn't very quiet, I guess."

"No," I said, still busy with the pencil. "Sounds like you've got it coming at you from all sides."

He smiled. I decided to try camaraderie.

"I've had that brand of trouble myself lately," I said. "Not much fun."

"No," he said, shaking his head.

"Maybe you should try my approach," I said, setting the drawing down and taking a seat. I took my lifeless cell phone from my pocket and held it up for him to see. "If you just push this little red button and hold it down for a few seconds, it won't ring all day. You should try it."

He laughed.

"The name's Tony," I said, and offered him my hand.

"Reid."

"Now, Reid, I'm no expert, but I'd say you're not from these parts."

"No," he said, and gave a slight laugh. "Louisiana. It's the accent."

"Actually, it's the manners. Nobody here would be that polite to a building contractor."

"How did you know it was a contractor?"

I looked down at my paint-bespattered outfit and then back at him.

"Oh, you're *that* kind of painter."

"Uh, yes," I said. "But I also come from a family of construction contractors and they get lots of phone messages from people like you, although none so polite."

"I don't know that I was all that polite in either conversation," he said, blushing again.

"Well, we all have our lapses, gaps in our personal protocol. If that's as bad as it gets, I'm sure we'll get along fine. What is that you're drinking?"

We talked over a few beers and he told me all about his messy breakup (six-year relationship, boyfriend was lazy and a leech), and about his job (moved to Denver to take a job as a newspaper photographer), and about the drama of his house renovation (job almost done, contractor nowhere to be found), and I listened, asked a lot of questions, and told him not much at all about myself. Then I looked at my watch, said I needed to go for some reason—to read to the blind, volunteer at the homeless shelter, save the whales, stop world hunger, I don't remember exactly what it was that time—and gave him my number. Then I said goodbye, holding the hand he offered a second longer than would be platonically appropriate, and left.

Swaggering down the tree-lined street back to my van, I felt better than I'd felt all evening. But the feeling was spoiled when I heard the distinct sound of a bike whizzing up behind me, the sound of a person pedaling hard with no intention of stopping. I did not turn around, did not even move to one side or the other. I didn't need to. I knew exactly who it was and I knew his technical abilities on two wheels so I just stopped. The bicyclist sped past me on the right, so closely that my arm brushed against his thigh. He skidded to a stop in front of me, blocking my path.

I groaned and closed my eyes. When I opened them again I saw him straddling the bike, arms crossed on his chest, head shaking from side to side.

"I see you haven't changed your MO much," he said.

I just smiled and admired his legs.

"You really should be a little more original," he scolded. "I think you used the same lines on me, and drew almost the same fucking picture."

Like I said, from my vantage point at the bar I could see *most* of the seats on the patio, but obviously not *all* of them, or I would have seen Tom. And had I seen Tom, I would have done an abrupt turn and gone somewhere else.

"I wanted to jump up from where I was sitting and yell, 'Hey, wait a minute! I've seen this movie before! Watch out! Danger! It looks good in the beginning but the ending sucks. It's a real heartbreaker. Breaks your heart and then stomps on the pieces.' "

I stepped in the gutter to get around him and continued on my way. He followed alongside, balancing on the two narrow wheels, his legs as smooth and muscular as ever.

"So, are you single again, Anthony, or just being a slut?"

I stopped, glared at him and remembered why I was glad he was no longer my boyfriend.

"That's a nice choice of words, Tom. Good to see you, too. Single or a slut? Hmm, let's see, I guess I'm both. The first—being single—is a transitory state, especially for me. The second—sluttiness—is more my essence."

He smiled, in spite of himself. I continued:

"Think of the difference between the Spanish verbs *ser* and *estar*. '*Estoy* single' is a temporary state. '*Soy* a slut,' that's more a part of the fabric of my being. So in answer to your question, yes, I'm both right now."

"So it's all over with you and that wig-winding cunt?"

I nodded.

"Serves her ass right after what she did to me," he said.

(What "she," meaning Roy, "did" was give in to my advances when I was still living with Tom.)

"So Tony's single again," he said, and then gave a whistle. "That won't last long."

"Probably not," I said, resuming my progress toward my van,

"so get your application in early. I'm not sure if your prior experience will be a help or a hindrance."

That threw him for a minute, and I realized I probably shouldn't have said it.

"Listen," I said, and stopped walking again. "I'm sorry. I didn't mean that."

"That's okay," he said. "It's taken a while, but I'm getting over you."

"Good," I said. "I'm a good thing to get over." We went on side by side for another block without speaking. He stopped a few feet ahead and turned to face me.

"Then why don't I feel good?" he asked. "Why do I still look at you and my heart beats faster and my dick gets hard? Why do I go crazy when I see you talking to another guy? Why do I still want to be the one you're sketching?"

He was crying in spite of himself, and he wiped away the tears as quickly as he could.

"You're a fucking prick, you know that? And you did some really shitty things to me, but I still miss you sometimes, Tony."

I stood staring down at a crack in the pavement, wishing it would split open, swallow me whole, and then close up again.

"I'm out of your life," I said softly. "That sounds like something you should be happy about."

"Yeah, you'd think so," he said, "but fuck, I still miss you, Tony. I miss doing things and going places with you and thinking there might be a future with you. I hate that it didn't last; in a lot of ways I fucking hate you, but I can't forget, no matter how hard I fucking try, how you made me feel; how, like, just for a while, you made me think I was the most important person in your world. Was that all a lie? Can you answer me that?"

I could and I couldn't. It was and it wasn't a lie. At the time, in the beginning, it wasn't a lie, but for me truth is, like my single status, more transitive than essential.

About Tom:

Without discounting his importance, let me try and abbreviate the flashback here by saying that I met him at St. Mark's and I sketched his legs, truly remarkable appendages that only a bike messenger could possess. I approached and gave him the portrait in the usual way, learned that he was single, that he had fallen out of a tree when he was seven and broken his collarbone, that his fa-vorite movie was *The Philadelphia Story*, and that he'd always wanted to go to Italy but couldn't afford it. I gave him my number and left. That was a Wednesday. Thursday he called and Friday af-ternoon I called him back and asked him to come over for dinner Saturday night.

I'm no great cook but I wooed Tom with Italian food, basil pesto to be specific, made with basil I harvested that Saturday morning from Peter's garden.

To make basil pesto, you'll need:

    2 cups fresh basil leaves
    5 cloves garlic, peeled
    ⅓ cup pine nuts (walnuts will work fine)
    ⅓ cup Romano cheese
    +/- 1 cup Olive oil
    1 teaspoon red pepper flakes
    salt to taste

Put all the ingredients in a Cuisinart (if you don't have a Cuisinart, a blender will work fine) and run it until everything is evenly pureed, usually about 15-20 sec-onds. If it won't blend easily, add more olive oil. Follow those directions and it's almost impossible to ruin. Pour the sauce over fresh pasta and serve with a baguette, a salad and a bottle of very cold white wine.

The meal was good as far as my cooking abilities go, and it prob-ably would have done the job by itself, but since for me wooing that is worth doing is certainly worth overdoing, I made the evening into an event.

I went to Home Depot and bought four 6-foot by 8-foot by ¼-inch pieces of plywood and painted them flat black. When they dried, I painted a different night view of Venice on each one using glow-in-the-dark paint. I drilled tiny holes through all the win-dows of the buildings so that when they were backlit, it would ap-pear that the light was coming from the buildings. Then I cut triangular pieces of plywood and glued them to the backsides of the four panels so that they would stand up on their own and I arranged them in a square. On the ceiling (this was a rental, mind you, so I was essentially kissing my deposit goodbye), I painted a night sky filled with constellations, from the center of which I hung a single refrigerator lightbulb covered in an origami shade I'd fashioned into the shape of a crescent moon. I had nothing but a card table then so I covered it with a piece of one-inch plywood that I'd painted to look like marble, and in the center of that I drilled three holes just big enough to hold candles. Then I set up three halogen lamps that I used for my painting work behind the panels and wired them to a single switch so that they would all go on at the same time, instantly illuminating the city.

When Tom knocked on the door, I had just finished getting dressed, à la Cary Grant, in a pair of black pants, a nautical sweater, and yes, I'm embarrassed to say it, a red ascot. My hair, shoulder-length then, was slicked back. On my way to the door, I turned on a disc of accordion music, lit the candles, waited a minute for my eyes to adjust to the darkness, and then opened the door and let him in. He was surprised, yes, and a little alarmed when I led him blindfolded into the plywood Venice. Then I removed the blindfold, switched on the lights, and suddenly there we were, smack dab in the middle of the Blanche DuBois world of paper lantern enchantment.

And it worked. Oh boy, did it ever! Better than even I had expected. He took one long look around, took one long, melting look at me, and in less than three minutes our clothes were off and those amazing legs were up in the air.

Not that sex was the goal. Or rather, it was, but with men (especially with gay men), it's never much of a challenge to reach that goal. No, the real challenge for me was to win him over, heart and soul, as quickly and passionately as I could, and I knew, by his response that night, that I had succeeded.

The problem—the one fatal flaw in my plan—was that I never understood the gravity of what I was doing. That I was actually going to such an extreme to make him fall in love with me and was doing it on our first date didn't seem at all strange to me. I was going after his heart when it was far too early to know if I even wanted it.

It is only now that I see how self-indulgent I was being. It was *my* little art project. I wanted to make him happy, yes, wanted to give him something he'd always remember but more than that I wanted an excuse to do something creative and silly and not feel stupid about doing it. A new lover gives you the chance and the liberty to do those things. Oh, you can still do them once you've won him over, but it's never the same, never as intense. It feels like you are preaching to those who already believe and that is rarely, if ever, as exciting as winning over a new convert. Of course, people say love naturally changes after that first blush, it develops in new and deeper ways, but I don't know that I've ever seen that except in the movies.

"Listen," I said, putting my hand over his on the handlebars. "I know I was a shit but at least that should tell you that there's nothing wrong with you."

"Yeah," he said, tears welling up in his eyes, "you just didn't love me."

"No, I didn't say that. And that's not true. I loved you and I didn't. I, oh I don't know, Tom, I can love someone a lot but only for a little while, then something happens, something shuts off inside of me, and that's the part I don't understand. It wasn't just you—It was the same with all the guys before you and'll probably be the same with all the guys after you."

He nodded and wiped his eyes with his fingers. He pulled his shoulder bag from his back to the front and lifted the Velcro flap. He dug around inside and pulled out a book.

"Here," he said, handing it to me. "I don't really go in for this touchy-feely crap, but a friend gave this to me after week three of watching me sit in the dark in my apartment sucking on a bong and trying to get over you. I read it. It helped me. Maybe there's something in it for you."

I took the book and looked at the title: *Lessons of Love*.

"Sometimes," I said, "I think I know almost too much about love."

"No," he said, sternly, "you know about lust. There's a difference."

Then, without another word, he rode off.

Lessons of Love. I'd read books like that before. When you break up with someone roughly every six months for a decade and you are always the one doing the breaking, you can't help but wonder if maybe, just possibly, it might have something to do with you. Self-help books are an affordable form of therapy, I'll grant them that much, but they've never helped me much, or at least not in the way the author intended. If anything, they always gave me a warped solace. Especially the chapter that seems to be in each and every one: the one explaining how pain is really an opportunity for personal growth and can only make you stronger. I used to read those chapters and think, "Hey, I'm all right! Instead of chasing me around and yelling at me, my exes should all be thanking me! I've brought nothing but opportunities for personal growth and increased strength into their lives."

It's a wonder someone didn't shoot me years earlier.

The way I brought that opportunity for personal growth and increased strength into Tom's life was like this: I got caught with my hand in the cookie jar. Or to be more precise, my hair. Like I said, it had been long then (you know, the tortured arty look) and it began getting gradually shorter and shorter. Not enough for Tom to be suspicious, just a trim from time to time. He didn't question it until he noticed that in two weeks my hair had changed styles three times, and that obviously I wasn't the one doing the changing. Bike messengers, as most of us know who have ever witnessed one of them weaving effortlessly in and out of downtown traffic, are slippery. Tom began tailing me and I never even knew it. Soon there were confrontations, denials, the usual ugliness. Which brings us to the two types of reactions you can expect to encounter when you get caught straying:

1. The Seeming Worst

The seeming worst would be Tom's reaction when he discovered without a doubt that I was cheating. We were sharing a house at the time and had, earlier that morning, had a bust-up argument. An argument I'd been in danger of losing, so I told him he was being irrational and I left. When I came home that night (after yet another haircut), expecting round two, I was surprised to find him already in bed. Not wanting to wake him, I snuck into the bathroom to pee and brush my teeth. Only after I'd been brushing for a good minute and was leaning over to spit did I notice that something had been shoved under the bathroom door. I bent down, picked up a Polaroid, and saw that it was a picture of my toothbrush, the bristles buried in Meth's ass.

2. The Actual Worst

The actual worst would be the look on Tom's face when he realized that I was leaving (that it was not just another fight) and that it was over between us. The moment when the anger collapsed and I saw the sadness. It was the catch in #2's voice as he said goodbye, Peter's façade of quiet grace, Jason's attempted indifference, Roy's frantic telephone messages . . .

To sum it up in a graphic and perhaps inappropriate way, it is much worse to realize that you are a misery-causing shit, than to have something miserable and shitty in your mouth.

Chapter Ten

"I did some reading over the weekend," Arabella said.

I nodded, and tried to focus on what I was doing. We were finished with the Helen of Troy niche and were now working on Leda, or Clytemnestra, or Persephone, I forget exactly which. Arabella was back in her Greek drapery, posing on one of the many plaster "ruins" she'd purchased.

"I went to the Tattered Cover," she said proudly, "and got a big, expensive book—one with an index and pictures—and I found a whole bunch of other goddesses that you didn't tell me anything about."

"I never claimed to know them all," I said.

"No, but you must have known about those singing girls, oh, what were they called, who could make a guy drive his ship into the rocks?"

"The Sirens?"

"Yeah."

"What about them?"

"You never *told* me about them. I mean, they're pretty important, don't you think. I mean, if I was still a stripper, I think I could've worked that into a kickass name; Sirena maybe, or Sirenessa."

"Mmmm," I said, "but do you think the men in the audience would've got it? Or cared?"

"Probably not, but you should have told me about them! We could have added them to the gallery. They would have made a perfect addition to all the other badass Greek chicks we've got already."

She paused and looked at the completed niches. "I suppose we could paint over that dumb Penelope, and maybe some of the others. But how would you paint the Sirens?" she asked, turning to face me. "The book just had this line drawing of some mermaidy-looking women leaning over a cliff with their mouths open. I think we could do better than that."

My phone rang. I picked it up and looked at the number. It was Peter. Arabella fell into the chair with a bothered sigh and contemplated her nails.

"Hello, Peter," I said, and headed toward the kitchen for some privacy.

"Good morning, how's it going?"

"Ah, well, you know, another day here in mini-Olympus. What's up?"

"I keep forgetting to tell you but we're planning a birthday party for Lola next Sunday and I wanted to be sure you can come. It will be after church so I think about noon or so."

"Great," I said, "but, well . . ."

"You can't make it," he said, his voice deflating.

"No, no, I'll make it. I'm just wonder if she'll know what's going on."

"Yes," he said, "I know what you mean. She's gotten worse, hasn't she?"

"I think so."

"Sometimes it's hard for us to notice since we see her every day. You don't see her as often so it must be more obvious."

I felt like there was some unintended criticism in there, but it was probably just my own guilty conscience.

"Anyway," Peter continued, "I talked to the doctor last week and he says she can still enjoy things in the present, she just won't remember them, so I think we could make her happy and maybe let all the ladies from the church come by and see her again."

"That would be nice. Let me know what I can do to help."

"Okay, we'll talk tonight."

I was about to hang up when a thought came into my head.

"Hey, are you guys going out tonight?" I asked.

"Not that I know of. Why?"

"Oh, I was just thinking, I saw that *Giant* is out on DVD so I bought you a copy. I was thinking maybe we could watch it together. I could grab some Thai food. What do you think?"

For a moment, there was silence.

"Peter?"

"Yes, I'm here."

"Well, what do you think?"

"That sounds great," he said, "but, well, never mind."

"All right then, I'll see you tonight about seven, seven-thirty?"

"Perfect. See you then."

I hung up and got back to work. Or tried to anyway.

"Was that Peter?" Arabella asked.

"Yes."

"You're ex-boyfriend?"

"Yes."

"The one that married your mother?"

"Yes," I sighed.

"And you just made a date with him?"

"No! Well, no, not a date, really."

"Uh-huh. Whatever. Your life's even weirder than the Greeks."

"Okay," I said, a touch impatiently. "How about we don't talk about me today. Now what were you asking about before? The Lorelei?"

Her face went blank. "The who?"

"Isn't that what we were talking about?"

"No!" she cried, breaking her pose and putting her hands on her hips. "I was talking about the Sirens. Who's this Laura Lie chick? Is that another one you didn't tell me about?"

"No," I said, lifting my glasses and rubbing my eyes. "My mistake. That's the German version, I think."

"What!" she cried. "There's a German version?"

I began to understand Gabriel's aggravation.

"Sort of," I said. "They have their own legends and that one happens to be similar to the Greeks. Maybe it's borrowed. I don't know."

"Hey, don't confuse me with some other country's hooey," she scolded. "I'm already confused enough by this new book. There's, like, twice as many people as in the other book, and then they throw in all these Roman names, to boot. God, I don't know how anyone could keep track of them all. No wonder our one little Jesus got so popular."

She shook out her hair, rearranged her drapery, and resumed her pose. A minute later she asked,

"What do you know about Seerka?"

"Who?"

"Seerka. It says in the new book that she lived on one of the islands that Odysseus visited and that she turned all the guys into pigs, I think she's supposed to be a witch."

"I think it's pronounced 'Seer-say,' " I said, and bit my lip.

"Are you sure?"

"Pretty sure."

"Funny, I thought her name was Circle at first, and that maybe they just left out the *i*. Whatever. Anyway, I was reading about her this weekend and I think she must be your ancestor, or something."

I didn't at all like where this was heading. I gave her a confused look. She didn't buy it.

"Oh please!" she scoffed. "Don't act all dumb. You know what I mean. She's probably my ancestor, too. We're cut from the same cloth, you, me, and Circe. Don't tell me you don't know what I'm talking about."

Fortunately, my phone rang again interrupting her analysis. Unfortunately, it was Roy doing the interrupting. I decided to answer it.

"Hello,"

"Look, don't hang up," he said. "Can we talk for just a minute?"

"Sure. Hang on and let me move someplace else."

"Okay, just don't hang up."

I wrapped up my brush in a piece of aluminum foil, held the phone to my chest, and whispered to Arabella, "I need to take a little break. I'll be back in five."

She had already broken her pose and settled into the chair with a magazine.

"Anything you say, Seeeeer-saaaay."

I scowled at her, went out onto the back porch, and shut the door. I pulled a chair up next to the pool and sat down. Then I took a deep breath, cracked my neck, and prepared for the worst.

"Okay, I'm back," I said.

"Listen," Roy said, "I've been thinking, and well, maybe you could come over for dinner tonight. We could talk."

Again I lifted my glasses and rubbed my eyes.

"Tony?"

"Yeah, I'm here."

"Well?"

"Roy, do you really think that's a good idea?"

"You don't?"

I could sense his temper rising, could almost feel the electricity of it passing through the phone.

"Well . . ." I said. "No, not really. I mean, what more is there to say? I did all the things you accused me of; I'd probably do them again. You don't deserve that."

Silence.

"I don't believe you're that way, Tony."

"Well, I don't know what to tell you."

"Can't we just meet and talk, face to face?"

The phone beeped. indicating another call.

"Roy, can you hold on a minute."

"You'll come back?"

"Yes, of course. Just a minute." I switched over to the other line. "Hello."

"Hello, could I please speak with Tony Romero?"

It was the Southern-accented forearm from *The Thin Man*. I perked up instantly.

"This is Tony."

"I thought it was you," he said, his voice and inflections the polar opposite of Roy's. "This is Reid, we met the other night, at that bar on Seventeenth."

"Yes, of course, Reid, how are you?"

"I'm well, thank you. Very well."

"Listen," I said, "I got your call, and have been meaning to call you back but I got really swamped with work and I just haven't had the chance."

Lie #1 to Reid.

"Can you talk now?"

"Sure, sure, but can you hang on a minute. I'm on the other line."

"Maybe I should call back lat—"

"No, no, hang on, this won't take a minute."

I switched back to Roy.

"Roy?"

"Yes."

"Listen, I've got some work problems I've got to deal with."

Lie # 847 to Roy.

"Will you call me back?"

"Of course."

#848.

"Today?"

"Yes."

#849.

"It's someone else, isn't it?"

"What?"

"On the other line. You're talking to another guy."

"Please," I scoffed. "You're paranoid. I'm talking to Gabriel."

#850.

"Oohhh, Tony," he said, his voice catching. "I know you. I know when you're up to something."

"What! Listen, I'm not up to anything."

#851.

"I'll call you later."

#852.

I said goodbye and switched back to Reid.

"Hey, sorry about that. I had to answer some questions for a guy that works with me."

#2.

"You sound like a busy guy."

"Sometimes, yes," I chuckled. "But I've always got time for someone with forearms and nice manners like yours."

He laughed. "Thanks again for the drawing, by the way."

"Don't mention it."

"I can honestly say I've never received anything like it."

"I'm glad you like it, if that is what you're saying."

"Yes, I love it. And that's why I'm calling. I was hoping maybe I could repay you, maybe take you to dinner and a movie."

My heart sank and I thought to myself: *Dinner and a movie, criminal lack of imagination, guy may be a dolt and not worth pursuing for anything more than a lay.*

"Are you there?" he asked.

"Uh, yes, I'm here," I said. "But I've got to be honest about something."

"Okay."

"Dinner and a movie, well, that doesn't sound very inspired to me, so here's what we'll do. I'll pick you up at, say, five-thirty on Saturday evening, will that work?"

"Yes, but—"

"Good. Wear something you can golf in."

"Uh, okay, but I don't gol—"

"Doesn't matter. What's your address?"

When I hung up, I reclined in the chair, exhaled a whistle of relief and closed my eyes. I was in that pose less than five seconds when I heard someone making that "shame on you" snickering noise above and behind me. For a minute, I thought it might be a squirrel but then I looked up and saw Arabella, sitting on the upper balustrade, still wearing her drapery and licking the edge of the joint she was rolling.

"Golf, eh?" she said in a deadpan voice.

"Are you always such a nosy little eavesdropper?"

"Yes," she said, lighting the joint and taking a hit. "And are you always such a fast talker? God, you sound like the hog auctioneer at the state fair."

"You shouldn't listen in on people's private conversations," I said reproachfully. "It's not nice."

"Why not?"

"Because it's not right."

"Uh-huh. You know, I've been thinking about that Circe . . ."

"Oh yeah, what about her?"

"Well, I think they got it all wrong."

"Oh, do you?"

"I do."

"And how so?"

"I don't think she turned men into pigs at all," she said, flicking the ash from the joint down on me. "She probably just gave them a mirror."

Chapter Eleven

I spent most of the week before the date with Reid speculating on what we should do, scrolling through all the usual ideas for an urban Saturday afternoon/evening date, but when Saturday rolled around, the only thing I knew for sure was that I wouldn't be picking him up in my van since I was having a hard time getting the musty smell out of it from all my wet clothes. That meant I either had to borrow Peter's car (not really an option) or that I had to retrieve my motorcycle from Roy's garage. Doing the latter meant that I would have to sneak over to Roy's while he was at work in order to avoid a scene. Luckily, Saturday is a hairdresser's busiest day, so I didn't have any trouble.

When I left his house, I went to the ATM to get money for the evening and then headed back to my mom and Peter's. Since Meth wasn't racing until the following weekend, I took her out for a run. We ran hard for about an hour and then walked a half hour more to ensure that her muscles didn't tighten up. When we got home, I fed and brushed her, played with her in the yard for a while, and then went upstairs to shower and attend to my own grooming.

I dressed casually, the way I almost always dress for a first date, in jeans and a T-shirt, black boots and a black belt. Normally I would have chosen a black T-shirt since black always makes for a nice echo of my hair color, but since my face was tanned from the run, I chose white instead, to maximize the contrast. Once dressed, I went downstairs, took a blue ice pack, a corkscrew, a few candles, and some cloth napkins, and headed out to the bike.

Since I was pressed for time, and since I'd been unable to think of an appropriate restaurant (and certainly didn't have a place where I could make him dinner), I decided to fall back on that old standby I told you about: the picnic. Or at least a modified version thereof. I went to one of the fancy grocery stores in Cherry Creek and bought several little plastic containers of exotic fare: curried chicken salad, Greek olives, herbed hummus, a strange-looking pâté that the saleswoman assured me contained some sort of aphrodisiac, Brie cheese, a small baguette, some grainy crackers, a bunch of black grapes, and five shockingly expensive apricots. I paid, put everything that needed to be kept cold in the one of the saddlebags with the ice pack, and put everything else in the other. Then I zipped over to the liquor store and selected a bottle of Chilean red wine, solely because of the label, which depicted a group of darting pelicans. I placed it in the unrefrigerated saddlebag, and then headed over to the address in the Highlands that Reid had given me over the phone.

His house was a turn-of-the-century two-story on a corner lot. The outside had been nicely painted, but from all the building permits posted in the front window, I could tell that it was still very much a work in progress. I parked the bike in the shade of a large, aromatic linden tree, and bounded up the walkway to the front door. When Reid answered, he wasn't wearing a shirt.

"I'm sorry," he said, "I got carried away working on a project and lost track of time. I just got out of the shower. Come in, come in," he said, stepping to the side. "Make yourself at home. I'll be ready in five minutes."

I went in and he disappeared up the stairs, leaving me standing in the foyer. I closed the door, walked toward the end of the hall, and immediately saw the project he'd mentioned: tiling the kitchen floor. Then I saw the stack of paint chips and the empty pill bottles, and when I looked around, sure enough, there was the wall covered in giraffe patches, most of them a variation on green. There was a sage that I liked, so I took note of the name (Forest Ash) that he'd penciled alongside it. I looked around the rest of the downstairs, examining the furniture and windows and tstchockas, the books on the shelf and on the coffee table. There were definitely possibilities, and I let myself imagine what it might be like to live there.

"Sorry about that," he said, jogging down the stairs. "Like I said, I completely lost track of the time."

"That's all right, no hurry."

He had chosen a navy T-shirt that fit tightly across his chest and a pair of faded jeans. I wondered if he had deliberately waited to get dressed so that he could see what I was wearing and then dress himself accordingly, or if he was really clever and wanted to give me a preview of coming attractions.

"You've been tiling," I said, looking down at the floor.

"Yes. I just started setting the tiles today."

"You made a good choice," I said. "Slate always looks good."

"I'm glad to hear that," he said. "I wasn't so sure when I opened the crate. It seems to fall apart pretty easily."

"Once you get it set, it'll be fine. My mom and stepdad have had it in their kitchen for about five years now and it's held up great."

"I've also been trying to decide on paint colors," he said, guiding me into the living room. "Maybe you could tell me what you think."

This was dangerous territory.

"Now, why do you want my opinion?" I asked, hoping he would have a good answer.

"Well, because you're an artist," he said, "and a painter. But mostly because I can't decide, and I'm so sick of trying, I'm about to just paint it all white."

"That's not always such a bad thing," I said, breaking my rule about never giving an opinion. "But I think the green you've chosen is good."

"The green!" he cried, pointing at the giraffe wall. "*Which* green? I've got about a hundred of them blotched on there now."

I walked over to the wall and pointed to the Forest Ash.

"I know you take pictures for work," I said, "so I imagine you probably take some that are artistic as well. Framed black and whites would probably look very nice against this color."

"You think?"

I nodded. Of course, I was also thinking how nice my framed sketches would look there, too.

"Since you brought up the subject of pictures," he said, "let me show you the one room in the house that is finished."

He led me to a room behind the kitchen that had obviously been intended as a laundry room. Instead, he had blacked out the window, installed several long, low sinks, and turned it into a dark room.

"This," he said, "is where I like to spend most of my time."

He pulled some of the prints down from the drying line and handed them to me. They were a series of shots of the church down the street from his house.

"They're nothing spectacular," he said modestly, "just some shots I took this morning."

I studied them a moment, admiring the texture and shadows.

"They're really good," I said, and meant it. "You have a great eye."

He blushed, shuffled his feet and then abruptly turned out the light, indicating that we should exit. I set the photograph on the table next to me, walked toward the door, and as I passed, kissed him, barely brushing my lips against his. He smiled and leaned into me so I kissed him again, longer this time. He was a good kisser and the second kiss lasted about thirty seconds. Then I leaned back and looked at my watch.

"Shall we go?"

He nodded.

There are two benefits of taking a motorcycle on a first date. First, it lends the driver an air of masculinity, which is rarely, if ever, a bad thing, especially if you're gay, and second, it enables you to gauge the progression of intimacy over the course of the evening. How that works is like this: When the two of you start out, his hands will inevitably rest primly on your hips (as Reid's were when we left the house and sped down I-25). He'll hold on to your shirt or your belt loops just tightly enough to keep from falling off. Later, his hands should actually be gripping your waist or your shoulders. Later still, and if the date has gone well, his arms should be around your chest, his own chest and groin pressed up against your back so that you can feel his heart beating as you bank the turns.

We got off I-25 at Sixth Avenue and took it to Broadway. Then we went south for about a mile until we arrived at our first destination: The Polynesian.

Built in the sixties as a cheap knockoff of Trader Vic's, The Polynesian was a monument to a monument of kitsch, as well as a relatively cheap and entertaining place to get drunk. Out front, there were rusting metal palm trees, a faded plastic palapa roof, and on either side of the front door, two fiberglass Easter Island heads with emerald eyes that lit up. These statues, so I've been told, used to emit smoke from their mouths, although that feature has never been active when I've been there.

"I thought we'd get a drink here," I said, walking the motorcycle back into the curb. "Then if we're happy with each other, we can go on with the rest of the date."

He gave me a playful pinch and stepped off the bike. I turned off the ignition and together we walked through the keyhole-shaped door. Inside, all the walls and ceilings had been painted black. Small tiki torches illuminated the hostess station, behind which an aged and unnaturally pale "Island Beauty" in a red and white floral moomoo sat doodling on the empty reservation book.

"Two for dinner?" she asked, rousing herself and reaching for the stack of grubby menus.

"I think we're just going to have a few drinks at the bar," I said.

She nodded, parted the beaded curtain, and smiled weakly as we passed through. We walked over to the bamboo bar and sat on stools shaped like bongo drums, the perfect spot from which to observe the pot-bellied diver, should he emerge to juggle his flaming torches. I ordered a pitcher of Mai Tais and, when they arrived, offered a toast:

"To choosing the right paint color."

"Here, here."

Then, as we slowly drank the pitcher, I began flipping through the mental Rolodex of quirky, offbeat questions that I always have ready on first dates in order to avoid the usual and mundane, "So, what did you major in?" or "How long have you worked there?" I pelted him with questions about himself, and showed intense interest in his answers. He told me about places in the world he'd traveled (Europe, China, Brazil); bones he'd broken (wrist and kneecap, rollerblading); relatives he was fond of (Aunt Betty and

Uncle Vern, who owned a goat farm); his favorite book and movie (*The Bridges of Madison County* for both; not surprising, given his profession); how he loved singing Nina Simone songs at karaoke; and how he was an avid pheasant hunter.

"So tell me," I said, pouring out the last drops from the pitcher, feeling flush and bold, "what happened with the last boyfriend, the one I overheard you talking to?"

He sighed and set down his drink.

"You don't have to tell me if you don't want to," I said. "It's really not my business."

"No," he said, smiling and shaking his head. "I don't mind. The thing is there's not really much to tell. We were together for six years, and then . . . we weren't."

"Just like that?"

"Just like that."

"Do you miss him?"

"There's not a lot to miss," he said, running his finger around the rim of the glass.

I nodded, although I didn't understand.

"Are you still in love with him?" I asked.

He considered the question. "Hmmm, how to say this?" he wondered. "I guess you could say we were together a lot longer than we should have been, so when we broke up, it wasn't a big deal. I had a job I really hated in Louisiana, so when I got the job offer here, I knew right away I'd take it. But I also knew he wouldn't come with me, and in the back of my head I guess I also knew I didn't want him to. So I came home one evening after work, sat down with him, and told him I was taking the job and that I wanted to sell the house and move."

"And what'd he say?"

"He wasn't even fazed, to tell you the truth, he just started looking around the room at all the stuff we'd acquired over the years and I knew he was calculating how we would divide things up. All he asked was when I thought I might be leaving. Then his friends phoned to say they were waiting for him outside and he got up and went to dinner with them just as he'd planned. It was very anticlimactic."

"That didn't really answer my question."

"Oh, sorry. Still in love with him? No," he said. "Still in love with the person I thought he was? Yes, I suppose I am a bit."

"He wasn't who you thought he was?" I asked, imagining some false identity scandal.

"No, not really. At first he was great, but then it all changed and I was nothing more than an accessory to parade around when he needed one, usually at his boring office parties."

He downed the rest of his drink and set the glass down on the bar.

"The last two years we were together he forgot my birthday entirely."

Realizing I'd taken the conversation to a place in which he felt uncomfortable, I decided it was time to change the venue as well as the subject so I summoned the bartender for the bill.

"Do you like golf?" I asked.

"Well, like I said, I've never done it before."

"But you're not averse to trying new things."

"No, in fact, it would probably be good for me but I'm pretty sure it will be dark soon and, well, don't they shut down the course, or something?"

"Most of them, yes, but not this one. Come on,"

Taking him by the hand, I led him outside and down the street about seven blocks until we arrived at the Putt-Putt Emporium. In exchange for a small admission price, I was given balls, putters, and a scorecard. I turned to hand him his ball and putter and was glad to see an eager grin on his face.

"I haven't done this since I was a kid!" he said, bustling past me to get to the start. We had to wait for two other groups ahead of us, but once we got on the course, we putted and laughed our way through the Dutch windmill, the Eiffel Tower, and the Taj Mahal. We crossed a small Tower Bridge spanning a Thames the color of Windex, and putted past pyramids and pagodas, talking all the while about silly, harmless things, until we arrived at the birthday cake.

I've often wondered who chooses the obstacles to install on a putt putt course (probably the same person who chooses the names of paint colors), and whether it was memories of a world tour, or just a tour of *the World Book Encyclopedia*, that had inspired someone to nail together the archetypical images of each particular country.

That, at least, would explain most of them. But then there were the anomalies: the giant clown head, pockmarked from all the balls that missed the rouged hole that was supposed to be its mouth, the ladybug, the running shoe, all plopped down pell-mell in the middle of the world tour, shattering any semblance of a theme. The birthday cake was just such an anomaly. A rotating, drum-shaped, multilayered, pink and white painted confection with flicker bulb candles on top. On the sides there were several small holes and the object was to get your ball in one of these holes and have it come out on the other side before the cake could rotate back around and spit your ball back at you. Sober, it would not have been an easy shot. Mai Tai'd as we were, it was nearly impossible and twice we were forced to step aside so that groups of less chemically impaired juveniles could play through.

Perhaps it was because we were there staring at it for so long, unable to get by, that I came up with the question. Perhaps it was because of our conversation in The Polynesian about his forgetful boyfriend. I don't know. All I do know is that it seemed like such a simple question at the time.

"So tell me," I said, standing smugly on the opposite end of the cake, having somehow managed to tap my ball through while Reid continued to putt and strike the side of it. "What's the best cake you had for your birthday when you were a kid?"

"That's easy," he said. "I had the same kind every year from the time I was five."

"Chocolate?"

He shook his head distastefully and made another unsuccessful putt.

"So that probably nixes German chocolate then too."

He nodded.

"Yellow with white icing?"

"Nope," he said, kneeling down and lining up the shot with his putter. "You'll never ever guess so you might as well give up."

"Give me a clue?"

He stood up and made a few gentle practice swings over the ball. "It would seem like . . ." he said, sticking his tongue out of the side of his mouth, trying to concentrate on his shot. "It would seem like the ideal cake for a gay child."

"Hmmmm," I said, tapping the rotating cake with my putter. "White with pink icing?"

He hit the ball and this time it went in one of the holes and came popping out in front of me.

"Yes!" he cried, and did a victory lap around the cake. He gave the ball one more gentle tap into the cup and retrieved it. Then he looked up and said, "But no, pink with white icing was not the right answer. What a stereotypical thing to say. Do you give up?"

I nodded.

"Fruit," he said.

"Fruit! As in the brown, poopy-looking thing you get at Christmas?"

"The very same."

"Boy, you must have had some disappointed friends at your parties."

"Oh, they always got something else," he said. "Usually boring old chocolate cupcakes."

"Why fruit?" I asked, still shocked. "Is your birthday near Christmas, or something?"

"Nope," he said, "It's in August. I just like fruitcake. Everyone thinks it's strange but that's because they haven't had the really good kind. If it's made just right, it can be one of the best foods known to man. Mmmm, what I wouldn't give for a piece right now."

"Gross," I said and walked toward the next hole, but the wheels inside my head had already begun turning.

Later that evening, after we'd returned to his house and I'd surprised him with the picnic, after we'd made love on the stairs and then once more in the bedroom, after we were lying spooned in bed and he was just about to drift off into sleep, I subtly recommenced the questioning.

"What is it that you like about it?" I asked.

"Huh? About what?"

"Fruitcake."

His eyes stayed shut but his mouth curved up.

"Mmm, I guess it's the way it tastes, and how those candied fruits look like little gems embedded in the mix."

"And what was it," I said, encircling him in my arms from behind and whispering in his ear, "that made it so special?"

"Scotch," he said drowsily. "Usually it's made with brandy. But my parents always used scotch."

His breathing became steady after that so I knew he was asleep. I lay awake in the gauzy light from the street lamp, gazing at his face; at the stubble on his cheek and the long, brown lashes. I kissed the back of his neck a few times and then closed my eyes, just for a minute or two.

I had not intended to spend the night. Mindful of Peter's feelings, I thought it best, at least while I was living in his house, and occasionally sleeping with him, not to let on that I was seeing someone else. Not that it would have surprised him all that much. Peter knew me too well to be surprised by anything I pulled, but I knew he would be hurt by it, and that was something I had done a thousand times and hoped to avoid doing for the thousand and first. So, when Reid woke me the next morning and told me it was ten o'clock, my first instinct was to jump out of bed, dress, and leave. But, there was Reid, breakfast tray in one hand, Sunday paper in the other, so I masked my feelings of dread and regret. He crawled in bed next to me and we ate and read the funnies. Then we pushed everything aside and made love again, after which I glanced at the clock on the bedside table and saw that it was half past twelve. I had the gnawing feeling that something was wrong, something more than just the guilt of being there. It was something I was forgetting, some appointment or something. Then like a blow to the head, it hit me—the horror of what I'd forgotten: Lola's birthday party.

I leapt out of bed so quickly that Reid thought something in the bed had bitten me and he leapt out himself.

"I'm sorry," I said, digging through the pile of my clothes on the floor. "I just, I totally forgot about something I have to do today. I have to leave right now."

There was no time to shower, no time to even look in the mirror. I pulled on my clothes and vaulted down the stairs. Reid put on a pair of boxers and followed. I gave him a quick kiss at the door before bounding down the sidewalk to my motorcycle. I got on the bike and zoomed down Thirty-Eighth to Federal Boulevard, cursing my stupidity and selfishness, my arrogant asinine egotistical vanity, as I went. Then I slowed down and began scanning the strip malls, looking to the left and to the right, until I spied one of the *miscellanea* shops. I pulled in, parked the bike, ran in, and grabbed as many bags of candy as I could carry on my way up to the register. I took off my sunglasses and looked up at the selection of piñatas dangling from the ceiling, trying to decide which one I could possibly carry on the motorcycle. There were donkeys and bunnies; Pokemon and Sponge Bob—all staring down at me with eyes as wide and frantic as my own. Eventually, I selected a large-beaked toucan and pleaded with the woman behind the counter to stuff it with the candy. While she did that, I looked around again and noticed some plastic trumpets on a shelf. I grabbed all of them and headed back to the register. On the way, I saw a bin full of gaudy, plastic tiaras and took as many as I could carry. There was an adolescent mannequin next to the register dressed in a lacy, white *quinciniera* outfit. She had been crowned with a much larger tiara that had a fake ruby in the middle of it. I plucked it from her static head and set it on the counter with the other items. The woman protested that the bigger tiara was part of the display and wasn't for sale, but a twenty-dollar bill quickly changed her mind. As she totaled everything up, I surveyed the loot and prayed to Mary, mother of God (whose rose-encircled visage was regarding me from several places throughout the store), that it would be sufficient.

If only I had the van, I thought, *I could get much more.*

Again, I felt the wave of dread and regret wash over me, and for about twenty seconds I thought I would not be able to stop myself from crying. The woman was still punching in prices on the cash register. I took a deep, deep breath, and held it. I put my sunglasses back on, clenched my fists and managed to stop the feeling of a collapse in my chest. She finished totaling and told me the amount. I paid and asked if she had any string. She cut me off a piece from a spool behind the counter and I took it, and everything else outside. I stuck the tiaras and other party favors in the saddlebags, but the piñata I would have to carry so I straddled the bike, set it on the gas tank between my legs, and tied it with the string to my body. It was not a great system, but at least I would be able to steer and work the gears, although once I got going, I was not able to go very fast without pieces of the piñata shedding off in the wind. Ten agonizing minutes later, I was back at *Casa Turquesa*. I parked the bike, took the tiaras and noisemakers from my saddlebags, and ran, as fast as I could with the cumbersome piñata, to the house. I heard laughter out back so I went around the side and saw them—my grandmother, Gabriel, Cleve, all of Lola's friends from church, even the priest—sitting around the long picnic table, while the two Great Danes cleared away the plates from the lavish Mexican luncheon they had prepared. Purple and green streamers (to match Lola's rather juvenile dress) festooned the yard, from the house to the fence to the garage to the black walnut tree and then back to the house, making a circle around the table. I took another deep breath, forced a smile, and dove in.

"Feliz Cumpleaños!" I shouted, blowing one of the horns and swinging the piñata.

My grandmother gasped and clapped her hands; everyone else turned and smiled. I smiled back and went around the table outfitting everyone with tiaras and giving them a noisemaker. When I got to my grandmother, I leaned down, gave her a kiss and then attached the large ruby tiara to her head. She was thrilled and pulled me into an embrace.

"Fernando," she sighed, "I'm so glad you're here. So glad!"

She pushed the woman seated next to her into another chair so that I could take her seat and then proceeded to introduce her "son" to everyone. I just smiled and played along while she beamed and held my hand like a vise. I ventured a glance at Peter and my mother, both standing on the back deck. They were smiling, although Peter's smile was somewhat forced. I smiled my way around the table until I got to Cleve, who gave me a frosty, narrow-eyed glare, and to Gabriel, whose look was less frosty but clearly of the disappointed variety.

My mother approached and in a low voice said, "We've already eaten and we're about to serve cake and ice cream. We saved you a plate, so if you want, I can bring you lunch instead."

"No, no," I said, "That's okay. I'm sorry I'm late. I'll just have cake. Don't slow down the show because of me."

She nodded and went back inside. A few moments later, she returned and whispered something in Spanish to Lola. Lola looked at her like she was crazy and gestured at me with both hands. My mother gave me a weary look.

"What is it?" I asked. She leaned in and whispered to me in Danish, "It's your father."

"What!"

"I know," she said, "I was surprised, too. He's on the phone and wants to wish her a happy birthday."

I nodded. I saw the problem. How could he be on the phone when he was sitting right next to her?

"Look," I said, again in Danish, "why don't I disappear inside for a while. Then tell her I want her to come to the phone."

She nodded and I got up, prying Lola's fingers off my hand and assuring her in Spanish that I was just going to the bathroom and would be right back. On the way inside, I passed Peter holding the phone to his chest.

"Is she coming?" he asked, not looking at me.

"Give her a minute," I said. "She's confused. She thinks I'm him. I'll hide in the laundry room till it's over."

He nodded.

Meth and the two other hounds were curled up together on one of the giant beanbag dog beds. They lifted their heads like periscopes when I opened the door. Then they jumped up and greeted me with licks and whimpers of excitement. I closed the door, quieted them down and took a seat on the dog bed. They all situated their bony bodies around me and were soon snoozing again.

I sat, absently stroking their soft fur, listening to the clothes turning in the dryer, and I wondered about my father calling from God-only-knew-where. How long had it been? I hadn't spoken to him, hadn't heard anything from him, for at least eight years. Then, suddenly, he remembered his mother's birthday. I tried to remember the last time he had remembered mine. There had been the *Sports Illustrated* swimsuit calendar and nudie playing cards one year at Christmas, the Rolex he'd sent for my graduation (without a card or greeting of any sort), and before that there were the birthday cards—always late, always containing a fifty—but for the last eight years there'd been nothing, not even any word to let us know that he was alive. I wondered where he was, and who he was with, and how many bastard half brothers and sisters I had running around the country. I imagined two of us meeting on a crowded transcontinental flight, or at a cocktail party, and unwittingly falling in love with each other and marrying and then having the awful truth revealed on the Maury Povich *Show*. And then, I guess I must have dozed off, because the next thing I remember was my mother standing in the doorway.

"Tony," she said, "we're about to start with the cake and ice cream."

"Okay," I said, rubbing my eyes and pulling myself up. "How'd it go with Dad?"

She hesitated, and looked over my head out the window behind me.

"Oh, okay, I guess. Of course she won't tell me anything about it and he hung up before I could get the phone back."

"Where was he?" I asked.

She shook her head. Then she stepped into the room, closed the door behind her, and gave me a hug.

"I'm sorry," she said. "You know how he is. He prob—"

"It's okay," I said. "Really. It's okay. You're right. I know how he is. At least he called her."

She nodded and brushed the hair back from my forehead. I tucked in my shirt and together we went back out to the party.

When I went through the kitchen, Peter was just putting the finishing touches on a cake the circumference of a truck tire; a garish, marshmallow-frostinged Mexican cream cake elaborately decorated with green icing borders and huge daisies made of purple sugar. Just looking at it made you think seriously about the possibility of diabetic shock. Cleve was standing next to Peter plopping scoops of ice cream onto the line of awaiting plates. Peter looked down as I passed. Cleve frowned and shook his head. Neither one said anything.

In the backyard, I took my seat once again next to Lola, who squeezed my hand and spoke to me in that strange nonsensical language of hers. A few moments later, out came the cake, complete with sparklers and five giant candles, which seemed appropriate since that was about the mental age my grandmother had reverted to. We all sang "Happy Birthday," during which Lola gleefully clapped her hands. Peter set the enormous cake in front of her, and as she leaned forward to blow out the candles, her happy face illuminated, I wondered what simple thing she'd wish for. Then, as if on cue, she inhaled, narrowed her eyes malevolently at my mother, and blew.

While the guests were eating the cake and ice cream, and while

Peter and Cleve went around serving coffee and tea, Gabriel and I got a stepladder from the garage and got to work stringing up the moulting toucan. I'd forgotten to buy rope and the only substitute I could find were some bungee cords, which, once we hooked them end-to-end, were still too short. The piñata was about ten feet off the ground, which was a problem since the average height of the elderly attendees was about five-four. Since there was no way to lengthen them, we got the longest broom handle we could find and hoped that it would be long enough. It wasn't. Peter and Cleve lined up the guests and they took turns at bat, but it didn't work. They were old and weak so none of their hits (when indeed they could straighten their armadillo torsos enough to hit at all) had much effect. Nor did it help that the woman at the *miscellanea* store had packed the piñata so tight with candy that it required a severe whack even to get it swinging.

When it was my turn, I approached Cleve and Peter. Cleve handed me the broom handle and Peter stood behind me and began tying the blindfold around my head.

"Your hair is a little messy in the back," he said, tugging gently at it as he tightened the blindfold. "I guess you forgot to comb it this morning."

I gave a nervous laugh. "It must be from the tiara," I said, realizing how phony I sounded.

"I don't think so," Peter said, his mouth right up against my ear. "Although I'm sure some queen is responsible for it. You also stink of a cologne that is not your own."

"I, uh. It's a new kind."

"I know you well enough," Peter said, his fingers pressing into my shoulders. "You never wear anything. You always smell just like yourself, and you don't smell like that now."

Before I could say anything more, he pushed me over to Cleve, who began spinning me around and around and around. Then he stopped abruptly and I was pushed forward. I stumbled, recovered myself, and then just stood there, listening to the cheers of encouragement all around me, half expecting, and half wishing, to be hit with the broom handle myself. It was all so awful and sad, all the more so because in the crowd of cheering voices I distinctly heard Lola yelling, "Swing, Fernando, swing!"

So I swung, but it was useless. I struck nothing but air. I made a few more swings and tapped at the thing but then stepped back and lifted the blindfold. For a moment, I couldn't see Peter and that worried me. I knew he was mad and I regretted trying to lie. I scanned the crowd of guests—my mother, Cleve, Gabriel, Lola, the ladies, and the priest, all silent now, staring expectantly at me, but no Peter. A moment later, he appeared from the garage, bearing a long two by four. My eyes widened and I got ready to run, but he was too close. He plucked the broom handle out of my hands, gave me the two by four, and then refastened my blindfold. He and Cleve were pushing me forward again but I locked my legs and stopped.

"No," I said. "I won't." I was annoyed and I lifted the blindfold. They let go of me and I handed the board to Cleve.

"No," I said again. Then I removed the blindfold and approached Peter, tying it around his smoldering eyes.

"It's your turn now," I said, and spun him around gently. Cleve gave the board to Peter, and the crowd started cheering. I stood behind him gripping his shoulders and said, in a voice loud enough for him to hear over the crowd, "Go ahead. Pretend it is me. Just knock the shit out of it." Then I pushed him forward. He shuffled to a stop but did not move. He looked more like a rag doll or a scarecrow than anything, and I realized that again I'd gone too far. Shaking his head in disgust, Cleve looked at me and said, "Don't be such a jerk."

He grabbed the board from Peter, held it with both hands, and lifted it back behind his head. Then with as much force as his skinny arms could muster, he slammed it forward, shattering the piñata. The candy ricocheted off the tree trunk and the fence and came back at the crowd like buckshot. There were shrieks and cries as people jumped to get out of the way, and then, everyone got very quiet and still. Cleve was bright red, from anger or embarrassment, I couldn't tell. Peter just looked sad. Everyone else was in shock. No one made a move. It was as if we'd all looked into the eyes of Medusa and been turned to stone.

Then I heard it, the sound of tiny toenails on hollow metal, the unmistakable chattering. I looked up and there they were, inching their fat, graying, toothless bodies down the drain pipe, pausing every few feet to wag their bushy tails, moving ever closer to the awaiting candy.

* * *

Later that evening, after all the party guests had gone and the residents of *Casa Turquesa* had returned to their respective corners, I sat in Lola's attic room helping her put away her presents and get ready for bed. Maybe it was all the sugar in the cake or the piñata guts/squirrel food that she'd been munching on, but she was talking a mile a minute, and saying something vaguely sensible about once every thirty seconds.

"Fernando," she said, taking my hands in hers and looking in my eyes. "Listen to me. That wife of yours is no good. Trash! she batteries of my glasses broke this yesterday. Hot, hot, hot, and the tanks of turtles, did you see them?"

I nodded.

"The beauty shop drawers were open, can you believe it! I can't believe it. No good. And there is something going on with *El Rubio*—"

That would be Peter.

"He is nice, a good man, but that *vaca*—"

That would be my mother.

"She is . . . You, Fernando, you deserve better!"

I laid out her nightgown and went in the bathroom to get her denture cup. I filled it with water and then dropped in one of the bubbling tablets—something I'd always loved doing as a child. I closed the lid of the toilet and sat on it, watching the cheery, pink effervescence until I figured she'd had enough time to get undressed and into bed. When I returned, I was relieved to see that the nightgown was on, and was not on backward or inside out. Although she was still talking, her avalanche of speech seemed to be losing momentum. I set the fizzing cup next to her bed, and without a break in her monologue, she popped out her teeth out and dropped them in. Then she went on with more Fernando this, and Fernando that. Fernando, Fernando, Fernando! The name sounded the same with or without teeth, and as I sat there, I wondered if maybe she had confused the two of us not because she was crazy but because we were so similar. It was an unpleasant thought, and yet one I couldn't ignore. Physically, we did not look similar. I was taller than my father and my skin was lighter, not to mention the fact that I was twenty-five years younger, but it wasn't the physical similarities I was worried about. I'd always known we were alike when it came to wooing. I'd have been worse off than my grandmother if I'd not known that. No, the similarity that I found most alarming that night was the stunt I'd pulled: the grand entrance with the armload of gifts designed to compensate for the tardy arrival, for the cologne and the messed-up hair, for the lame lies and excuses. A stunt that was highly reminiscent, if not identical, to stunts my dad had pulled during my youth.

I thought about my father then, about a time, years earlier, not long after my parents' divorce, when I'd been sent to visit him in Florida for a month during summer vacation. It had been an awkward visit for us both but the thing I remember most was not the awkwardness but, rather, his apartment: the quintessential seventies bachelor pad designed to wow the ladies. There were plants hanging in macramé from the ceiling and the chalky scent of burning incense, a fancy stereo system and a wine rack, beaded curtains separating the rooms instead of doors, even an aquarium. But what I remembered most were the women—more women in a single month than my ten-year-old math mind could keep track of—all tip toeing past my open bedroom door on their way to the Master Suite, with its giant water bed concealed under an elaborate mosque of superfluous mosquito netting. In the morning, I always saw the women emerge again, never quite as pretty as when they'd gone in, walking unsteadily on their high-heeled shoes out to their awaiting Pintos or Camaros.

Yes, I remembered the apartment and the women, but what I also remembered was how much time I spent alone. How many days of game shows and soap operas I watched, waiting for my dad to come home; waiting for him to get up and send Little Miss Last Night on her way; waiting for him to do the things he'd promised we'd do together: the deep-sea fishing, the trip to Disney World, the tour of NASA.

I looked back down at Lola, finally quiet and asleep, and wondered if my father was the way he was because of something she or my grandfather did or didn't do. Had it been nature or nurture for him? A stupid question, really, since either way you can blame your parents.

I turned out the light and went downstairs. The house was dark but Peter was sitting on the couch in the living room staring out at the blue evening light in the backyard. I went and sat next to him.

"I'm sorry about today," I said, not looking at him. "And about everything."

He looked down at his palm and made circles around it with his thumb.

"Maybe your going back to Denmark isn't such a bad idea," I said, but as soon as the words were out of my mouth, I was afraid they sounded wrong.

"I don't mean that I want you to leave, because that's not it. I, it's just, well, I know you love me and, well, you shouldn't. You should get over me."

He was silent for a moment, still staring at his palm. Then he gave a deep laugh and said, "*Should!* Of course, I should get over you. Of course, I shouldn't love you! '*Should*' doesn't have anything to do with it! I can't just turn it on and off like you." Then he looked at me and his expression softened.

"But you can't see that, can you?"

I didn't know what to say. Wasn't even sure what he meant.

"You're so bad sometimes," he said, shaking his head, "and you think I don't know. You think I don't know about James's radio show and all your sketches of boys. You think I don't know that those scabs on your face were done by you to hide someone's bite. But I know, and sometimes I want to kill you. Sometimes I want to have nothing to do with you, to be rid of you, but then you go and do something so nice, like the piñata and the plastic crowns, and somehow, for some stupid reason, I realize how much I love you."

He put his arm around me and pulled me close so that my head was resting on his shoulder. He ran his fingers through my hair.

"But you're right," he said, "and I know it. I love you but you don't feel the same," he said. "And probably will not ever feel the same."

It was moments like that, moments when Peter had almost completely given up, and there was no pressure, no expectation that I would be good, that I felt I really could love him and be happy with him. I probably shouldn't have done it, but I sat up and kissed him then. That kiss led to another, and to undoing buttons, and to what that sort of behavior always led to with us. It was the third time, and the second person I'd had sex with that day, and although it sounds callous, I couldn't help contrasting the two.

The sex with Reid had been exciting, in the way that opening a present, or seeing a good movie for the first time, is exciting—it was the discovery, the examining of new equipment and comparison of technique but more than anything else, it was a chance to perform. It was Tony on stage doing his damndest to entertain, to make it a night to remember, to hear the roar of applause at the climax. Really more of an ego fuck for me than an actual one.

With Peter, I could relax. There was a richness, a depth. It was less a primary color and more like one of the classic shades you'd find in the Benjamin Moore historical deck: Princeton Gold, or Hale Navy. Peter knew my body, what I liked and disliked; had knowledge of what worked and what didn't, but it was more than that. With Peter, there was a freedom, a lack of inhibition, that expanded the things I was able to do and say and feel. There was a connection, a union, a moment in time and space when we would join together like two soap bubbles floating in the air and, for an instant, for a brief few seconds, become one. Unfortunately, like a soap bubble, my realization of that intimacy didn't last. As soon as the sex was over, or at least in the few hours after it was over, the intimacy would pop and disappear.

"I've still got to clean up all this mess," Peter said, looking back into the kitchen at all of the dishes from the party.

"Come on," I said, standing up and offering him my hand. "I'll help you."

We pulled on our boxers and went into the kitchen. Peter had installed an expensive German dishwasher, but he never liked to use it, preferring instead to wash the dishes by hand. I used to chide him about it, but that night it was nice to be standing there in the soft light of the kitchen, the rest of the house dark around us, while he washed and I dried. Seen from the outside it would have seemed like a perfect diorama of postparty, postcoital, urban domestic bliss, which I then had to destroy by asking, in an offhand way,

"Do you know anything about making fruitcake?"

I don't know why I did it, it was almost criminal given the circumstances and in the moment after I said it, I felt the whoosh of horrors as they escaped from the Pandora's box that was my mouth.

"Fruitcake?" he said, his soapy hands suspended above the water, his brow wrinkled.

"Yeah, you know, the stuff you get in the round metal tins at Christmas."

"Yes," he said, "I know what it is. Why are you asking about it?"

Again, almost without thinking, I opened the box and responded with the first semiplausible lie I could think of. One of those sudden, terrible lies that we say without considering the possible consequences.

"Oh, I don't know, when I was painting with Gabriel the other day, we got talking about birthdays, I can't remember exactly why, must have been because of Lola's party, and then we started talking about cake, and what kinds we liked, you know, that sort of thing."

"And who brought up the fruitcake?" Peter asked.

"Gabriel," I said, and then, as if that wasn't bad enough, I improvised:

"He said the nuns always made it for them in the orphanage for, um, when it was fall, you know, when the weather started changing, and I thought it might be nice to try and make one for him."

Again, Peter held his hands suspended above the water and he looked straight ahead. From his reflection in the window I couldn't tell if he bought it, or not. Then he turned and I saw that look—the look you'd give someone if they just rescued a puppy from a burning building, or after they'd given a twenty-dollar bill to a homeless beggar. The look you'd give someone who had just succeeded in painting a very favorable self-portrait, and before I knew what was happening, he was kissing me again and the clothes were coming off, and well, you can guess the rest.

Thus, the charm was wound up. Peter and I researched fruitcake recipes on the Internet and in old cookbooks from the library and spent many a late evening together laughing, and baking and making love. We probably made ten different recipes; about half of them inedible, but the best we created was actually the first recipe we tried. It came from a little metal recipe box that Peter had discovered some years back at an estate sale and was written on a grease-stained card in loopy cursive that looked more like drunken Arabic and took nearly an hour to decipher. But the result was good. Or as good as fruitcake can get.

Peace reigned in all aspects of my life during those two weeks, although it was, of course, little more than the clichéd calm before the storm. Gabriel and I neared completion on the work at Arabella's, Meth won two races and advanced to a higher class, giving Cleve and me a nice little packet of money, and the four of us—my mother, Peter, Cleve, and I—had several lovely dinners together. If, as was often the case, my mother and Peter had to work late on a project or had some social commitment, I would toddle over to Reid's, ostensibly to help him work on his house but, more often than not, to lie naked in a pile, from which I would, like Cinderella, carefully extricate myself at the appointed time—in my case, 11:00 at the very latest. Then I would shower to remove the scent of Reid's cologne (I would not be so foolish twice), dress once again in my filthy work clothes, drive home, and exhibit my hard-working self to anyone still awake to witness, shower once more, and then crawl, understandably exhausted, into bed next to Peter.

We finished up with the fruitcakes on a Friday night, and three of them sat glazed and ready to be wrapped up the next morning and given to Reid. I was, of course, concerned about Gabriel and how he would react to being given his loaf, as he surely would be when he came to pick up Lola for church on Sunday, but I had prepared him for that possibility earlier in the week by telling him that it was a Danish tradition to give fruitcakes in August, and not to be at all surprised if he got one.

Arabella, eavesdropping on the conversation, as was her habit, chimed in with,

"What kind of hokey tradition is that?"

"Yes," Gabriel wondered.

"Well, it's a cultural tradition," I said, in what I hoped was an authoritative, documentary-sounding voice. "A celebration of the end of the Great Nordic Famine, I forget exactly the year, and the fruitcake is to, well, celebrate the end of the famine. You know, because it has, like, all of the food groups of the forest in it. The ones that they're thankful for."

As if that wasn't bad enough, I added, "And if you get one, you're supposed to kiss the cake and shed mock tears."

Cold? Calculating? Conniving? Callous? Yes. And my being thus brings up an interesting point, illustrated, as so many things are these days, with a psychological buzzword: my being cold, calculating, conniving, and callous enabled me to compartmentalize my life, and that compartmentalization enabled me to work with one unknowing lover on a gift for another and not be overcome with guilty remorse. Of course, "compartmentalize" as I am using it here is really nothing more than a euphemism for "rationalize," which is itself nothing more than a euphemism for "make lame excuses to oneself and others for one's scandalously bad behavior," which is exactly what I did. And, I suspect, exactly what the Nazis, and Joseph Stalin, and probably even Woody Allen and Bill Clinton did, too. In the back of their minds, in the deepest darkest recesses of their consciences, they knew they were doing something wrong but they went ahead and did it anyway, ignoring the human costs and collateral damage. Indeed, they had to ignore it. To actually consider what they were doing, to know, and own their deeds, would not have been pleasant, and would not have allowed them to keep doing them.

But, probably it is even simpler than that: None of us (Stalin, Allen, Clinton, me) ever imagined we would get caught, and as long as no one found out, as long as we could maintain a smiling façade, no one would get hurt. But, of course, that didn't happen.

Chapter Twelve

Saturday, July Seventeenth, was not a busy day. In fact, there were only two things on my list:

    1. Take the dog to the track in time for her race at 1:00.
    2. Meet Reid for a date at 7:00.

The first should have been easy. I'd been looking forward to it all week, ever since Meth had advanced in her standings the week before. Cleve was very excited, too, and we had spoken about the race when he'd arrived home the night before and found Peter and me in the kitchen, still cleaning up from the last batch of fruitcake.

"You'll have her there by noon," Cleve said. "Right?"

I nodded.

"Because she's in the first race at one o'clock and she's got to be checked in and weighed."

"Not a problem."

In the list of definitions at the end of Arabella's expensive and weighty tome on Greek mythology, the word "hubris" is defined as *"a presumption toward the gods; excessive pride and self-confidence, esp. by a mortal."*

When I look back on that simple Saturday, I see that it was a Molotov cocktail of hubris, impatience, and the requisite dash of vanity that eventually caused everything to explode. Put plainly, I was too proud of my (okay, *our*) little baked creation to wait until that night to deliver it, so, on my way to the track that morning, Meth rested and ready in the seat next to me, I decided to swing by Reid's house and leave one of the fruitcakes on his doorstep. I imagined him stepping out to get the paper, or returning from a trip to the hardware store, to discover the little foil-wrapped ring of joy I'd left for him. The happy warmth he'd get from that discovery would simmer all through the day, stewing into feelings of adoration and lust for me by nightfall, and my nerves did an excited little conga just thinking about it.

Of course, it didn't quite work that way. I got to his house at about ten-thirty, but since it was such a beautiful day, the home improvement project he'd decided to tackle was the front porch itself. I should have just driven by at that point and waited until evening, and maybe I would have had he not seen my van and waved and, well, what could I do? I parked, took the fruitcake in one hand, the dog's leash in the other, and the two of us jogged up the steps.

"Hello," he said, advancing open-armed to greet me. He was wearing a short pair of cutoffs and a tool belt and had bits of sawdust in his hair. He kissed me and then looked at his watch. "You're a little early for our date."

"Yeah, I know," I said, giving a sheepish shrug of my shoulders. "I was on my way to the track, she's got a big race today. I was just going to drop by and leave this for you. But you're here so you've ruined it."

Unceremoniously, I handed him the fruitcake.

He took the package and I could tell by the expression on his face that he suspected what it was. He pulled back some of the foil, peeked in, and then looked at me, his eyes all misty. My heart gave a smug beat of satisfaction although I was surprised, and yes, I'll admit, a little alarmed, by the strength of his reaction.

"You made this?" he asked, his voice cracking. "Just for me?"

"No," I said, "I made it for that other guy I like so much who loves fruitcake."

He laughed, pushed me up against the door, and gave me a kiss, and before I knew what was happening, he had pulled me, the dog, and the fruitcake into the house. He set the fruitcake on the hall table, grabbed me around the waist, and carried me up the stairs to the bedroom, Meth barking and jumping behind us.

"We have to hurry," I said, laughing as he pulled my shirt over my head and began undoing the buttons of my pants. As I was falling back on the bed, I glanced over at the clock on the table and reckoned we had a maximum of fifteen minutes. It took only about seven, and then three more to get dressed and skip back down the stairs, where I saw Meth, who had, I uselessly reflected, been suspiciously quiet during our time in the bedroom. She was surrounded by shredded tin foil and was wolfing down the last large chunk of fruitcake, which she wolfed even faster when she saw me on the stairs.

"Oh, fuck," I said, and then plopped down on one of the steps.

"Oh, no!" Reid cried, but then couldn't stifle a laugh.

"No, no," I said gravely. "It's not funny. She's got to race today."

We sat and watched as Meth attempted to swallow the last mouthful.

"Should I . . . I don't know, get her some water, maybe?" Reid asked.

"No. Shit! We should give her the doggy Heimlich, or the Princess Diana finger, or, I don't know! Shit!" I said, smacking my forehead, "I am so fucked!"

Reid, still naked, stepped past me down the stairs and went to the kitchen. The dog, trailing her leash, followed him. A moment later, I heard rhythmic lapping sounds and Reid's gentle, Mayberry-accented scolding.

"That was a very, very, naughty thing to do out there, little critter."

When they returned, I could see that Meth's torso was noticeably distended. I looked at my watch again.

"Okay," I said, trying not to hyperventilate. "For better or worse I've got to get her to the track." Reid nodded and handed me the leash. I shook my head at the dog and took her out on the porch.

"Hey, Tony," Reid whispered, shyly peeking out from behind the door. "I know it's a bad time, but thank you."

"I'll get you another one," I said, and then vaulted down the steps, Meth walking and burping behind me. I lifted her into the van and sped off, trying to think of something to tell Cleve. When we got to the track, I still hadn't thought of anything and was sorry to see that he was standing out front waiting for us, pacing back and forth and puffing on a cigarette. I knew he had a lot money on Meth (as did I), and that that would make the whole thing even worse.

I got out of the van, woke the napping Meth, and together we walked slowly toward Cleve. When we were about fifty yards away, I could tell that he could tell something was wrong. He squinted and shielded his eyes, wondering, no doubt, why I seemed to have replaced our slender and speedy greyhound with an ambling bovine.

"What the hell!" he cried, looking from the dog to me and back again.

"It was an accident," I said. "I went to the bathroom and she got into one of the fruitcakes. I didn't see her until it was too late."

"Oh, fuck," he cried, spinning around and throwing his hands up in the air, "oh fuck, she has to be weighed in fifteen minutes! You know how she is with food, why didn't you watch her?"

Why, indeed.

"God, I want to kill you," Cleve cried, and pushed me in the chest.

"I'm sorry!" I said, wanting to kill myself. "I'm sorry. What can we do? There must be something we can do."

I was hoping, of course, that he would have some surefire way to fix her, some doggy laxatives, maybe, or syrup of ipecac, but he didn't. He sat down hard on the curb, stuck his cigarette in his mouth and pulled his hair back tight with both hands. For a few seconds he remained that way, staring down at the pavement, puffing in and out like a dragon, trying to come up with something. Meth gave a fruity burp.

"We're gonna have to just run her anyway," he said. Then he lowered his voice and whispered, "Oh *Jesus*, I've got money on this one, do you know how much money I've got on this one?"

"I know! I'm sorry!" I cried. "Here, you take the dog, I'll go see if I can bet on some others for you. Come on, who's the next best shot?"

He clenched his eyes for a minute and said, "Nitro Bess."

"Nitro Bess," I repeated. "Okay, and next?"

"Um, shit, ummmm," he said, mentally scrolling through the

names and records of the other dogs in the race, "try CK Dexter Haven."

"Nitro Bess and CK Dexter Haven. Got it!"

Then Cleve, still not quite believing the mess, took Meth and went one way, while I took my ATM card and the two names and went the other.

After I'd drained my checking account and made all the betting combinations I could possibly think of, I went to the stands and waited for the announcement that I knew somehow was going to come. The announcement that dog number four, TC Methamphetamine, had been scratched. There was a flurry as people flipped through their forms and then rose to return to the betting counter.

After the race, I got up, and walked slowly toward the kennels, wondering how Cleve would react. When I got there, he wasn't back yet. The other two dogs were whimpering to be let out of their crates, but I didn't dare. I just waited and paced and waited and paced. When Cleve and Meth finally did return, she looked better, but Cleve certainly did not. He came in wordlessly and handed me the leash.

"Was it . . . bad?" I asked, not wanting to know, but not wanting to sit there in silence, either. He sat down on a chair, twisted his head to one side, and whistled.

"It wasn't good," he said, and took a cigarette from the pack on the table. He lit it, inhaled deeply, and told the rest of the story.

"I took her down, checked her in, and there were a few strange looks, but everything seemed cool, and she made it through. Then they took her in for the vet check and weigh-in so I ran outside to watch from the window. The dude knew something was up when they had her step on the scale. They checked and double-checked and then the vet comes over and starts looking her over. Got right down next to her, which was too bad for him because, man, as soon as he started feeling her neck, she puked red and green all over him."

I groaned and covered my eyes.

"They gave her back to me a few minutes later and axed her from the lineup."

The awkward silence returned. I waited for Cleve to blow up at me, but he didn't, and I didn't know how to handle him not doing so. When someone is really angry, it's always easier if he yells and screams and shakes his fists because then, no matter how much the outburst has been provoked, you can calmly raise your defenses and exit the scene saying something like, "Hey, whoa, I'll talk to you later, once you've calmed down." That will probably just enrage him even more, but it will give you an interval to assess the situation and come up with an appropriate alibi or excuse. It was a tactic I'd used many times in my relationships with Tom and Roy, but clearly it wasn't going to work with Cleve because he wasn't ranting and raving. He just looked annoyed and disappointed. Of course, I felt guilty. Guilty for having stopped at Reid's, guilty for not watching the dog, guilty for the whole fruitcake lie. Not guilty enough to confess, mind you, but guilty nonetheless.

"Did you at least remember to put the money down on Nitro and CK?" he asked wearily.

I nodded.

"All right then," he sighed, resigned to this round of bad luck. "How about we go upstairs and you and me try to win back some of what we lost."

I nodded and we went back out to the track.

The rest of the afternoon we spent poring over the forms, eating hotdogs, smoking cigarettes, and running back and forth to the betting counter. When the last afternoon race was over, it was almost six o'clock and we were still in the hole. Cleve stayed on for the evening races, in which our other two dogs were racing, but I went and got Meth, who had now gone from burping to farting, and took her home with me.

On the way, I decided to stop by Reid's again to ask if we could reschedule the date for another time. I should have called, especially in light of how my first unannounced arrival had turned out, but I didn't, and when I arrived, it was to discover that Reid, anticipating my arrival, was boiling lobsters. The table was set (not, I presumed, with the china he and the ex-boyfriend had been bickering over) and there was a bottle of wine in an ice bucket (an ice bucket!). He had put so much effort into it and was so happy to see me that I couldn't really back out.

His yard was fenced so we put Meth (who was so gaseous that her name could then have been short for Methane) outside. I eagerly accepted the glass of wine he offered me and downed it in one gulp. Then we sat, and ate, and talked and cooed at each other until precisely eleven o'clock (the time at which I had programmed my cell phone to vibrate) when I reluctantly got up to leave.

"You really have to go?" he purred, running his hand up under my shirt.

"I really do," I said, clipping the leash on Meth. "I, uh, have to take my grandmother to church in the morning."

Not a complete lie, nevertheless I tensed my shoulders for the lightning bolt I felt sure was about to strike me. Instead, I got the warm, aawww-burning-building-puppy-rescue, helps-out-with-Special-Olympics, takes-his-sick-grandmother-to-church look I'd gotten a few nights before from Peter.

When I got home, Cleve was in the kitchen making a sandwich.

"Where'd you go?" he asked, eyeing me, then his watch, then me again.

"Oh, I took Meth to the park," I said, lying for something like the ten-thousandth time that week. "The fruitcake isn't sitting well with her," I said, waving my hand in front of my nose.

"It's good she only ate one," he said, pointing to the remaining four on the counter.

"Yes."

He knelt down and scratched her ears.

"She looks better," he said.

I shuffled my feet and mumbled, "I'm sorry about today."

He just shrugged and sat down at the table to eat and read the paper.

Meth and the two other dogs took off barking down the hall and I heard my mother and Peter come in. I had hoped Cleve would be in bed when they arrived so as not to have to witness my next performance, but there was no way around it.

"How was the party?" I asked, before either one of them had the chance to ask the question I knew would be coming. My mother kissed me on the forehead, then walked over and kissed the top of Cleve's, which made him blush.

"It was fine, fine," she said. "Did you both get something to eat?"

We nodded. Peter stood behind me and gave my shoulder a squeeze.

"You smell fishy," he said.

"Who all was there?" I asked, not even sure whose party it had been or why they'd been having it, but wanting to quickly deflect attention away from me.

"Oh, let's see," my mother said, and began listing off names.

"Never mind about that," Peter said, interrupting her and bending down to greet Meth. "How did the race go?"

I opened the refrigerator door and pretended to look for something.

"Oh, yes," my mother said, taking a seat at the table next to Cleve. "Tell us. Did she win? Tony, don't hold that open, please."

I shut the door and stared at it. There was an expectant silence which neither Cleve nor I attempted to fill. I knew Cleve was glaring at me, waiting for me to tell them. Soon, my mother and Peter would follow his gaze and be staring, too.

"No," I said, turning and seeing the scene just as I'd imagined, all eyes on me. "She didn't win. In fact, she didn't race because she was sick because I was busy talking on the phone before the race and Meth got hold of one of the fruitcakes and ate it."

"I thought you said you were in the bathroom," Cleve said.

"I was," I said. "I was on the phone in the bathroom. It's called multitasking. Anyway, she was too sick to race and it's my fault, okay, so I'm sorry."

"Oh, Tony," my mother said, dropping her hands into her lap. Then she turned to Cleve. "Did you lose much money?"

His reply was matter-of-fact: "Yes."

"Oh, Tony," in chorus this time from both my mother and Peter.

"You've got to be more careful," she scolded. "It's like having a small child."

"I know, I know, I'm sorry. I won't let it happen again."

More silence. Then thankfully, my mother turned back to Cleve and asked how the other two dogs had done in their races.

A little while later, when Cleve had gone to bed and my mother was headed that way, I stopped her on the stairs and embarked on the next mess:

"I think I'll go to church with Lola and Gabriel tomorrow," I said, "so, you don't have to get up and get her ready if you don't want to."

She turned and cocked her head suspiciously.

"I just want to go," I said. "I thought maybe you'd want to sleep in."

Peter approached, his head similarly cocked. And of course, they were right to be suspicious since my motive for wanting to go was because I felt somewhat less than confident that my spiel about the fruitcake had convinced Gabriel, and I wanted to keep some distance between him and my mother and Peter until their interest in the subject waned. In short, I thought that the proverbial tangled web I'd been weaving was tangled enough so if I couldn't untangle it, I could at least keep it from becoming more tangled.

Or something like that.

So the next morning, true to my word (the only time I was true to it that entire weekend), I got up, got Lola dressed and ready, and the two of us, *avec* fruitcake, met Gabriel on the front steps of the cathedral and all went in together. Had my life been a novel or a movie, or had God taken a personal interest in me, the homily that morning would have been on the theme of lying, but instead it was about the evils of contraception, which didn't seem directed at me at all, and made me think that maybe, if I was lucky, God's attention was elsewhere just then. I listened politely, and afterward, instead of returning to *Casa Turquesa* for some of Peter's waffles (where I was afraid the conversation might again turn to fruitcake), I made it a special occasion and took Lola and Gabriel out to breakfast.

Chapter Thirteen

The next morning at Arabella's, I did not need to search for the key to her front door on my key ring because the door wasn't locked, was not even closed all the way. When Gabriel and I walked in, there was the obvious evidence of a little party: two of the dining room chairs had been pulled into the foyer next to the large, overstuffed one, and there were sticky shot glasses and an ashtray on the floor, full of lipsticky butts. A trail of female garments left behind on the mauve-carpeted semicircular stairway seemed to indicate that "heat" had driven the partygoers to the upper level of the house. Gabriel and I looked at the scene, looked at each other, shrugged, and then each went to our respective areas of the house, where for two hours we were able to work unmolested.

I always enjoyed those quiet mornings when Arabella was sleeping it off or was otherwise occupied, though I'll confess they made me worry that maybe she'd overdosed. At eleven-thirty, my worries were dispelled when I heard drawers in her bedroom opening and closing. Soon thereafter, she emerged at the top of the stairs clad in a violet bra and panties, her blond tresses sloppily pinned up. She squinted at the light and then descended the stairs like a zombie, dragging her toga behind her. Without a word, or even an indication that she saw I was there, she walked through the foyer and into the kitchen, where I heard a cupboard door slam followed by the violent whir of the coffee grinder.

I went back to my work. I was sketching the Circe niche that morning but was not happy with certain aspects of it. In the background, off in the distance, there was the ocean and a boat meant to be the *Argo*, bobbing patiently in the harbor, waiting for her crew to return. Closer in, on the island, I'd painted Odysseus, reclining on a shaded divan, being fed grapes by two fair maidens. In the foreground, I'd sketched Circe—a beautiful woman whose face vaguely resembled, as did the faces of all the women in the niches, Arabella's. Circe/Arabella was gazing fondly at Odysseus while simultaneously waving a wand over a group of enchanted pigs, and it was those two things—the wand and the pigs—that were the problem. I'd made the wand look too much like a conductor's baton and, consequently, the pigs gazing up at it, looked like a choir about to burst into song. They reminded me of those taxidermied frogs that have been outfitted with little wooden instruments and arranged into a band. What's worse, Arabella had insisted that I assign to each of the three pigs the facial features of her three ex-husbands, helpfully supplying me with fading snapshots of each of them.

The whole drawing was just about to go from being kitsch to being absolute cartoon trash, which, given the subject matter and setting, was not a long journey, but one which I nevertheless hoped to avoid. Therefore, I had spent most of the quiet morning trying to improve it without changing the whole arrangement. It was aggravating, so I decided to wait and get some input from Arabella before I began the actual painting.

When she emerged from the kitchen, coffee cup in one hand, toga in the other, she was still not quite present. She sat down, blew on the coffee, and stared blankly ahead.

"Long night?" I asked.

"Mmmm," she said, and then took another sip of coffee. "Long and densely populated. They just left, like, an hour before you guys got here."

"They?"

"Yes, there were five or so, but only two stayed the night. Brothers, or cousins, or something. I can't remember. Dmitri and Menelaus, or maybe it was Nicholas. Something like that."

"Greeks?"

"Yes. Met them at a restaurant. They're waiters. It was great, but I don't think it's going anywhere. Neither one can speak English very well and they were both wearing wedding rings. Listen," she yawned, "do I have to pose this morning? I really don't feel up to it."

I looked at my watch and made a scolding sound.

"Considering there are only about twenty minutes left in the morning, I guess you can be excused until afternoon."

She sighed and eased back into the chair with her coffee. Once the caffeine began pumping in her bloodstream, she sat up and narrated some more of the details of her evening. I waited for her to finish and then asked her about the problems I saw with Circe and the anthropomorphic pigs.

"I think they're fine," she said, gazing at them thoughtfully. "It kind of reminds me of a scene from *Charlotte's Web*. Don't you think?"

I was about to argue that I didn't think that was a good thing when Gabriel appeared at the top of the stairs, ready to go to lunch.

When I left for work earlier that morning, I took one of the fruit-cakes with me and wrote the following in an old Christmas card:

> Reid,
>
> Here's a second attempt with the cake. I hope you'll enjoy this one as much as the dog seemed to enjoy the first. And while I'm on the subject of second attempts, let me use this card to tell you again how much I've enjoyed getting to know you these past few weeks. I hope I'll be seeing much more of you in the future.
>
> Tony

I had intended to deliver the cake and the card on my lunch hour. I had not intended that Gabriel accompany me on the delivery, but the man from his building who usually made sandwiches for him had been sick that morning, so he didn't have a lunch. We ate at a bar downtown, and after we finished, as we were walking back to the van, I mentioned that I had a small errand to run.

"It won't take me ten minutes," I said. "Do you mind?"

He shrugged, and we got in the van and drove through downtown on Fifteenth Street, heading toward the Highlands.

During that trip, I happened to look in the rearview mirror and saw a bicycle messenger darting in and out of traffic. He was wearing a yellow jersey and had on a pair of oversized black sunglasses that made him look like a bee. I got so flustered and was so busy looking back that I ran a red light and nearly hit another car.

"Hey!" Gabriel cried, grabbing the dash with both hands. "What are you doing?"

"Sorry. I'm sorry. I wasn't looking," I said, and turned my attention forward. When we came to a stop at the next block, I looked back again. We were out of the shadows of the skyscrapers and the sun was reflecting off the rear window of the van so I couldn't see behind me. I looked in the side mirror and saw nothing at first. Then, as if teasing me, the slender half circle of a spoked wheel poked out from behind my rear bumper. I adjusted the mirror to get a better look.

"The light's green," Gabriel said. Someone behind me honked. I accelerated slowly, hoping the bicyclist would pass me, but he didn't, and try as I might, I couldn't see him. The subsequent traffic lights were synchronized so we did not stop again.

"Do you see a bicyclist back there?" I asked. Gabriel looked in the side mirror.

"I do," he said. "Two of them. Why?"

I shrugged, and tried to convince myself I was being paranoid. Then, as we were leaving downtown, speeding up and going under all of the railroad bridges before crossing the Platte River I saw the yellow jersey and the sunglasses two car lengths behind. I sped up. This was a notorious stretch of road for getting a ticket but I decided to risk it. Gabriel looked over at me. The light ahead had turned yellow. I pushed the gas pedal down and sped through the intersection at least three seconds after the light had turned red.

"Hey!" Gabriel yelled. "What are you doing?"

"Sorry."

We sped up the hill to where Fifteenth turns into Twenty-Ninth, and as we made the gradual left turn, I looked back once more and saw nothing. Surely, we'd lose him on the next uphill stretch. When we got to the intersection of Federal and Speer Boulevards, I relaxed. I looked back to see that the fruitcake had not been smashed (it hadn't) and then turned around and again glanced in the mirror. He was there, about a hundred yards back, standing up on the pedals, the bike tilting from side to side with each rotation. I knew those legs. I knew it was him. I turned back to the light. Still red. A steady stream of cars going both directions in front of me. I drummed my fingers impatiently on the gear shift and looked back again. He was about fifty yards away. Finally, the light changed and I made it through the intersection. I assumed that he had, too, but I stopped looking back and focused on getting to Reid's, dropping off the fruitcake, and then getting away as fast as I could. I turned left onto Thirty-Second and then zoomed the five blocks up to his street and took a right. I came to an abrupt stop under the linden tree, but left the engine running. I grabbed the fruitcake and the card, ran up the steps to Reid's porch, deposited them behind one of the planters so that they were out of the sun, ran back down the steps to the van, hopped in the still open door, put it in gear, and took off. Gabriel was too bewildered to speak.

In retrospect (what a menacing word!), I should have stopped. I should have gotten out of the van, and should have spoken to Tom. But I was a coward and I didn't, and I paid for it later.

When we returned to the job site, a highly caffeinated Arabella came squealing down the stairs and ran to turn on the radio. Gabriel sighed, put on his headphones, and passed her going the other direction. I contemplated walking right back out the door, but decided I'd better just let her have her ten minutes of fun and then be done with it for the day. The radio came on and I immediately heard James's voice echoing throughout the house.

" . . . and the possibility of severe afternoon thundershowers. Right now outside the KLZY studios we've got a partly cloudy seventy-nine degrees.

"This is James Tower, ladies and gents, playing all your favorite songs from yesterday. I'll be with you for another three hours this afternoon and we've got some great music coming up, let me tell you. Looking at my watch, I see that it's ten minutes past one o'clock, my friends, which can mean only one thing. Yeeeeessss, that's right, it's time once again for the most popular part of our program. The part where we play a song about all the rascals, rogues, and scallywags out there. Those men and women who take a heart and break a heart. We've all had one in our lives at some time or another, and today we're taking requests from you, our listening audience. So if you have a song you'd like to hear, a song you'd like to dedicate to that *special* someone, well, go right ahead and pick up the phone. Our request line number is 720-570-0544. That's 720-570-0544. Whoa! Will you look at the switchboard light up! Let's take our first call.

"Hello there, do you have a song you'd like to hear today?"

"Hello?" (an elderly female voice)

"Yes, hello, who is this?"

"Hello?"

"Yes, hello. I need you to turn down your radio, ma'am."

"The radio?"

"Yes, *turn down the radio!*"

"Just a minute."

There was the sound of a phone clattering on some hard surface. James chuckled. The woman returned.

"Can you hear me now?" she asked.

"Much better, much better, with whom am I speaking this afternoon?"

"This is Gladys. Gladys Holik."

"Why, hello, Gladys, this is James Tower from KLZY. You're our first caller for Radio Romeo today."

"I'm the first caller?"

"You're number one, Gladys! Where are you calling from?"

"Yes, I'm over here at the Heather Gardens."

"Heather Gardens," he said, "lovely place, lovely people. I think we had a busload of you come out for Swing Bingo a few weeks back, am I right?"

"Bingo? Yes, I believe so."

"Boy oh boy, we sure had a good time that night."

"I couldn't make it."

"No?"

"I don't get out on account of my hip and all, and then of course I have cataracts so I don't do well at nigh—"

"Well, I'm sorry you couldn't make it. It's always a good time. I know we've got a lot of loyal KLZY listeners out there at Heather Gardens."

"That's right, we listen every day. But you got too many comm—"

"Excellent. Always a pleasure to talk to fans. Now, Gladys, did you have a song in mind that you'd like me to play for Radio Romeo today?"

"A song?"

"Yes, dear, which song would you like me to play?"

"Yes," she said, "I'd like to hear that one song you played the other day."

Pause.

"Er, could you be just a bit more specific?"

"I think it was maybe that Ellen Fitzgerald song you all played the other day."

"Hmmmm, well, you know, we play a lot of her songs. And there are probably close to ten thousand that she recorded."

"Yes, it's that one, the one about the trick with the knife."

"Trick with a knife . . . Ahh, yes, yes. I've got it. That's an old favorite of Radio Romeo listeners. A classic, really. The old Rogers and Hart tune, 'Everything I've Got.'"

"Why, yes, I suppose so."

"Excellent choice, Gladys. Excellent choice. And who are we sending that out to today?"

"I'd like to send it out to Harold Jurwitz—"

"No last names, Gladys, please! Remember our rules."

"Oh, yes, sorry. It don't matter, though, he's been dead awhile."

"Well, then," James laughed, "you be sure and turn up the volume."

Gladys laughed. James laughed.

"Now tell us a short story about that old scamp Harold. Can you do that?"

"Yes. I sure can."

"Excellent! Let's hear it, and remember, no last names."

"Okay, well, this was back a while, I was in my twenties, working at the Denver Dry Goods. That's where we met, see. I sold him a tie and he asked me out. We courted for a while and then we got engaged, see, had the ring and everything, and I took him home to meet my family. They—my family—were living out in Kiowa at the time but he had a car so we drove instead of having to take the train or the bus. Of course, since we weren't married yet, Mother and Dad wouldn't let us share a room, so every night we'd say good night in the hall and I'd go off to my room and he'd go off to the guest room."

"Or so you thought!" James interjected.

"Or so I thought."

"Uh-oh, uh-oh. I think I know where this is going."

"Yes, well, we'd been there about three days when my mother came in to my room one morning and gave me a note from him saying he'd run off with my baby sister."

"No!" James cried. "With your own sister?"

"My own flesh and blood."

"Gee, Gladys I'm sorry. That's terrible."

"Oh, thank you, but it all worked out for the best. A couple months later I found my Travis, and he was good to me for almost thirty-seven wonderful years."

"Wonderful, wonderful! One man's trash is, well, er, never mind. That's just great. So what about your sister and Harold, what happened to them?"

"Them? Oh, they went ahead and got married and my sister had a baby that was retarded so that slut got wh—"

"Whoa, Gladys, I think we lost you there. Hello? Hello? Yup, Gladys must have been on a cell phone and gone through a tunnel. It happens. Well, without further ado then, from Gladys to Harold, here's the honeyed voice of the incomparable Miss *Ella* Fitzgerald singing the Rogers and Hart classic 'Everything I've Got.' "

As the morbidly cheerful song droned on, Arabella emerged from the Media Room doing a uniquely inappropriate dance, which I tried to ignore by preparing my palette. When the song was over, she turned down the volume and returned to the foyer to begin her afternoon shift on the pedestal.

"That was great!" she exclaimed, pausing in front of the mirror by the front door to freshen her lip gloss. "Maybe the best one ever. What a horribly perfect song!"

"Someone's certainly feeling better than they were this morning," I said.

She stepped up on the stubby column and arranged the drapery.

"Yes," she said. "Plain coffee wasn't doing it for me so I put a couple shots of ouzo in it. That perked me right up."

"Ouzo. How nice. And where did you get that idea?"

"It was my own idea," she said, "but I got the bottle from the two Greeks last night. It's good. I'll make you one if you want. The stuff's clear in the bottle but it looks just like cream when you pour it in coffee. Makes it taste sort of like black jellybeans."

"I'm sure it's all the rage at the Athens Starbucks."

She was quiet for a while, watching me paint, and she actually managed to hold a pose for almost a record fifteen minutes, but then, not surprisingly, she gave an exhausted moan and returned to the chair. She fished a package of cigarettes out of the cushions and lit one, exhaling her licoricey breath in my direction. She got up again, danced her way into the kitchen, and returned with a fresh cup of coffee and the half-empty bottle of ouzo.

"You sure you don't want one?" she asked, pouring a few shots in her mug. "That song was pretty rough."

"I'm sure. Thanks, though."

She settled back in the chair.

"So how many Gladyses do you think you have in your life?" she asked.

I pretended not to hear, hoping the question might just evaporate if it hung in the air long enough. When I didn't answer, she did it for me.

"Quite a few, I'll bet," and she began counting them on her fingers. "I know about Peter and James, and Roy, but I'm sure you've got others that I don't know about at all. Imagine all those people carrying around that spite for you even years after you're dead."

I could imagine it all too well.

Arabella went on talking but I tried to tune her out and focus instead on painting the pigs' faces. The afternoon wore on and on and on. In between shots of ouzo, Arabella worked on the color novel and treated me to more analyses of my character. Just a normal afternoon, until . . .

She'd resumed her posing and was perched unsteadily on the pedestal, coyly twirling a strand of hair around her index finger.

"Wouldn't it be something," she sighed, "if you were bisexual."

That was new, although somehow not unexpected. I felt my shoulders tense up. I tried to ignore her, tried to focus on the niche.

"I mean, have you ever slept with a woman?"

"Never," I said, adamantly shaking my head.

"Do you ever think about it?"

"Never."

"It's too bad, really. I mean, you should try it sometime. Just so you'd know what it was like."

I gave a nervous, artificial laugh.

"Don't laugh," she said. "I'm serious. Imagine what fun we could have together. Two players with no shame! Both beautiful and fun, and full of beautiful fun."

"That stuff will give you an awful headache," I said, getting up and taking the bottle from her. She fell forward and clasped her hands around my neck.

"I could really show you a good time!" she murmured.

"Yes, okay, good-time girl, you're about to fall off the pedestal."

I lifted her up, set her feet on the floor and escorted her back to the chair. She kept her arms around my neck and began pulling my face close to hers whispering again and again, "Imagine, just imagine," and then she kissed me. I pursed my lips like a schoolmarm and turned my face to the side. I tried to unclasp her hands from my neck, but she resisted, giggling.

"Stop it," I said, twisting my neck and trying to get away. "You're going to make me mad." But she didn't stop. I got my hands on her shoulders and pushed her back into the chair, with more force than I'd intended or she'd expected. She released her grasp and I stood up and took a step back, wiping my mouth. She sat up, perfectly erect, and glared at me. Her face was red, and I knew it wasn't from the ouzo. If she'd been a character in a comic strip, the conversation balloon above her head would have been filled with nothing but exclamation points. I turned away to spare her some embarrassment. I righted the pedestal, went back to my seat, and picked up the palette and brush. The silence was heavy. My hands were shaking. There was no way I could paint.

Then she started laughing. A thin, bitter laugh at first, which slowly grew louder. I laughed, too, again with the hope it might lessen her embarrassment.

"I guess," she said, her voice low and breathy, "it's better for all women that you're not straight." Then she stood up, walked up behind me, and ran a long fingernail up the back of my neck. I shivered but did not turn around. I heard her walk slowly up the stairs and then heard her bedroom door click shut.

I looked at my watch. It was three o'clock. The air in the room felt muggy and I wanted to get out. I wrapped up my brushes and paints and crept quietly up the stairs to see if maybe Gabriel was at a place where he could stop so we could leave early. I found him in one of the back bedrooms rolling out a ceiling and I knew he wouldn't want to stop. I knocked on the door. He turned around and lifted the headphones from one ear.

"Hey, I've got to run to the hardware store. Do you need anything?"

He shook his head. I turned, snuck back down the stairs, went out to the van and drove away.

I did go to the hardware store but once there I just sat in the van in the parking lot thinking about the awkward mess that would be tomorrow. I knew, despite Arabella's attempts to pooh-pooh it, that something terrible had happened. A shift had occurred in our already dysfunctional "professional" relationship, a shift that was going to make it even more difficult and awkward to continue working for her than it already was. And yet, the dread that I felt about that was absolutely eclipsed by the horrible sight that I saw when I returned to her house: there, sitting on the porch with his bucket of tools, was Gabriel, holding the three remaining rings of foil-wrapped fruitcake. My mouth fell open. He noticed, and that erased any confusion that might have been lingering in his mind. His face hardened. He got up, fruitcakes in one hand, tool bucket in the other, and approached the van. He pulled open the sliding door, put the bucket and the fruitcakes inside, closed the door again, and got in the cab. There was another heavy silence, during which I tried to concentrate on driving. After about five minutes, he said,

"Peter stopped by."

He let the words hang there for a minute, waiting to see if I'd respond. When I didn't, he continued,

"He was in that part of town running some errands and just thought he'd stop by."

More silence.

"Thought he'd stop by since he didn't get the chance to see me on Sunday."

I tried to swallow but my mouth had gone completely dry. I knew it was bad but I wasn't sure just how bad so I decided to let him reveal what he knew before I said anything. He was silent for the rest of the ride. He made me suffer and squirm until we got right in front of his building. Then he put both hands on his knees and said,

"I am quitting."

I stared at the steering wheel.

"I'm sorry but I won't be giving you two weeks' notice. I appreciate the work you have given me, but I cannot work for you anymore because I don't respect you and because you are dishonest. I know there is a lot of dishonesty in the world but I don't want to be around it, or be a part of it."

He paused then but made no move to get out of the car. Maybe he was waiting for me to respond. When I didn't, he said, "You know I've never approved of your homosexuality, because it's a sin and—"

I started to protest but he held up a hand and cut me short.

"I've never approved of it," he repeated, almost yelling, "but I'm aware that that kind of sin is not contagious. Lying and dishonesty, on the other hand, are, and I want to protect myself from them.

"When Peter handed me those fruitcakes, I was confused. Oh, you'd told me about the tradition, and the famine, and all that. You'd laid the groundwork for one lie with another lie and I believed you. I even made a fool out of myself by kissing the cakes, just like you said to do. But then we got to talking, Peter and I, and I realized that he had made the cakes for me, and that you had lied to me and lied to him. I'm not sure what the story is and I don't think I want to know. He was so happy about it, Tony, so, rather than confuse him and hurt his feelings, rather than expose you for the liar that you are, I played along. I was complicit in your lie. It was easy to do. Too easy. And I don't ever want to be in the position of having to do it again.

"And that," he said, "brings me back to my point about homosexuality. You are like all the people of the world who don't know Christ. It is a sin, I'm sure of that, but not a sin that you have chosen, and so I believe God will be merciful. But the lying, Tony! The dishonesty! The playing with people's hearts! You choose to do those things. You do them willfully. You and that woman! You both shrug off the pain you cause, you laugh at it, and to me that is almost unforgivable."

Without another word, he got out of the van, retrieved his tools, and walked to his building without looking back.

That night, dinner with Peter, Louisa, and Cleve was a bitter affair for me, all the more so because the three of them were so jovial. They discussed Peter's departure, which my mother was slowly resigning herself to, and plans that each of them were contemplating for the future. They talked to Cleve about the dogs and how he had been offered a job by one of the bigger breeders to work as a trainer, and of course, they talked to me, and told me how kind and thoughtful I'd been to make the fruitcakes for Gabriel and how happy he'd been when Peter had arrived with the extras.

"It was so touching when I gave them to him. For a minute he looked confused, but then he got a little emotional," Peter said. "I was sorry I missed you, Tony. I had to go out that way to pick up some lumber and saw that the extra fruitcakes were on the counter. Although I have a newfound respect for the stuff, I didn't think we'd eat them so I thought I'd take them to Gabriel and maybe get a look at what you've been working on. You aren't angry that I stopped by, are you?"

"No," I said, not looking up from my plate.

"I mean, I didn't want to take away from your good deed," he said.

"No, you didn't. It was fine."

"The house was interesting," he said, his words directed at all of us again. "I can't say I liked the color choices, that orange in the foyer especially, but Tony's work, those niches, and the mural in the dining room, just great! Does that woman drink? She certainly smelled like liquor."

I nodded, still staring down at my plate.

"Oh, what a shame," said my mother. "Is she alone?"

I nodded.

"Tony," she said, putting her hand on my arm. "Are you all right? You look like you're about to choke."

I looked up, and truly felt like choking. "I think, yes, I think I don't feel so well," I said and pushed my chair back from the table. "I'm just going to go lie down."

I went down the hall and ran up the stairs.

"Do you think you need a doctor?" she called, getting up and coming after me.

"No," I said. "I just need to lie down."

I went into one of the bathrooms on the second floor, slammed the door, and threw up. Peter and Cleve were knocking, asking if I was okay.

"I'll be fine," I said, in between flushes. "Really." But as I looked at my pale reflection in the toilet water, I realized that again I was lying.

Chapter Fourteen

Not surprisingly, Arabella wasn't at home the day after our "encounter," so I had the house to myself and was able to finish all of the niches in the foyer and start on Gabriel's unfinished work in the upstairs bedroom. The next day, Arabella was home, although much less desirous of my company. In fact, she did not emerge from her bedroom until nearly two o'clock. Then she descended the stairs, wearing a prim sundress and dark glasses, and went straight out the front door without a word, or a glance in my direction.

I spent the rest of that second afternoon working on all the areas I'd avoided painting until the end—the closets and the insides of little cupboards, the undersides of window frames. The boring, tedious areas that I'd always left to Gabriel. While I did so, I thought about Reid. It had been two days since I left the fruitcake and card on his doorstep and I hadn't heard from him. Several times, I'd thought about calling and leaving a message, but then I didn't do it because, to be honest, I really didn't want to hear another thing about the stupid fruitcake and was seriously weighing whether I wanted to pursue anything further with Reid. Not because I thought he was unattractive, or unworthy of attention, but because everything associated with him—every meeting and date and gift—had resulted in so much trouble that I was starting to think our relationship was jinxed or, heaven forbid, that maybe I was losing my touch.

At about four o'clock that afternoon, my phone rang and it was him.

"I was just thinking about you," I said, and felt something stir in the terrain below my belt.

"Really?"

"Yes, and wondering if you were going to call again."

"Yes, I'm sorry, I got real busy with work. Listen, maybe you could come by tonight?" he asked, a hopeful ring in his voice. "Then I can thank you properly for the fruitcake."

"So you did get it," I said.

"Oh yes, I got it."

"Good."

"So you'll come by?" he asked.

"Sure, what time?"

"Oh, maybe around six. Will that work?"

"Sure. Should I bring anything?"

"Just yourself."

"Okay then, I'll see you at six," I said brightly.

He hung up without saying goodbye.

Maybe I should have heard something suspicious in his request. Maybe I should have had my guard up, especially in light of our other ill-fated meetings and the fact that it had taken him two days to call back, but for whatever reason, I trusted that he just wanted to see me to say thanks and have another roll in the hay. And I'll admit, as I drove to his house that evening, my spirits (and again, parts farther south) were buoyed by the possibility of the latter.

When I arrived, I was surprised (and yes, annoyed) when Reid opened the door and snapped my picture with a Polaroid camera. Blinded by the flash, I barely had time to recover before he snapped another, and another.

"Hey," I said. "What's the deal? Stop!"

He stopped. I could barely see him as he stood there in the doorway, fanning the three photos in his right hand. I rubbed my eyes and blinked several times. As soon as the spots had faded enough that I could actually see, Reid had turned and was walking down the hallway into the kitchen.

Again, I should have known something was wrong, but I didn't know him all that well and anytime a Polaroid had appeared in my past, (the incident with the toothbrush notwithstanding), it was usually employed in the documentation of some new sexual position. Little did I dream that he would use it for more sadistic purposes.

"What's this about?" I asked when I got to the kitchen, a sly smile on my face, my dick as rigid as a tree branch.

He didn't say anything, or even look at me. He set the three black-and-white Polaroids on the kitchen counter and stared at them, as if studying which one he liked best. Then he uncapped a red Magic Marker and drew horns on my head in the third picture, the one he'd taken last, in which I was frowning. When he'd finished, he recapped the marker, set it aside and picked up a black one. On another picture, the first one, in which I'm smiling like a naïve idiot, he drew a circle over my head that was supposed to represent a halo.

Of course, at that point, the tree branch was more like a wilted flower stem and I knew there was going to be trouble, but I decided to stick around and see just how bad it would get. I pulled out one of the bar stools and sat down.

"What's the third option?" I asked, pointing to the last picture, the one in which I looked dazed and expressionless. He scowled at me.

"I think that's for you to say."

He reached below the counter and produced a plain white envelope, which he set down and pushed toward me. I looked at it, then up at him. He nudged it closer.

"Open it."

I stared at it. Then, figuring that if he was still in the room, it probably didn't contain anthrax or anything explosive, I picked it up. It had already been opened neatly along the top with a knife or a letter opener, and contained a single sheet of paper. I removed the paper and, before I had even unfolded it all the way, recognized Tom's angry scrawl. It was a letter. A poisonous, bitter letter. More bitter than aspirin washed down with grapefruit juice. More bitter than a shitty toothbrush. The kind of letter that should have been written in blood, or with individual words cut from magazines. In short, just the kind of letter I would have expected Tom to write:

> *You don't know me and I don't know you, but I'm going to warn you about something, the way I wish someone had warned me. It's about Tony Romero and how dangerous an affair with him ~~can be~~ is. By dangerous I don't mean he'll give you AIDS, or anything. A case of crabs, maybe, but probably not AIDS. No, I mean emotionally dangerous. I mean he'll blow up your heart like a balloon and then just let go, or worse, jab it with a pin. He'll get interested in you, make you feel like the king of the universe, and then dump you on your ASS! Partly this is because he is a love and sex addict who can't <u>EVER</u> keep his dick in his pants. Partly, it is because he is an <u>ASSHOLE</u>! Just ask any of his other boyfriends, they'll totally back me up, I guarantee. We all got fucking cards like yours, and flowers and dinners and dates and gifts. I don't know what the gift he left for you means, that round thing in the foil (I peeked, sorry), but I'm sure it means something. He's very, VERY clever that way—finding out what you like and what's important to you and then using it to make you fucking melt. He is a DISTURBED man, fucked in the head. I know you are probably way under his spell right now and believe me, I know what that's like. I know how easy it is to get caught up in the tornado of that charm, and I know you'll probably think this note is just sour grapes on my part, just some whiney ex who got the shaft, but <u>BELIEVE ME,</u> I am not the only one who feels this way. I'm not the only one who's been fucked over. There are many, many more. If you don't believe me, try getting a haircut from a guy named Roy at the Ruben Blades Salon (but I probably wouldn't mention Tony's name when he's got the scissors near your head). Or just for laughs, get a radio and tune it to the AM station KLZY at about 1:00 P.M. Monday through Friday. Better yet, talk to his <u>own</u> <u>mother</u> and her "husband"—Tony's "stepfather"—I'm sure they'll give you an earful!*

*Again, I say all this FOR YOUR OWN GOOD. Things are
not as they appear.*
<u>*BEWARE!*</u>

I finished reading and set the letter back on the counter. I wasn't
surprised, not in the least. Tom was, after all, the same boyfriend
who had gone down to the post office when I left him and had all
my mail forwarded to the dog pound. The same boyfriend who
had snuck over during the night and slashed my tires *and* Roy's
tires. The same boyfriend who, after one of our bigger fights about
my infidelity, gave me an elaborately wrapped "peace offering": a
box containing an axe and a note that read: *Take this hatchet and symbolically bury it in the backyard, with the knowledge that if you ever do
something like that to me again, I'll dig it up and kill you with it.* The
same boyfriend who had once bought me ten pairs of tight black
underwear so that when he did the laundry, he could examine
them for tell-tale semen tracks. So, no, I was not a bit surprised by
the note. Disappointed, yes. Surprised, no.

Reid stared at me waiting for an explanation, which, of course, I
did not have. Oh, I could have rallied my old defenses, could have
argued my way out of it by explaining how insanely jealous (or just
insane) Tom was, but I didn't. Reid had probably taken at least
some of Tom's advice and listened to Radio Romeo; maybe he'd
even spoken to Roy or to Peter or to my mother; I didn't know, and
at that point I didn't want to know.

"Don't you have anything to say for yourself?" Reid demanded.

I did not. I folded the letter, put it back in the envelope, and set
it on the counter. Then, as if they were playing cards, I flipped the
photo with the halo and the photo he hadn't graffiteed so that they
were facing down on the counter and I walked back toward the
front door. Reid came running after me. He grabbed me by the arm
and spun me around.

"Wait a minute. Don't you have *anything* to say?" he cried.

I shook my head and looked longingly at my van parked in the
street.

"Well, I do," he said, and slammed the door.

I thought he might so I leaned back against the wall and waited.
Evidently, he did not realize how many times I'd found myself in

situations like this. He seemed to expect outrage, or denial or claims of a misunderstanding. Either that, or pleas for forgiveness, but I knew it was past that point. I knew there'd been too much damage done to lie. There was nothing for me to do except politely wait for him to say what he had to say and then leave. He didn't make me wait long.

"You've been playing a game," he said, pacing from one side of the small foyer to the other, shaking a finger at me. "But you need to learn, my friend, that there are games you shouldn't play, especially when you're over the age of thirty. They're not even okay to play in your teens or twenties, but when you're in your thirties, they are pathetic, inexcusable! They are nothing but selfish, egotistical meanness."

He paused and glared at me, again to see if I had anything to say for myself. I didn't. He continued:

"I've had philandering boyfriends before, Tony. Mean, lower-than-the-belly-of-a-snake, underhanded men in my life, but I think you, sir, take the cake! I wish it had been a pie so I could smash it in your face!"

Then he whipped opened the door again and stood next to it, an obvious indication that I should leave, which I did.

Having no place else to go, I returned to Curtis Park, where, I felt certain, I was about to get a similar tongue-lashing from Peter, and probably from my mother. Surely, if everyone else now knew about the goddamned, stupid, mother-fucking fruitcake, then they must too. Gabriel, or Tom, or Reid, or maybe even James had surely reached one or both of them and told all the gory details. There was no use in avoiding it, so I decided to go home and just get it over with.

As I drove, I envisioned a real Barbara Stanwyck moment for myself, just like the one at the end of *Double Indemnity* when she's confronted by Fred MacMurray and confesses everything but then he lets her have it anyway. Bang! Right in the stomach.

But when I got to the house, there was to be no such drama. Peter and my mother were out on the back deck barbecuing salmon steaks and sharing a bottle of wine. They were talking and laughing and didn't appear the least bit upset about anything. But since appearances that day had been alarmingly deceiving, I thought it wise to retreat to my room until I could better gauge the situation. I was almost to the stairs when Peter spotted me from outside and called,

"Get a glass, Tony, come join us."

My mother turned and smiled, a look of relief on her face. The look she always had whenever my arrival made Peter happy instead of sad.

"Yes, Tony, come and join us."

I hesitated for a second, but then decided to take the risk and went to the kitchen and got a glass. After talking to them for a while, it was clear that Peter didn't know anything about the fruitcake, or Gabriel, or Tom, or Reid, so I allowed myself to relax and enjoy their company, at least for that night, figuring I might as well since when they did find out, which they surely would, I was more likely to have a glass of wine thrown at, instead of poured for, me.

The next few days were difficult. Although certain that Peter was going to find out, I couldn't bring myself to confess, so I spent as little time as possible at the house. When I was there, with Peter or my mother, I was as chatty as a parrot, always driving the conversation so that I could be sure of its direction and destination.

In addition to being anxiety-riddled, the week was (what with Gabriel gone, Arabella avoiding me, and Reid no longer calling me during his lunch break) pretty lonely. To occupy the time, I threw myself into work and painted like a madman, trying hard to finish Arabella's project so I could get out of that house and breathe a little easier.

One evening, as I was washing out brushes, about to leave for the day, my phone rang. I saw that it was Peter and my stomach made a little leap. This was it, I thought. The jig was up. With true fear in my heart, I answered.

"Uh, hello."

"Tony? It's me. Peter."

"Yes."

"Listen, Louisa's out tonight so I was thinking maybe you and I could have dinner together."

"Dinner?"

"Yes. Do you have some other plans?"

"Plans? No."

"Good, then let's have dinner together. We can pretend it's a date. I'll cook and we can watch a movie. Nothing fancy. What do you say?"

"Sure," I said. "Great," although I felt certain his invitation was a ruse, just as Reid's had been, to get me home so he could rip me apart.

"Are you all right?" he asked. "You sound funny."

"Yes. No. I'm all right. Fine. Sorry. Just a little spacey. I'll, uh, see you tonight."

Again, all my prophecies of doom were proven untrue and the evening went exactly as Peter had planned: we had an excellent dinner and after dinner retired to the couch, where we watched a video. He'd rented a movie we both liked, *The Umbrellas of Cherbourg*, but I fell asleep before it was over and Peter carried me up to the bedroom like a child. I listlessly undressed and went to sleep, Peter joining me a few minutes later.

I wish I could remember more about that night, but when I really think about it, there is nothing remarkable to remember, nothing out of the ordinary. The next morning, Peter woke me before he left for work, kissed me goodbye, told me he loved me, and that was it.

That day at Arabella's I remember I worked on the baseboards, the things I hate the most and always leave for last. I was crawling around on the floor in the dining room when I heard her emerge from her bedroom, descend the stairs, and click across the marble floor to where I was working. I looked up. She was dressed in a black, sleeveless chemise. Her hair was pulled back tightly and she was wearing a little pillbox hat with a veil, underneath which her eyes were further concealed by a pair of black sunglasses. She was either going to a funeral that day or had gone to the plastic surgeon the day before.

"Do you think you'll be done soon?" she demanded, arms imperiously folded across her chest.

I nodded. The hostility bit was really getting old, but I played along.

"When exactly?"

She was trying to be stern, but beneath the veil, I could see her lips trembling.

"Tomorrow," I said, "but maybe the next day if I don't finish everything tomorrow."

"Well, I'd appreciate if you could put a fire under it," she said, examining the clear polish on her nails. "I'm having guests for the weekend and I'd like to have all this done and your equipment out of here by Friday at the latest. Can you do that?"

For a second I considered telling her I was sorry, but sorry for what, I couldn't really say. Sorry that I wasn't bisexual, sorry that she'd developed a schoolgirl crush on her gay housepainter, sorry that maybe somehow I'd encouraged that crush, sorry that I'd witnessed her make a drunken fool of herself, sorry that she was lonely and miserable and that money and men and substances hadn't been able to remedy that. The list could've gone on and on. And I *was* sorry. I felt terrible, but I really didn't know what to say to convey that without further offending her so I figured the best thing would be to shut up, finish the job, and get out of her house and her life so all I said was, "Yes, I can do that. I'll be gone by tomorrow at the latest."

She hesitated a moment, as if she'd been expecting me to argue, to say I needed more time. She shifted her weight from one foot to the other and seemed about to say something but couldn't find the words. She stood there for a few seconds, then abruptly turned and clicked her way back across the foyer and out the front door.

Around twelve-thirty, I broke for lunch, taking my sandwich out by the pool to eat in the sun. Then, around one o'clock, because I am vain or masochistic, take your pick, I decided to listen to James's radio program. I got up from my chair and walked inside to the Media Room. I'd never actually been in that room of the house and was surprised to see that, like Arabella's outfit, it was all black. Carpeting, walls, ceiling, furniture, entertainment center— black. Somehow, I made my way through that monochromatic darkness, found the black remote control for the black stereo, and turned it on. It was already set to the correct station. Since it had taken me so long to find the remote, I had missed all of James's introductory banter and the song was already playing. It was Nat King Cole. I listened for a few bars but didn't recognize it.

"Ahhh, there you have it, my friends." It was James's voice. "The incomparable Mr. Nat King Cole. "'The Party's Over'." A fitting song to end with. And I'm afraid this is the end, my faithful, lovelorn listeners. Yes, that's right, the swan song of Radio Romero, er, I mean Romeo. Time to move on to bigger, better, more optimistic things and leave the bad past behind us. It's been fun, our little game of revenge, but on Monday we'll turn over a fresh new leaf. Yes, we'll move away from our tales of love gone wrong to a new program devoted to love gone right! Yes, on Monday, we'll begin Radio Romance, a few minutes each day devoted to your musical memories of true love. We'll be taking your requests and listening to your recollections, so get those love letters and diaries out from the basement or the attic and let us know about a song that was special to you and your sweetie. Again, that's Monday afternoons at one o'clock, right here on the station that swings Colorado, KLZ—"

I turned off the stereo and tossed the remote back into the black room. So, my days as a radio star were at an end, eh? I didn't know what to make of that. I'd wished for the program to end so many times, but now that it had, I felt more nostalgic than relieved. Felt like my fifteen minutes of fame were over and I hadn't fully appreciated them. I felt the extreme darkness of suddenly being removed from the spotlight.

I worked at Arabella's until seven o'clock and, to my surprise, finished the job. I got all of my supplies, all my ladders and drop cloths and brushes, packed into and on top of the van just before it started to rain. As I walked back to the house to turn out the lights and close the door, I calculated that I'd been working there for nearly eleven months. An absurdly long time in which I should have produced something comparable to the Sistine Chapel, and which, I realized as I walked along the Gallery of Badass Greek Chicks, I had not done. Oh, technically the work was good, but the subject matter and the colors were ridiculous, and there was no reason that it should have taken so long to complete. No reason, that is, except for the obvious one, that in eleven months I had probably worked only a month of full days, and had, I figured, seduced and slept with at least thirty different guys. I looked over the final invoice and realized that in spite of the wasted time, I'd made good money on the job. Had I worked a little harder, I could have made great money.

The invoice.

I had had it with me, printed and ready that morning, but had wisely refrained from presenting it to Arabella before the job was actually finished. As I stood there in the foyer, looking for a place to leave it so that she'd be sure and find it, I considered writing a note, maybe thanking her for the work, telling her what a pleasure it had been and how much I'd miss her company, but I decided that would sound too phony and I was tired of lying so I just put the invoice on the dining room table with the key, and I left.

As I was leaving, just as I reached the end of her street and was about to turn, I spied her car. She had parked beneath the drooping branches of a large willow tree in an obvious attempt to conceal herself. If her windshield wipers hadn't made their arc across the windshield just when they did, I would not have noticed the car at all, let alone the person in it. The tree concealed a lot, but not all. The grill and hood were exposed, as was the windshield, and it was through that freshly wiped surface that I saw her, sitting, veil still in place, smoking. Obviously, she'd been waiting, hiding out until I left and it was safe for her to go back home. Safe for her to return to her own house. Unfortunately, at the same moment I saw her, she saw me, too, and saw that I had seen her, which made it even worse. I quickly drove through the intersection and went on my way.

For a moment I considered going back to try to talk to her, to try and end all this awkward silliness, but for whatever reason, I didn't, and just drove back home.

Or perhaps it would be more accurate to say that I drove from the lair of one middle-aged, hysterical, blond woman to that of another.

Chapter Fifteen

"**G**one! But why? Why didn't he tell me? Why didn't he say goodbye?"

I was in the living room with my mother, who was sitting on the couch, all three dogs arranged around her.

"I don't know, Tony, but he asked me not to tell you, so I didn't. It was probably all the last-minute things he had to do."

"What? That's bullshit!" I said, and began pacing the room. "You don't just pull out of someplace, someplace you've lived for ten years, and not tell people you're leaving."

"He told you," she said, "and I told you. Months ago. But you wouldn't listen. You didn't believe it."

I rolled my eyes.

"Maybe if you'd—" she began, but then stopped herself and looked away.

"Maybe if I'd what?"

"No," she said, shaking her head.

"You started to say something. You might as well just say it."

"Maybe," she said, her voice low and cold, "if you'd been around and not out chasing boys all the time, you would have noticed. He probably didn't tell you because he didn't want to see—again—that you didn't care."

"Didn't care!" I exclaimed. "Wh—How—Why would he think I didn't care?"

She laughed at that, but it was a dry, humorless laugh.

"And what does that mean? Why are you laughing?"

She looked at me, as if genuinely surprised that I would ask such a question.

"Oh, Tony, come on! You've treated him badly almost since the day you brought him home. I've said this before but I'll say it again, the way you've treated Peter makes me ashamed."

She glared at me from the pile of dogs, a look of disgust on her face.

"Peter did so many wonderful things for so many people. Just look where you're standing right now. Look around. Do you think any of this," she said, extricating herself and standing up and then making a grand upward sweep with her arms, "anything here would be the way it is if he hadn't helped us? If he hadn't shown us how to do it? Don't you remember what it was like all those years when you were growing up, the disaster this place was, the rotten plumbing and the goddamned squirrels in the attic?"

She was shouting now, and the dogs, frightened, crept off the couch, heads down, tails between their legs. Cleve and Lola, hearing the shouting, appeared at the top of the stairs. They stared down at the two of us.

"But it's not just all this," she continued. "No, the thing I wish you could see is how he did it all for you. How he stayed here any way he could. Stayed here, in your house, married your mother, took care of your family, just so he could somehow, anyhow, be close to you. And he tried, Tony. He waited. For ten years! And yes, you're right, you don't just leave someone you've loved for ten years and not say goodbye. Not unless they've done something really bad. And you've done a lifetime's worth of really bad things to him. I don't know what it was—the thing that broke him—but I know it started at Lola's party. What you've done since then I can only imagine."

I could tell this was going to get even uglier if I stuck around so I turned and headed up the stairs. I had not taken two steps when I heard her voice, low and bitter, say, "At least your father had the sense to stay away after he left."

I stopped but did not turn around. Yes, this was going to get uglier. I took a deep breath.

"But you," she continued, "you had to keep jumping back into his life, giving him hope each time you returned. Falling back into the familiar when your latest love affair turned sour. And they all do go sour, Tony. Why is that? Do you never wonder why?"

I resumed my progress up the stairs. Cleve and Lola moved aside to let me pass.

"I'm not finished!" my mother yelled, her voice hoarse. "Do not walk away from me while I'm speaking. You will hear me!" I turned around and looked at her. Her face was red, her hands at her sides clenched into fists. Cleve looked truly frightened. He had never seen her this angry, and to tell the truth, neither had I. He put an arm on Lola's shoulder, whispered something to her, and the two of them went back upstairs. I stood on the steps and waited.

"There's nothing wrong," my mother continued, "with the men you choose, Tony. The problem is with you. Do you know that?"

Several seconds passed. The ticking of the grandfather clock seemed suddenly very loud. I nodded.

"What is it you're going after with all your drawings and your boys? Is it the sex?"

Oh boy, I thought. Nothing quite like having your mother scream at you about your sex life.

"What is it you want? I've never been able to figure that out. It can't be making you happy, having your life always up in the air and getting thrown out all the time. I'd like to throw you out myself right now but that would teach you nothing. That is what you're used to."

I didn't move. I was wondering how this crimson-faced Viking had somehow replaced the calm, cool Scandinavian that had once been my mother.

"No," she said, "I won't throw you out, Tony, but I do want you out of here right now. Just go away for a while."

I hesitated.

"Now!" she shrieked. "Get out!"

I went upstairs. Meth was in Peter's room, her long nose poking out from under the bed, her eyes wide and frightened.

"It's all right, girl," I said, and got down on the floor to pet her. When she realized I wasn't mad, she crept out and began licking my face. I scratched her neck and stroked her long, narrow head. Downstairs I could hear the muffled voices of Cleve and my mother, she apologizing and he trying to calm her. I got up, went to the closet, and threw some socks and underwear and a clean T-shirt (and my sketchbook, of course) in a bag. Meth was whining under my heels the whole time and I realized that she thought it was happening again. She knew what was going on and she was terrified of being left behind, and that was what broke me. I bent down and tried to tell her it was okay, that it wasn't like the other times, but there was no way to do that. She was so scared she was trembling.

"It's okay, girl," I said. "It's okay, it's okay," but I was crying and that only made her more frightened. She went and stood by the door, waiting for me to open it. When I did, she took a few steps out into the hallway and then turned back to make sure I was following. As we were going down the stairs, I saw Cleve standing at the front door staring out at the rain coming down.

"There's no hurry, man," he said, "she's gone."

"Where?"

He shrugged. "Just went out back to the garage and then came right back through and left. Drove away. Didn't even take her purse or anything."

"Did she take her car?"

"What other car would she take?" he asked.

"Where's Peter's car?"

"He drove it."

"What do you mean, he drove it? He went back to Denmark."

"Yeah," he said, still staring out at the street where my mother's car had been, "but he's driving to New York. He's gonna sell the car there."

I stared at Cleve's calm profile and was suddenly angry.

"You knew about this," I said.

"About what?"

"About Peter leaving."

He nodded.

"And you didn't tell me."

He shook his head.

"Why?"

"You were busy," he shrugged. "And she was right, you didn't care."

I didn't say anything else. I opened the door, and before I could stop her, Meth ran out into the rain. I ran after her.

"You're taking the dog?" Cleve cried, coming out after us.

"No, I'm not."

Meth was waiting by the door of the van. I grabbed her collar and pulled her back. Cleve took hold of her and held her with both hands as she thrashed and whined.

"You gotta stay, girl," I said, in the most upbeat, talking-to-the-doggie voice I could manage. "Stay here. Stay here. Good dog."

I opened the van door and got in. Meth bucked and Cleve struggled to pull her back toward the house. As quickly as I could, I started the van and drove away.

There really shouldn't be any suspense about where I went. I had no place else to go so I drove to St. Mark's. When I arrived, I took the clothes out of the bag, leaving just the sketchbook and pencils and some other junk, and then walked as quickly as I could through the rain. It was a Friday night and St Mark's was packed, not a single seat open, which wasn't all that disappointing since I felt like shit and didn't even want to be there. I looked around for a minute, but then decided to try my luck next door at The Thin Man. A martini or a giant glass of bourbon sounded better than coffee, but before I even opened the door, I could tell from the roar inside that it would be just as crowded as next door. I opened it anyway, looked in, and it was just as I'd expected: All the tables and stools were full and the crowd was three deep trying to get to the bar. I gave up. I just stood on the sidewalk in the rain. I was so miserable and so disgusted with myself I would have taken pretty much any drug—heroine, crystal, ecstasy, soma—anything that would have taken me out of myself. Since there wasn't anything, I headed back to the van. As we know, I didn't quite make it.

Chapter Sixteen

Which brings us up to the moment all of this art therapy has been leading to. The climax. The dénouement. The part in the story where I should have had a pivotal moment of change, where I should have learned something and moved forward in my personal development. The moment when I'd been pushed down so low there was nowhere to go but up. Here was my own pain from which growth was supposed to sprout. I was supposed to walk away from that crowded, smoky bar, symbolically baptized by the rain, vowing that my life would be different. The violins were supposed to start up and a brand new me was supposed to walk down the street, but alas, too late.

Bang! Bang!

A real film noir moment.

"He'd resolved to be good . . ." the narrator's deep voice would say. Maybe it would be my voice speaking about me in the third person, the way the narrator does in *Sunset Boulevard*.

"He'd resolved to be good," my dead narrator would say, *"but alas, too late."*

And that angle might have played out very nicely if:

1. I had resolved to be good, and
2. I had been killed.

But since life, and especially my life, is annoyingly unlike the movies, neither of those things happened. If it hadn't been Friday night and raining, if I'd been able to find a table inside, I'm sure I would have gone into St. Mark's, sat down, found some new masculine specimen to draw, and the whole thing would have started all over again, so no, obviously, I had not resolved to be good. Nor was there much resolve on the part of the lame-aim, weak-willed shooter, whoever that shadowy person may be.

It's been about three months since the shooting, and in that time I haven't done much except write about the past and try to catch up to the present, and to tell you the truth, I'm tired of it. I never seem to catch up. I keep writing and writing trying to contain the past and make some sense of it, but in the meantime the present just keeps spilling more and more, making it spread outward like a stain. So, for the sake of brevity, and to get current, I'm going to summarize here what's happened in the past few months. Admittedly, this is the part where I get lazy. The part where I have to ask you to keep thinking cinematically. Time will pass here like it passes in B-movies, so just close your eyes and imagine the pages flying off an old daily calendar, or a few edited scenes showing the rapid change of the seasons.

As I said in the beginning, the stream of suspects began arriving to wish me well, sign my cast, and accept my apologies. Apologies that I was more than happy to give since I was a bit concerned about having my IV spiked with bleach, or a pillow held down over my dozing head. Roy, Gabriel, Jason, Arabella, James, Reid, Tom, Edmund, Cleve, and even Peter—all came to witness what one of them had done, and all of them left with the smug satisfaction that at least I *appeared* to be remorseful for my actions, at least I was not getting away with them, at least I was (dare they say it?) suffering.

Peter, hearing in a telephone call from my mother that I'd been shot, turned around in Kansas, or Nebraska, or wherever he'd been on the Eastern Plains and drove back to Denver to make sure I was all right. He stayed about three weeks, brought me a different flower each day, and more books and magazines than I could read in a lifetime, but then he left again to go through with his original plan to return to Denmark, where he was to help his uncle, who was retiring from the paintball business, pack up and sell his house.

But the most significant event that happened in the past three months was the end of my poor, crazy grandmother, who died in her sleep one night, leaving her squirrels without their advocate, and finally freeing my mother.

While Peter was here, helping with me, and then with the funeral arrangements, he and my mother got to talking about how, with Lola gone, my mother would be able to fulfill her desire to go to Mexico. Soon, that discussion evolved (or mutated, take your pick) into a plan for both of them to move to a town in the Mexican part of the Sonoran Desert where they decided to start a new, and inevitably successful, business manufacturing and selling the line of furniture that Peter and I had designed so many summers ago. Leaving me alone for a week, they took a fact-finding trip south of the border and managed to find an abandoned cannery for sale on the coast of the Sea of Cortez, which they determined would make an ideal furniture factory. When they returned, Peter took leave of my mother and returned to Denmark to help his uncle, vowing to rendezvous with her in Mexico two months later. In the meantime my mother got busy taking classes in web design and Spanish so that she could better handle the business end of things and leave the creativity up to Peter. She put the house up for sale (with an obscenely high asking price that caused a collective gasp among the neighbors) and made plans to leave at the end of the month, regardless of whether the house had sold or not.

As for me, I've been out of the hospital for two months now and am back, for the time being, living at *Casa Turquesa*, which is a little creepy since I've been relegated to the third-floor lunatic mother-in-law apartment. The rationale for that has been that the elevator is large enough to hold a wheelchair, and the bathroom is equipped with the "old-person bars" I need to get my sorry ass in and out of the bathtub, and on and off the toilet. But really I was stuck up there so that my mother could keep the rest of the house pristine and clean for the open house days and private showings planned by Bob, the world's most annoying realtor, who does everything in his power to get me out of the way when people are coming. I'm afraid I haven't been very cooperative. Maybe it's a reluctance to let go of the house, maybe it's just a desire to aggravate Bob, but for the first few showings I made it a point to descend dramatically in the elevator just as the prospective buyers reached the kitchen, spouting nonsense *à la* Violet Venerable in *Suddenly Last Summer*.

Needless to say, my mother and Bob did not see the humor in that and so last week the elevator was turned off. The wheelchair, too, was taken away and has been replaced with a fancy new walking stick, lovingly carved by Peter, and I'm being encouraged (for my therapy, of course) to use the stairs. That gives Bob time, when he hears my heavy tread on the steps, to usher the prospective buyers out to the garden, where he can warn them, in private, of my eccentricities.

Not wanting to use the stairs, and not wanting to leave the house much at all, I've spent most of my time up here doing my onanistic art therapy, hoping that one day soon I'll get to the end of it.

Chapter Seventeen

"Tony," my mother called. "I'm leaving now."

I put the pen and pad away and stood up. The room was almost bare. There was a card table, a folding chair, and suspended from two hooks in opposite corners of the room, a hammock. All of the bedroom furniture, in fact most of the furniture in the house, had been sold, and what hadn't had been crated up and sent south of the border. As long as I didn't interfere with Bob the realtor, I was told, I could stay in the house until it sold, which seemed like a good deal but really wasn't because I was totally alone. Even Cleve had gone. He'd rented an apartment out east and had finished moving himself in two days before.

I got up and hobbled down the stairs to the main level. There was the detective, dressed very nicely in a two-piece navy suit, a handkerchief in the breast pocket to match his tie. His head was shaved, and his skin tone much improved. He picked up my mother's two suitcases, took them out to his awaiting car, and put them in the trunk. Then he opened the passenger side door and stood, like a footman, waiting for her arrival. She stood in the foyer, watching me descend. She had her sunglasses on and was nervously consulting her watch.

"Listen," she said, smiling up at me, "you probably won't be able to get in touch with me for a few days. I'll call you as soon as I'm settled and get a phone connected. You know what to do if Bob calls, right?"

"Right," I said.

"And you won't give him any more trouble."

"I won't. I promise."

"As soon as Bob says 'go,' you have to go."

"I know."

She then ran through the list of things I was to remember to do and the list of things I should please not do. I nodded but didn't write anything down. We had been through all of this *ad nauseum* in the past week and I knew that she was just reciting it all again because she was nervous.

"All right then," she said, taking a deep breath. She leaned over and gave me a kiss on the cheek. "I think I'm really going to miss you," she added, and sounded surprised by it. I rolled my eyes.

"No, really, Tony. It's been fun these past few weeks."

The past few weeks had indeed been good for the mother-son relationship. My shooting had made her more inclined to be sympathetic, but she was also happy that I was there to help. There is nothing like having to sift through and pack up thirty years of family history to bring estranged family members back together. We had worked all day, every day sorting and packing and throwing things away, and then spent the evenings sitting on the back deck with a bottle of wine talking about our strange family and the directions fate had led, and was still leading us.

Repeatedly during those discussions, she inquired about me and what I was going to do. An inquiry to which I had no answer. I didn't have much money, didn't have any real prospects, other than the dog, whose career was being managed by Cleve, and I had no idea what I wanted to do. I was a boat without rudder or sail.

"You know you are always welcome to come," she said as I limped down the walk with her to the awaiting car and detective. "The country is so beautiful, Tony, I can't even tell you. Huge saguaro cactus everywhere! You'd just love it."

I nodded, said I'd think about it and kissed her goodbye. She got in the car. The detective closed the door and walked around to the driver's side. She rolled down her window.

"Think about it," she said, "won't you?"

"Sure. Call me when you can."

We said a final goodbye. Then she nodded to the detective and the car pulled away.

For a long time after the car had gone, I just stood staring down the street, not wanting to go back into the big empty house.

In Roman Catholic theology, limbo is defined as the quiet place between heaven and hell; the place where souls who have not become Christians must stay. They are not condemned to punishment, but are deprived of the joy of eternal existence with God. Many devout people view their time on earth as nothing more than a boring limbo that must be endured. I looked at my time alone in the house in the same way. It was not hell, but it was not heaven. It just was.

Since the present for me was still and stagnant, and the future so uncertain, I'm afraid I sought solace once again in the familiar past. I pulled out my sketchbook, went back to the cafés and again started picking up tricks. But something had changed. Something was different. The appeal had dimmed. I seemed to be doing nothing more than mechanically going through the motions and, more often than not, I found that once I had the guy in my pocket, once I had the phone number or the whispered invitation back to his place, I really didn't want it. I was just doing it because I didn't know what else to do.

Whenever he had free time, the detective joined me on my outings and I gave him pointers on what to say and do to approach and pick up women. Since he had no artistic talent, he had to rely on words and actions to do his bidding, and I became a sort of coach or mentor. Increasingly I found that I was indifferent to my own success, but intensely interested in the success of my protégé. Watching him was fun but, like most fun things, was not without an edge of guilt.

"How about that one?" he asked, pointing to a slender blonde wearing ridiculously tiny eyeglass. I studied her for a moment while she waited in line. She was dressed all in black and carried a smart little handbag.

"She looks like a younger, trendier version of my mother."

"Yeah, I know," he said, rubbing his hands together. "She's perfect."

I looked at him leering at her and was reminded of the cartoon where the starving coyote looks at the roadrunner and sees it morphing into a roast chicken.

"Okay," I sighed, "and how are you going to start, Romeo?"

He thought for a moment. "Well, I guess I could say something complimentary about her hair."

I shook my head. He tried again.

"I just heard her order a latte with half-and-half instead of milk so I could comment on how I like a girl who isn't afraid of calories."

I gave him a look over the rim of my sunglasses. A look that said "don't be stupid."

"Look at her again," I said. "Find a way in. It's there. I can see it."

He studied her intensely. So intensely that he looked almost constipated.

"Okay, okay, I got it," he said. "How about this: I'll go up to her and say, 'I know that boys usually don't make passes at girls who wear glasses, but you are so beautiful I'm going to have to make an exception.'"

I groaned.

"No?"

"No. *Look.* What do you see?"

Again, he studied her.

"The bag," I said. He squinted at it.

"What about it?" he asked.

"It's Kate Spade."

"What! How can you tell that from here?"

Again, I looked at him over the rim of my sunglasses.

"Okay, okay," he said, "so what about it? What do I say? C'mon, hurry!"

I sat up and we both leaned forward, hovering over the table.

"If I were you," I said, "I'd touch her gently on the sleeve, comment on what a beautiful bag she has, and then caution her to be careful with it."

He was about to interrupt but I stopped him.

"She'll ask why, and you'll tell her that Kate Spade bags are the favorite of urban purse snatchers."

"Is that true?"

"Probably not, but who cares? It doesn't matter. First of all, she'll be thrilled to meet a straight man who can identify a Kate Spade bag."

"Ahhhh."

"Second, she'll be curious to know how you would know such a statistic, which will give you the opportunity to tell her all about the exciting and romantic field of detective work."

"That's great!"

"Not really, but it will probably work. And the shoes are expensive, too. I'm not sure what kind they are but ask if they're Blahniks. She'll be impressed."

He got up, smoothed his goatee, popped an Altoid in his mouth, and strode up to her. A few minutes later they were seated together at a table on the other side of the café and he had her foot in his hand and was examining her shoe.

I decided to focus on my own prospects. Across the room, sitting alone, I spotted a handsome, dark-haired guy. For a moment, we made eye contact, then I looked away. I flipped the page of my sketchbook, got a sharp pencil from my bag, and then subtly, oh, so subtly, looked up again. He picked the same moment to steal a glance at me and I'm afraid I got nervous and looked back down at the page. A few seconds later, I ventured another glance and it was then that I realized the handsome devil I'd been about to draw was none other than myself, reflected in the mirrored wall. I blushed, had a hearty laugh at, and with, myself and then closed the sketchbook. But a second later I opened it again. I'd never really done a self-portrait. At least not since college when it had been an assignment. Strangely enough, it had always seemed too vain to me, when the truth was that it was probably too intimate. In a way, I didn't want to look closely at myself out of a fear that if I knew my physical faults, it might shake my confidence. Might make me more self-conscious.

Self-consciousness.

When, I wondered, had that become a bad thing?

I glanced up at the mirrored wall and myself reflected in it and tried instead to focus, as I did with all the men I sketched, on my strong points, but all I could come up with was a good head of hair (albeit beginning to gray) and a cleft chin, which I had hated when younger but had grown to tolerate. I started sketching, tentatively at first, trying to capture an expression, but each time I looked up, all I saw was a nervous concentration, a timidity in the eyes that I certainly never would have imagined myself possessing. I drew and I erased, then I drew some more, erasing it all a minute later. I was about to turn over to another page and begin again, when I became aware of someone standing behind me. I turned around, looked up, and saw Reid, coffee cup in one hand, newspaper rolled up under his arm.

"Mind if I sit down?" he asked.

"Look," I said, "I'm really sorry."

He wrinkled his brow.

"I know you have a lot to be sorry for, but I'm not sure what you mean right at the moment. Does that mean I can't sit down?"

"No, no," I said, closing my sketchbook and clearing a place for his cup. "Please. Sit."

He sat, and just stared at me. I fidgeted with the zipper on my jacket.

"How have you been?" he asked.

Not knowing how to answer, I gave a circular nod and said, "Okay."

"You're looking much better than the last time I saw you," he said, emptying a sugar packet into his coffee and stirring it. The last time had been at the hospital. I was still hooked up to the self-dosing morphine machine then and I remembered frantically pushing the button when I noticed his broad-shouldered frame in the doorway. The time before that had been when I'd been summoned to his house and confronted about the fruitcake. If only I'd had the morphine pump then.

"Yes," I said. "I was pretty out of it that day," meaning the day in the hospital. "I'm much better now." And to prove it, I flexed my fingers and bent my leg a few times. "No more wheelchair, and my hand's almost as good as new."

"So I see," he said, frowning at the sketchbook. "Whose forearm or ear or kneecap is it this time?"

I heard the deep laugh of the detective and looked over at him, still locked in giggly shoe talk with the blonde, completely unaware that one of the prime suspects had just joined me.

"I was trying to draw my—, er, some still life," I said. He raised an eyebrow and set down his cup. There was another, longer silence, in which I zipped the zipper up and down. He sat, legs crossed at the knee, one hand resting on the handle of the cup.

"Any idea who might have done it?" he asked.

I looked up at him and tried to read his face. He didn't flinch.

"I'm actually here with the detective," I said, gesturing over at the lovers' corner, "but he doesn't seem to think there's much possibility of finding the guy."

"So it was a guy?"

"I'd assume so, but, well, I guess we really don't know."

He nodded. Again, I looked over at the detective and the girl and wondered which conversational avenue he had chosen to wander down. She appeared to be doing most of the talking, and from what I could tell, he was just nodding and smiling and looking intensely interested, interjecting some little pun or compliment every now and then to keep the conversation light and engaging and to show that he was paying attention. I turned back to Reid.

"Look," I said, "I know this will sound completely hollow coming from me, and there's no reason you should believe me, but I am sorry. About everything."

"I know," he said.

"I did some really shitty things, and if I could go back and not do them, I would."

He raised an eyebrow.

"Okay, that's a lie," I said. "It makes me sick to say this, but if I could somehow go back in time, I probably would do some of the same things again—I'd just be more careful about getting caught and hurting people's feelings. It sucks, but there it is."

For a moment, he didn't say anything. Then he actually laughed.

"I don't know for sure," he said, "but I think you may have taken a step forward just then with your honesty. A small step, maybe, and you seem to take two steps back for each one you take forward, but it might be progress."

Progress. Great. Toward what, I didn't ask.

We talked about less serious subjects after that, about his house and his job and about the new guy he was dating, which prompted him to ask, "And how about you, Tony? You're on the mend now, you must be dating someone."

I shook my head.

"Oh, come on, nobody?"

"Nobody. I don't think I should inflict myself on anyone for a while."

He laughed.

"Look," Reid said, downing the remains of his coffee and setting the cup back in the saucer. "Maybe you're being too hard on yourself."

I started to protest but he stopped me.

"You made some trouble, caused some pain, you haven't been a good guy."

"That's an understatement."

"I'm from the South, remember? We're always polite. But fine, you were a prick. Is that better?"

I nodded.

"But you're certainly capable of being a very nice guy. I do know that. The fact that you took the time to be so thoughtful about that damn cake is evidence of that. And since you have that capability, since you are not without redeeming qualities, I'm going to give you some advice."

I was looking at the floor, hoping the encounter would end soon. He reached over, put his finger on my chin, and gently lifted my head so that I was forced to look at him.

"Put your energy toward the right thing," he said. "Spend some time thinking about what you really want, who you really want, even if you really want anybody at all. We're not here forever. The clock is always ticking."

Then he stood up. I stood to say goodbye and extended my hand. He pushed it away and gave me a hug.

"Take care of yourself," he said. I nodded, but then wondered how, exactly, one was supposed to do that.

Chapter Eighteen

For weeks after my grandmother's death, we (Peter, my mother, the ubiquitous detective, and I) had tried, without success, to locate my father and tell him the news. We knew he was no longer in Denver, but that was about all we knew. We tried the numbers of some women in Florida, who put us in touch with women in South Carolina, who put us in touch with women in Seattle, who gave us the number of a woman in Montreal, who cursed and hung up when she heard his name, and after that we just gave up. Given all that, it was a surprise when, a week after my mother's departure, I opened the front door one Saturday afternoon headed to the track and saw my father coming up the front steps. I recognized him immediately but was too shocked to say anything.

"It's been a long time," he said. "Do you know who I am?"

It had been almost fifteen years but he was not greatly changed. He was still tan, still sharply dressed, still had cigars peeking out of the front pocket of his blazer. He was wearing enormous wraparound sunglasses that, together with his white hair, made me think of Aristotle Onassis.

"We've been trying to find you," I blurted out. "To tell you, I mean. Do you know? About Lola?"

He nodded.

"I'm so sorry," I said, but then wondered why I was saying I was sorry to him for the loss of a woman he had abandoned years ago. His eyes, hidden behind the dark glasses, were making me uneasy so I looked over his shoulder at the street and saw a powder blue Thunderbird parked at the curb with a woman sitting inside, staring straight ahead.

"Would you like to come in?" I asked.

He hesitated.

"It's okay," I said. "She's not here. No one's here except me."

He nodded and then slowly stepped in. I was about to close the door behind him, but before I did, I asked, "What about her?"

"Her?"

"My new mommy," I sneered, nodding at the Thunderbird, "or sister, or whoever she is."

He turned and looked at the car, then back at me, a wry smile on his face. "She'll be fine. She is very good at keeping herself entertained. Where is your mother?"

"Mexico."

He was surprised, but not as surprised as I would have thought.

"She always wanted to go," he said. "Is she there to stay?"

"It looks that way. She sold everything or took it with her."

I then explained the business that she and Peter were planning to start. He listened attentively, and when I finished talking, he removed his sunglasses and looked around. Immediately I noticed that he had had his eyes done. The skin around them, like Arabella's, had an unnatural tautness and sheen, and the eyes themselves looked like slightly upturned almonds. It was as if everyone who underwent that type of surgery was initiated into a special ethnic group all their own.

"Peter is . . . her husband?" he asked.

I nodded, not really wanting to explain the particulars just then.

"And do you like him?"

"Peter? Yes. Everybody likes him."

"Has he been like a father to you?" he asked.

I laughed and said, "If you mean has he been there for me, does he care about me, does he remember my birthday, then yes, he's been like a father. Just not like *my* father."

"You're angry," he said. "I expected that."

"I don't know that I'm angry," I countered, "but I can't really say what I'm feeling right now."

He stood, hands clasped behind his back, gazing at me.

"You've grown into a handsome man."

I grinned and wanted to slap myself for doing so.

"But what's happened that you need a cane?" he asked, pointing at my walking stick.

"Uh, someone got a little angry with me," I said, tapping it on the floor.

He waited for more.

"With a gun."

"A gun!"

"Yes. An ex-lover probably, no one knows for sure. Well, at least one person knows, but so far that person is keeping quiet about it."

"But you are all right," he said, and seemed to want to reassure me, more than himself.

"Yes," I said. "I'm all right." Then I explained the circumstances of the shooting and told him about the surgeries and recovery. When I'd finished, we stood facing each other for a long, awkward moment. He looked around the foyer and peered up the staircase, noticing the changes.

"Renovation and restoration," I said. "It's what Mom and Peter did for a living."

"It's beautiful," he said. "I barely recognize it."

To ease some of the awkwardness, I gave him a tour of the house, mechanically reciting the list of improvements that had been made: the elevator, the third-floor deck, the mother-in-law apartment, the salvaged woodwork, the window replacements. He was respectfully silent throughout, and when we were finished, I looked at my watch.

"I don't mean to be rude," I said, "but I really have to go. I've got a dog in the fourth race this afternoon and I promised to meet a friend at the track."

"You own a dog?" he asked, his face brightening.

"Yes."

"A greyhound?"

"Yes."

He was beaming. It was almost as if I'd told him he had a grandchild. I wanted very much to be mad at him, felt I was entitled to some indignation, but it wasn't working and instead I heard myself saying,

"Hey, I don't know what all you've got planned, but you're welcome to come along. I could take you to the cemetery afterwards and show you Lola's grave. If you want, I mean."

He hesitated, trying to detect some underlying motivation in what I'd proposed. Finding none, his shoulders relaxed and he said, "I'd like that."

Together, we walked back down the stairs and out the front door. I locked it behind us and deposited the key in the lock box for Bob.

"I'll drive," my father said, nodding toward the Thunderbird, which was, I couldn't help noticing, almost the same hideous color the house had been.

While we'd been inside, the woman had put the top down. She had long, red hair; pale, freckled skin; and was at least five years my junior.

"Anna," my father said, addressing the girl, "this is my son, Tony."

She said hello and offered her pale hand for me to shake. There was a wedding band on her finger but it was almost totally hidden by the giant rock in the engagement ring.

"He's got a dog racing today and would like to take us to the track," my father said. "You don't mind, do you, darling?"

"I don't mind," she said, still holding my hand. "I would like to go."

"Good," I said, and climbed into the tiny backseat. "Then we'd better hurry."

They got in and my father started the car and pulled out into traffic. I was prepared to give him directions, but he seemed to remember how to get there so I spent most of the drive talking to Anna, who was full of questions about Denver and the mountains. In her voice I had detected a foreign, although still familiar, accent and inquired where she was from.

"Denmark," she replied and somehow I was not surprised. She looked like an *au pair* or a nanny, and I figured my father had met and seduced her, just as he had met and seduced my mother. But that still didn't explain the rock.

When we got to the track, I led them to the stands and then went looking for Cleve. I found him on the west side taking Meth to the weigh station and called his name. Both he and Meth turned.

To me there are few things in the world better than the reaction of a dog when it sees its owner. Meth's tail whipped back and forth when she spotted me and she hopped a good two feet off the ground. I felt like a celebrity approaching an excited fan.

"I wondered if you were going to make it today," Cleve said.

"I had some unexpected company."

I squatted down and let Meth lick my face.

"My dad's here," I said, standing up and wiping the dog slobber on my sleeve.

"Not here at the track!" he cried.

I nodded. Cleve had heard so many stories about the man, most of them bad, so I knew he was curious to see him in the flesh.

"He's in the stands right now. He's got some girl with him."

"No!"

"Yes, and she's Danish."

"No!"

"Yes."

"Where the hell's he been all this time?"

I shrugged, and then wondered why I hadn't asked him that question myself.

"Are you, like, okay?" Cleve asked.

I had to think about that one. I was not feeling quite "okay," whatever that meant, but again, I couldn't really tell how, or what, I felt. Cleve put his hand on my shoulder and we walked toward the weigh station.

"Dude, this has gotta be weird for you."

"Yeah, but whatever," I said.

He clapped his hand on my shoulder a few times.

"Look, I've got to get her in here now," he said, winding Meth's leash around his wrist. "You gonna be all right?"

"Yeah, sure. Look for us in the stands when you're done checking her in."

The two then disappeared into the building and I went back to the main area of the track. It was about one-thirty and the sky was cloudless. Dressed as they were, my father in his expensive suit, with his straw hat and sunglasses, and Anna in a yellow and white gingham dress, they stuck out like, well, dog balls, and were easy to spot in the middle of the crowd gathered at the finish line. It was easier to imagine them strolling the boardwalk at Nice or Cannes than to actually see them leaning on the dog track fence in Commerce City. I watched them for a moment—a lot of people were watching them—and then chuckled to myself and went inside to get some beers and a betting form.

As I was tottering back, trying to carry the drink tray and my cane, someone behind me called out,

"You going to drink all those yourself?"

It was the detective. We had planned to meet an hour before but I'd forgotten.

"Hey, I'm sorry," I said. "I didn't blow you off."

"Yeah, right," he said, relieving me of the drink tray.

"No, really," I said. "My dad showed up just as I was about to leave. It kind of threw me off schedule."

He scrunched up his face and whistled.

"So, the prodigal father returns, eh? Where's he been?"

"You're not going to believe this, but I forgot to ask," I said. "He's got a girl with him. Come on. You're going to like her."

We walked back out to the stands and I pointed them out to him. He whistled again. We approached, I made the appropriate introductions, and together we claimed a section of seats about five rows up in the stands.

As soon as we sat down, the detective began asking Anna a lot of idiotic questions like, *Is it true that redheads have fiery tempers to match their hair?* and I could almost see his dick get hard as she giggled her responses. I left them to chat and turned my attention to my father, handing him the betting form.

"That's my dog, Meth," I said, pointing to her name in the roster.

He studied the paragraph of history and analysis of her that was listed at the bottom of the page and nodded.

"She's got a good chance in this one," I said, "and if you want to make some money, I'd do a box with her in first, Land Rover in second, and Terry's Pride in third."

He took a silver pen from the inside pocket of his blazer and scribbled some notes in the margins of the form. Once we had our choices all mapped out, he got the detective, who had been busy reading Anna's palm, and the two of them went down to place the bets, leaving me alone with Anna. She was perched on the edge of the aluminum bench, and clutched one of her knees with both hands. Her sandaled foot was swinging back and forth. It was a beautiful foot and the nails had been given a French manicure. The upper portion of her dress was close fitting and revealed that her body was slender with small, firm breasts. She wasn't wearing a bra, either, which was making her very popular with many of the male patrons. As I looked at her profile, I again concluded that she was at the very least five years younger than me.

"So," I said, trying to decide how to begin.

"So," she replied, her foot swinging faster.

"Do you like traveling with my father?" I asked.

"Your father? Oh, very much," she said, tossing her hair back from her shoulders. "He's very charming."

Again, I noticed the ring.

"Are you two . . . married?"

She laughed.

"I only asked because of your rings," I said.

She spread her hand out in front of her, and gazed at the rings.

"I am married," she said, "just not to your father."

Again I wondered if maybe she was a half sister, but her porcelain features made that seem not very likely.

"Your dad is my lover," she said, clarifying the matter. "That sounds funny. Especially to me since I've known him so long. He is a good friend of my parents."

If her parents' "good friend" was banging their teenage daughter, I wondered what someone would have to do to qualify as an enemy. I was also curious how old she'd been when they first met, but I didn't want to be rude so instead I asked, "And how long has he known them? Your parents, I mean."

"Oh, for years, since I was a girl."

I was about to ask how she would classify herself now, but stopped myself.

"He and my father are in business together," she said, and her tone was slightly impatient, as if she was restating the obvious.

"I'm sorry to ask so many questions but this is all new to me. What type of business are they in?"

The foot stopped swinging.

"That," she replied, "is a good question. My father does a lot of different things. The business he runs with Fernando . . . they say it's import-export, but I've never been clear on what it is. They travel a lot."

"And where is all this happening?" I asked. "Where does he live?"

"Your father? In Denmark, of course. Just outside of Copenhagen."

I dropped my betting form and stared at her.

"He lives in Denmark."

"Yes, of course," she said.

"No," I said testily, "not '*of course*.' "

I finished my beer and picked up the one my father had left behind. I took a big drink.

"Look," I said, "maybe you don't get it, but I haven't heard anything from the guy in ten years. I had no idea where he was, what he was doing, even if he was alive. I've imagined him living in every corner of the world. But Denmark! That's the last place I would have considered."

"He called you," she protested. "On your grandmother's birthday. I was there. I heard him."

"Yes, he did," I said, aware that my voice was getting louder and my words more clipped, "but we had no idea where the fuck he was. My grandmother had Alzheimer's. She was crazy. I didn't even get to talk to him."

"That I didn't know," she said, releasing her knee and setting both feet on the ground. She swiveled around to face me. "It was a very hard call for him to make. I know how upset about it he was after he hung up."

I didn't bother responding. We both turned to face the empty track and were quiet. She played with the clasp on her white, patent leather purse and I tapped nervously on my walking stick.

"I know this must be hard for you," she said, still staring down at the purse, "and I probably should not have come."

"Oh, it's all righ—"

"No. You two should be alone. I know you're angry about him and it probably only makes it worse to have me here. It's just that it was a chance to see where he was from, and to get away for a while and have a little holiday, so I took it."

"No, it's okay," I said, surprised at my wanting to make her feel better. "It's just awkward, that's all. I'm sure if the situation were different, if he hadn't just come back, I mean, I'd be glad to have you here. If nothing else, I'm glad to see that my father has such good taste in women."

She blushed.

"I don't mean to pry," I said, "but can I ask you another, sort of personal question?"

"Sure."

"Okay, it's obvious what my dad sees in you. You're beautiful, you're young and smart and you certainly know how to dress."

She blushed again, gave my arm a pat, and said, "It's easy to see you are your father's son."

I gave the approximation of a grin and continued, "But what I want to know is what you see in him?"

She stared down at the track, thinking. Again, she clutched her knee and swung her foot.

"Oh, a lot of things," she said. "He's funny and charming, and I know this will be strange to hear—it would be strange if someone said it to me about my father—but he is a very sexy man. I know he's not a perfect man," she said, tilting her head to the side, "but then, neither is my father. In fact, your father and my father are very much alike when it comes to screwing around. Granted, my mother is worse than my father, but, well, never mind. What I mean," she said, the speed of her speech increasing, "is that maybe the reason I like your father so much is because he's so much like my father. I know that sounds crazy, or at least so my friends think. And my mother. And your dad, too. Think it's crazy, I mean. But it seems to me that in life you either grow up and become your parents or you spend your time trying to find them in another person. And maybe that's what I'm trying to do here, in this affair, I mean. Or at least that's what my therapist says."

I set down my beer, feeling like I'd had enough, although it was probably not the beer that was making my head spin.

"You, on the other hand," she said, "are probably trying really hard to avoid being like your father in any way, shape, or form, am I right?"

I nodded.

"But you're not succeeding, are you?"

I didn't respond.

"Are you?" she demanded.

"Maybe I just haven't tried very hard," I said.

"Try as hard as you like," she scoffed, "it probably won't do any good. Our destinies are shaped by our parents, by what we see going on when we're growing up, by what we learn and don't learn. There's no escaping it. Simon—that's my therapist—says you can learn to deal with it, adapt it to your life, maybe harness it and direct it toward something else, but the absolute worst thing you can do is deny that it exists."

I attempted to interrupt but she stopped me.

"It's not the sins of the father that are visited upon the son," she said archly, "it's the baggage."

She went on talking about her therapist, and about her husband and their therapist, about her Sri Lankan healer, and her aromatherapist, but I tuned her out, nodding and pretending to listen, but always with one eye on what was happening on the track. Eventually, my dad and the detective returned, although just long enough to collect Anna and head down to the fence to watch Meth's race.

"Aren't you coming, Tony?" my father asked.

"No, I think I'll watch from up here," I said. "Meth's number six. She should be in the green jersey."

He gave Anna an arm, the detective gave her another, and thus linked, the three of them descended the steps. They looked like something out of an old musical comedy and I half expected them to burst into song and rhythmic kicks. They arrived at the main level and squeezed in near the finish line just as Rusty, the mechanical rabbit, began making his way around the track.

Meth came out of the chutes well, which is to say that she was ahead and thus less likely to head-butt the other dogs. As long as she stayed in front and didn't get crowded, there wouldn't be a problem. She was on the outside at the first turn and lost some ground but she made it up on the straightaway and by the second turn had gained the inside advantage. It was always at the end of that turn that the dogs began to slow down and you could really see them work. The movement of their bodies, so sleek and piston-like in the beginning, became a series of slow, bobbing thrusts. Meth and another dog were two lengths ahead of the other pack.

She was pushing hard and I stood up, clenching my betting form and rocking back and forth, as if by doing so I might help her along. And maybe it did help, because in the last fifteen yards she pulled ahead of the other dog and finished in front. I smacked one palm into the other, emitted a loud "Yessss!" and then dropped back into the chair.

I looked down at the crowd. The detective and Anna were hugging and dancing around, thrilled that their bets were winners. My father was more sedate and was looking up at the stands, waiting for me to look at him. When I did, and he saw that I saw him, he lifted his hat in a kind of salute. It was a small, stupid gesture, but it made me grin like a retard. I quickly sat down and pretended to scan the betting form.

A few minutes later, my dad came walking up the stairs alone.

"Where's Anna?" I asked.

"Your little friend," he said, short of breath from the hike up the steps, "has taken a liking to her, I think. They've gone to buy some souvenirs with his winnings.

"That is a wonderful dog, Tony, I must say."

Again, the retarded grin.

"Did you train her yourself?" he asked, taking a seat and counting out my winnings for me. I told him that Cleve had done most of the work with her, and then gave him an abbreviated version of Cleve's story.

"He sounds like an interesting kid," he said.

"He is. And he's heard a lot about you over the years. Not all of it good, I'm afraid, and he has a crush on Mom so don't expect him to be nice. He's got a crush on her husband, too, so that might make it even worse. It's complicated, but he does want to meet you and said he'll come by later."

"That will be fine," he said. "I'd enjoy meeting some of the people in your life."

I imagined him meeting Roy and Tom and James, and couldn't help thinking he'd probably find those meetings something less than enjoyable.

"But tell me, Tony, is there any special girl you're seeing?"

I laughed.

"No?" he asked, giving me a teasing poke in the ribs.

I laughed again.

"You really don't know, do you. You've been gone that long."

He was confused. I didn't really care how he reacted so I figured I might as well just tell him. What, after all, did I have to lose?

"Dad," I said, the word sounding foreign coming out of my mouth, "I'm gay."

An eyebrow crept up over the rim of his sunglasses and for at least a solid minute he was silent.

"Well, then," he said, trying to mask his surprise, "let me ask the question another way. Is there any special someone in your life?"

"At the moment, no. No special someone."

"How long have you, er, how did you . . ."

"How long have I been gay?" I said, supplying the word he was having difficulty with.

He nodded.

"It happened right after you left," I said with a wink. "It's completely your fault. You know, absent father, dominant mother, all that."

"Yes, I know about that," he said with a weary sigh, "My Anna is a great fan of psychoanalytic theory. But seriously, can we be serious for a moment? Are you happy, that's all I want to know?"

I didn't have to think about it very long.

"No," I said. "I'm not."

"I'm sorry," he said, but offered nothing more.

"And what about you?" I asked. "Are you happy?"

He examined his nails and then brushed a piece of lint from his cuff. "I guess I have more happiness now," he said. "Now that I have simplified things. Now that I have quieted down and stopped making so much trouble for myself."

"So, you've stopped making trouble for yourself," I said.

"Yes."

"And, um, having an affair with the married daughter of your business partner. That simplifies life somehow?"

He laughed.

"I mean, I can see how her age would simplify the intellectual level of conversation," I said, "but as far as simplifying life, I don't think so."

"You're a smart boy," he said, patting my thigh. "Maybe too smart. Maybe that has something to do with your unhappiness."

I rolled my eyes.

"No," he said, "you're right. With women, I've made trouble for myself and I still make trouble for myself. I search and search (and thoroughly enjoy the search) but I have yet to find just the right woman."

I wanted to vomit, but more because I recognized my own words coming out of his mouth than because what he said was offensive.

"And who would she be?" I asked. "This 'right woman'? Does she exist anywhere on the planet? Can you describe her?"

He paused and tilted his head to one side, thinking.

"She would be," he mused, "a lot like your mother."

I wanted to smack him. Instead, I took a deep breath, gritted my teeth, and asked, as calmly as I could, "Then why did you leave her?"

"I knew that was coming," he said, grinning and staring down at the crowd beginning to gather at the finish line, ready for the next race to begin. I followed his gaze and saw Anna and the detective leaning on the fence, each holding a beer and laughing.

"I left your mother," he said, "because I wanted to remain true to her."

I made a dismissive grunt.

"I knew that was coming, too," he said.

"Well, come on!" I cried. "I know you weren't *true* to her," I said, making little quotation marks with my fingers when I said the word "true". "I remember you picking up women at the grocery store. Even better, I remember you taking me clothes shopping and screwing the fitting room attendant while I was in the next booth. I remember you taking me to the playground, where I watched you seducing all the lonely, unhappy mothers and *au pairs* with flowers you stole from the botanic gardens, so don't tell me that you left because you wanted to remain *true*. I haven't seen you for fifteen years, but in that time I haven't acquired Lola's Alzheimer's."

"Perhaps," he said, "you misunderstood."

"Please! I don't think so. It was pretty clear, even back then, what you were doing."

"No," he corrected, "perhaps you misunderstood what I mean now by the word 'true.' "

I crossed my arms and waited for him to explain. He took his time doing so, pausing to cut the end off his cigar with a tiny pair of silver scissors attached to a chain in his wallet. From his pants pocket he produced a silver Zippo and lit the freshly cut end, puffing several times to get it going. I wondered what Anna's therapist would have to say about the cigars.

"By saying that I wanted to remain true to your mother," he began, leaning forward and holding the cigar like a wand, "I meant that I wanted the image of me that she had in her head to remain intact."

"I don't know that you were successful there," I said with a laugh. "I know she used to love you but she really hates you now."

"Yes, and that is my point," he said, pointing the cigar at me. "Hate is much better than indifference. Or boredom, which are the feelings about me that she would have had if I'd stayed."

Again, I rolled my eyes, but with less vigor than the time before. He went on:

"Love and hate are at the opposite ends of the spectrum," he said, stretching his arms wide, "but they each burn white hot and clear."

This was the cheap sophistry I remembered him using when I'd been a child to weasel his way out of arguments with my mother.

"White hot and clear, eh? As opposed to what?"

He leaned his back on the bench and delicately flicked the ash from the end of his cigar.

"As opposed to all the muddy emotions in the middle.

"I left Louisa because that was the only way I could remain the man that she had fallen in love with."

That made some sense to me, although I never would have admitted it. Instead I said, "But don't you think you cheated her out of something?"

He gave me a questioning look

"I don't mean money, or anything like that, although there were some lean years after you left. I mean, don't you think you cheated her out of, oh, I don't know, the rest of the story."

He considered that.

"Maybe that is what women want," he said, "but that is not what I could give. Not what I *can* give. I make an excellent lover, but an awful husband. I'm not proud of it, but there it is. And in the long run your mother was probably better off without me. Look at what a wonderful match she made with—what was his name—Peter?"

I took that as my cue to tell him about the odd, triangular relationship between Peter, my mother, and me. At first, he seemed surprised, almost upset, by the details, but by the time I got to the description of the fantasy wedding Peter had staged (a wedding I had not attended and was describing from hearsay and photographs), it was clear that he was relishing the tale.

"Poor Louisa," he said with a laugh. "She's had some strange men in her life."

I raised my nearly empty plastic cup in a toast to that one.

The fifth and sixth races were over, but still the detective and Anna were leaning on the fence, their heads close together, as if whispering. I knew in a moment, his arm would encircle her; his hand would be resting on her hip.

"I'm a lot like you," I said to my father. "And I don't think that's a good thing."

"How do you mean?" he asked.

"I mean, look down at him, flirting with her," I said. He followed my gaze. "I taught him how to do that. Oh, not the way that you taught me. I learned from you by watching, witnessing you in action. His training was more hands on. There is even a manual."

I gazed down at my student; employing so well the tools I had given him. Then I looked over at my anguished father and for a moment, I had the sadistic hope that the detective would steal Anna away from him. The hope that, for once, my father would get a taste of his own medicine, cruelly administered by me, his abandoned son. Then I looked at my father again. When he wasn't smiling (and he certainly wasn't smiling then), he looked tired and old.

Cleve joined us shortly thereafter and together we watched the remaining races. Far from the fireworks I had expected, the two got along well, my father disarming him early on with charm and compliments, and Cleve earning my father's admiration with his street smarts and knowledge of dog racing. I was almost jealous.

Once the races were over, we found the detective and Anna, both slightly drunk, and Cleve gave the three of them a tour of the kennels. I waited on a bench in front of the track, watching all the people coming and going and musing at the signs posted in the parking lot reminding race fans not to leave their children or pets unattended while inside.

When they came out, we said goodbye to Cleve and then drove to the cemetery, as planned. Since the detective had driven alone, and since he seemed intent on tagging along, I rode with him, my father and Anna following behind in the Thunderbird.

Riverside Cemetery is one of the most pathetic and most interesting places in the city. Pathetic because it is next to a shallow, muddy, polluted stretch of the Platte River, and has a lovely view of a refinery. Interesting because the graves are old, many dating back into the 1800s. Initially, these older bodies had been buried on a sloping hillside uptown, with a view of the western mountains, but they were dug up and reburied at Riverside when the city claimed the original land for the botanic gardens and a park.

Because my family had been poor in the 1960s, they buried my grandfather at Riverside instead of the ritzier Fairmount or Crown Hill, and although we certainly could have afforded a better place for Lola when she died, we decided that she would rather be next to her husband, so we buried her at Riverside, too. In the end, what does it really matter? Most people don't bother visiting graves, and soon I would be the only family member remaining in Denver.

The ride with the detective was interesting. The beer and the sunshine and Anna's attentions had made him giddy and inclined to talk.

"I don't know how your old man did it," he said. "She is one hot babe."

Although his grooming and style of dress had been moved into the current decade, his vocabulary was still stuck in the 1980s.

"Not to be mean," he went on, "but what is someone her age, just a girl, really, doing with an old dude like him?"

I shrugged.

"Do you think she likes me?" he asked, eyeing her in the rearview mirror.

"I do," I said, egging him on. I envisioned him on a horse galloping up alongside and scooping her up as he passed, leaving my father bewildered in the dust.

"Really? You're not just saying that to be nice? You think she's into me?"

"Oh, totally."

When we got to the cemetery, I directed him along the deserted, single-lane road until we got to the spot where my grandmother had been buried two months before. We got out and I escorted my father to the two small headstones, while Anna and the detective went off to look at the other graves.

In two months the grass on Lola's grave had grown out evenly but the earth was still raised, whereas the ground covering my grandfather had sunk a good six inches. The unevenness struck me as funny somehow.

My dad was solemn, his head bowed respectfully, but I noticed his eyes were on Anna and the detective. I knew he was uneasy and I felt a little surge of satisfaction. Then, as if reading my mind, he gave a nod to the sunken grave and said, "I know it's hard to believe, but I hated that bastard even more than you hate me."

For a minute, I was too shocked to say anything. Then, following my instinct, I lied and said, "I don't hate you."

I tried to sound soft and conciliatory, but it didn't work.

"It's okay to hate me," he said. "I haven't done much to make you feel otherwise. We can talk about it if you'd like."

I stared at him, unsure how to respond. He looked even smaller than I remembered. Harmless, almost.

"Please," he said. "Let's walk. Go ahead. Say what you need or want to say. Anna has to meet her husband in San Diego on Monday so we're leaving early tomorrow morning. This may be our only chance to talk."

Whether he said that deliberately to whip me into anger, or whether he was actually that callous, I don't know, but it had the desired effect and I exploded.

"You haven't changed a bit! You'll bend over backwards to make time for some piece of ass, but when it comes to your own son, you're always in a fucking hurry."

As the volume of my voice increased, he kept walking toward the river, trying to get out of earshot of Anna and the detective. I caught up to him, grabbed him by the sleeve, and pulled him around.

"It's okay for you to say you make a better lover than a husband. That's fine. I don't care. But what about being a fucking father?"

He exhaled noisily, lifted his glasses, and rubbed his eyes. It was almost a gesture of impatience, and I really considered hitting him.

"Why don't we walk a bit more," he said, and started off across the graves, farther from Anna and the detective, who had turned now and were watching us. I followed him, a few steps behind. We walked until we were at a hillside overlooking the refinery and the river. He dusted off one of the head stones and sat on it. I stood, gripping the top of my walking stick with both hands, my knuckles white.

"About the parenting," he said, "It's going to sound stupid but I just got scared. I'll admit it. Oh, I was selfish, too, no denying that, but the truth is I got scared."

"Scared of what?" I asked.

"The usual. Scared of screwing it up and setting a bad example, scared of having someone need me, scared of the whole thing."

"So that's why you left, that's why you never had any contact with me? Christ, you weren't even around long enough to set a bad example!"

He looked at me over the rim of his glasses, a faint smile on his face.

"Judging by what you've told me about your injuries, and by what you say you've been teaching your friend," he said with a nod toward the detective, "I don't think I left soon enough."

I could think of nothing else to say, no retort, had no other questions to ask.

"It's not a nice thing to say, Tony, but I truly think you were better off without me in your life."

We sat not saying anything, staring at the refinery, for a long time after that, until Anna and the detective shouted for us to come, saying they had something they wanted to show us. My father got up, waved at them, and then came over to where I was sitting and offered me his hand. I took it and he pulled me up, and together we joined the others.

The four of us strolled around for a while, looking at the various monuments and mausoleums, but my leg was starting to hurt so I decided to walk back to the car, telling the others to take their time since, at the rate I was going, it would take me a while to get there. I'd gone about a hundred yards when I heard Anna's jewelry jingling behind me.

"They're watching a fox eat a bird," she said, scrunching up her face in disgust, "so I thought I would go back with you."

I nodded and kept walking.

"I didn't tell you everything earlier," she said, walking alongside me. "About why I stay with him, I mean."

I was getting annoyed and bored with the subject.

"You don't have to tell me," I said. "It's really none of my business."

"He's very lonely," she said.

I walked faster. She kept pace and continued talking.

"I know he seems like a loner, all cavalier and tough, but he's really not. On the evenings he's not with me, your father goes to a Philippino karaoke bar down by the harbor. He gets drunk with all the sailors and whores and sings."

"He had a family," I snapped. "He's the one that left us."

She went on talking wistfully, as if she hadn't heard me, almost as if I wasn't there.

"Such sad songs—Hank Williams and Johnny Mathis."

We got to the cars. Neither one of us had keys so we leaned against the low hood of the Thunderbird.

My father and the detective joined us a few minutes later, all smiles and pats on the back. I knew my father had resorted to a divide-and-conquer strategy. He had wooed the detective just as he had wooed me earlier with his camaraderie about the dog and now they were the best of friends. I looked at him, so lively and handsome, such a master of conversation and social graces, and tried hard to imagine him drunk, in some dark bar, holding a sticky microphone and making everyone miserable with his flat, strangely-accented version of "There's a Tear in My Beer."

We discussed dinner options and then drove to a restaurant not far from downtown. The brittle truce held throughout the meal and my father told an interesting, although vague and probably untrue, story about the import-export business he ran with Anna's father.

Since they were to leave early the next day, we agreed to say goodbye that evening. I would go back to the empty house, they would go back to their hotel, and in the morning they would get up and drive on to San Diego. In the back of my mind I knew that once he drove away, I would not see my dad again. I knew that the next

I heard of him would be in a telephone call from some woman, possibly Anna but probably another, telling me that he was dead. In spite of that, my goodbye to him was unceremonious. No tears were shed, no promises to keep in touch were made, just a handshake and a hug in an obscenely bright parking lot.

Chapter Nineteen

The week after my dad left, I decided it was time, for better or for worse, to resume living my life instead of just sitting around writing about it, so I made some calls, lined up a painting job, and returned to work. The only one still eager to hire me was Arabella, who had, in our time apart, discovered minimalism and had decided that instead of murals she now wanted her entire house to be nothing but clean, white, unadorned surfaces. It was depressing to paint over all the intricate work I'd done the year before, but in my many years of painting, I had learned to maintain a degree of detachment from my work, because no matter how great or beautiful it may have turned out, it never really belonged to me and the time always came when I had to pack up my tools and leave it behind.

In addition to minimalism, Arabella had also discovered a new man. He was a shadowy figure about whom she was vague but who was, judging by the number of mornings I arrived at her empty house to find a bed that had not been slept in, very real. I cornered her in the kitchen one morning when she came sauntering in, still dressed in evening clothes, and asked her about him.

"His name is Charles," she sighed, holding her coffee cup and

gazing dreamily out the window at the birds frolicking in their concrete bath.

"Charles. Go on, tell me more."

There was a coy little pause.

"Hmmmm, well, he's a plastic surgeon."

"Ahhhhh."

"Yes, we've had a few dates now and it seems to be going well.
He's very concerned about my skin so I've quit smoking and he
wants me to quit drinking, too, but I don't know about that."

I set down my coffee and went and stood between her and the
window.

"You quit smoking for him?" I asked, not concealing my surprise.

"Ultimately I did it for myself."

"Yes, but ultimately you did it because he asked you, right?"

"He's very concerned about my skin. Smoking does horrible
damage to your epidermis, almost as much as the sun," she said,
turning away from the window and returning to the coffeepot to
refill her mug. "So I've got to be very careful, especially living in
this dry climate."

"Uh-huh. Now, are you going after this one because you're hoping to get some discount on a face-lift, or something?" I asked.

"No, heavens no," she chuckled. "They're not all that expensive.
Or so I've heard. And I've got more than enough money," she said,
waving an indifferent hand at the fresh, white walls surrounding
us.

"Then what is it?" I asked, genuinely curious.

"What is what?"

"Oh, come on! What is it about him that's making you clean up
your act?"

"I don't know what you mean," she said, all wide-eyed innocence. I gave her a look. The same narrow-eyed look she'd given
me countless times when I'd evaded the truth.

"No, really," she said. "He's just a nice guy that likes me."

"Oh, I don't doubt that, but what is it that you like about him? It
can't be his money since, as you've said, you've got enough of that,
so there must be something else, something about him that's a challenge. What could it be?" I pondered. "Is he married?"

She shook her head and lowered her eyelids.

"Under thirty and devastatingly attractive?"

"He's forty-eight if he's a day, and he's got a spare tire."

"Hmmmm, let me think. Royalty with a title?"

"Nope."

"I bet he's a workaholic. Yes, that must be it. Not married to a woman but married to his job."

"No, he wants to book us a month-long Aegean cruise. I'm the one having trouble finding the time for that."

"Then I don't get it," I said.

She shook her head, tilted it to the side, and gave me a pitying smile.

"It's like I said, he's a nice guy who likes me."

Then she disappeared upstairs to shower and get dressed.

I had been working at Arabella's for about ten days when I got a call from Bob telling me that the house had sold and I would have to be out by the end of the week. Of course, my marching orders weren't unexpected but they did pose a problem because they demanded that I take action, and that was one thing I really did not want to do. I hadn't been looking for a place to live and now I had to do so in a relatively short amount of time.

Since it was a "renter's market," finding a new apartment should have been easy, and since I really had no possessions, once I did find a place, I would not have a difficult move. But until the very day that I was forced to surrender the keys to *Casa Turquesa*, I didn't even bother to go out and look, and when I did, I took the first apartment I visited without even bothering to see the bathroom. I moved myself in, tried to turn the page and start another chapter in my life, but I couldn't seem to get away from the past and felt like I was just acting my way through the present. I got up every morning and went to work, painted all day, and even thought again (albeit with dread) of hiring an assistant, but I was only going through the motions. Pretending to be interested in it. In the evenings, I hung out at the track with Cleve, but there really wasn't much for me to do, and I soon grew bored and lonely and stopped going. Instead, I went home to my apartment after work and tried to get excited about decorating or buying new furniture, but that didn't work either and I never moved beyond half-heartedly dog-earing some pages of the Pottery Barn catalog. Consequently, I ended up sleeping on a cot, pulling clothes from a giant duffle bag as I needed them, and eating all my meals out. Even my sketching was put on hold, and when I went to coffee shops, it was, more often than not, just to drink coffee. Or to meet the detective, who I still hooked up with once a week, although more because I was lonely than because he needed further coaching.

Ninety-five percent of the time, painting is a mindless task. There is always time to think and exist in your own head, and that's not always such a good thing. Gabriel had dealt with that empty time by listening to books on tape. I, on the other hand, had used it to develop new wooing methods and mentally plan future dates. Or more often, to think of lies and stories to get me out of the trouble that the wooing methods and dates had gotten me into. But this time around, working alone at Arabella's and soured on the prospect of finding another O.O.D., I struggled to find something to think about to fill in all the lonely hours.

Much of the time, I thought about Peter, and each time I did, it was like I took a step down—like the feeling I used to get in dance clubs when the ecstasy started wearing off and I began my gradual descent back to reality. It was a sad feeling, a feeling of regret, maybe, that I could not always live my life feeling that high, and that I really hadn't fully appreciated it when I was there. I regretted that I had let Peter go, yes, but that regret was made even worse by the gnawing knowledge that someday in the not-too-distant future he would surely be with someone else and the torch he had carried for me would dim and go out.

Having nothing else to think about, I tortured myself by imagining Peter living in a large, airy hacienda. It would have long, gently flowing sheer curtains and be tastefully decorated with all of the realized furniture he and I had designed together. There would be an arched colonnade connecting my mother's wing of the house to the section Peter shared with his doe-eyed, artistically accomplished, muscular, tall, and adoring Latin lover. A lover my mother would love like a son. I tried to imagine a similar ridiculous future for myself but I just couldn't do it. Couldn't seem to create the escape fantasies or, rather, couldn't make myself believe them like I used to.

So, night after night I went "home" to my pathetic apartment and tried to make myself feel better, or worse, I'm not quite sure which, by indulging in my favorite act of self-pity: I put a relaxing CD in the player, filled the bathtub with water as hot as I could possibly stand it, and then sat there and smoked cigarette after cigarette until the water went cold or the music stopped. It was pathetic really, and never more so than in that apartment with the tub too small for even my short frame. Nevertheless, there I wallowed, adding my briny tears to the soapy water.

One night, after just such a bath, I was asleep on my cot and I awoke in a sweat, with a feeling of panic. I stared up at the off-white, semigloss rental apartment ceiling and, in one of those middle-of-the-night moments of crystal clarity, knew that I would go after Peter, knew that a life with him was exactly what I wanted, and almost without thinking, I got up and started preparing to leave, started doing all the things necessary to get out of the country. I got all my papers and my passport together; sorted my clothes and put those I wanted to take with me in one pile, and all those that I would give to Goodwill in another. Then, I made coffee and wrote some e-mails on my laptop until the sun came up, certain I was doing the right thing. With daybreak, my early-morning clarity became clouded and I had second thoughts. The prosecuting attorney inside my head pointed out my history and said that, if I was anything close to a decent human being, I would leave Peter alone and not drag him back into the Soap Opera Life of Tony Romero. Then I made another cup of coffee, watched the sunrise, and argued my defense: I had undergone a life-changing event, had suffered eye for an eye (or, uh, elbow and leg for broken hearts) justice, and so would surely settle down and stop being a tramp. Or at least I would really, really, really try. And besides, didn't I owe it to Peter to try and undo all the damage I'd done? Of course I did. It was really the only decent thing to do. In addition, think of how helpful I could be with the new furniture business. And didn't I have a right to take part in it since they were, after all, using my designs?

The latter argument proved more persuasive and by eight o'clock I was dressed and waiting at the door of the bank where, when allowed to enter, I closed my account and bought some traveler's checks. From there, I hurried over to see the lawyer who had been handling Lola's estate and the sale of the house. I told him where I was going, and arranged for him to transfer ownership of my van and my painting business over to Gabriel. Next, I went to an Internet café and booked a ticket for the following day: Denver to Frankfurt, Frankfurt to Copenhagen. I was optimistic and bought a one-way fare, figuring the next ticket I purchased would be from Copenhagen to Mexico City. Once in Copenhagen I would take the ferry—the same ferry on which I had first glimpsed and sketched Peter—to the smaller island and then take a train north. I tapped in my credit card and passport information and arranged to pick up the ticket at the airport. Then I called my landlord and told him I'd changed my mind and would be leaving the following day.

"You're not getting the rent back!" he said sharply. I said that sounded fair, which prompted him to add, "And I'm keeping the deposit, too." Again, I didn't argue, wasn't even upset, was almost giddy about it. I said I would spend one more night there and leave the keys under the mat when I left. Then I hung up and drove over to Arabella's where I passed the rest of the afternoon getting bids for subcontractors to do the work my hasty departure would prevent me from finishing.

"Are you sure you're doing the right thing?" Arabella asked, head at an angle, one eyebrow raised. She was looking at me the way I'd imagine you'd look at someone when they say they're dropping out of AA because they're all cured and have their drinking under control.

"No," I confessed. "I'm not sure. But I *think* it may just possibly be the right thing to do."

The look didn't change.

"You wanna know what I think?" she asked. I did not, but gave a shrug anyway.

"I think you're afraid."

Another shrug.

"And I don't think it's ever wise to act on decisions made out of fear."

"Uh huh, and which self-help book did you mine that little gem from?" I asked, but before she could answer, I said, "Not that it matters, because it's really bullshit. Look, I'll admit I'm afraid, but what I'm afraid of is losing Peter. Forever, I mean. I know I probably deserve to lose him, but I don't want to. And as far as acting out of fear goes, I think sometimes it's not just the right, but the only, thing to do. Look at World War Two."

She was confused.

"Do you think World War Two would ever have been won if we hadn't acted out of fear? No, we'd all be speaking German, eating really fattening food and living in Neo classical Hell. Or maybe Japanese."

"Oh, brother!"

"And what about Scheherazade? There wouldn't be the *Tales from the Arabian Nights* if she hadn't been scared. Or the Great Wall of China, one of the wonders of the worl—"

"You're crazy. You know that, right?"

I did. I was afraid and crazy and lonely and stupid but not so stupid as not to realize that the more people I told of my plan, the more arguments against it I would have to endure. So, for that reason I decided to conceal the fact of my departure from all but a select few, who, for logistical reasons, had to know. The rest I would e-mail from Denmark or Mexico, once I was settled and living in monogamous bliss with Peter. Also, if things didn't work out—a remote yet distinct possibility—I would not have to explain the folly of my failed visit when I returned and could say instead that I'd been away on, say, some vague Mediterranean vacation, or maybe even that I'd spent a month in rehab.

On the day I was to leave I was busy packing up my last few things in the apartment and was about to carry my suitcases down to the van when the detective appeared in the doorway. We had a standing Wednesday afternoon meeting time at The Market. A date I'd forgotten about in my haste.

"So, here you are," he said.

I stood up, met his eyes, and then followed them to my duffel bag. I knew I would probably have to tell him.

"When you didn't show, or answer your phone," he said, "I thought something might be wrong so I decided to swing by."

"I must've left the phone in the van," I said, patting down my pockets. "Anyway, I couldn't make it today. Some other stuff sort of came up."

"No matter," he said, stepping inside and closing the door behind him. "The girl of my dreams must have been busy somewhere else because she sure wasn't at The Market today." Then he leaned to the side to try and see what was behind me and said, in an almost offhand way, "Hey, are you . . . going somewhere?"

He wasn't smiling. In fact, he was looking more like a detective than at any time since I'd met him so I decided I'd better not lie. I told him all about my plan. He listened. When I finished, he just shook his head and said, "I don't think you should bother."

I thought he was probably going to tell me something similar to what Arabella had told me—that he knew me, that the leopard shouldn't try and change its spots, or something along those lines. I was sure that was what he'd say, but I asked him anyway:

"Why not? Why shouldn't I bother?"

His sly little smile was making me uneasy.

"Well, because," he said. "Because they'll probably both be coming back to Colorado soon."

I waited, but he didn't explain.

"What do you mean by that?" I asked.

"I mean that Mexico and Denmark both have extradition treaties with the U.S., so once they're formally charged, they'll probably both be sent back here for trial."

"Trial!"

"Yes."

"What for?"

He exhaled and made a rough whistling noise.

"This is hard for me to say, Tony, but one of them, possibly the two of them conspiring together, perpetrated the whole thing."

"What whole thing?" I demanded, imagining some shady business dealing, but certain that he was mistaken.

"The shooting."

"What!"

He held up his hand indicating that I should wait, then he turned, went back outside to his car, and returned a moment later carrying a hard-sided briefcase. He came in and walked past me to the kitchen. He set the case on its side on the counter and pushed the two release buttons with his thumbs. He opened the case and the spring-loaded clasps popped up and he took out a thick manila envelope. I was standing in the doorway to the kitchen, leaning against the frame. My hands had gone ice cold.

"I know this will be upsetting to hear, but let me tell you what we think happened that night."

"I don't thin—"

"No, please," he interrupted. "Save your questions till the end."

"But this is ridiculous,"

"I'll grant you that, but hear me out."

I listened and he told me a tale of how my mother, enraged at the loss of Peter, had gone into the garage, retrieved the gun, and then waited outside, probably in her car somewhere down the street. When I left, she must have followed me to St. Mark's and then into the alley, possibly for another verbal confrontation. Too angry to talk, she had just pulled out the gun and pow!

I listened, shaking my head. In some ways, it sounded plausible. She was certainly angry enough to have pulled the trigger, but in addition to motivation, she had an alibi and had, after our fight, driven two blocks to the house of some lesbian neighbors. They had consoled her with cocktails on their back deck (a deck, incidentally, that Peter had built).

"So it couldn't have been her," I said. "Or Peter. He'd already left by then. How could he be two places at once?"

The detective came around the counter and leaned his hips against it, his arms crossed on his chest and his legs crossed at the ankle.

"He couldn't," he said, shaking his head, the sly smile expanding into a smirk. He stifled it, tried to look grave and serious, and went on:

"I checked out his alibi, of course. Not as water tight as your mom's, but still pretty good. He put a lot of thought into it. He checked into a motel in Kansas early that afternoon and then went out again and didn't return until late that evening. Said he went to a movie but couldn't say which one or produce a ticket stub. So what I'm thinking is that in that time he could easily have driven back across the border, tracked you down, shot you, and then crept back across to his motel room, making a point to talk to the owner before he turned in for the night."

"Except that he didn't," I said, rolling my eyes.

"No?"

"No! Now come on," I said, more impatient than nervous, "that's stupid. They were pissed off at me, no denying that, but even so, do you really think they would have plotted out something so stupid?"

"No," he said, "I don't. But in the absence of anyone else, they seem to be the obvious choices, wouldn't you say?"

"No! I wouldn't."

He uncrossed his arms and ankles and approached me, leaning in close to my face.

"Then why don't you tell me," he said, "who *you* think did it."

I tried to laugh but it sounded cheap and fake.

"If I had any real idea who it was, don't you think I would have told you by now?"

He shrugged and went back to the briefcase, removing another thick manila envelope. He opened it and pulled out a stack of papers. He set the papers aside and then reached in the envelope again, producing a clear plastic bag containing a gun. It was closed with a twist tie at the top. He untwisted it and removed the gun with his bare hands, setting it on the counter in front of me.

"Does this look familiar?" he asked.

It did. It was my mother's gun. The gun she'd used to shoot the squirrels out of the trees. A .22 pistol she'd purchased at Gart Brothers in the early eighties. It was rusty, like it had been at the bottom of a lake. Or a sewer. I tried to swallow but my mouth had gone completely dry.

"Shouldn't you, uh, wear gloves, or something?"

He gave me a questioning look, but the smile was still there.

"I mean, you know, to protect the fingerprints."

"I think we both know whose prints would be on this gun," he said, lifting it up and taking aim at several different random objects in the room.

"Not my mother's," I said. "Or Peter's."

"No," he said, laughing and shaking his head. "Not your mother's. Or Peter's. It is registered in your mom's name but she's not the one who fired it at you."

"No?"

"No," he said. Then he turned and pointed the rusty thing at me. My heart was racing, but my mind was racing even faster, running from one possible lie to the next, wondering which one he might possibly believe. Then it hit me—the realization that he would not believe any of my lies because he already knew, with certainty, the whole, ridiculous, pathetic truth.

"How long have you known?" I asked, looking at my luggage on the floor and wondering if I might be taking it to another, more restrictive destination.

He lowered the gun and laughed.

"Oh, I've known pretty much since the beginning," he said. "I didn't say anything at first because I was waiting to see if you were trying to pull some insurance scam, or were trying to set someone up to take the rap."

"How did you know?" I asked, my voice almost a whisper.

Again, he laughed. "Let's see, two shots at close range, one of them in the elbow, with a very low caliber pistol. Of course, I knew. The trouble was hoodwinking the other guys involved in the case that that wasn't what happened."

"Why?" I asked. "Why did you do that? Why did you wait?"

He bobbed his head, as if wondering the same thing.

"Curiosity, maybe. At first I just thought, here's a messed-up guy, starved for attention, like those mothers who make their kids sick so that they can look like martyrs, but when you didn't play it that way, I decided to stick around and see if I could figure it out for myself."

I sat down on the duffel bag and rested my chin on my walking stick.

"So far, I can't," he said. "Figure it out, I mean. So, first, why don't you tell me what happened. And then you can tell me why."

If it had been at all scripted correctly, this confrontation would have taken place at night, in the fog, preferably under a bridge or in a dark bungalow. A perfect film noir moment. Instead, the sun was shining from a cloudless sky and what must have been a flock of giddy sparrows was chirping away outside the window. I gave a disappointed sigh and began:

"It was after the last big fight with my mom," I said. "The day after Peter left. The day when pretty much everybody in my whole world was pissed off at me."

The detective had produced a small tape recorder and set it on the counter.

"My mom told me to leave," I continued. "I hadn't been kicked out, per se, but she wanted me gone. If she'd just been angry, I could have dealt with it. But she was sad, too, and not just because Peter was gone, but because of me and what a shit I was proving to be. Coming on top of everything else that had happened that week with Reid and Arabella and Gabriel and Tom, I just couldn't take it. It was too much. So after she left, I went in the garage and got the gun. It took me a while to find the bullets but eventually I did and started loading them. I remember taking them out of the box and just staring at them rolling back and forth across my palm, knowing that they'd soon be inside me. I thought of doing it—killing myself—right then and there in the garage, but I knew that would be the worst thing I could do. I'll admit I'm a selfish prick sometimes, but I'm not that selfish. Suicide would only have made everyone more miserable, and I'd done enough of that already. I knew that they didn't want me dead, but they did want me to hurt, so that's how I got the idea . . ."

"Of shooting yourself."

"Yes."

"So you went to St. Mark's . . ."

"So I went to St. Mark's. My will was fading at that point so I thought I'd sit down, have a cup of coffee, maybe think things out a little more, but it was raining and all the seats inside were taken, so again, I decided to just do it. I turned around and went back out of the café, but I was wet and shaking. It was raining hard. One of those weird, early-evening, midsummer thunderstorms where the rain comes down but the sky is still blue. I tried to go next door to the bar to get a drink—"

"But you didn't."

"No, it was too crowded and noisy so I walked back to the alley. I stood in the rain for about ten minutes, thinking, shaking. But then my thoughts sort of funneled to a point and I just took out the gun and did it, my leg and then my arm. It didn't really hurt at first, and that surprised me, but it sure started bleeding right away, and I know it sounds stupid, but that surprised me, too. Then I realized I still had the gun in my hand and that I hadn't thought about what to do with it. I looked around in a panic, like I'd just pulled the pin out of a grenade. I tried to toss it up on the roof of the building, but it was too high, and I've never been good at throwing things so it came right back down, smack! Right on my forehead."

"That explains the gash."

"Yeah," I said, smiling at the recollection and running my finger over the fading scar. "That's probably the part that really could have killed me. Still, I tried to toss it up again but I was getting scared by all the blood and was starting to see stars, so I gave it up."

"How did it get in the sewer?"

"I put it there," I said. "I stumbled out onto Seventeeth, and before anyone could see me, I just dropped it between one of the holes in the grate."

I stopped talking at that point and looked up at him.

"I guess you know the rest," I said. He nodded. The tape recorder kept running. I went back to staring at the floor. He was still leaning on the counter, arms crossed on his chest. I wanted a drink, or something to slow me down, but there was nothing in the cupboards or the refrigerator, not even any ice cube trays in the freezer, so, like the nervous, guilty person that I was, I started talking again, faster and faster.

"I don't know what else to tell you," I said. "I didn't do it for the attention—in fact, I could have done without most of that—and I didn't do it to pin the blame on anybody else, you can see that, can't you? I did it, well, I did it *for* them, really. To make them think that finally I got what I deserved, that finally someone got even, finally someone had the courage to do that crazy, irrational thing they all dreamed of doing. It doesn't really matter that that someone was me, does it? It's probably better that way. Don't you think?"

His face was stern, the skin between his brows creased in concentration. He stared at the wall behind me. It was a moment, I reflected, not unlike the many moments in my life when my boyfriend *du jour* first began to have suspicions about my infidelity. I'd argue to make him think he was wrong, crazy, and paranoid, and he'd stand there, looking at me, questioning my truth and his own sanity. But this time I was telling the truth, and was upset to realize that lies are often much easier to make people believe than the truth, especially when the truth sounds more stupid and ridiculous than any lie I ever could've pulled out of my ass.

After about a million (or at least twenty) silent, agonizing seconds, the detective shook his head and focused his eyes on me.

"I spent twelve years in Catholic school," he said. "It was as fucked up and miserable as you've heard—angry priests and bitter nuns into corporal punishment and guilt trips."

I nodded and gave a hearty laugh, trying to seem like an ex-Catholic comrade, a brother in arms. He knew me well enough by then, or maybe he was just a good detective, because he detected my phoniness and frowned at me.

"My point is, that what you did, what you did to yourself, I mean, sounds almost like something the nuns and priests would have taught us to do to atone for our sins. And I can't help thinking they'd be proud of the way you handled it."

After a few seconds, I asked, "And you? What do you think?"

"Me?" he said, focusing on me, all amusement gone from his face. "I think it was stupid, over the top, unnecessary, and danger-ous. And I could put together a list of charges that would get you in a whole lot of trouble."

He paused then and glared at me with a glare that could only have been learned from angry nuns and priests.

"But I won't," he said. The tension in my shoulders relaxed. "You didn't do any real harm to anyone but yourself and you proved your point, I guess. Sort of. In a really twisted, fucked-up way."

Again, there was silence. I heard my watch ticking and looked down at it. My flight was scheduled to leave in a little less than three hours.

"So . . . " I said.

"So . . . What?"

"Does that mean I can go?" I asked.

In response, he stopped the tape recorder, popped out the tape, and handed it to me.

"You sure you know what you're doing?" he asked as we were carrying my luggage to the van.

"No," I said. "I'm not, but I guess this is one way to find out."

We said our goodbyes. I got in the van and started it up. As I was about to drive away, I rolled down the window and called out his name. He turned around.

"You know that little manual I made for you when I was in the hospital, that thing the art therapist had me do?"

He nodded.

"Do you still have it?" I asked.

"Of course."

"Do me, and yourself a favor," I said, "and burn it." Then I put the van in gear and pulled away. I drove as fast as I could to the greyhound track, parked, and went down to the kennels, where I found Cleve busy clipping a dog's toenails. He looked up and smiled but at the same time I could see he was wondering why I was there in the middle of the day. There wasn't much time for niceties and I knew he'd be angry when he heard what I had to say so I said it right away, as quickly as I could.

"I'm leaving. You can have the motorcycle and anything else I left behind at my storage unit. Here's the key. The rent's paid until the end of the month. Also, I was hoping you could maybe get my van over to Gabriel, oh, and give me a ride to the airport."

He stopped clipping and stared at me like I'd just spit out a stream of druggy nonsense.

"I know I don't want to know," he sighed, "but where are you going?"

"Denmark."

He closed his eyes and shook his head. When he spoke, his tone was that of a weary parent.

"Tony, tell me someplace else, anyplace else, or at least tell me you're going to stay with your dad."

I ignored him and went on:

"I was hoping maybe you could keep Meth. She's always sort of belonged to both of us anyway and I don't think they have a greyhound track in Denmark."

"No," he said, standing up slowly and rubbing his temples. "No track in Denmark. There's one in Finland, but they don't allow betting."

"Kind of pointless then, eh?"

He locked his eyes on mine.

"Not if you're doing it for the joy of the competitive sport," he said. "That *is* why you're going, isn't it? This is just a bigger challenge, right?"

I didn't know how to answer that truthfully and I didn't want to lie. I hoped that it wasn't, but I wasn't totally convinced myself. I fully intended to be good and honest but I knew that hopes and intentions didn't mean much, especially when they came out of my mouth.

"Can you give me a ride?" I asked again.

"You don't deserve him," Cleve said, shaking his head. He led the dog whose nails he'd been trimming back into her kennel and brought out another, which he began brushing.

"I know I don't," I said.

"I don't think you ever will."

"I know."

"But you know he'll take you back without any questions."

I didn't know that, at least not completely, but I nodded my head anyway.

"So why don't you just leave him alone?"

"Because I love him," I said, and knew that again, coming from me, that sounded hollow. Cleve shook his head.

"Give me a break!" he said, and the dog he was brushing, a little too vigorously, let out a whimper. "You don't love anyone, not even yourself all that much. Why are you doing this?"

"I . . . don't really know what else to tell you," I shrugged.

"Well, you better think of something," he said, "because I'm not taking you anywhere until you do."

I sat down and put my face in my hands. Then I jumped back up again and said, "Okay, if you really want to know, I'm going because I'm sick of jumping from one place to the next, always setting little fires and then leaving before I can get really burned. I'm going because I'm sick of being a fake, and lying, and never saying what I really like, or feel, or want, just so someone will want me. For whatever fucked-up reason, and I really don't know what that reason is, Peter does love me, and he's about the only one in the whole world that I don't have to pretend with. But mostly I'm going because I'm scared."

He started to interrupt, undoubtedly with an argument similar to Arabella's on the folly of acting out of fear, but I stopped him.

"Yes, because I'm fucking scared, all right? I know that sounds like a shitty reason but I'm not going to lie about it. I'm going because I'm scared of losing Peter and any life we might somehow have together."

Cleve gave a disgusted grunt. I ignored him and went on, my voice getting louder, "And because I'm scared of what I've turned into, all cold, and mechanical, always playing games, not caring who gets fucked over. And because I don't want to end up in some dirty waterfront swill house singing Johnny Mathis songs with a bunch of alcoholic whores!"

Cleve stopped and held the brush suspended above the dog's back.

"And I'll try to be good this time," I added. "It's not sport. It's not the challenge. I will try to be good. And if I can't do that, I'll be honest about it. Please just give me a ride."

I didn't really need a ride, I could have called a taxi, or even taken the bus, but before I left, I wanted to explain my motives to Cleve. Of course, I wasn't naïve enough to think I could get his blessing, or even his unspoken approval—it would have been easier to make the dogs bark in French—but I did want a chance to argue my case and let him see that my motives were maybe not as dark as he imagined.

He sat for a long time with his eyes closed. Then he opened them, stood up, led the dog he'd been brushing back to her kennel, and brought out Meth.

"Say goodbye," he said, without looking at me. "Put her back in the kennel when you're done. I'll be out front."

He grabbed his keys from a hook by the door, straightened his ball cap, and without another word or a glance in my direction, headed out to the parking lot.

We were silent all the way to the airport. Only when I'd gotten out of the car and had my luggage on the curb did Cleve speak.

"You better not fuck it up this time," he said, wagging a finger at me. "And you better not fuck him up, 'cause if you do, I'll come after you and fuck you up."

He walked away and was about to get back in the van, but then turned, came back, and gripped me in a hug.

"Just try to be good," he whispered. "Trust me. It'll make your life a hell of a lot easier."

The flight from Denver to Frankfurt is direct and lasts nine and a half hours. Probably because it was the middle of the week, the plane wasn't crowded and I had a whole row of seats to myself. Because the flight was so empty, the attendants were especially attentive, striding up and down the aisles handing out magazines and headsets and smart little nylon zippered bags containing a toothbrush, an eyeshade, and a pair of travel socks. The attendants all had that youthful, blond, just-off-the-slopes-of-Zermat look, and one in particular—the male one, of course—stood out from the rest. He was a good six inches taller than the other attendants and had clinically white teeth. His nose had obviously been broken at some point in the past, and had that sexy lopsided Z shape. Almost without thinking, I got up and retrieved my sketchbook from the overhead compartment. I sat down, lowered the tray table, and flipped open to an empty page. I took a good, long, admiring look at him and then made a few initial strokes with the pencil. I looked up again. He was facing me, pushing the drink cart, a navy blue apron protecting his suit. He caught me looking and smiled. I smiled back, looked down at the page, and then realized what I was doing and stopped myself. I closed the sketchbook and tossed it onto the empty seat next to me.

You can still draw, I told myself, *just not him. Anything but him.*

I put the headphones on and idly flipped through the in-flight magazine, ever aware of the approaching drink cart. When it got to me, I pretended not to hear him and he touched me on the shoulder. I looked up and saw his name tag: KONRAD.

"Something to drink?"

His voice was low.

"Just water, please."

While he was putting ice in a glass, he nodded at the sketch-book. "Are you an artist?"

"No, not really. I just draw sometimes."

He handed me the drink and a package of peanuts. I set them down on the tray table and was about to put the headphones back on when I sensed that he was waiting for something else. I looked up again. He was still staring at the sketchbook. He focused on me again and smiled, nearly blinding me with his toothpaste ad smile. And that nose! It was even better up close.

"I draw some, too," he said, "so I like to see how other people do it."

There was an awkward pause. A pause in which seeds could have sprouted and grown to maturity; or a spider have woven an intricate, sticky web.

"Mine aren't very good," I said, wishing he would move on.

"Ahhh, maybe you are too modest," he said, resting a blond-haired paw on my shoulder.

What was happening was a scenario that I'd left out of the woo-ing manual. A scenario in which the O.O.D. turned the tables and began wooing me. In the recent past, before I decided to change my ways and become a one-man man (i.e., the day before), I looked on situations like the one described above as a bit of good fortune—like putting money in a vending machine and then, because of some glitch in the works, getting the candy I wanted *and* my money back. It didn't happen often, but when it did, I always enjoyed it and thought somehow that some little lesser god had given me a gift. This time I felt like the gods, in true Greek mythological fashion, were tempting me, teasing me almost, to resist something they knew I was too weak to resist. Nevertheless, I decided to try.

"I, uh, I don't like to show my work to people," I said, giving Konrad a lopsided grin. "Strangers, I mean. Really, I'm sorry. It's not anything against you. I just don't like to show it."

He gave my shoulder a squeeze, smiled, and moved down along the line. My shoulders relaxed. I picked up the in-flight magazine and began reading a long article about the life of a jet-set socialite who had just died and bequeathed her large art collection to a New York museum. It also noted that she was an avid traveler who hated winter and so kept houses in New York and Sydney, Paris and Johannesburg, so that no matter what time of year, she could always be where it was springtime.

I closed the magazine and tried to sleep but was soon awakened by Konrad bearing the dinner tray. He set it down but then lingered, offering small bottles of champagne and a box of chocolates he'd nicked from the first-class section. I was polite and as gracious as I could be, but really tried not to be flirty, which only seemed to inflame his curiosity even more. Throughout the flight, he stood at the head of the cabin and stared at me, even while speaking to the other attendants. He smiled directly at me whenever he walked by and always rested his hand on my shoulder or my forearm when he leaned in to speak to me. Then, when we were midway across the Atlantic, the trouble really began.

The dinner service was done and everyone in the cabin was either engrossed in the movie or asleep. Konrad, standing in the light of the attendants' station, was making googly eyes at me and indicating, with his eyebrows mostly, that I should join him in the bathroom. The mercury inched its way up the thermometer. It was bad. So bad that I almost couldn't resist it. I didn't want to be rude but I knew I might have to be. Knew that if I were to join him, it would make null and void all the resolutions I'd made to myself. No, what I needed was to tie myself to the mast and ignore the Siren's song (or, in this case, the song of Laura Lie). I took the eyeshade from its little zippered pouch and put it on. Then I tried to replace my erectile thoughts of entering the Mile High Club with tall, Teutonic Konrad, with thoughts of Peter, and what I hoped would be our future life together. It wasn't easy. The thoughts of Peter were good, and I looked forward to realizing them, but the thoughts of naked Konrad were good too, and it was hard to shut them out. I gritted my teeth and again I wondered if I was doing the right thing. Wondered if I would be able to resist the inevitable temptation in the future, if I would ever be even remotely worthy of having Peter as a boyfriend. Somehow, I must have fallen asleep because the next thing I knew someone was nudging me awake. I lifted the eyeshade and was almost blinded by the sun glinting off Konrad's white teeth. I squinted and, as my eyes adjusted, was glad to notice that he seemed less beautiful and irresistible in the morning light. His eyes were red-rimmed, and his orange tan obviously fake. As he slammed my breakfast tray onto the table and quickly moved on, I was glad that he was behaving more like a normal flight attendant stuck working in coach than the irresistible ski hunk I'd imagined the night before, and I felt a smug satisfaction at having resisted his advances.

Once on the ground, I maneuvered through Frankfurt Airport and then boarded an SAS flight to Copenhagen, on which, I was relieved to notice, all the attendants were women. Younger versions of my mother. I hadn't slept well, or for very long, during the first flight, but I was too nervous and excited to sleep, thinking of Peter and his reaction to my arrival. Probably he would be happy, maybe even relieved when he heard what I had to say. Probably. Although, maybe he wouldn't. Maybe it would go badly. Maybe he'd throw me out and I'd have to go back to the airport and completely retrace my steps. Maybe, probably, I shouldn't be doing this at all.

We landed in Copenhagen, and once I'd cleared customs and immigration, I took a short train ride to the ferry. The boat was smaller this time, and less crowded. Again, I wanted to sleep, but was too wound up and ended up just staring out the rain-streaked window. I thought of calling Peter, just a casual call (in which I would neglect to tell him that I just happened to be in Denmark) to try and gauge his mood, maybe determine what I might expect, but I decided against it. Decided that the element of complete surprise might be better. I'd just present myself, tell him what I had to say, tell him that I'd decided to really try to change, and then ask him if he might consider taking me back. The words "delusional" and "lunacy" made recurring appearances in my mind, but I quickly ushered them out again.

When the ferry docked, I lumbered off into the gray, wet weather and walked the two soggy blocks to the train station. There were only two trains a day during the week and I'd just missed the first. The second wouldn't come for another five hours. I was getting so anxious I considered hitchhiking, but I hadn't been to Denmark in a decade and figured I might just get more lost, and that might make my journey even longer and more tedious than it had already been, so I sat back and tried to be patient. I knew I should try and sleep since when I arrived there would probably be a lot that we needed to talk about, but I was too afraid of missing the train so I drank a succession of espressos and paced around the station.

By the time the train arrived, I knew without a doubt that I was crazy, that Peter would reject me, and that I really ought to just turn right back around and begin the long journey back to Denver, flogging myself all the way for my stupidity. Or maybe even go to Copenhagen and shack up with my father. We could hang out all day and drink and gamble and flirt and then, well, I could just kill myself. My pessimism deepened as the train clicked and clacked along, and by the time it pulled into the station, I was so tired and raw I really thought I would just go home again. The train stopped. I got up and got off. I'd come this far, I told myself, had crossed an ocean and eight time zones—I might as well play it out.

From the station, I hired a taxi but then realized I didn't know the exact address so we ended up driving around and around the suburbs of the small town, while I tried to recognize landmarks in a place I'd spent three weeks ten years earlier. It was ludicrous, and at that point I should have just had the driver pull over at a pay phone so that I could call, but I didn't, and for another twenty minutes we drove around and around and around until I noticed the hedge, and then, peeking over it, the thatched roof of the house. The cab stopped and I asked the driver to wait. If it went badly, I didn't want to have to call for another cab. I got out and walked into the yard. It was dark by then and late autumn, so of course they weren't outside. There were lights on in the house and, as I approached, I saw the uncle sitting at the kitchen table, puffing away on his pipe and reading the paper. He looked up when I knocked, got up, and opened the door. I stood in the light spilling out from inside, and looked at him. His eyebrows shot up when he realized it was me and he removed the pipe from his mouth. We stood facing each other, not saying anything. I could feel the heat from the house escaping into the night. He moved aside so I could come in. Nearly everything in the house was packed up in boxes. The bookshelves were empty and there were shadows on the walls where the pictures had been. The only things still up were the guns and the taxidermied heads. I stepped in, my heart racing.

"Peter," the uncle called. He turned his head to the side, but kept his eyes on me. Then, as if I'd been away for a week instead of a decade, he added, "Your little friend is back."

I heard footsteps coming down the stairs and then heard them slow down and stop. I looked up and saw him, looking blond, and beautiful and kind, and he saw me. For several seconds neither one of us made a move; the whole world seemed to have frozen. Then, in that subtle, honest, transparent way of his, Peter smiled.